An Army of Heroes

The Last Great Hero
Book 3

Scott J. Robinson

All characters and events portrayed
in this book are fictional,
and any resemblance to real people
or incidents is coincidental.

For more information visit
www.tengama.com
or email
scott@tengama.com

Please help support
independent writers and publishers.
Your money is wonderful.
So are your reviews,
comments, mentions, tweets,
emails, blogs, likes
and deliveries of chocolate.

An Army of Heroes

Sunday

RAWK, THE LAST OF THE GREAT HEROES, didn't know how long he should wait. Sitting at a table near the back of the taproom he squinted into the fug and the noise again, as if Prince Weaver's disguise might actually be working for the first time in history, as if Rawk wouldn't have been annoyed by his presence before he even saw him. But there was just the usual rabble, hunched over their meals and their drinks and their shady deals. There were no guards and certainly no prince. Weaver was notoriously late, but this was getting ridiculous.

In the babble of half–heard conversations, with the smell of sweat and ale and over–cooked pork heavy in the air, Rawk leaned back in his chair and closed his eyes. The only good thing about meeting Weaver for lunch was the opportunity it gave him to sit and pretend he was a normal person. Everyone knew he had lunch with the prince, and it seemed to be the only time they didn't feel the right to annoy him with questions and requests. Conversations continued around him as if he wasn't even there.

"...said the canal is almost done. If the bloody dwarves don't stuff it up..."

"...troop of mercenaries came in on the Fernal Dance. Had one ale each at the Golden Crown, then marched away north..."

"...another riot yesterday..."

A few minutes later, Rawk grunted, deciding he'd waited more than long enough. He scratched at his short chin–beard. The Blue Caravan was a terrible place for lunch anyway. The kitchen wasn't visible from his seat but, judging by the tankard he'd been forced to drink from, he doubted it had been cleaned any time in the last year; even the more entrenched drinkers seemed to be wary of the food.

But Weaver appeared in the doorway just as he was pushing his chair away from the table.

"Path, damn it." He sighed and sank back down, laying his big hands on the rough timber of the table as if to keep them away from his weapons.

The prince spotted him and wove his way though the clutter of tables, trying to look nonchalant. The effect was ruined when he stubbed his toe on a loose board, stumbled into the back of a sailor and nearly flipped a table and all its contents onto the floor. Normally, in a place like this, that would have resulted in a fight, but everyone in the room knew who Weaver was, disguise and all, and reluctantly passed up on the chance for some light entertainment. The sailors muttered apologies and serving girls hurried out to clean up the mess.

Rawk shook his head. "If you're going to make me wait half an hour, Weaver, then next time I won't be turning up."

"I'm not Weaver," Weaver hissed, looking around to see who was watching, completely forgetting about the fight that didn't happen a moment before. Then he spoke more loudly. "My name is Juspert. I am a merchant from Frenable." He sat on the seat next to Rawk and sent his two guards away with a gesture.

Rawk watched them go. "Do you honestly believe that nobody recognizes you? A stupid hat and a fake beard aren't a disguise."

"What's wrong with my hat?" Weaver straightened the item in question. It didn't improve the look in any way.

"Those things have been out of style in Frenable for at least ten years, Weaver."

"Well, I don't get out as much as I used to; you know that. Anyway, you chose to come, Rawk. You are the last of the great Heroes and I can't *make* you do anything."

"Of course you can't. But you can whine constantly if I don't. And you can make my life difficult by not paying me or by doing any of a dozen other things." He didn't actually need the money, but Weaver didn't need to know that.

"Do you really think I would do that?"

Rawk didn't bother answering. He rubbed his hand over his bald head and looked about the room.

Weaver sulked. "You come because you want to, Rawk. You come because you know what we had is not something you find every day."

"What we had?" Rawk sighed. "This is about the damn 'good old days' again? When will you admit that they're gone?"

"They might be gone, Rawk, but we can bring them back." Weaver looked intensely at Rawk. "I love you and I think..."

Rawk blinked. He sat for a moment, thinking. "What? What did you just say?"

But Weaver looked at his fingers, fiddling with an ithel coin. "Nothing."

"No. You—"

"All right. I said 'I love you'. Isn't it obvious?" Weaver reached out and took Rawk's hand.

Rawk pulled away. "What in Path's name..."

"I know you love me too, Rawk. You just have to—"

"I don't love you, Weaver."

"But what about that time..." Weaver leaned in closer and Rawk leaned back.

"What time?"

"In Mesatip."

"Mesatip?" Rawk shook his head trying to remember. He knew he was getting old but, as far as he knew, he wasn't starting to forget things. Not important things anyway. "I have no idea—"

"We'd just fought the gabanochs."

"Right, yes, I remember that."

"And that night..."

Rawk tried to think. They'd fought the stinking gabanochs a few miles up the side of a mountain and been stuck in a blizzard over night.

"I will never forget that night, Rawk. The way you held me..."

"Held you?" Rawk said. Now he remembered, though he obviously didn't remember the same thing Weaver did. "Are you kidding? It wasn't some romantic evening with candles and flowers. We were freezing. We would've died." All they'd done was share body warmth.

"I know you love me too, Rawk," Weaver said, as if Rawk hadn't said anything at all.

"That was forty years ago."

"I've never forgotten that night, Rawk."

"I had until a minute ago. And you've been wandering around all this time... What? Pining after me?" Rawk grunted. "You're an idiot, Weaver, and you need to get over your fantasies." He started rise, but the prince grabbed his shirt and held on tight.

"Fantasies? What do you think this is all about, Rawk? Katamood? Prince Weaver?"

"What are you talking about?"

"I did this all for you." He waved his free hand, encompassing the tavern and the city beyond. "Everything. I was never going to be a great Hero like you, but I could do this. I wanted to be worthy of you."

Rawk pulled the prince's hand away from his shirt but Weaver grabbed him again and pulled him in close.

"You are not going to walk out on me. Not now. Not after everything I have done." His eyes were wild, his jaw tense and quivering.

Rawk grabbed the other man's hand again, slowly pulling the fingers away from the cloth. "I have things to do, Weaver."

He headed towards the door and resisted the urge to look back. "Path, what was that all about?" He almost tripped on the same board Weaver had found earlier, apologized randomly, and finally got outside. Ducking under the sagging roof on the front porch, Rawk stepped down onto the street with a sigh of relief and unconsciously fished a few coins from a pouch on his belt for the gaggle of children who were waiting.

"Tell us a story, Rawk," one of them shouted. The others took up the chorus.

Rawk rubbed his hand over his head again as he tried to focus his thoughts. He straightened the white cotton of his shirt where Weaver had grabbed it. He retied the laces down the front. "All right, all right. Yes. A story." *About the good old days.* He held up his hand and waited for what amounted to silence amongst a group of children. A few adults were hanging around the back as well, as if they had just happened to pause there for reasons completely unrelated to stories. *No, the good old days were gone.* "Not so long ago, a... troll came to our fair city. It was a huge creature almost twice my height, and looked as fierce as a northern winter. But it wasn't fierce. Not really. It was sad and alone and was looking for something it had lost. I killed it anyway, without thinking." The crowd was a bit restless. Rawk didn't care. "And a few days later, I journeyed into the Old Forest to see if I could find any more of the creatures." By the time Rawk got to the bit where a dwarf saved him most of the children had gone, but there were at least a dozen adults listening in stunned silence. He shrugged. "So we killed the entire family that day, plus their pets. But only after a dwarf saved me. And then I came home and was treated like a hero. Prince Weaver gave me money. People asked me to tell them the tale, or tales of when I killed other creatures, while they swore at and spat at the dwarves who were doing the work that kept Katamood running."

There was a moment of silence.

"Is that true, Rawk? Were you really saved by a dwarf?"

It probably wouldn't matter what Rawk said in response; the story would soon be spreading around the city, one way or the other. He sighed. "Of course not. That would be crazy, wouldn't it? It's just a story."

Everyone started talking at once and Rawk was worried it was going to degenerate very quickly. Perhaps there would be walnuts thrown in tribute as everyone ignored the bits of the world they didn't like. On the other hand, there might be a riot. Admittedly it would be a very *small* riot, but he really didn't feel up to it. Not today. Not now. Once again he resisted the urge to look back to see if Weaver was following him. He was saved, from riots and looking both, by a scream that he wasn't sure he even heard. Maybe he hadn't. Maybe he was looking to be saved. But a team of dwarves were working on the sewers not far away and, though those down in the trench continued to work, throwing dirt up to the street like an endlessly erupting volcano, all the others had paused, heads cocked, trying to listen as well.

The scream came again. Louder this time.

Rawk drew *Kaj* and the closest of his crowd reared back. They parted before him and he darted across the ancient cobbles of the road and into an alley, jumping rubbish, splashing through puddles left over from last night's rain. Buildings crowded close on either side, plaster in−fills dirty and grimy between the exposed timber frames. Another scream, from a different person this time, but at least Rawk knew he was getting close.

He barreled into an intersection, sliding to a stop. He rubbed at his sore knee and looked around. An old man was standing there on his doorstep, bucket of vegetable scraps in his hand. He pointed without saying anything. Rawk nodded his thanks and left with the same lack of words. In just a few seconds he slowed to a limping walk as the alley opened out slightly at a dead−end. The buildings may have stepped back, but they loomed over the little square like priests of Path around a Caramas Altar. On the far side was a stable. A body was lying twisted and bloody on the hay−strewn cobbles just outside the open door. A crow was standing nearby, with ruffled feathers and a highly offended expression. The bird squawked indignantly and hopped backwards as another body sailed out the loft window and landed with a soft, wet, thud.

Rawk swallowed. "That doesn't look good."

The crow squawked again.

There was movement in the higher of the two doors, a shadow slinking through the shadows, but nothing emerged and it was several minutes before anything else happened. Then, a creature came out on ground level, scraping its dull grey scales on the doorframe, sauntering into the sunlight as if it was Prince Weaver entering a throne room. It was huge, twice as tall as a draught horse, with six tree—trunk legs, a long tail and a snout like a battering ram. A battering ram with bloody fangs. And there was a bloody spike on the end of its tail. The creature shook its head, sending a spray of glistening, red droplets across the dirty plaster of the walls. It blinked slowly up at the sun, then spun about and went back the way it had come.

Rawk started to breathe again. He almost gagged on the smell of death.

"Where's the exot?"

Two Heroes were standing not far away, swords drawn, faces flushed from running.

"You haven't killed it already, have you?"

Rawk shook his head. "It's in there, but I'd take a minute to think if I was..."

The two men were racing each other towards the stables, wordless battle cries letting every creature in the neighborhood know they were there, though only one creature really mattered at the moment. A second later, the first of the men reappeared, flying through the air and screaming. He hit the cobbles and rolled. He sat up, apparently all right, but made no effort to go back and help his friend. By the sound of the screaming, the friend needed all the help he could get.

Rawk took a step forward, cursing under his breath, but any thought of a rescue mission was cut short when the sounds suddenly stopped. He shifted his grip on *Kaj*. He shifted his feet and turned to look at the man on the ground. "What happened?"

The man winced, holding his ribs. "Its tail."

Rawk nodded and moved carefully forward.

Inside, it took a moment for his eyes to adjust. A rope with a hook on the end, for taking supplies up to the loft, was hanging down into a shaft of bright sunlight that lanced down through a skylight. There were two dead horses in the shadows, both of them half eaten. Flies, dancing through golden dust motes, were creating a background hum that drowned out the sounds of the city. The dead Hero was lying on a pile of hay as if he was just having a bit of a rest while the exot sniffed him, obviously choosing the leanest cut. Rawk had seen men being eaten before. You would think it really couldn't be any worse than seeing any animal eaten raw, but it was. It was considerably worse. He cleared his throat. He didn't do it to get the creature's attention, but it was always going to.

Cold green eyes turned towards him. The tail flickered, brushing the hay on the floor, sending up storms of dust. It was mesmerizing. Rawk blinked. *Kaj* seemed very heavy.

"How do I end up in situations like this?" He'd hired Heroes to stand on corners so he didn't have to run around saving the city. And yet here he was. Two Heroes had even arrived before him, sort of, and done nothing at all that helped him stay outside. All they'd done was force him into the stables sooner than he wanted, before he'd had a chance to think. He couldn't be too hard on them though, because a few months ago he'd have been the one doing the rushing, bad knee and all.

Rawk took a chance and looked around again.

He turned back in time to jump the scything tail and slash with his sword. The blade encountered flesh but didn't do anything interesting. He raced towards the other side of the room. As he went, he grabbed the hook hanging from above and swung it as hard as possible. It sailed harmlessly past the exot as it stalked along behind.

Rawk turned, sword ready, and wished he were somewhere else. He licked his lips, tasting hay–dust. A couple of yards away, the creature gathered itself to attack. Rawk felt his own muscles tensing as well. He wanted to look around, to see where he could run, but he knew there was no helpful exit nearby.

The hook, swinging back the other direction, struck the exot on the shoulder. The creature spun around violently to meet the unexpected attack. And Rawk darted forward. He stabbed up under one of the front legs, a hard, teeth–clenching thrust, grunting with the effort. He knew that if he failed to kill it quickly he would probably die himself.

The exot screeched and bawled as blood gushed forth. It turned and the huge head slammed into Rawk, knocking him across the room where he struck the rough timber wall hard enough to shake a saddle down from its hook. He fell into a pile of hay, sending out a golden explosion, gasping for air and coughing all at once. His ribs ached but, if only he would get some air into his lungs, he would live. That was more than could be said for the exot. The creature was on the floor, writhing in the final throes of life, scraping straw aside with its weakening limbs. It screamed like a wagon full of stuck pigs.

Taking a deep breath and wincing at the pain, Rawk carefully levered himself into a sitting position and leaned against the wall. His head pounded. "That went just like I planned," he said, watching the hook as it swung in ever decreasing arcs over the top of the exot. *Kaj* was lying on the floor not far away as well but the sword wasn't going to go any where for the moment. Rawk was still sitting, and starting to get the hang of it, when he heard someone outside the door. He looked up in time to see a dwarf with one of the camera things. The pop and the flash of light came, as usual, and when Rawk could see again, blinking away tears, he was on his own.

"Just leave me alone," he shouted.

Waydin carefully poked his head through the door. "Leave you alone? What are you talking about?"

Rawk grunted. "You'd starve if you were a Hero, Waydin. You always arrive five minutes too late."

"I can't arrive at all until someone orders me too." The soldier looked around. "Is that your new sword? I've heard about it. Nice."

"A dwarf made it for me."

"Really?" He wrinkled his nose. "Maybe you should get someone to look at it, just to make sure it isn't going to break any time soon."

"You know a human smith who's better than dwarf smiths?"

Waydin shrugged. "Just because they *can* make a good sword, doesn't mean they aren't too lazy to actually do it."

Rawk shook his head and sighed. Anyone who said dwarves were lazy was either blind or willfully stupid. Maybe even both. Dwarves were noisy and smelly and either overly jovial or overly cranky. But they weren't lazy and if they did something, they did the best job they could.

"So, what sort of creature is this one?" Waydin asked. Half a dozen more soldiers had come in to have a look. There were a few more outside keeping the crowd at bay.

"No idea. But its big, so make sure..." He cleared his throat. "Make sure Weaver takes the price off my bill."

"Are you still paying off that room?"

"I have the feeling I'll be paying for the rest of my life." *One way or the other.* Rawk clambered to his feet and his head took its complaint to an all-new level.

When he had his sword he limped outside. The crowd was slowly growing, encouraged by the lack of screams. Most of them were human but there were some of the other races, though none seemed to be dwarves with a camera. The crow, sleek and black against the sky, called from the peak of a roof, flapped its wings against the afternoon sky then settled down to watch again.

Rawk didn't return to the *Hero's Rest*. Sylvia's place wasn't all that much further and, the way he was feeling, it seemed appropriate. And while he was there he would take the opportunity to purchase a few things. So he crossed the river and then a few hundred yards past that, after avoiding 2 stories and an offer of ale, the canal as well. Down in the bottom, the machines rattled and clanked and pounded, making the ground shake and sending out equal amounts of steam and dust. There were so many dwarves milling about in the deep, still−dry ditch that Rawk wondered if the machines were really any use at all. Then he scaled the street up the side of Mount Grace like he was actually scaling an actual mountain. Each step seemed a monumental effort that was beyond him. But he climbed on anyway, ever upwards. Half way to the top, and still some distance from his destination, up he stopped and looked back the way he'd come.

The river and the canal were both swarming with activity. Ships of all shapes and sizes clogged the brown sheen of the former, dancing their crazy, lazy never−ending dance. And machinery and dwarves continued to dance their dustier, rhythmic dance as the two ragged ends of canal slowly crept towards each other. It was a dance that would be ending very soon. A week at most, he guessed, though he didn't really know much about the intricacies of digging up and shifting a few thousand ton of rock. Let alone the intricacies of letting in the water. And the dwarves would probably want to clean up before they did all that anyway. They seemed to like saving a symbolic, last little piece of work so they could hammer the last nail, or pat down the last shovel full of earth, and say the job was done without then having to spend the rest of the week making the place look tidy again. Maybe two weeks then, and they'd see how crazy Weaver really was.

A few minutes later Rawk pushed in through the door of Sylvia's shop, the bell clanging dully over his head. He sat down on the stool by the counter to wait. The shop was neat and tidy with rows of jars and containers in solemn ranks on the shelves. Everything was in its place. He had never been upstairs to her home and wondered if it was the same. He decided it would be tidy, but without the same pristine, cold feeling. It would be comfortable and lived in, like a favorite pair of boots that had just been polished.

It wasn't long until Sylvia emerged from the back room, smoothing down her long hair with one hand and holding a box of jars in the other. "Rawk. Good afternoon."

"Hello." He had noticed Sylvia was attractive before, once he got around to not trying to kill her, but she seemed to get more beautiful every time he saw her. He decided that most elvish women ticked all the boxes for beauty but he'd never really looked at them in the past.

Sylvia looked a bit nervous. She smoothed her hair again. "How can I help you today?"

Rawk looked away to examine the shelf where the tea usually sat. "Firstly, I need some more tea. And some cream for my knee."

"So, it is working?"

"The cream or my knee? Both work, when I remember to put the one on the other."

"Good. And is the tea for a poultice or for drinking?" She looked him up and down, as if looking for a gaping wound that needed healing.

"It's for drinking. Why do you always think I'm injured?" He clenched his fist to avoid rubbing his ribs. He was pretty sure there would be an impressive bruise there soon enough though there was no way he could show her now.

"Well, you have gone right through my usual supply, but I have managed to get some more from a merchant ship that arrived in Westport a few days ago."

"I'll take it."

"You cannot have all of it."

"Why not?"

"What if somebody requires a poultice? I am a healer, remember, not a... not a tavern."

"What tavern would serve tea as a drink?" No tavern would because nobody really knew about tea. They didn't understand. "Well, I'll take as much as you'll give me."

She collected a package, already wrapped, from under the counter. "The cream is in there as well. I surmise that I must to add it to you bill?"

"If you could."

"It is getting rather high."

"Don't worry, I'll have someone sort it out."

"Thank you."

"And now for the other thing."

Sylvia sighed. "Of course there is another thing."

"Why are there still exots everywhere?"

"What do you mean?"

"We took care of the sorcerers, so how come there are just as many exots appearing as there were before we killed everyone?"

"Many of the ohoga portals are natural."

"Many?"

"Some." Sylvia cleared her throat and started stacking the jars from her box onto the shelf behind the counter. They were filled with a dozen different flower petals of a dozen different colors. "They are probably appearing because all the magical activity weakened the veil between the worlds."

"Some?"

"Yes."

"Then what about the rest?"

"I really do not know, Rawk."

"Could there be another cabal?" They hadn't killed *all* the members of the last one, but surely there weren't enough left to keep things going.

"Of course it is possible, but I think it is very unlikely. That was a lot of sorcerers. And if General Ramaner was the one pulling the strings to get his revenge…"

"What about that other man we saw at the meeting?"

"What of him?"

"Well, he didn't look like a warrior and you said he wasn't a sorcerer."

"I am positive he was not. Magic clings to anyone who has used it like… like grass seeds cling to a shirt."

"So why was he there? I doubt it was for the lunch special."

"What are you suggesting?"

"Maybe he was the one in charge, not Ramaner. And now he's found a way to set his plans in motion again."

Sylvia hesitated again, then sighed, as if this were an argument she had already had with herself. "If I am to find out what is happening, I will need to use your library. Perhaps there is something in there that will give me a clue." She collected her scarf from a hook behind the counter and started to wrap it around her head and face.

"What? Now?"

"I have no appointments and every portal that opens means more innocent people could die. And each portal that opens by magic weakens the veil and makes it easier for portals to open naturally."

"Come on then." Rawk hoped she didn't solve the puzzle *too* quickly because he didn't know if his ribs were up to a fight. He didn't know if they were up to the walk home. His knee wasn't doing too well either. He pushed himself to his feet and headed slowly for the door.

"Why are you walking like that?"

"Like what? I always walk like this."

She didn't say anything as she finished wrapping her scarf.

Halfway down the side of Mount Grace, in a small market that clung to the side of the street, Sylvia suddenly stopped. It took Rawk a few steps to realize and, when he looked back, the elf was staring. He followed her gaze and saw a woman, scarf wrapped around her face, standing in the shade of a jewelry stall.

"What's the problem?"

Sylvia took a moment to gather herself. "The woman's scarf."

"What of it?"

"It is almost wrapped in the manner of silfon, but not quite."

"Like your one, you mean? That special thing they do in your mother's village?"

"Yes. I thought... But it is just a human. Someone from around here. How would they even know of silfon?"

Rawk laughed and hurt his ribs. He winced. "It was bound to happen. Women have seen you with me. Or maybe they've seen you in the newspaper."

"I do not understand."

"Everyone tries to copy what I do. The things I wear, the paces I go. Why do you think tavern owners are willing to pay for me to have lunch at their establishments? Now, they're copying you as well."

"You are sure? It seems ridiculous."

"Of course it is. If I wanted, I could have men in Katamood painting stars on their faces within the week. Welcome to my life." And as if on queue, a crowd was starting to gather. Rawk pulled out a few coins to throw to the closest children, then waved to everyone else. "Have a good afternoon everyone. Hopefully the rains stay away."

The crowd grumbled but most of them took the hint and started to drift away, leaving Rawk free to continue down the hill. He was managing to avoid things nicely today.

—O—

17

Natan was coming out of the Ostler's Yard when Rawk led Sylvia down the side of the *Hero's Rest*. He was dressed in black, as usual, but had gone with the addition of a broad brimmed hat and a tall, colorful feather.

"Good afternoon, Rawk. I heard there was some excitement earlier. How did you fare?"

Rawk spread his hands. "I'm still alive and the creature isn't."

"A win then." Natan eyed Sylvia up and down as he dabbed at his face with his handkerchief. "And who is your friend?"

"This is Sylvia. She's my healer."

"You take your healer with you everywhere now? If you are at that point, then perhaps you should retire."

"I did, but it didn't stick with all the exots about. And if I'm injured, the next exot may be the one that kills me."

"Very wise." Natan spoke to Sylvia in elvish. "*Katamood is a long way from Amaraton, sister.*"

Sylvia's face was hidden under her scarf, but Rawk didn't doubt that she was surprised. It was a long time since he had heard the language himself— if he wasn't chasing and killing elves there wasn't a lot of opportunity— but it seemed that Natan's grasp of the intricacies was profound.

"*Yes, it is. And where is your home?*"

Natan laughed and gestured to the *Hero's Rest*. "*This is more of a home than I have ever had. I have travelled far enough and long enough to know that home is a state of mind.*"

"*I wish it were so,*" Sylvia replied.

"It is different for each of us, is it not? What would life be if we were all the same?" Natan laughed. "Rawk, please don't work Travis too hard. I have not seen nearly enough of him recently."

"I don't see much of him either these days. It must be his actual job at the tavern that's keeping him busy."

"Ahh, well, perhaps I should go and speak with his employers at *Keeto Alata*."

"Perhaps you should. And see if you can talk Yardi into dropping the price of our lodging while you're there."

"I am sure you would have more luck than I in that area."

Rawk shrugged. "I think Yardi likes profits more than she likes me."

"That she may." Natan mopped at his brow one more time before turning and continuing on his way.

"He is a surprising man," Sylvia said.

Rawk watched as Natan straightened his feather. "I suppose."

"A strange man."

"*That* I can agree with. Come on."

Shadows filled the Ostler's Yard, stretching out from the stone of the western wall, clutching at the side of the stables. Valen was sitting at the table outside the kitchen door, attacking a bowl of stew as only a young man could, before the dinner rush filled the rest of his day.

Rawk was about to greet the lad when a clatter from the corner of the yard spun him around, *Kaj* was in his hand in an instant, the long blade a gleam in the shadows.

"It is merely a cat," Sylvia informed him.

"It's always round about here somewhere," Valen added around a mouthful of food. "I reckon that's the one what's been leaving the dead mice on the back stairs."

The cat had been hanging around quite a bit in that case. Rawk grunted and headed inside, hoping Kalesie was too busy to notice Sylvia trailing in his wake. If the old cook caught a cat in her kitchen she might just let it go— and elf was a different matter entirely.

Down in the library— which wasn't really much more than an office with a desk, a couple of chairs and a shelf for the ever-growing collection of books— Rawk stood *Kaj* in the corner. He put a taper to the glowing lamp hanging on the wall by the door and used it to light the one on the desk. "Make yourself at home."

But Sylvia was already perusing the bookshelf. She picked out a small volume, examined it for a moment then slid it back in a different place.

"I didn't say you could rearrange anything." He sat down and leaned back in his chair. "I've spent hours getting them in order."

"Which order is that?"

Rawk shrugged. "It depends. What day is it?"

Sylvia chose another book and took it to her usual seat. She began reading and Rawk knew she could very well sit like that for the rest of the day, as if she was the only person in the room. A lot of time she *was* the only person in the room because Rawk couldn't keep up and got in trouble if he interrupted too much. So he looked around for something to do. There were lots of books *he* could read, which might somehow help with their mission, but he didn't want to read. That sounded a bit too much like work at the moment. When he noticed a jug and a brazier taking pride of place on a small table in the corner, he was glad of the distraction. With a groan he got back to his feet and went over to open the lid of the jug. He sniffed as a slightly bitter cloud of steam was released. *Tea.* There were small tankards near the brazier, plus spoons and honey. Travis had outdone himself this time.

Rawk made himself a cup and was about to head back to his desk to enjoy it when he remembered Sylvia. He looked at his cup for a moment, sighed, and took it to her instead.

"Thank you," she said, without really paying attention to what she was getting. But the cup was hot, so she looked up quickly enough when her fingers touched the steel. She eyed it and Rawk suspiciously. "What is it?"

"Tea." He gestured to the brazier and the jug. "Travis didn't leave the package, but it's Harish Dark, if I'm not mistaken. Have a sniff."

"I know what Harish Dark smells like, Rawk."

"Yes, but..." He sighed. "Don't think of it as medicine. Think of it as something to enjoy." He went back and made a cup for himself.

"You put honey in it?"

"Yes. Milk can be good too, but a bit hard to keep down here, obviously. Is it hot enough? I imagine the brazier was Travis' idea but I don't know how well it will work or how long it's been going. The taste gets stronger and... fuller... the longer you leave it."

"It is not wine."

"Really? Thanks for letting me know." He took his cup back to the desk but half the enjoyment had been taken out of the experience now. It was supposed to be relaxing, not an argument. "Drink it or don't, just don't sit there looking at me like I'm an idiot."

Rawk watched as Sylvia took a careful sip of the tea. The elf blinked her large green eyes. She didn't say anything, but neither did she put down the cup as she went back to reading. That made Rawk feel a bit better. He took a sip of his own and sat back in his chair, closing his eyes to rest.

−O−

Rawk woke with a start and almost fell off his chair. He looked around the office, rubbing his eyes. "What? What is it?"

"You are getting old, Rawk," Sylvia said from the doorway. She was looking out into the larger storage room, as if she could see through the next door and down the hallway. She had a book in one hand and was straightening her dress with the other.

"You woke me up to tell me I'm getting old?"

"No. I believe Celeste and Grint are here."

"What time is it?" Rawk rose to his feet, every joint and muscle creaking like his chair, and joined Sylvia at the door. "They aren't working tonight." The lamps in the office stretched his shadow across the dim, cluttered room beyond.

"It is just after sundown. And I did not say they were working; I merely said they were here."

And just then Grint opened the door to the storeroom and stomped in, like dwarves tended to do. His sister, slimmer, with dark skin and hair like their fermi, followed a moment later in an entirely more quiet and demure manner. She smiled and nodded but didn't say anything.

Grint nodded a greeting as well as he looked around. "I thought you were going to clean this room up?"

Rawk looked around as well. There was still stuff everywhere, the flotsam of a life spent traveling the world. A lot of it was stuff he would never use again, if he had ever used it in the first place, but it was his life. Each piece came with a memory, even if he struggled to remember what some of those memories were. He pointed at something he did recognize. "I got that hat from Princess Miramelle of Gardon thirty years ago."

"What for?" Grint asked. "It's horrible."

"It *is* interesting," Celeste agreed, blinking her large brown eyes as if she was attempting to make a hat manifest from the motley bundle of rags.

Rawk shrugged and cleared his throat. Even if Celeste wanted to hear the story about the rest of the reward he was given for saving the princess's life, he didn't want to tell it. "I can't remember now." He changed the subject. "Why are you two here anyway?"

"We came to listen to your new fiddler."

"Ferran? He's pretty good. Might do you two out of a job."

Grint shrugged. "We've got a contract. We can stay at home all week if you want, as long as you keep paying us."

Rawk grunted. "Let's go and get something to eat then, so we don't miss the start of the show."

"Who says you're invited?" Grint replied with a smile.

Rawk glanced at Celeste but she had gone to examine the books for a moment. "You'll be lucky to get in to see Ferran, the way you're going."

In *The Vault,* people were ordering drinks and making themselves comfortable before the rush came. There was always a rush these days, with a lot of people forced to stand down the back, which pleased Rawk no end. The *Hero's Rest* was becoming known as a place that offered great entertainment every night of the week. *The Vault* had only been open a few weeks and it already rivaled *Harker's Hall* over the south of the river, and the *Veteran's Club.* He decided if he could just work out a sensible way to get meals down the stairs then he would soon be able to gild his gold before he rolled in it.

But, as it was, even famous Heroes still had to go up to the common room to have a meal. With a sigh, Rawk turned away from his reserved table and wound his way across the room, stopping at the base of the stairs up to the common room to let a worker pass.

Celeste spoke into the pause. "Let's not go to the common room," she said. "Let's go somewhere else."

Rawk looked at his companions. A dwarf, and a fermi. And Sylvia didn't have her scarf wrapped around her face yet but, even if she did, she would still be recognizable as an elf. What would all the people out on the street say about that? "Do we have time?"

"We have plenty of time," Celeste said. "I know somewhere that isn't far."

The door opened at the top of the stairs again and a wave of noise tumbled down along with a drunken man who shouldn't have been using those stairs at all.

"Rawk!" the stranger shouted. He stumbled all the way to the bottom and leaned against Rawk as if he was a lamppost. "Tell me a story, Rawk. The one about when you killed that elf witch."

23

Rawk glanced at Sylvia. The other man didn't seem to notice her.

He waved away Rawk's unvoiced protests. "Or something else. It doesn't matter."

Rawk wondered if this man was one of the people he had been trying to impress all his life. "This place isn't far?" he asked Celeste. "All right then. Let's go." He pushed the man away, leaning him against the wall and standing ready for a moment, in case he didn't quite have the angle right.

As they headed for the main stairs up to the street, Sylvia started wrapping her scarf around her face. Rawk had seen the intricate process so many times he was sure he'd be able to do it himself.

"Will you be able to eat with that on?"

"Of course not. I will simply transfer the food to my stomach via magic."

Rawk knew she wasn't serious, but looked at her suspiciously anyway. "You aren't willing to do magic to save me but you'll do it to avoid removing your scarf?"

"It is handy if you don't like what your host has supplied for dinner; you don't have to taste it."

The place Celeste led them to was just a couple of blocks down the hill towards the Old Forest. A dwarf on stilts was working his way down the dead end street, lighting the lamps as he went, bringing a slow wave of light towards the tavern. The front porch had been removed and replaced with a garden that crept up the wall and onto the low, sloping roof. Rawk had visited the place five years ago and it hadn't looked anything like this.

"When did all this happen? This used to be a dingy little tavern with flat ale and overcooked roast." Though that described most taverns in Katamood. Especially the ones that Weaver seemed to like.

Celeste looked the building up and down. She shrugged, a slight lifting of the shoulders of her dusky rose shirt. "I don't know."

Grint did. "Azure Sky bought the building about three years ago. She closed it down for a month to have the remodeling done and opened it up again as *The Sky Tree*." He pulled on his beard. "Gunter and Gan did most of the carpentry, I think. Hadner did the tree."

"The tree?" Rawk looked at the plants but couldn't work out which one was *the tree.*

Celeste went inside, brushing leaves away from her face. Sylvia followed and Grint did as well. Rawk grunted. He didn't have any choice. Inside, he realized that the front wall was made up of huge, folding doors that could be pushed aside to bring the plants into the room. There was also a huge skylight overhead letting the starlight in to add to the soft glow of the lanterns. And in the back corner stood a huge metal tree. Branches reached out into the room and hundreds of colored–glass leaves, like butterflies, filtered the light. Rawk stared. It was like he'd entered a magical glade somewhere deep in the Old Forest, a special place where fairies gathered to gossip and play. Celeste was waiting just inside, her face painted green and red and yellow.

"Do you like it?" she asked. The colors played across her face.

After a moment, Rawk turned away from her to look at the tree again. "Hadner was a genius," he said eventually. When he looked back, Celeste was still looking at him. "It's beautiful."

"Where are we going to sit?" Grint asked.

Celeste blinked and looked around. "Anywhere."

The chairs and tables were rough looking things, made from crooked branches and roughly cut wood. They suited the surrounds but looked like they'd fall apart at the slightest touch. "So Gunter and Gan made the furniture?"

Grint nodded. "Went out and cut each piece themselves."

Rawk nodded too. If dwarves made it, he'd trust that it wouldn't fall apart.

There were a dozen other people in the place, none of them human. A party of elves laughed a babbling brook in the corner. Another elf brooded alone. And three tables of dwarves argued good-naturedly amongst themselves.

Rawk picked a small, almost-round table in a corner; there was still rough, dark bark running around the edge. "So, I take it Azure Sky is an elf? I'm surprised Weaver let her buy the place."

Sylvia unwrapped the scarf from her face. "Perhaps Azure did not buy it; I believe her husband is human."

"So what sort of food do they have?" Rawk remembered something Grint had told him a while ago. "And do they pay human prices for their ale or dwarf prices?"

"They don't sell ale," Celeste said. She picked up a small book from the table and handed it to him.

Rawk's eyes narrowed. "What sort of tavern is this?"

"Who said it was a tavern?"

"Well..."

"They call themselves a bistro."

"What in Path's name does that mean?"

"I don't know. But they sell food and wine and cider and you don't have to put up with all the drunks."

Rawk didn't know why he was complaining; it also meant he wouldn't actually have to drink any ale. He looked at the book Celeste had given him. "And what's this?"

"A menu." Celeste informed him.

"Why don't they just have a board on the wall?" But when he opened the book he knew why. There were about twenty different meals listed, though it took a few seconds of blinking before he could actually make out the words. "They've got all these things waiting out the back there?" Customers at the *Hero's Rest* had two or three choices at most.

Celeste smiled. "They cook it fresh once you've told them what you want. It takes a bit longer but..."

"You don't like the meals at the *Rest?*"

Celeste pursed her lips. "Meals at the *Rest* cost five ithel and that is how much they are worth."

Rawk looked back at the menu and saw prices listed as well. Most of the things were between fifteen and twenty ithel by the looks of it. "Twenty ithel? That's ridiculous." But he read the description of the first dish and it sounded delicious. "I'll have one of these," he said. "The *Kepler Venagoon,* whatever in Path's name that means."

Celeste smiled. "All the names of the dishes come from poetry."

"Really? How... interesting." Rawk got a cider as well and it was worth the extra money to not have to force his way through a mug of ale. He pulled his cutlery from the pouch on his belt and tested the edge of the knife.

"*Kepler Venagoon* is one of my favorite poems. It is only short, but there is so much emotion in it."

"I've never really read poetry. Thok did loan me a book though; I should get around to reading it some time."

"Our mother used to read to us all the time. I guess it stopped us from running around the streets and getting into trouble."

Rawk grunted. "My father never read me poetry and look where I am now."

"Yes, you're sitting in a tavern with an elf, a dwarf and a fermi. I'm guessing your father would be very disappointed."

Rawk laughed. "Yes, he would."

A few minutes later, Celeste was smiling as she told a story about Grint trying to build their mother a rocking chair when he was just ten years old. She had obviously told the tale before, and it almost came out as a song. The words danced and flowed like the notes from her mandolin and her eyes shone in the colored light filtering through the leaves of the tree. Grint kept trying to say that she'd been involved in the chair's construction as well while Celeste protested her innocence. Rawk wasn't sure he believed her. Sylvia was soon laughing, tears streaming down her face, in a very un-elfish manner.

When the meals came it did not signal an end to the conversation. Talk moved from rocking chairs to canals to music. "I wish I could play something," Rawk said. "It's as if my mind understands music but just can't manage to translate it for my fingers."

"Have you really tried to play?" Grint asked.

"Of course. I've tried just about every instrument there is over the years."

Celeste smiled. "But for how long? Did you play it five times and then give up? Or did you play it every day for a year, even though you were terrible?"

Rawk cleared his throat and examined the bone handle of his knife. "More than five times."

Grint laughed. "Six doesn't count. Did you pick up a sword for the first time and expect to win a fight? Of course not."

"Well, actually..."

Grint's eyes narrowed. "You expected to win or you did win?"

"I *did* win."

"Of course you did."

Rawk looked around at the others. "It was only against Yardi though. We were about twelve years old."

Grint laughed. Celeste threw a heel of bread at him.

Above the sound of laughter Rawk could hear music, a cascade of sound that drifted away amidst the colored leaf-shadows. No, not music because he couldn't actually hear it at all. He could see the sounds. Feel them in his bones.

"You felt it too," Sylvia muttered.

"The portal?"

The elf rose to her feet. "Yes. I believe it is very close by."

Rawk stood up. "That's what I thought." He looked around as if the exot might emerge from beneath a table in the bistro. "But where?" He stalked quickly out through the greenery, brushing it out of his face, and onto the street. He drew his sword as he went.

There were four creatures standing in the yellow light of the lamps. One was shorter even then Grint, seemingly as solid as a tree stump and just as weathered. It had only one arm and used it to hold a shield that was taller than it was. The second was tall and slim and had one arm as well. The opposite arm. Instead of a shield it held a sword. Neither of them had any eyes that Rawk could see, or even a place where eyes might once have been. Their wide, toothy mouths were grinning stupidly. The last two creatures were like rotund, long nosed pigs, though they stood on two legs. They had no arms at all but each had a single, large, green eye.

Both of Rawk's eyes narrowed. "What in Path's name?"

The two sightless creatures came forward as one, taking tiny steps on the rough cobbles. They crowded together, their own defensive line. At the same time the pigs spread out, as if trying to get a better view.

Rawk almost forgot to raise his sword. He did at the last moment as both the armed creatures rushed forward. He blocked a swing form the sword, like blocking a falling tree, and was shoved back by the shield. He stumbled, righted himself, and got himself some breathing space.

As long as it was a shallow breath. The two creatures attacked again, seemingly moving with more confidence than they had last time. Trying to be nice to his arm, Rawk deflected the blow instead of blocking it. Then he spun around behind the sword wielder, swinging powerfully at its unprotected back. Except it blocked without turning, displaying strange joints that meant back and front might well have been the same. And Rawk was pushed away by the shield once more.

"How can they even see me?" Rawk said, breathing deep.

"Rawk, I think..."

Rawk shifted his grip on *Kaj*, waiting. "That's very enlightening," he said eventually.

"I think there is only one creature."

"So we're all hallucinating the others?"

"No, I mean, they are all the one creature. The two with the eyes are seeing for the others. They have spread out so their depth perception is improved and their sight is not blocked by the others."

"You can't be serious."

"You think I am joking."

"Well..." It probably wasn't the time the elf would take up comedy. "So, I have to attack the ones with the eyes so these other ones can't see me?"

"Yes." She nodded but seemed unsure.

But that wasn't as easy as it sounded. Not because they fought back, but because they could apparently work in perfect unison with their comrades to make sure they never got anywhere near the fight. After another unsuccessful flanking maneuver, Rawk stopped to look around for inspiration. Not having any luck, he was about to ask for suggestions when Grint charged out of the bistro with a couple of dwarves and an elf on his heels. They had armed themselves with chairs and shouted as they split up and headed for the two exots with the eyes.

Rawk was distracted almost as much as the enemy but, before the eyes had even been engaged, he scuttled forward and dispatched the sword creature with a thrust between its shoulders. He spun, shouldered the shield aside, and killed its owner as well. The two eye−men were brought down by the dwarves, dying silently.

Rawk leaned on his sword, looking from one creature to the next. "Well, that was weird."

But Celeste was crying.

"What's the matter?" Grint asked her. "Nobody even got hurt."

"They were a family. They were..." She turned and walked away from the bistro, towards the main street.

Rawk took a step to follow, but he didn't know what to say. So he stood silently with Grint, watching her, while Sylvia rushed to follow. There were three crows watching from up under the eaves across the street. They complained loudly about the noise, ruffled their feathers, and settled back down.

Munday

RAWK WOKE EARLY AND WISHED HE HADN'T. He then spent an hour exercising in the gymna and that wasn't a good idea either. By the time he was done his arms and legs ached and he didn't know if he'd be able to make it down the stairs for breakfast. He decided to have a shower before he even bothered making the effort. He stood under the spray for a long time, letting the hot water wash away the sweat and sooth his muscles.

"I'm getting old," he said.

"You were old a long time ago."

Rawk jumped, heart hammering.

"Sorry, did I frighten the great Hero?"

"Travis, I wish you wouldn't do that."

"I wish I didn't have to walk all the way up those stairs just to tell you Weaver's here; I have to get *some* type of reward."

"You do; the highest pay of any tavern manager in the world."

"I think you're making that up."

"You aren't paid enough to think."

"I'm not paid enough to deal with Weaver either. He's down there disturbing your customers."

"As long as he still doesn't *know* they're my customers." Rawk sighed. "I'll be down in a minute."

But he waited where he was, under the hot water, for at least another five minutes, trying to find some calm for the start of his day that was not starting out well.

When he decided he really couldn't delay any longer, he dressed in clean clothes and headed for the taproom. But he didn't make it that far. Weaver was standing at the bottom of the stairs, leaning against the wall, without a fake beard or bad hat in sight.

"Good morning, Rawk."

"I suppose."

He was looking very serious. "About yesterday."

"Don't worry about it."

"Our friendship means too much to me to—"

Rawk waved away whatever Weaver was going to say. It would probably be a lie anyway. "Let's just forget it."

Weaver nodded, but Rawk knew that wouldn't be the end of it. For Weaver, it wouldn't be over until he got what he wanted.

"You didn't just come here for that. What else do you want? It's still a bit early for me to do a lot of thinking."

"Did you have a late night?"

"There was a new act down in *The Vault*. They did overtime."

"Really?"

Rawk winced. He knew what was coming but couldn't help himself. "Yes."

"Really? I heard that you didn't go to *The Vault* at all. A little birdie told me that you spent hours at some cheap elf tavern. I heard that you were there with an elf, a dwarf and a fermi."

"Is that what you heard?"

"I don't understand you, Rawk. You won't spend time with me and yet—"

"I thought we weren't going to talk about that?" He raised his eyebrows. "The elf was my healer and the other two were Grint and Celeste. And the tavern wasn't cheap."

The prince looked slightly mollified. "People will talk."

Rawk wondered why it mattered. They were an elf, a dwarf and a fermi. Or, at least, close enough that for any witnesses it wouldn't matter. But did it actually make any difference which *particular* elf, dwarf and fermi they were? "People always talk. But we just went out and had something to eat. We were intending to go back to *The Vault* to listen to the new act, but got caught up and ended up staying where we were for a few hours."

Weaver didn't say anything. His lip twitched.

Rawk sat down on a step. "Grint and Celeste have lived in Katamood their whole lives. Did you know that their father helped build the battering ram you used to knock down the door of the North Watch?"

Weaver's lip twitched again. "No, I didn't know that."

"He died a couple of days later, repairing a wall that was hit by one of your catapults. It fell on him. Celeste was only ten years old so she barely remembers him."

"A lot of people died before the city was free."

"I know. There are a few statues around commemorating them, but they all seem to show only humans."

"Nobody wants to see a statue of a dwarf."

"Dwarves might. Celeste's grandmother moved in with her recently because her home was taken so you could build your canal."

Rawk knew he should let it rest, but Weaver could never take a hint so he knew he would have to move him on— to either another place or another conversation— in another way.

There was a moment of silence. "You told me there were no more trolls in the Old Forest. You told me Galad died when a branch fell on him."

"Yes."

"Well, there's a rumor."

"There usually is."

"About you and the trolls and a dwarf."

"Well, you shouldn't believe everything you hear."

Weaver nodded slowly. "Perhaps. But I may have to look into it. The safety of Katamood is at stake."

"I can guarantee you that Katamood is completely safe from trolls. You have enough things to worry about without adding that to your pile as well."

"Such as what?"

"All the other exots turning up in the city every day? I killed some more last night." He was going to say *another one*, just because it was a really interesting idea, but that would mean he'd get paid less. "Four of them, with weapons."

"I did hear something about that."

"And then there's the Sorcerers holding meetings with the leader of the City Guard?"

"That is not proven."

Rawk laughed. "So you believe a rumor the old ladies are spreading through the city but you won't believe me?"

"Well…"

"Exactly. I have things to do, Weaver." Rawk got back up and pushed past Weaver. He didn't look back as he went through to the taproom. And halfway to the front door, he bumped into Natan coming the other way.

"Watch it." The big man looked around, a touch of heat in his voice. His dark eyes opened wide when he saw Rawk. "Oh, it's you. Apologies. I've been working all night and am quite exhausted." He looked away for a moment and Rawk turned to follow his gaze. It was only Weaver, staring as if force of will alone could make him give up the trolls. "I see you have been busy, too." Natan said. "Now, excuse me, I must go and get some sleep."

"Sure." Rawk glanced at Weaver then hurried from the tavern. He didn't care what the people thought.

Making his way down the hill, Rawk caught glimpses of the incomplete section of canal. The dwarves never seemed to stop. And not just those ones; there were dwarves everywhere doing the hard, dirty work that nobody else wanted to do. They were still working on the sewers, digging the deep drains along each street and carting the dirt and stone off to who–knew–where. They were probably adding it all to some huge pile and had a plan for what they would do with it all at the end. Whatever they did, Weaver would take the credit. He was already taking the credit for the canal and the sewers but Rawk doubted he was being completely honest.

There was a shout and Rawk had *Kaj* in his hand before he thought. He looked around, but all he saw was a woman shouting at a dwarf work gang, waving her fist like she could hurt them if she wanted. When she stormed away with threats of calling the City Guard, Rawk stayed where he was. The dwarves were all standing around a timber–framed machine, poking and prodding and tinkering. And standing in the middle of them was Clinker.

Rawk had not seen the lad since he'd shouted at him for something that wasn't his fault.

"Path."

Rawk looked around and started through the traffic towards the dwarves as one of them climbed onto a seat to work the machine with his feet. Another shifted a lever and they all stood back to watch as big, spinning brushes moved jerkily forward and scrubbed at the wall.

Rawk read the graffiti they were cleaning. *Here comes the storm. Let it wash us clean—* Words of Wisdom. "What does that even mean?"

A couple of the dwarves turned to look at him. One of them shrugged. He was big for a dwarf, with a mismatch of blond hair and an unkempt red beard tied with five guild ribbons of different colors, all in various stages of coming undone. "Storms is generally considered ta be bad things, but they clean the city better than a dozen dwarf work gangs could. Bad things can lead ta good things."

Rawk raised an eyebrow and the dwarf shrugged.

"Maybe." He laughed. "I'm an engineer, not a philosopher."

For a minute, Rawk watched the machine as it worked. "Hello, Clinker," he said eventually, without turning from the machine.

The lad was making an effort not to look at him too. He didn't reply.

"I see you got your machine working."

The contraption was doing a great job. The wall was almost clean already; the task would have taken a great deal longer with scrubbing brushes, though it wasn't clear how long it had taken to haul the machine up the hill. Clinker still didn't reply.

"I want to apologize, Clinker."

The whole work gang was making an effort to mind their own business.

Rawk turned to look at the boy properly. "I was wrong. You were doing a great job and it was only because Falling Leaves used magic that you failed at the end. Nobody could have done any better."

Clinker finally turned in his direction. He cocked his head to one side. "Magic?"

"Sylvia didn't tell you?"

"I haven't seen her."

"Don't stop seeing Sylvia because of me. She probably can't get by without your help and you don't punish all of your friends just because one is a bit of an idiot."

"*Are* you my friend?"

Rawk hesitated. He looked at the dwarves, who were still looking anywhere but at him. And in that moment, Clinker sighed and looked away. The boy was still shorter than he should have been, even for a dwarf of his age, and his hair still stood up at all sorts of crazy angles, but he had changed. There was a stillness to him that had not been there before. And not just a stillness of body; a stillness of his soul. Rawk wasn't sure if that was a good thing.

"Of course I'm your friend," he said.

Clinked looked back again. "Kikum stole my money," he said after a moment.

Rawk sighed this time. Kikum had said he was Clinker's friend too though that had always been doubtful. "Well, I don't need your money."

"He didn't get all of it. Just ten ithel."

"Just ten ithel?" That was a fortune for most street urchins.

"I hid some coins and told him about it, just like it was an accident and all. The next day the money was gone and he hasn't talked to me since. Larsi says it was probably worth the money."

"Do you trust Larsi though? She's just a girl, right?"

Clinker blushed and looked away. Yes, he'd changed.

"Sylvia has the rest of your money?"

"I guess I'll have to see her some day."

"And will Thacker buy your machine?"

The dwarf who'd spoke earlier laughed. "Too right Thacker will buy the machine. We can keep the whole city clean with a couple of these things, even without a storm ta help. We might even be able ta adjust it to clean the streets."

"And how much will he pay?"

The dwarf pursed his lips and examined the machine as it finished removing the graffiti. "Maybe a hundred ithel up front and a few ithel a month in royalties for each one."

"Path! Really? You're rich, Clinker."

The boy motioned to the older dwarf. "I need to give some to Kristun."

But the dwarf held up his hands. "I don't want your money."

"But you helped."

"Barely. One little idea."

Clinker wrinkled his nose and didn't look pleased.

Rawk turned to Kristun, remembering what Clinker had said when he'd mentioned him all those weeks ago. "Ah, you must be Kristun ga Meyer, the engineer, not Kristun ga Lund the tanner."

"That's right. How do you know that?"

"I know everything."

"Clinker been talking about me, has he?"

"Perhaps. Anyway, the *Hero's Rest* isn't far away, so if you aren't going to take Clinker's money, at least go up there and have a drink. Tell Travis to put it on my bill."

Kristun narrowed his eyes.

"Not just you. The whole gang." All of the dwarves were looking at him. He cleared his throat. "Anyway, I've got to go. But, Clinker, you'll come and talk to me if you see me now, right?"

The boy nodded.

"Good. Good." Standing there with all the dwarves looking at him was making Rawk nervous. "I've got to go." But when he turned to leave, he discovered there were a handful of humans looking at him as well. They all looked a little shocked. Some looked disgusted. One held up two fingers in the sign of the Great Path.

"Mind your business," Rawk said and stalked off.

Fifty yards down the hill, Rawk slowed down to catch his breath and look around. Nobody was looking at him. Well, no more than usual. They hadn't heard the conversation though that probably wouldn't matter. There'd be a rumor spreading through the city by the time he'd had lunch. Actually, he'd probably be Clinker's father by lunch.

A fleet of wagons rumbled slowly past, tarps hiding the mountainous loads. A crow flapped down amongst some doves, scaring them away and inspecting the breakfast they'd left behind. A horse clattered along the canyon of the street. On the far side, a woman was standing in the doorway of a shop, holding the door open with long fingers covered in bejeweled rings. She smiled at Rawk and, after a moment, sauntered across the street to his side.

"Hello, Rawk." She was as slim as an elf, but with full breasts and a little nub of a nose. "I am Redella."

"Hello, Redella."

Her breasts were threatening to spill from her dress every time she breathed.

"I like your dress."

"Thank you." She pulled herself up straighter, which made Rawk like the dress even more. "It is my own design."

Rawk looked back at the shop she'd been haunting. He could see racks of dresses through the rippled glass of the windows. "It's your shop?"

"Yes."

"How's business?"

Redella shrugged and Rawk was distracted enough that he didn't catch what she said.

"Pardon?"

She smiled. "Business is good. In fact, I was going to have a celebratory drink tonight and was wondering if you would join me."

Rawk raised his eyebrows.

"I will be at the *Mayflower* after sundown."

"Well, my schedule changes by the minute these days, but I just might join you."

There was a shout up the street and Rawk reached for his sword. He pushed Redella behind him, Hero that he was, and turned to face the threat. But, again, there was no threat. Not to anyone around here, anyway.

Rawk relaxed and Redella asked, "What is it?"

Two-dozen men came into view, marching double time Rawk recognized the leader and called out to him. "Paker, what's going on?"

The captain looked his way for a moment. "There's trouble brewing south of the river again. Looks like there might be another riot." He smiled. "Come on down, you might get to break some dwarf heads too."

"Maybe I will." But he stayed where he was as they continued down the hill.

Redella shaded her eyes to watch as well. "I don't know why we put up with them."

"The Guard?"

"No, the dwarves. And all the others."

"Others?"

"Elves and kedda and fermi and all the rest of races. They should be thankful we let them live in Katamood."

Fermi were *human*. Rawk wondered who decided which humans were worthy of respect and which were just like dwarves and elves. "Most of them were probably here before us, you know. Do you think Katamood is a human word?"

"What are you suggesting?"

"Should they be thankful that they lost their houses so Weaver can have his damn canal?"

"Prince Weaver cannot fix every problem, now can he?"

"Then he shouldn't create the problems." Rawk knew that Thacker and the dwarves had made preparations for all the people who would be made homeless, but they had yet to convince Weaver that their plans were a good idea. Celeste's grandmother had been thrown out of her home; it could have been Celeste. He looked at Redella. "I just remembered that I have things to do this afternoon. I won't be able to make it to the *Mayflower*."

"Some other day, perhaps."

"Maybe." He managed a smile before he hurried down towards the river.

–O–

Rawk crossed over Dragon Bridge in the wake of Paker and his troop of City Guard. A few weeks ago the square on the far side had been filled with tents and ramshackle houses cobbled together from the detritus of the city. The settlement had looked like it had been washed up by the river, and it didn't look any better now. Just bigger and more crowded. Moving along the path that wandered from the bridge to the road on the far side, Rawk noticed four other troops of soldiers hiding in the empty, haphazard streets. He knew what men looked like when they were teetering on the edge of a battle. There was a restlessness about them, an energy that pushed them towards the fray, even if they wanted to go the other direction. These men were one shout, one misheard word, away from charging. Of course, it helped that their opponents would be largely unarmed civilians.

But, at the moment, those opponents were nowhere to be seen. They possibly didn't even know the soldiers were there. Rawk started to run, as much as his knee would allow.

In the center of the square, the ersatz buildings hung back from the cistern, leaving a small clear space. This was where the gathering of locals had started. It was where the most vocal of them were. It was where the riot would live or die. There was no obvious leader, nobody urging them towards action, so Rawk started to push his way forward. The cistern would let him get up above the crowd. He had almost made it but a dwarf climbed up first and shouted for attention.

"Fellow citizens..."

Rawk swore. The other noises slowly died down.

"How long are we going to sit and wait for Weaver to throw us some scraps from the food that he stole from us?" The dwarf looked around. "This is our city. This is..."

Rawk jumped up onto the edge of the cistern. Heart racing, he held up his hands to silence the muttering from the crowd. It didn't work. "There are soldiers watching you right now," he said. "Trained, professional soldiers." Some of the audience fell silent then, other shouted to let the soldiers come.

"This is the way he treats us," the dwarf shouted, trying to wrest back the initiative. "He sends soldiers instead of emissaries."

"Have you talked to Thacker about what you intend to do?" Rawk asked. "Have you told him that you are going to defeat the soldiers here and then storm the palace? He might be interested to know."

"Thacker is useless," the dwarf shouted. "I am Gupter. I am one of you. I have worked with you to build shelters and to keep warm at night. I have found food for you. What does *the great Rawk* know of our lives?"

The crowd cheered.

"I know of life," Rawk said. "And going out to fight those soldiers is a quick way to lose it."

"I would rather die on my feet than live on my knees."

Rawk had to hold up his hands for quiet again and it was a long time coming. "Gupter is an idiot," he said eventually. Gupter was furious, but Rawk kept going. "If you die on your feet, you are dead a long time. In some situations, like this one where you have no hope of winning, that is the same as giving up. But if you live on your knees for another day, then there's a chance that the day after that you will get a chance to live on your feet."

"We are already dying. Our children are starving."

Rawk found that hard to believe. He doubted very much that Thacker would let anyone die. He wondered which local thug he would have to beat up to get the food moving in the right direction again. "I will see what I can do to help."

"What will you do, Rawk?"

"I will talk to Thacker today to see what can be done. I will talk to Prince Weaver. People are already working on your behalf. Let them keep doing that before you do something that cannot be undone."

Gupter could obviously see he was losing them. "Why should we believe you? You're Prince Weaver's friend. You're as bad as the rest."

Rawk kept going. "I'm here Gupter. And, in the past, I may not have helped many who weren't humans, but I've always been a man of my word. Go back to your homes. Don't give the City Guard an excuse to hurt you."

The mob was gone. The people were individuals again. They became smaller, slumping down, shifting nervously. They turned and spoke to those next to them. One by one, and in small groups, they drifted away into the tents and the shanties. Down one of the streets, Rawk watched as Paker shook his head and led his men away. None of them looked to be very happy.

Gupter certainly wasn't happy. "What in Path's name do you think you're doing? You think you're helping? You don't know anything about what's going on here."

"I know what was going to happen, Gupter. Innocent people were going to die."

The dwarf shook his head and jumped down from the edge of the cistern. He stalked away with a half dozen others close behind.

Standing under a tree in the corner of the small square, birds raucous above him, was someone Rawk knew. He wasn't quite sure how he hadn't noticed him in the first place; Thok towered above everyone else. He gave the man a nod. "Hello, Thok. I didn't expect to see you here." He never really expected to see Thok anywhere really; he just kind of turned up and disappeared completely. If Rawk didn't like him it would have been a bit creepy.

The big man nodded in reply.

"So, do *you* think I should mind my own business?"

He shrugged. "Who's to say this isn't your business? Given your history, I'm not sure what your motivation is, but I'm not totally clear on Gupter's motivation either."

"What would you have done?"

"If there was a riot? Run the other direction."

"You could have talked them around. They probably see you as one them."

"I'm not one for speeches. I prefer to write my messages down if I've got any choice."

Rawk took a deep breath and looked around. "Do you want to get some lunch?"

"Sure. Why not?" He motioned down to a street leading away from the river. "Come on."

Thok led the way to a tavern half way up Mount Grace. It was obviously a regular hang out, for he was greeted by name and seemed to know everyone, even the customers. There was only one choice for lunch, but it was a thick, rich stew that came in a bowl large enough to feed a horse. There was also a piece of bread with butter and a mug of ale. Rawk took his spoon from the pouch on his belt and set to.

"I realize you can do whatever you want, but it was still surprising to see you down there."

Rawk ate in silence for a while. "I've spent my whole life being a Hero. When I was younger, I needed to do what was expected if I wanted to make a living. But now..." He shrugged. "I guess I've just been wondering who I'm trying to impress."

"Some people are worth impressing."

"Of course. But most of the people worth impressing aren't impressed by the whole Hero thing anyway." He picked up his mug of ale but stopped with it half way to his mouth. He looked at Thok. He looked back at mug. And he put it down. "Can I get some water? I've been drinking ale all my life and still haven't grown to like it."

"I'm sure Tessa can manage something." Thok waved to a waitress and explained the situation.

A minute later, Rawk was taking a long drink of cool, clear water. He set the mug down gave an appreciative shake of his head and returned his concentration to his food.

"Shouldn't you be having lunch... somewhere?" Thok asked.

Rawk tapped his spoon on the side of his bowl as he gave it some thought. Of course, he should have been, he just couldn't think of where. "I haven't been going to the usual places much at all lately. Ever since..."

"Since Maris died?"

"Was *killed*. Yes." He pushed the last of the stew around in his bowl. "I killed the damn sorcerers... Most of them..."

"So the rumors are true?"

"Surprising, I know." He shrugged. "I thought I was finally, really, going to get to retire."

"You don't actually seem all that keen on the idea."

Rawk shrugged. "I don't think I want to be a Hero any more, but I don't think I want to be a *retired Hero* either. That doesn't sound like much fun."

"Are you a Hero? Or are you Rawk?"

Rawk shrugged. He wasn't quite sure he understood the question. "It doesn't matter now anyway. The portals are still opening. The exots are still coming."

"So there are more sorcerers?"

"I'm not sure. We aren't sure."

"We? You and Weaver?"

Rawk almost laughed. "Weaver's carrying on as if nothing unusual is happening. He doesn't care, as long as nothing appears in his palace. Sylvia is helping me."

"The healer? How can she help?"

"Sylvia knows all sorts of things. And speaking of which, I'm meeting her this afternoon. And now I have to go and see Thacker as well so I really have to get going." He wiped his spoon on his shirt and put it back in the pouch with the knife and fork and threw some coins on the table.

"Well, good luck. A waster appeared just down the road from my place the other day. It killed three people before one of your street–corner–Heroes managed to kill it."

"You saw it?"

"No. I only heard about it. I've seen wasters before though and I have to say I'm not overly disappointed."

"They aren't very impressive, are they? But," Rawk shrugged, "it killed three people so maybe we should stop looking at how things look and worry about how they act." Exot, man or dwarf.

"Perhaps we should."

Rawk left him there, sitting at the table, staring into his mug.

–O–

A goat—cab took him up the mountain to the first of the stairs and from there it wasn't far to the gate into Caldera. He went between the carved columns and into the tunnel that led straight into the mountain. There was a right angle bend to the left about half way along and a bend the other direction not long after that, just enough to halt the momentum of any charge. Then he came out into the light in the circular valley at the top of the mountain.

The city that filled it was still part of Katamood technically, but looked completely out of place. Colorful panels of timber and silk were splashed of added splashes of color to the red stone buildings that blended together along the sides of curving, winding streets. Gardens overflowed from rooftops like colorful waterfalls.

Rawk stood and stared and wondered when he would really get used to the place. He might have stayed there for longer still, had not the rattle and clank of a tram bought his attention back to the business at hand. He hurried down and climbed on the contraption as just before it pulled out of the station and rode it all the way around to Thacker's offices, listening to an old dwife behind him tell a fried about her new granddaughter. It sounded no different to a conversation any two old ladies might have.

Thacker was sitting in his office, working at a large, leather bound ledger when a guard let Rawk through a short time later. He looked up, seemingly pleased for the distraction. Rawk doubted the feeling would last.

"What can I do for you, Rawk?" He was at lest fifteen years younger than Rawk and unusually well groomed for a dwarf. His beard was combed and all the guild ribbons in his beard were neatly tied.

"Food."

"You've missed lunch, I'm afraid. I don't think I could get away with stopping again." It looked as if he was giving the idea some serious thought.

"No, food for the canal refugees down in the square."

Thacker's eyes narrowed. "They have food."

"They don't agree. I just hobbled a riot in that crazy makeshift town but I don't know how long that will work."

"Food was sent down yesterday. I have the work order here…" Thacker looked about on his desk, but it had obviously been tidied recently because the ledger was the only thing on it.

"It may be leaving Caldera, or your warehouse somewhere," Rawk said, "but after that, I'm not so sure. Who's in charge of the operation?"

"Berker ga Mund." He picked up the ledger but that didn't reveal the paperwork he was after.

"Well, you may want to have a word with him."

"I've known him for years."

"Well, maybe it isn't him, but you need to have a word with him anyway so you can start to work out what's going on."

The dwarf nodded and called out to his unseen assistant. The dwife stuck her head in from an adjoining room. "Salo, I need to talk to Berker."

"Very well. I'll see if I can find him."

"Thank you."

"You have that under control then?" Rawk asked. "I can't give you any more information so I'll be on my way. I have to meet with Sylvia."

"Yes, I can handle it from here. If that food was diverted along the way I'll rip off someone's ears."

"You should really delegate stuff like that."

Thacker threw down his pen and left a spot of ink on the page. "Don't worry, I will."

Back on the outside of Mount Grace, Rawk found a goat–cab at the first opportunity and rode it all the way down to the river and back up Two Watch Hill as far as Juskin's bookshop. He sent up a cloud of dust as he opened the door and discovered the little old man sitting behind the counter. He was repairing a book that looked like it had come out second best in a tavern brawl.

"Good afternoon, Rawk." He eyed him shrewdly over the top of his spectacles. "You look different today."

"It's my hair. Do you like it?" He rubbed his hand over his bald scalp.

Juskin looked at his head. "That's it... I can see your head. I *have* seen your head before, but your hood is always up when you first come in."

Rawk hadn't realized, either that he usually had his hood up or that today he didn't. He resisted the urge to rub his head again. "Well, I..." He smiled. "I decided a little while ago that I was done with impressing anyone. So, I now no longer care if people see me in a bookshop consorting with the likes of you."

"Good for you. I wish more people were seen in bookshops. This one in particular. Though I assume you still don't want anyone to know you are after books on magic."

"That would probably be for the best. Speaking of which..."

Juskin tapped the book he was working on. "If you just give me a minute you can have this one. Plus I have a couple of others. Travis came in this morning but a supplier dropped these off a little while later." He went back to work, concentrating fiercely. Rawk didn't want to disturb him, so he wandered around looking at some of the other volumes on the shelves. When he discovered the poetry section he stopped to strain his eyes and read the titles more carefully. But the titles didn't help.

Rawk cleared his throat.

"Yes?" Juskin came to stand by his side, four small books clasped in his hand.

"Do you know the poem about Kepler Venagoon?"

"Of course." He adjusted his spectacles as he scanned the titles. He pulled one down and flicked through the pages. "Ah, yes, here you go."

Rawk took the book, waiting for his eyes to focus as much as they would. The poem was barely a dozen lines.

"White Paladin of time already revealed,
Kepler Venagoon was called again
to follow the Great Path, sword and shield,
between heaven's stars above and the life
sparks below. And every step of blood and faith,
was another step away from Salodie, his beloved wife.

And when the years brought him at last to the end
he had lost the sense of the stars above
and the sparks below. Kepler Venagoon
searched for the up and the down, one and the other,
the living world below and heaven above the moon
for beloved Salodie."

"So is this supposed to be good?"

Juskin shrugged. "It probably isn't one of his better works, according to the scholars."

"But what do they know, right?"

"Exactly. Many people love the poem."

"Well, I'll take this one too, I guess."

"Should I hide the fact that you are buying poetry books as well?"

"Is poetry against the law?"

"No, though I wish some of it was, particularly some of the later works that came out of Melange."

"Well, tell anyone you like then. I'm not impressing people any more, remember."

"Very well." Juskin handed over the four books he was holding as well. "I trust you, Rawk, but... Your bill is becoming quite large. Is there any chance..?"

"You want some money?" Rawk nodded. "I don't have much on me at the moment but I'll get Travis to pay you next time he's in. Everyone is calling in their debts." He considered the fact that he owed Weaver, or more accurately Katamood, a lot of money. He could pay it off any time he wanted, if he wasn't worried about arousing suspicion regarding the state of his finances, but he had never before thought that Weaver might actually ask him to pay.

Outside, someone screamed.

Rawk went to the door and watched as a wave of people surged up the street, looking behind as if they were being chased. He glanced at Juskin then hurried out onto the front steps to see if that helped sort out the mystery. Not really. More people were coming, rushing madly, but there was no evidence of anything that might be scaring them. Rawk drew *Kaj* and went the other direction, sticking close to the side of the street to avoid the worst of the current. He was still bumped and jostled but his size meant he was able to keep moving. He tried to ask what was happening, but the man shook him off and kept running without noticing who he was.

Soon the people were gone and Rawk could move more quickly. His knee hurt, but he started to run.

In the main lane way of Mount Cheese Market he skidded to a halt. That hurt even more than running but he didn't have time to think about it. The sent of carami and rosemary drifted to him from a spice merchant's tent and Frew was standing not far away. The little Hero glanced towards Rawk but couldn't really spare the attention. He was facing a dozen warriors with another bleeding out on the ground by his feet. For a moment, nobody moved, then Fabi rushed into the clear and almost fell over as he stopped in a hurry as well.

"What's going on?" the big black man asked.

"This lot came through a portal," Frew replied, not taking his eyes off the strangers this time. "Do you think the three of us can take them?"

Rawk doubted it very much and even at his best he would have thought it a bad idea to even try. A lot of them wore colored animal—mask helms and those that didn't had luminous tattoos of intricate design on their faces and necks. Rawk could see a hawk, a dragon and a scatter of strange symbols. Hundreds of ribbons, like butterflies, covered their cloaks. Beneath was chipped and dented armor.

They seemed to be normal men, and women, but it was obvious that they knew which end of the sword was the sharp bit.

"Did you talk to them?" Fabi slowly drew his sword.

"What do you mean?"

Rawk cleared his throat. "Fabi and I were talking about this the other day. Did they attack you? Or did you attack them?"

"They attacked me."

"Were you being friendly?"

"What?" Frew didn't let the conversation distract him.

"Did you run towards with your sword drawn?"

"Of course I did. I was pretty much on him before either of us realized."

Rawk nodded. He looked the strangers up and down; they were standing, calm but wary, not attacking anyone at all. After a moment he spoke to Fabi and Frew without looking at them. "Don't move."

Holding *Kaj* loosely out to the side, point down, Rawk walked slowly forward. When he got to Frew's side he paused for a moment, licking his lips, then continued forward again. The awnings protecting the market stalls from the weather flapped in the breeze and it was like the applause of a crowd.

"What in Path's name are you doing?"

From the corner of his eye, Rawk saw Frew do a two—fingered Y sign in his direction. "I didn't know you believe in the Great Path, Frew." *If not, it might be a good time to start,* he thought. He should be concentrating, not worrying about Frew and his gods. He kept walking. Each step he took, the strangers seemed to become a bit more tense. They subtly shifted their feet. They shifted their grip on their weapons. They made small adjustments to their armor. But, still, none of them attacked. A cloud passed across in front of the sun and Rawk paused for a moment, shivering.

Only one of the strangers was watching him. The rest were watching Fabi and Frew or keeping a more general eye out for trouble. Professionals then. Veterans. Rawk stooped down to lay *Kaj* on the cobbles. He licked his lips, standing silently with the sword by his feet. He didn't know if Frew or Fabi would be quick enough to help if some decided they wanted him dead.

He had left behind the scent of the spices and could now smell nothing but tallow. He didn't know where it was coming from. It was annoying him. Distracting. His nose twitched. The stalls and tents stopped flapping for a moment, as if they too were waiting

The leader of the warriors stayed where he was. He glanced around, perhaps looking for the surprise attack. He turned a full, slow circle as his companions waited, still and watchful. Once he was facing Rawk again, the man paused, then walked slowly forward, lithe as a cat. A few paces away, he stopped and slowly sheathed his sword with a whisper of steel on steel.

"I'm guessing you don't speak this language," Rawk said. Perhaps he should have just tried talking to them earlier, though they'd had plenty of chance to join the conversation. Which meant he didn't know what he was supposed to do to communicate, beyond the things he'd already done. Rawk looked at the man and shrugged. It was a gesture that anyone from this world would understand.

Rawk pointed to himself and said his name.

"Adonda Zid Har Weizu," came the reply.

Rawk breathed. Maybe everyone was going to live. "Adonda?" He glanced back. Well, everyone except the dead guy.

The man eyed him up and down. "Zid," he said.

Perhaps 'Adonda' was a title, or rank. Or perhaps 'Zid' was the rank and Rawk was being put in his place. Rawk wasn't sure how to clarify, but knew it didn't matter in the end.

Especially when Zid became alert and looked around. A moment later, Rawk heard it as well. The tramp of feet on the cobbles. Synchronized military feet. Zid wasn't happy but Rawk held up a hand to try to calm him.

"You know Weaver is unlikely to just let these men go to wander around the city," Fabi said, "no matter how friendly they appear."

Rawk hadn't thought of that. He should have, but for the last few minutes all he'd been thinking about was staying alive. Even if he could control the City Guard long enough to keep Zid and his companions alive, they were probably going to be locked up as a threat. "Path." He held up his other hand as well. *Keep them calm. Great. And then what?*

Zid said something though it wasn't immediately obvious if he was talking to Rawk or to his own men. But they still didn't attack. The canvas flapped and the boots came closer. There were people watching from amidst the stalls and the buildings further away.

Rawk did the only thing he could think of. He picked up his sword and walked quickly away from the sound of the approaching feet. He paused once and looked back to beckon the strangers to follow. He hoped he looked desperate enough for them to get the message. Frew didn't move, but Fabi came and stood by his side. The big man sheathed his sword, perhaps as a symbolic gesture, and Rawk decided to do the same. He gestured again then turned and walked, pushing between two of the braver spectators who were finally starting to get closer. If the exots didn't follow, then there was nothing more he could do that wasn't dangerous for someone— mainly himself. When he next looked back, Zid was looking towards the approaching footsteps, then gave an order in a surprisingly melodic language, and followed Rawk.

In the nearest alley, away from the prying eyes for a moment, Rawk sent Fabi ahead to look for trouble and paused amidst a stinking drift of rubbish— no spices here— to let everyone else catch up. He started moving again when Zid was a couple of yards away. Buildings leaned in, blocking out most of the sky. The world was reduced to just a sliver. But Rawk didn't know where he was going or what he was going to do. He couldn't just wander around in the alleys; the Guard were sure to catch up sooner rather than later. He ducked and weaved down one narrow, cluttered alley and crossed a major road into another twisting backstreet beyond. Rawk was positive he'd never been down that particular narrow, ambush–waiting–to– happen in his life but a green roof brought him up short. He was sure he knew it. The building it crowned was tall and narrow. It looked like it might be a shop on the ground floor and a house above.

Fabi was calling softly from one side and it sounded as if the City Guard were still following the trail of curious people they'd left behind. A swell of sound suggested someone was not far behind.

As Rawk turned to continue on, he spotted an old book lying on the ground beneath the back stairs of the building, tattered leather cover green with mold. And he knew where he was. He raced up the creaking stairs and tried the door. Locked. So he knocked and waited. Knocked again. Eventually, after what seemed a lifetime, Juskin opened the door a crack and looked out.

"Rawk? Is that you?"

"Yes, it's me. You have to let me and my friends in."

Juskin's eyes narrowed.

"Quickly." Rawk's heart pounded. He looked back down the alley but there was nothing to see. The source of the tramping feet was hidden by a bend. It wouldn't be long though so he pushed the door open, startling Juskin, and waved his followers in. A minute later the storeroom at the back of the bookshop was crowded with armored warriors. Someone upset a pile of books and the volumes thudded dully onto the floor.

"What is going on?" Juskin demanded.

Rawk shushed the old man and peeked out the small window at the back with Zid by his side. Everyone else waited silently while Juskin bustled around to move other precarious ziggurats further from the edge of benches and tables.

"Rawk, I don't—"

Rawk glared at him and he stuttered into silence as well.

Paker came into sight. The captain stalked purposefully along the alley. His men came along behind, swords at the ready, looking like they wanted some action. Rawk knew most of the men and none of them were known for their intelligence or for their accepting ways. He swore under his breath and sat down on a pile of books. *Paker?* What were the odds of him just randomly walking around the streets with a troop of the Guard at his back?

A minute later, Zid let out a relieved sigh and sat down on the edge of a table covered with a autumn scatter of leather–bound books. He took off his bird helm, revealing a round, blue–tinged face with a long nose and a tussock of white hair. His left cheek and neck was covered by a luminous tattoo that seemed to shift and swirl in the dim light.

"Who are these men?" Juskin asked.

"I don't know, Juskin. We can't understand a word they say."

"Then what is going on? Why are they hiding in my shop?"

"Don't you trust me?"

"I do. But these men..."

Another of the warriors took off their helm and she obviously wasn't a man. Rawk didn't know if he'd ever seen anyone so beautiful in his life, though it was an unsettling type of beauty he didn't quite know how to deal with. The woman said something to Zid in the musical language.

Juskin replied haltingly before anyone could say anything.

Rawk blinked at the old man. "Excuse me?"

Zid started talking as well, rising to his feet. The words were on the edge of aggressive and Juskin backed away before Zid made a concerted, noticeable effort to calm down. And that last act confirmed for Rawk that he had made the right decision.

"What's going on, Juskin?"

Juskin cleared his throat and glanced at Zid. "They are speaking Halote."

"That's a language?" Fabi asked from near the door. He had it open a crack and was looking down the alley after Paker. "I thought it was a city that was destroyed a few hundred years ago."

"It is both. They spoke Halote in the city of Halote before the volcano buried them. Though it was more like a few thousand years ago."

"Then how do *you* speak it?"

"Halote was the center of the world, long ago. There were schools and libraries where people from all around the world went to study. Many books were saved, so the language lives on. It is actually quite different from what your friends are speaking, but I think we would be able to understand each other enough to get by." He paused, narrowing his eyes. "How are they your friends if you cannot even speak to them?"

"Will you just ask Zid what's going on?"

"Zid?"

"Their leader."

Juskin nodded and turned to the other man. They spoke at length, but Rawk thought that most of the conversation was just the same thing repeated in different ways as they tried to understand each other.

"Well?"

"As far as I can tell, Zid and his... Jentre?— I'm not sure exactly what that is— were waiting to see the King, or something similar. The portal appeared and they were sucked into it."

"Sucked into it? It pulled them in?"

"Yes. Perhaps. No. Maybe it was a metaphorical pulling. Then someone attacked them..."

"Frew did."

Frew cleared his throat. "I didn't attack them, as such. I just ran towards them, in a general sort of way, with my sword drawn. It was more a misunderstanding than anything else."

"Of course. A Hero wouldn't attack without first finding out all the facts."

"Hey, there were still people everywhere at that stage."

Rawk held up a hand to stop Frew from going any further. "Right," he said. "So, what do we do now?"

"You are asking me?" Juskin laughed. "Zid doesn't seem the type to go around killing people for no reason, so... Did anyone see them with you?"

"Yes."

"So they need to go into hiding for a couple of days? At the least." Juskin cleaned his spectacles while he examined the warriors. "I suppose they could stay here."

Rawk looked around. "Here?" He raised an eyebrow.

"Not exactly *here*; you know that I live up stairs. It would be cramped but..."

"Do you want to study them? Do some research?"

Juskin blushed.

"Anyway, no. Weaver will send someone here soon enough. He has to know that I visit your shop fairly regularly."

"In that case, you should leave as soon as possible."

"Yes, you're right."

Juskin spoke to Zid, a long laborious process that involved lots of pauses. Juskin spent so long staring at the ceiling between words that Rawk was beginning to wonder if there was a Halote dictionary painted there. Eventually, he got a nod in reply and the soldiers started removing their helms and their long butterfly–cloaks. They folded the latter and put them in the former and placed them in a pile beneath the table. With their dark armor and unsettling beauty they were still going to attract attention, though not as much as before.

"I don't know where you want to go," Juskin said eventually, "but Zid and his Jentre will follow."

"Right. Good." Where did he want to go? It probably didn't matter at this stage, as long as it was away from Juskin's shop, where the search would probably come as soon as Weaver worked out how close it was to the Mount Cheese markets. He looked around, trying to think. "This group is too big, too noticeable. Let's split up. Frew and Fabi, each of you take four of our new friends and meet at the main *Keeto Alata* warehouse."

"At the warehouse?"

"Yes, there's a small door on the north side. This lot don't look like the sort to go into the offices, but they might be workers." He looked them up and down. "Or guards. Or something. Juskin, tell them what's happening."

A minute later, Rawk took a deep breath then led Zid and three others out into the front of the shop and from there out the door onto the street. His heart was racing but the locals were so used to exots now that it was almost as if they forgot about them after a few minutes of quiet; there was no screaming right now, so everyone carried on as if nothing had happened. And old lady tottered along with a basket of flowers. Three young men were trying to, alternatively, cajole and push and carry a reluctant goat down the street. A couple were wrangling a child in much the same way. Some passers by did pause to look, but the stranger's tattoos didn't glow as much in the sunlight, so they were just attractive foreigners. Rawk's hand twitched but he took it away from the hilt of his sword and hurried down the street. At the corner he looked back and saw Fabi emerge from the shop. He continued quickly down the street and his heart didn't slow at all.

The offices of *Keeto Alata* were back down towards the river. They weren't that far away, but every step increased Rawk's unease. Every corner was an opportunity to be surprised by Paker, or any of the City Guard. His back itched. He hurried on and tried project a mien of *I'm not going to tell you a story.* It seemed to work.

They came to the warehouse from a smelly, damp alley and Rawk went in through the small side door without pausing. There was a guard just inside. When he thought about it, it was obvious, but it still caught him by surprise.

"You can't come in here."

"What's your name?"

"Howser."

"Well, Howser, do you know who I am?"

Howser looked him up and down, as if it might be a trick question. "Rawk?"

"That's right."

"You still can't come in here. You might be able to kill me, but I don't really think you want to so it's unlikely to happen. But if I let you in, Yardi will probably fire me. And then my *wife* will kill me; she's pregnant."

"Congratulations. Is it your first?"

"Yes. There's less than a month to go."

"Right. Well, I understand completely." He looked back at his followers, who were still standing in the alley. "But you know Yardi is a friend of mine, right?"

"Yes."

"Do you really think she would mind letting me in?"

"I'm not paid to think, Rawk." It looked like he would be very good at the 'not thinking' part of the job.

Rawk sighed. He kept his ownership of *Keeto Alata* secret for a reason but he was starting to wonder if it was more trouble than it was worth. "Look, Howser, I have some friends out here, and some more coming soon, and we really need to get out of the open."

Howser leaned to the side slightly to look out the door.

"Do you really think I'm going to steal something?"

Howser gave it some thought and Rawk wondered if he was going to go to Yardi to request a pay rise.

"Let us in. I may not kill you, but I will knock you senseless and Yardi will still fire you for being incompetent."

Still nothing.

"Your conscientiousness is wonderful, but get out of the way."

Rawk pushed the man aside and made his way into the warehouse. Zid and his friends followed and they all crowed in a small clear space in the corner.

Fabi was not far behind. And a few minutes later, Frew led his small group in the door as well. The little man gave a sigh and loosened the muscles in his shoulders. "Well, that was uncomfortable."

Fabi laughed softly. "Now what, Rawk?"

"I've got to go talk to Yardi, I guess."

Up in the reception area, Hurno didn't look happy. "Rawk," he said. "Yardi is very busy at the moment."

Rawk sighed. "Are you going to make me go through all this again? Every time?"

"I am trying to do my job. I—"

"For a long time, I was just trying to do my job as well, Hurno, but sometimes you have to actually think for yourself. The world isn't black and white. And, in my experience, people are wrong as often as not, even if the rest of the world doesn't realize."

"Yardi told me..."

Rawk sighed and went across to Yardi's office. And for the first time that he'd ever seen, Yardi was actually doing some work. She had a big pile of papers on her battleship-desk and was marking off items in ink as red as blood.

"Here we be go," she said with the usual confusion of grammar and diction from all the languages she knew. "Who be you sleeping with this time?"

"Nobody."

Yardi raised her eyebrows.

"No, really; nobody." And he realized it was true. He gave a grunt.

She obviously didn't believe him.

"I have a dozen men who need jobs. Well, men and women." He paused and scratched his head. "Well..."

"They not be men *or* women?"

"They look like men and women, but I have no way of judging for sure."

"You could ask."

"They speak Halote. I don't suppose *you* do?" It wouldn't have surprised him.

"No. Not a lot of traders coming from Halote."

"I didn't say they came from there. They came through an ohoga portal."

Yardi sucked air through her teeth. "Exots?"

Rawk ignored the word. "They can be guards or they can load some stuff into wagons. It will just be for a couple of days until Weaver gets bored."

"Weaver is looking for them?"

"Maybe. Paker certainly was a little while ago."

"I don't have much in the way of work at the moment."

"Look, just give them somewhere to hide. You don't need to pay them or anything."

"They only speak Halote?"

Rawk nodded and Yardi sighed. She threw down her pen and rose to her feet. "Take me to them."

Yardi came up short, mouth open, when she saw the first of the strangers. He was bigger than the others and had a dragon design glittering on the shaven skin around his ear. His dark eyes were intense, his stillness mesmerizing, like a cobra ready to strike.

"Hello." Yardi recovered quickly, stepping forward as if nothing had happened.

The man's eyes narrowed and he glanced at Rawk, as if making sure the man in charge of the operation knew what was going on. After a moment, he gave a small nod and stepped aside so Zid could come forward.

But there wasn't much to say, beyond brief, awkward introductions.

Eventually, when it was obvious communication of any sort wasn't going to be easy, Yardi grunted. "There are a couple of empty workers rooms down back. There not be enough, but I'm sure if they warriors they be used to sharing. But we be having big shipment arriving in three days and workers be coming as well, already hired, so they will have to be gone by then." Her eyes narrowed. "How do you know they speak Halote?"

"I have an interpreter."

"You didn't be thinking to mention this before?"

"No. You didn't think to ask? Juskin owns a bookshop. He's working now and not one for either fighting or sneaking around in alleyways. I'll send him around when I can but until then you'll just have to make do."

"Me? You can take them down the back and explain to them. I have work to do."

"Oh, all right."

—O—

When Rawk made his way into the library, he felt like he was coming home after a month of campaigning. He was exhausted and his nerves were still jangling. Sylvia was already there, holding a cup while she examined the books on the shelf.

"You made a cup of tea?"

She looked at the cup in her hand. For a moment, she seemed to be at a loss for words. "I feel more... aware... when I drink the tea."

Rawk smiled. "And you thought I was crazy."

"I *know* you are crazy, Rawk. I am merely still trying to discover all of the causes and symptoms."

"Of course. Sorry." He sat down at his desk. "So, how's it going?"

Sylvia sighed, missing a perfect opportunity for a joke about causes and symptoms as far as Rawk was concerned. "It does not seem to be going at all. Your library is relatively small, when considering the depth and breadth of magic's history, and may not have an answer for us at all, but it is big enough that it could take me a year to discover that."

Rawk tapped the books he had just brought in. "Well, good news."

"There are answers in there?"

"Maybe."

"So, what you mean is that you have some more books for me to search through?"

"Yes."

Sylvia sighed. "Travis brought those ones in a while ago." There was a small pile on Rawk's desk. There was also a small, carefully wrapped parcel.

"Excellent. Do you need to hire an assistant?" Rawk took up the package, wondering what it could be.

"An assistant?"

"Yes." He pulled at the string to release the cloth covering. Inside, was a pair of spectacles— two circles of polished glass held by a thin wire frame. He pursed his lips, glanced at Sylvia, and put them in his drawer. "You tell them the sort of thing you are looking for and they can read some of the books and point out stuff you might be interested in."

"I understand how such a system might work, Rawk, but do you really expect me to go around looking for people to read books about magic for me? How long do you think it would be until *that* rumor began to spread?"

"Well..."

"Yes, so stop disturbing me so I can read." She pulled a book from the shelf, apparently at random, and took it back to her chair.

Rawk took a book as well and sat with his feet up on the desk. Then he had to get back up to get himself a cup of tea. Finally, he sat down, took a sip, and blinked his eyes into focus so he could read.

Some time later, Rawk started and nearly fell off his chair. His tankard, still half–full of tea, wobbled on the table but settled as he watched stupidly. Sylvia looked up from her book.

"What time is it?" But he could hear music coming from *The Vault*. Celeste and Grint were playing, dancing their melodies down the hall and in through the door. Rawk rubbed at his face and rose to his feet. "It must be dinner time. Are you coming?"

Sylvia sighed and put down her current book. It was different to the last one Rawk had seen.

Rawk's usual table was waiting for him, and Biki put down a drink almost before he arrived. He grabbed the dwife's arm. "I need something to eat, Biki. And Sylvia too."

Biki nodded and hurried away, ignoring the calls of several other customers as she went. She came back with two bowls. One was heaped with a steaming, chunky stew and the other almost over flowed with a salad. Then she was gone again, hardly even pausing.

"How is Biki working out?" Sylvia asked.

"Like a dwarf," Rawk replied, getting his cutlery from his belt pouch. He separated out his spoon and put the knife and fork back. "She doesn't stop. The bastards never leave her alone but she doesn't complain. I would have torn someone's head off by now."

"No, you would not, Rawk. Dwarves have been not complaining for thousands of years. Elves too, to an extent. Complaints and retaliation lead to retribution, even more so when the law is always against you, such as in Katamood."

Rawk ate his stew and listened to the music. He watched Celeste as she played her mandolin, marveling as her fingers danced across the strings. She was hardly better than dwarves and elves, really, according to most of the people of Katamood. She was just a native. Rawk wondered where the prejudice stopped.

The food was long gone when Weaver appeared and sat down at Rawk's table. "Rawk, I knew I'd find you here, listening to this pair. I don't know how you can do it."

Rawk sighed. "Sometime it doesn't stop."

"What?"

"Nothing, Weaver. No disguise tonight?"

"No, Rawk, not tonight. I have come to ask you about some more rumors."

"Rumors? Well, I hear that Franzo Winkle is selling his dry dock. And Drin Garbut is..."

"Rumors about you, Rawk. And some exots."

"Yes, I killed some more exots. You owe money. You always owe me money."

"I hear differently. I hear that you confronted some exots and led them away into the city."

Rawk took a drink. "Do I get paid for that?"

"The exots looked just like normal men, apparently."

"How do we know they were exots then?"

"They came through a portal. And you hid them in the city."

Rawk sighed again. "You really shouldn't believe the rumors, Weaver. I've died about ten times in the last twenty years, remember?"

Weaver wouldn't be distracted though. "Just because they look like men doesn't mean they *are* men. We cannot trust them. We cannot let them loose in Katamood."

"Look, Weaver—"

"They had these tattoos." He waggled his fingers near his face. "They almost glowed. That should make them easy enough to find. And if I discover that you helped them in any way..."

Rawk turned to look at the Prince. He looked very serious. He looked half mad. "That guy?"

"What?"

"There was one guy with a strange tattoo but Frew killed him before I even arrived. One guy." He waved a hand. "I'm sure you found the body."

"Well, yes."

"Right. Just one guy," he said again. "That was it. There was no army of them. How would I hide them? As usual the details got blown out of proportion. Frew never even mentioned a portal. He was just some crazy foreigner, from somewhere out past Frenable, maybe." He started to sit back in his seat, but realized Sylvia was trying to hide in the shadows behind him and changed his mind. Instead, he rose to his feet and pulled Weaver up as well. "You really have to stop believing everything you hear on the street, Weaver. You know how every little tale grows with each mile it moves." Rawk gave a laugh. "I mean, come on, we stretched enough stories back in the day."

"There was only one man?"

"That's what Frew told me." He started leading the prince towards the door. "And why would Frew talk himself out of a payment?"

Weaver gave a reluctant nod. "I better not find out you are lying to me, Rawk. I say who lives and dies in Katamood. Not you. Do you understand?"

Rawk swallowed as the prince stalked away through the tables.

"Is it true?" Sylvia asked quietly once Rawk had sat back down. "You are *rescuing* exots now?"

Rawk took a drink and suddenly wished for something stronger than water. "The portals open randomly— at least the natural ones do— so they can't *all* appear in the midst of a vicious pack of wild animals. Sometimes, people must come through. Normal people like you and me."

He looked at the elf and wondered when she had become a normal person.

"I had not thought about it."

"Well, I had. And now I've got another job to do tonight, Path damn it." He sighed and sat back to enjoy the music while he could.

Half an hour later, Rawk headed to the storage room outside his library and found a blue, rough spun woolen cloak that he had never worn in his life. He couldn't even remember where it had come from. It was too short, but that just added to the disguise. Pulling the hood down low, he collected *Kaj* and headed back across *The Vault* and up the stairs to the taproom. He waited a couple of minutes in a dark corner near the door, trying not to cough on the smoke, then attached himself to a drunken group as they squeezed out onto the porch. He hunched his shoulders to make himself look smaller. Someone stumbled down the stairs and the rest of the group followed. Across the road, reasonably quiet at this time of night, one of Weaver's men was sitting on a step in the half–dark where the street lamps didn't quite meet. He was whittling, the age–old pastime of men on a stakeout. The man glanced up at the group but dismissed it immediately and went back to his wood and his blade, sending out long, curling shavings.

Breathing a sigh of relief and trying to calm his racing heart, Rawk stayed with the group, mouthing the words to their song when they started to lurch down the hill. Around the first corner, he straightened his shoulders and almost struck off on his own, but movement a little way down the street caught his attention. Shrinking again, he pushed towards the center of his disguise as they argued about lyrics and weather dwarves should be allowed to sing in taverns on the north side of the river. Rawk bit his tongue and kept an eye on the dark corner where he'd seen the movement.

There was another spy, standing in an alcove between two whitewashed buildings. But a Hero would never sneak anywhere, so the incognito–soldier hardly even looked at Rawk and his companions.

"Hey, do you think dwarves should be able to work north of the river?" someone asked.

Rawk's heart raced when he realized his companions had stopped to ask the opinion of Weaver's man.

"Go home."

Nobody seemed offended at all and the singing resumed. It was one of the songs Grint had been singing earlier. Rawk was pretty sure it was one of the dwarf's own compositions.

Further down the hill, Rawk finally felt it was safe to leave his new friends behind. They didn't even notice when he slipped away, heading for Mistook Alley. It was a narrow, winding thing, barely more than a yard wide at some points, that wound its way southwards for almost half a mile before spitting the brave travelers out near the cistern in Carker Square. Rawk drew *Kaj*. He hadn't been into Mistook for years; it was scary enough during the day.

Rawk tried to watch his footing but the only light was seeping into the alleyway out through grimy windows and through the cracks in badly made doors. He almost slipped in a pool of half dry blood. He almost tripped over a moldering pile of rubbish. He also tried to watch out for trouble of the more pointy kind. His heart was hammering in his chest. His mouth was dry. Weaver and his men would never find him in here, not even when he was dead and rotting. Someone stepped out of a narrow door squeezed between two downpipes, his shadow stretching up the wall on the far side.

"You lost? It ain't safe here."

Somehow, Rawk doubted the man was really concerned about his health. "No, I've got this under control," Rawk told him. He pushed back his hood, clearing his peripheral vision. He should have done it earlier.

"Rawk? Is that you?"

Rawk looked around. "Ummm... Yes. Do I know you?"

"Course not. Doubt you got many friends in Mistook, right."

"Not a lot, no."

"What you doing here? I saw you kill that bano a few days ago."

"Bano?" Rawk breathed shallowly, trying not to inhale too much of the stench.

"The shark with legs."

It didn't feel right, chatting to the cutthroat in the most dangerous place in the city. He didn't really have time, but didn't want to anger the man. "Where did you get *that* name? I've never heard of it."

"My papa used to tell me stories, before my ma slit his throat. He was from the mountains up near Kenkona and he used to talk about them all the time. Maybe your shark was something different though."

"Perhaps." It was an interesting thought that the portals might not be leading to other worlds at all. "I would love to stay and chat..."

"Of course. You obviously on a mission of some kind. Didn't come here for fun. You want some company?"

Rawk looked around, licking his lips. One less person trying to sneak up behind him might be a good thing. "Sure. Come on then."

"My name's Fix." Fix held out his hand to be shaken.

"Hello, Fix. Good to meet you."

"So, where are you off to?"

"I have to get to—"

"Ah, a secret mission. Obviously. I wouldn't trust me either." Fix showed a row of perfect teeth in a smile. He noticed Rawk noticing. "My papa always said to look after your teeth 'cause you can't go next door and steal some more."

"A wise man, it would seem. My father always said, 'Money can be stolen, but a good work ethic can't.' Something to keep in mind, if you're ever looking for a good work ethic."

Fix laughed. "Two wise fathers, it would seem. "

Rawk smiled. "Yes. Though apparently neither of them were really the best for making up catchy slogans."

"You're friends with Prince Weaver?"

Rawk grunted noncommittally.

"You gotta thank him for me. One of his Heroes saved my daughter the other day."

"One of his Heroes?"

"Yeah, you know, the ones he's got standing on corners everywhere looking for trouble. Yeah, my little darlin' was breakin' into a shop when a bear–looking thing, with green fur and a long tail, appeared out of nowhere and attacked her. A Hero came and fought it off. He was so quick I didn't even have a chance to move."

"Well, I'm glad to hear it, Fix. Just so you know, though, I'm the one paying the Heroes."

"Really?"

"Yes. I don't think Weaver has come up with an original idea in his life."

"What about the canal? And all the pipes and taps and what–not."

"Dwarves. All of it is the dwarves."

"You've got to be joking. Those little buggers are too stupid to come up with their own ideas."

"What are you basing this on?"

"Well..."

"I can assure you, Weaver sits in his palace taking credit for everyone else's work."

"I thought you said he was your friend."

"I thought I grunted noncommittally."

Rawk raised *Kaj* in an instant as three men landed lightly on the street in front of him, daggers in hand. Their faces were dramatic patchworks of light and shadow. There were probably a couple more men to the rear. Either that or it was the stupidest ambush ever.

"I hope these aren't friends of yours, Fix. I was starting to like you."

"I *know* Johnny, Rawk, but he isn't a friend."

Rawk smiled. "Good, then you won't mind if I kill him."

Johnny stood up straight, backing away slightly. "Sorry, Rawk. I didn't realize it was you." Rawk risked a look over his shoulder. There were two more men there. They were lowering their weapons too, though they didn't look sure about it. Perhaps they thought they should just rob Fix instead.

"So, you're going to let me go on my way?"

"Of course."

Rawk looked up. There was a balcony five yards up, with sagging boards and twisted metal railing barely more than a darker shadow in the darkness. "That's an impressive jump," he said.

Johnny smiled. "Can you tell us a story? One in the city? I've never been outside Katamood, so I don't really know much about the country side."

"Well, I'm actually in a hurry at the moment, Johnny, but I'd be glad to come back some time." He looked at his surroundings, wondering how many people were listening in. Wondering how many of them liked Heroes more than they liked money. "As long as you can guarantee my safety."

"Of course I can."

Johnny obviously knew that was a lie. Rawk certainly did.

"Great. Then once I get this mess cleaned up I'll come and visit Mistook alley again."

Rawk started to walk again, brushing past his would−be muggers and continuing on. His neck prickled but no attack came. He doubted he would be so lucky next time.

The alley continued to wind its way down the hill. Fix talked continually at his back, giving information about the people who lived behind the lopsided, rotting doors. A matron who cut her hair once a year and sold it to a wig maker. A family of five kids, none of them older than fourteen, who got by collecting scraps of paper to sell to paper makers. There was a man who hunted rats and made shoes from the skins.

Patches of murky light reached out to hold hands in the darkness, but never quite succeeded. At one point the buildings of each side joined overhead, creating a tunnel as black as pitch. Rawk ran his hand along the wall, worried about splinters and things unknown, worrying about being mugged again, watching the grey rectangle in front of him like a starving man watches a jam filled pastry. He kicked through a drift of trash and sent a pair of dogs skittering away under a rotting building. He suspected they were actually rats, but he didn't want to imagine any rats that big.

He came out into the open again and looked up at narrow strip of stars overhead. "Nice weather we're having recently." The talk calmed him, let him pretend it was all just a normal stroll through the city. Thankfully it was only half a mile.

When Rawk stepped out of the alley into Carker Square he took a deep breath. It felt like the first breath he had taken for a long time. A weight shifted from his chest. Quickly stepping back out of the light thrown by the lamps he took a moment to look around.

"Who are you looking for?" Fix asked. "Who's going to be watching at this of night?"

"I don't know. I'll let you know when I do."

"Oh."

"I thank you for your assistance, Fix, but I think I should be fine from here. You should get back to your daughter." Rawk pulled a ten−ithel piece form his pouch. "Buy something nice for her."

Fix gave a smile and a nod. "That I will, Rawk. That I will." And he drifted away into the darkness like... like a thief with the easiest ten ithel he'd ever made.

Rawk waited in the shadows. There was no reason to think anyone would be waiting for him in such a random place, but he watched and listened for five minutes, just in case. There were people coming and going though it must have been almost midnight. There were two lovers holding each other close on a bench, but there was nobody lurking suspiciously. Apart from himself. Finally, he pulled his hood up, gathering the shadows of Mistook about his face, and slipped out into the square.

Crossing quickly to the other side, he paused just into the next alley. It was not nearly as narrow or as famous as Mistook but good enough for his purposes. Rawk faded into the shadows and looked back the way he'd come. There was no change in the rhythm and flow of life. A wagon, piled high with produce went slowly by, iron−rimmed wheels grinding on the pavers. A washerwoman went even slower, heading for her tubs with a full basket on her hip. The lovers kissed.

A few minutes later, Rawk was satisfied and hurried on. It wasn't until he was almost at his destination that he slowed down once more. If Weaver suspected him of hiding the exots, he may well have men watching some strategic locations other than the *Hero's Rest*. If that were the case, the main offices and warehouses of *Keeto Alata* would be one of those locations. Across the road from the worker's quarters, he stopped to watch and wait again. He didn't see any sentries, but held his breath when a troop of the City Guard marched through an intersection not far away, swearing at a few civilians who didn't move fast enough. They didn't slow, even when they knocked somebody over.

"Maybe Weaver is even more stupid than I thought." Rawk hurried across the street and mounted the stairs to knocked at the first door. "Zid, are you in there? It's Rawk?" Of course, amongst all those words there were only two that Zid or his followers would recognize. "Zid? Rawk." He pushed back his hood. The shadow of Mistook had fled long ago, but the stench remained.

The door opened a crack and a stranger peeked out. Rawk saw the glimmer from a tattoo and slipped inside. It wasn't Zid, though. The woman, Jali, tall and slim and muscled like one of the gymnasts from the circus, led him out a second door and into a hallway. Zid was a couple of rooms down.

"Zid, we have to go now." Rawk said as soon as he saw the man. Zid didn't understand and Rawk couldn't work out how to explain. "You need to get everyone together and follow me." He got Zid's sword from where it leant against the wall and gave it to him. Then he took the arms of Zid and Jali and pulled them back into the hall. Then he went to the next door and woke the two men in the room beyond. He motioned to their swords and beckoned them out into the hall as well. Everyone seemed to get the idea and soon all twelve of the strangers were filling the hallway, fully dressed and ready to go. They waited silently to find out what was going on. Rawk couldn't explain, so he went back to the door he had entered the building by. When he saw that the coast as clear, he made his way quickly across to the mouth of the alley. The others followed silently, watchful and wary, but weapons still sheathed. Professionals.

Rawk kept moving, from alley to alley, darting across streets or moving slowly, trying to look nonchalant; he wasn't sure if he was that good at acting. He wiped sweat from his face, and tried to avoid looking at every person they passed. He had his hood up, so it was doubtful anyone would recognize him but it felt as if everyone was watching. Several times they had to hide in the shadows, or rush out of sight when patrols went past.

They were in a small square, trying to look as if they should be there, when Zid stopped and his companions spread out, looking around, hands poised near weapons. Rawk sensed the portal a moment before it opened in their midst. Weapons flashed out. Warriors dropped into fighting stances. They paused, holding their breath as one. Rawk slowly drew *Kaj,* a long cold rasp in the quiet.

Creatures came through, seven of them, a swirling confusion of wings and claws. But still the warriors waited. Buzt, the big man with the dragon tattoo, called out and Rawk saw a line of blood across the man's forehead. A second later another batted away a claw that was far from accidental. Zid and his followers finally started to fight. They moved with deadly precision, striking at the exots, working in teams as if they had been doing it all their lives. Perhaps they had. Wings brushed against Rawk's face, a fluttering darkness that felt hot and oily. Rawk dodged and slashed wildly. He missed and something came at him from another direction. Claws clattered across his blade. He ducked and spun, almost hitting a man with a blue tattoo-lizard slinking cross his cheek and nose. The man lunged forward, stabbing over Rawk's shoulder and using his sword to lift an exot up and away like a puppeteer, even as the long claws slashed. The creature's claws missed, barely, the tail brushed Rawk's head as it passed him by, before it slammed into the ground headfirst. Rawk looked away, spinning, stumbling as he searched wildly for the next attack. But the last of the creatures was dying, killed by a deadly whirlwind of blue flesh and steel.

Rawk breathed, blinked, as he tried to let the world catch up with his racing senses. He discovered that a crowd was starting to gather, shuffling in from the side streets or leaning out windows and doors. They were still at the *staring—at—the—exot* stage of the process so Rawk took a moment to look at his companions. Nobody was hurt seriously, though perhaps there was poison but they didn't have time to wonder because, above the rumbling of the spectators, could be heard the sound of approaching soldiers.

Hood still shading his face, Rawk grabbed Zid and started moving again, stepping over the closest creature as he kept heading west. It was a huge thing of fur and wings and heavily muscled arms. It looked ferocious with teeth and claws impressive enough to keep children awake at night. He realized that, despite this, his companions had waited to see if they would attack. They knew from experience that looks could be deceiving.

"You there. Stop where you are."

Rawk glanced back and started to run. He found the nearest dark alley and ducked down with Zid and his jentre close behind. He skidded to a stop at the back door of a warehouse that was open just a crack. He slid it open a bit more and looked in at a team of dwarves working the night shift. They were unloading a wagon.

"In we go," Rawk said, waving Zid in. He closed the door when everyone was through, nodded to a dwarf and hurried across to the main entry.

Back out on the street he paused to wiped sweat from his face and look around. One way seemed much like the other, so he picked a direction and continued at a fast walk. At the next cross street they turned, and again at the one after that. They hurried along quiet streets, staying away from taverns, drifting through the shadows like ghosts, heading ever towards the forest. Rawk wondered if his heart would stop racing some time before they made it.

Tewsday

THE OLD FOREST WAS A DIFFERENT PLACE AT NIGHT. Rawk had only been there during the day previously when he could see that the things clutching at his feet and legs were nothing more than the undergrowth. He could see the animals that were making the noises. Beneath the trees, he had been afraid, but never of the forest itself. Struggling along the narrow path, all manner of creatures hiding in the dark and trying to pull him down, he wished he'd thought to bring a lantern, or even a torch. Slivers of moonlight silvered the world but seemed to conceal more than it showed. Shadows were ink−black patches that could have hidden an army of exots.

Rawk hacked at a vine with his sword and pushed on, happy he couldn't understand what Zid and his companions were saying. He had a feeling they were questioning his sanity. Or, at the very least, questioning if he had any idea where he was going. He was starting to wonder that himself. Glimpses of the stars and moon reassured him that he wasn't walking in circles at least. That little piece of knowledge may have been the only thing that kept him moving.

The forest crowded close.

In daylight, it took a couple of hours to reach the duen's abandoned cabin. When the sun started to rise four hours after they had stepped under the trees, filtered thought the canopy like the light at *The Sky Tree*, the duen's cabin still wasn't in sight. But Rawk breathed a sigh of relief anyway. He could see that he was not about to be attacked and he was also able to get his bearings. He knew it wasn't far away at all.

Half an hour later, they broke into the clearing around the big wooden building. Rawk sat down right where he was, massaging his knee and looking up at the sky like it was a long lost friend. Zid came and blocked his view. He didn't look all that impressed. Rawk sighed and climbed back to his feet. At least, he tried. Zid help him up and continued to glare at him.

"Come on."

Around the far side of the building, Rawk unsheathed *Kaj* and laid the sword on the ground. Then he lowered himself to the grass. He didn't kneel this time; he just sat and tried to get comfortable. Zid look at him for a moment, then glanced around. He started to say something, but a sound caught his attention. He drew his sword and spun in a fluid, startling instant and his companions followed suit.

At the edge of the forest, mace in hand, stood a duen. It was not Opok. The creature was bigger, about eleven feet tall, and younger. And it looked *much* meaner. Rawk quickly got to his feet, empty handed, and tried to calm everyone down.

"It's all right everyone. It's all right." His heart was racing.

Zid relaxed slightly so Rawk turned to the duen.

"My friends do not speak our language, so I cannot explain to them that you are also a friend." Rawk swallowed. "Is Opok with you?"

The duen stood silently for a second, two, then stepped slowly aside. Opok came out of the forest and Rawk started to breath again. He closed his eyes for a second.

"Greetings, Rawk. I be feeling the presence of warriors and was not knowing what to expect."

"I didn't know where else to take them."

Opok looked Zid up and down. He said something Rawk couldn't understand, and Zid replied.

"Thank Path for that," Rawk said. It made things much easier for him. "The Prince of Katamood is seeking these warriors. They will probably be killed, or imprisoned at the least, though they haven't done anything wrong."

Opok nodded. "And you wish for them to return to our village? You ask much of us, especially if your prince searches for them."

"I know, Opok. But, like you, they're hunted and far from home."

The duen nodded. After a moment of thought, he spoke to Zid again. The conversation lasted for some time. "They can come with us for now," he said eventually. "Beyond that I make no promises."

"Of course. Hopefully Weaver will forget about them soon enough and they can come back. Or they might be able to just go somewhere else once we know..." Rawk wasn't quite sure what they needed to know.

"Hope we will. Duen have spent much time away from other peoples. Having them in our village will be strange."

"Well, thank you, Opok. Your generosity continues to be a thing of great wonder."

"Do not flatter me, Rawk. But we must return to our village; the Kipro Ceremony is today and cannot be missed."

"Well, thank you. And tell Zid that I'll come to get him as soon as I can."

Opok nodded, said something to Zid. The younger duen made his way into the trees and Zid followed a moment later with his Jentre close behind, hands resting lightly on the hilts of their sheathed swords.

"You must pass a message to Sylvia for me, Rawk."

Rawk listened and nodded though he didn't really understand. "I'll let her know," he said once the duen had finished. "Thank you for your help."

Opok nodded. "We cannot be staying in the forest forever."

"I know." At least Zid's people could pass for human. Most humans would probably want to kill the duen on sight. If they could be convinced to get to know them though... Well, they'd know dwarves for thousands of years and still couldn't manage to be polite to them most of the time.

Opok nodded and followed the others, slipping into the trees and out of sight.

Rawk sighed. The whole day stretched out in front of him and it was a long walk home on his own.

–O–

Fire breathes new life into the forest.— *Words of Wisdom.*

Rawk grunted. He had never seen any of the graffiti this far west before. He wondered if it was one person or a group of them, spreading their resources. He wondered if they were ever going to actually *do* anything.

He continued up the hill.

"Rawk." A group of boys called out and raced down the street towards him. "Can you tell us a story? Have you been fighting exots this morning?"

"No. Why would you think that?"

"Because you're limping."

"Oh." Rawk rubbed at his knee and went through several options in his mind. Eventually he shook his head. "No. There haven't been any exots today."

"Then how come you're limping?"

"It's an old injury."

"An old injury?" another boy said, as if he couldn't quite grasp the idea.

"I've been injured hundreds of times over the last forty years, and now my body has decided that it just can't keep up."

It seemed that the idea was uncomfortable for the boys, so they decided to ignore it. "Can you tell us a story? Did you fight something this morning?"

Rawk shook his head and started to walk again. The boys followed. Rawk sighed. "One time, I was fighting trolls with two of my friends. We followed them into the forest to where they lived. It was a log cabin, with a table and beds and a fireplace for cooking the animals that they trapped. We killed their pets first and then attacked them. They were fighting to protect their family so they fought desperately." It was the second time Rawk had told the story, but it still wasn't very good. He needed to spice it up a bit. Some other time though. He couldn't be bothered today. "They fought bravely and they were going to defeat us. I fell and was waiting for the killing stroke, but a dwarf came from nowhere, from some hiding spot at the edge of the forest. He attacked the troll, which was twice his size, with a little dagger hardly longer than your hand."

The boys laughed, those that were left. A lot had already drifted away, probably unhappy with the way the story was going.

"It isn't funny," Rawk said, harsher than he meant to. "I was able to kill the troll, but not before the dwarf died."

"That didn't really happen."

"Yes, it did. I wouldn't be alive today if not for that dwarf. The dwarf would be alive though, if I had not gone hunting for a family of trolls to kill."

The boys were staring at him.

"Do you think I need to work on that story? Nobody seems to like it."

The last remnants of the audience stopped, but Rawk kept limping slowly up the hill.

If the boys had followed for just a few minutes more, they could have seen a story for themselves, though it was not a very exciting one and Rawk didn't even get involved. A leathery creature with four stubby legs and a long tail had latched onto someone's foot. The victim was screaming loudly and didn't stop even when one of Rawk's paid, street–corner Heroes stepped in and finished the exot off.

Rawk grunted, pleased he didn't have to make any effort, and waited for long enough to make sure the injured woman was being assisted, then continued on again. It felt as if he was starting a whole new journey that was bound to be as interminable as the one he had just finished. He didn't think he was ever going to get home. The day had hardly begun.

A crow cocked its head at him from the top of a sign. It didn't make a noise, but the sign screeched in the gentle breeze and set Rawk's teeth on edge.

"Are you following me, you bastard?" he asked the bird. At least it wasn't asking for a story.

A few minutes later Rawk sent another group of children on their way without a story. He was polite about it, but that didn't make them any happier. When a tall thin man and his gap-toothed wife strode up by his side and started to talk as if he were an old friend it was a different matter. They asked questions and made assumptions, neither of which Rawk was happy with.

"Leave me alone," he told them.

The pair of them stopped talking for a moment, then carried on as if he hadn't said anything at all.

"Shut up and go away," Rawk said, louder this time.

They stopped, mouths hanging open, and he kept going.

"I'm Jasp Keel. You can't talk to me like that," the man said when he managed to get his mouth working again. "Who do you think you are?"

Rawk stopped, though he knew it was going to take an effort to get himself moving up the hill again. He took a deep breath and rounded on the couple. "Jasp Keel? That two bit merchant who lost a fortune betting on ger seeds?" The man had gone to Yardi begging for work, for any contracts he could get his hands on, when ger seeds proved to be about as popular as tuberculosis.

Keel's eyes widened.

"Yes, I know about that." He limped down the hill towards him. "Can you see me?" he asked. "Do I look like I want to have a chat with every stranger that walks by? Do I look like I give a damn about your—"

There was a flash and a pop and Rawk spun about, twisting his knee, to see a dwarf with a camera ducking back down an alley.

"Path damn it." He started up the hill again. "Just leave me alone."

Eventually, Rawk made it all the way up to the top. He went in through the back gate of the *Hero's Rest* and stopped in the Ostler's yard, sitting down at the table by the kitchen door. He knew it was a bad idea, because he was just going to have to get up again in a minute, but he didn't care. He just wanted to sleep. He watched as a small, black shape stepped daintily out of the stables, stalking a tuft of seed that was moving slowly with the breeze. A cat. The cat. Not much more than a kitten. It concentrated fiercely, pausing for a moment before taking another step. It had almost reached its prey, but a clatter from the kitchen sent it skittering away, behind the water trough and out of sight. Rawk sighed, wondering if he would ever be able to give up the chase and run away to hide. He was beginning to think it would never happen.

Kalesie was shouting something, so he rose to his feet and scaled the stairs into the kitchen.

He discovered the cook standing near the big, central table, knife in hand. About half a dozen different vegetables, in various stages of dismemberment, lay scattered across the scarred surface.

"I've had about enough of you," the woman said, waving the knife dangerously close to Biki. "Just because Rawk and Travis like you, doesn't mean I have to put up with your crap."

Biki didn't say anything. She just held onto her big, over−full serving plate and stared at her shoes.

"You do what I tell you to do or I'll kick you all the way back over the river."

Rawk washed his face in the sink by the door and when he was done, Kalesie was still going. So he dried his face on his sleeve and wandered over to the table. "What's the problem?"

"This is none of your business, Rawk." Kalesie waved the knife in his face as well, for a moment, before seeming to come to the conclusion that that may be taking things a bit too far. "This Path cursed dwarf has been annoying me with questions all morning. And now she has the nerve to question the ingredients I was using in my stew."

"What ingredients are you using?"

"That's none of your business either." She turned to the table and started to chop violently at a carrot. "Both of you get out of my kitchen."

Biki looked at Rawk, then Kalesie, then back to Rawk. It was obvious she wanted to say something, but felt that she couldn't. Rawk motioned with his head then led the way from the room. Just through the door into the taproom he stopped to wait. Biki came through a moment later.

"What's the problem?" he asked.

"Nothing."

"Nothing?"

"Except she doesn't seem to care about what the customers want at all. She was told yesterday that people were complaining about the stew and today she is making the same one, I'm sure."

"Well, she's pretty set in her ways."

Biki narrowed her eyes.

Rawk cleared his throat.

"I need to give out these meals."

Rawk sighed and went through the next door. From there, one set of stairs went up to his room and another went down to *The Vault*. He paused for a moment, unsure, and was caught by Natan before he could make up his mind.

"Ho, Rawk."

"Natan. A late lunch today?"

"If it was my first lunch then it certainly would be late." It looked as if part of his first lunch had dribbled down the front of his black, lacy doublet. "I was just upstairs reading and thought I would come down for a drink and a bite to eat."

"Pork stew again today, I hear." He was starving as well but too sore and tired to actually make much of an effort to fix the problem.

"Oh."

"You don't like the stew?"

Natan glanced towards the kitchen door and didn't say anything.

"Right, then. Do you know where Travis is?"

"I know where he was last night and this morning." Natan smiled. "Since then though..." He shrugged his round shoulders apologetically.

"Well, I'm sure he's around somewhere."

"Of course he will be around somewhere. I'm not sure he ever goes home any more, what with all the hours he works and the nearness of my bed."

"It's a long walk to his place. I've never understood why he didn't move closer."

"He might soon. He keeps telling me about all the dwarves moving into the west of the city."

"They may be all over the city soon."

"Like rats? Don't say things like that." He took out his handkerchief and mopped at is brow as if just the thought of dwarves was enough to make him sweat.

Rawk felt his fake smile slip slightly. "No, I didn't mean like rats at all. Weaver has made getting a place to the south of the river so hard that they may not have a choice. Why would they choose to live up here when people, humans, treat them like second class citizens?"

Natan concentrated on his handkerchief for a moment. "I think I hear that pork stew calling to me after all."

"Pork stews can be very insistent," Rawk agreed.

Natan went through to the common room and Rawk made a decision as the sound washed over him again. He headed down the stairs.

Sylvia was sitting in her usual seat in the library.

"Did Travis give you a key or something?" Rawk asked.

She read from the big tattered book on her lap for a moment more before marking her place with a long, slim finger and looking up. "What is the matter?"

"Nothing."

She raised an eyebrow and Rawk sighed.

"Really, I'm fine."

"If you insist."

Rawk didn't insist, but he didn't know that he was ready to get into another of those conversations with Sylvia. He leaned his sword in the corner and checked the tea on the brazier.

"I put that back on not five minutes ago," she said.

It would be a while until it was ready then. Rawk went to his desk and sat down, stretching out his legs. He was teetering on the edge of sleep. "I have some good news," he said.

"More books? Travis brought another dozen or so from Lady Tapalar's collection today," Sylvia said. "I am not quite sure if you understand the meaning of 'good news'."

"No, this is better than more books. I spoke to Opok again today."

"You did? It is a bit early for you to be back already."

"I set out at about midnight."

"That was your task last night?"

"Yes."

"And what was so important that you had to go into the Old Forest at midnight?"

"Those exots that Weaver wanted to kill?"

"Yes?"

"He won't be finding them now."

"You took them to see Opok?"

"Yes. And he speaks their language."

"Right."

"They should be fine now."

"Good."

"Exactly."

"So is that the good news? I was hoping it would have more immediate benefits."

Rawk yawned and tried to gather his wandering thoughts. "Information. Opok says that magic is still being stored somewhere in Katamood."

"I dare say it is. There must be hundreds of small talismans and the like."

Rawk shook his head. "He says there's enough magic stored here to open two score portals. And he says that it isn't being stored in an object."

"Then what?"

"He wasn't sure earlier because the cabal thingy was muddling things, but he's sure that it's being stored in a person. Enough power to open forty more portals."

"He is incorrect," Sylvia said. "It is not possible." But she didn't look so sure. She looked a little bit frightened.

Rawk looked at her. "You know something?"

"There are legends about men who cannot draw magic but can hold it."

"Pardon."

"Think of magic as..." She looked around. "As the water in your teapot."

Rawk's eyes narrowed. "Right." He didn't know if he could think his way through another of her metaphors.

"I must first choose a flavor of tea and put it in, then I can pour a cup for myself, or I can pour one for you, or I can pour it on this book. *You* can't touch the pot at all because it is too hot but, because I am a sorcerer, I can."

Rawk stifled another yawn and gave it some thought. "Still with you. Different flavors are different spells." He slipped off his boots and wriggled his toes. The feeling was pleasant, the smell was not.

"Correct."

Rawk felt she looked a little bit relived that he was understanding. He was a bit impressed himself, seeing he was having trouble keeping his eyes open.

"The trouble is, all my tea cups have holes in them."

"If you don't use it straight away it goes away?"

"That is how it is for all sorcerers. But there are legends of people called spences. They cannot pour water from the pot either— they cannot even see the steam coming out, apparently— but they have a cup and it does not have a hole. And they can decide which flavor of tea after the water is in their cup."

"So, sorcerers supply the magic and then they use it?"

"Precisely."

"So how do we find this spence then?"

"I do not know. They are legends, remember? I am not willing to admit that they even exist. If this is a spence and not another cabal... Rawk, the spence does not have a teacup, they have a bucket. To hold enough power to make forty portals is inconceivable."

Rawk blinked several times. "Sylvia."

"Yes."

"We broke up that cabal weeks ago."

"Yes."

"Dozens of portals have opened since then. But the spence can still open forty *more* according to Opok? That doesn't sound like a bucket; it sounds like a whole dwarvish tank full of hot water."

"Path, you are right." She put her head in her hands for a moment. "There must be another cabal. There must."

"Or, that man with the cabal who you said was not a sorcerer?"

"Inconceivable, Rawk."

"So you keep saying. Perhaps we should keep an open mind."

"Perhaps." She looked up at the library. "I do not have enough time."

It looked as if she would say more, but Rawk was finally drifting off to sleep and didn't find out one way or the other.

—O—

"Rawk, where are you?"

Rawk came awake in an instant, sitting bolt upright in his chair and looking around. Sylvia and was still there. She looked very uncomfortable, looking at the door as if expecting something unpleasant.

"Are you down here?"

Rawk surged to his feet. He looked at *Kaj* in the corner but left it there and hurried out into the clutter of the storage room. He pulled the door closed behind him just as Weaver rounded the corner.

"Where did you go this morning?" Weaver said without even offering a greeting.

"Nowhere."

"Nowhere?" He gave a bark of laughter that held no amusement. "You never left the *Rest* but all of a sudden Hular sees you coming up the hill."

Rawk raised an eyebrow. "You have people watching me?"

Weaver paused. "No. Of course not."

Rawk shook his head. "Why would you do that, Weaver? That hurts. After all this time you think... Well, I don't know what you think I'm doing."

Weaver sighed and picked up a silver goblet from a large box of random items. "You are protecting exots, Rawk."

"You know this for sure?"

"Well..."

"And, even if it was true, who says it's against the law?"

"Well..."

"No, seriously, where has it ever been written that people can't protect exots? I saw some birds come through a portal the other day. Tiny little yellow and green things, they were. I'm pretty sure they weren't vampire birds. They weren't going to hurt anybody."

"So you didn't kill them? You just let them fly away?"

It was Rawk's turn to sigh. "They were the size of sparrows, Weaver. Even if I had wanted to kill them I don't think they would've sat around while I tried to run them through with *Kaj*. There are probably dozens of other creatures we don't know about, little things that came through and slunk away into the city, petrified."

"They could be dangerous, Rawk."

"They were tiny birds."

"Not them. The warriors."

"There was one warrior and he's dead. I didn't help anyone."

Weaver put the goblet down and picked up a battered helm from the same box. "Is this Kalanar's helm?" he asked.

Rawk was glad of the change in conversation. "Yes."

"I remember that. That was a great summer. We spent almost every day in the palace gardens. Swimming and picnics. And dancing every night." He looked wistfully at Rawk.

"You make it sound as if you and I were dancing together, Weaver. Do you remember Posy and... Who was the chambermaid you were with? Bethu?"

Weaver threw down the helm. If it hadn't been dented before it would have been now. "They were both using us. They thought we could take them away from there."

"We could have, but *we* were using *them*."

"Those exots don't belong here. I will find them and I will kill them." Weaver spun about and left the room.

Rawk went back into the office and slumped down onto his chair. "What time is it?" he asked.

Sylvia was staring at the door. "Mid–afternoon. You have slept for more than two hours."

"Well, I needed it." It felt like he hadn't slept at all. "You keep reading. I'll see if I can find you some help."

"Who?"

"Waydin, maybe."

Sylvia gave him a look.

"Trust me."

Rawk went upstairs first and had a shower, standing under water as hot as he could stand, letting it wash away the night before. When he put on some clean clothes he felt like a new man; it probably wouldn't last long. A few minutes later, carrying a purse full of money, he was on his way down the hill.

He spent a few ithel to avoid having to tell a story. Then spent some more on a pastry and on the porch to watch a dwarf work gang. Their wagon, half loaded with the huge pavers and supports to lay back over the sewer, had a broken wheel and wasn't going anywhere. But that didn't stop the work. The four bullocks had been unhitched from the front and were resting in the shade while the dwarves unloaded the supplies and moved them by hand, shuffling up the street.

A man, hardly taller than the dwarves but as skinny as spring sapling, stopped by the wagon. "Are you going to get out of the way? I need to buy a hat."

Rawk realized the wagon was stuck in front of a millinery shop.

"Sorry to inconvenience you, sir," the gang boss said, taking off his own broad brimmed leather hat as if the object might offend in the current circumstances. "Unfortunately the wagon won't be going anywhere in a hurry."

Rawk had heard the conversation a hundred times before. He kept chewing on his pastry, wondering what he could say. Possibly if he defended some dwarves Weaver would forget all about the exots.

"That's not good enough," the little man said, putting his hands on his hips and sneering. There was a crowd starting to gather and he was feeding off the attention.

"We're doing our best, sir. The wheelwright is on his way as we speak."

"I suppose he's a dwarf; the wheel will just break again. Aren't there any human wheelwrights?" The crowd was urging him on.

"I dare say there are dozens in Katamood, sir, but seeing they don't have to be members of the Wheelwrights' Guild, I couldn't say for sure."

"Well, go and get one. I don't have all day."

"Sir, if you just go next door, you can use the stairs there and then use the walkway to reach the hat–maker."

"I shouldn't have to waste my time because of your incompetence. Why don't you go back across the river?"

The dwarf grunted. "Where do you live, sir?"

"What? That's none of your business."

"Well, I just wanted to know so I can make sure we don't disturb you in the future."

"That would be wonderful."

"We won't put the sewers along your street so you'll have to keep using your chamber pots."

Rawk smiled. That was different. In all his days Rawk could not remember a dwarf in public being anything other than polite and respectful.

The little man's mouth was flapping as he tried to think of something to say. But the gang boss didn't give him the chance. "Except we won't send the privy wagon along your street, because you don't like dwarves. And we won't sweep your street and we won't light the lamps. And you can go down to the docks to unload your own food. And you can explain to your neighbors why the price of pumpkins has doubled. And why the trash is piling up outside their doors. And you can take their chamber pots away."

With every sentence the little man was wilting, collapsing in on himself. And the catcalls of the crowd had turned to an angry, confused muttering. The man suddenly turned and started to walk away.

"You forgot to get your hat," the gang boss called after him. "Perhaps you should get one with a veil so nobody will recognize you."

There was a rumbling from the crowd and Rawk swore. Licking the last of the pastry filling from his fingers, he wondered what to do. The angry noise started to grow as what had just happened started to sink in, and Rawk knew he was out of time.

"All right then," he called. A couple of people looked in his direction but not many. He found his battlefield–voice, long dormant, and put it to use. "Listen up." People started to turn in his direction so he held up a hand as he waited for some quiet. "I can sort this out for you."

"It's not right, Rawk. Dwarves shouldn't speak to us like that."

"Obviously. But we can fix everything."

"Come on then. Show these damn dwarves what it means to cross a human."

"What's your name?" Rawk asked the closest human.

"Het."

"Right. Het. So, tomorrow you can be in charge of sweeping the streets. Get some volunteers. And who will drive the privy wagon? I'd like to make sure we've got that covered before I go about showing theses dwarves who's boss."

"I'm not going to sweep any streets. I'm a shoemaker."

Rawk picked someone at random. "Will you drive the privy wagon? I imagine there's more than one of them so we'll need a few more volunteers."

"What?"

"Somebody has to do the jobs. Will it be you?"

Nobody said anything. They didn't even mutter. They looked at the dwarves, then back at Rawk.

"Right. Well, while you get all that organized, go on your way and let these dwarves get on with their work."

Nobody moved.

"Go, before I call the City Guard."

The people stood for a moment longer, then started to drift away. It probably wouldn't be the end of it, but Rawk couldn't do anything about that.

The gang boss gave Rawk a small nod, then turned back to his charges. "Don't just stand there, you lazy louts. Get back to work."

They hadn't even slowed. They had laid another five pavers while the conversation took place, though Rawk guessed they'd been ready to step in and help if it was required.

Rawk took a deep breath and continued down the hill. When he reached Juskin's shop, he found the little old man was sitting at the counter reading. It looked like he had been there some time.

"You are lucky you caught me," he said. "I was about to close up."

"No, you're lucky. I have money."

"What's the matter?"

"Why?"

"You look... Something."

Rawk shrugged. "I just saw a dwarf giving a human hell."

Juskin's eyes narrowed. "Are you sure?"

"That's what I thought."

"The world is changing."

"Don't I know *that*." Rawk took a deep breath. "So how's business?"

Juskin sighed. "You know that as well, Rawk. I am one of the last book shops in Katamood and I still cannot make any money."

Rawk took out his purse. "How much do I owe you?"

Juskin checked his ledger and Rawk counted out the coins. There were still a few left over when he was done. "Have you ever thought of getting out of the book business?"

"I'm too old to start over. What would I do?"

"You could work for me."

Juskin laughed. "I think I am too old to be a squire. And besides, the way Travis talks that position is already taken."

"He says that, does he?"

"Not blatantly."

"Well, anyway, no, I don't want a squire. I want... Well, I want someone to do all sorts of things."

"Such as?"

"This is between you and me, all right?"

"Yes."

Rawk looked around, as if someone might have magically appeared in the shop which, with all the portals opening around Katamood, was entirely possible. "I own the *Hero's Rest*."

"Really?"

"Yes. And Travis has recently been officially promoted to manager, but he could use some help with the accounts and things like that. My healer is also using my library for research and she could use some help as well; she is working to a bit of a deadline."

"And how much do you pay. I say the book business is going badly, and I complain, but it is still enough to let me keep a roof over my head and food on my table."

"I will pay you enough." He clinked his purse, as if that would prove he could pay. "Do you own this building or are you leasing it?"

"I own it."

"Well, there you are, you can lease out the shop and make a fortune."

"It is about to fall down."

"Look, I'm sure we can work something out."

"I heard that you hired a dwarf."

"You don't want to work with a dwarf?" Rawk had not given the matter much thought, but he had assumed that Juskin would have no problem with things like that.

He didn't know why. Not too long ago he'd thought it was normal and sensible to not like dwarves.

"I can work with a dwarf, I was just trying to work out where I fit in to everything."

"So you don't want a dwarf telling you what to do?"

"What I mean is, am I just another charity case or are my services genuinely required?"

"Oh, right. Biki is not a charity case. Not completely. Her services were required, and so are yours. I've owned the *Rest* for years, and some other businesses, but haven't really done much about growing them. I'm making a fortune because of the efforts of others, but I've taken a bit more interest in the businesses and also decided that it would be great to do some good for others while I'm doing some good for myself."

"Very well. I accept your offer."

"Excellent. The hours you work may be a bit strange, but you will be compensated appropriately."

Juskin's eyes narrowed. "You want me to start immediately, don't you? But I can't afford to just ignore the shop completely and leave all the stock sitting here."

"I'll buy the stock."

"Pardon."

"I'll buy it. Then I can sell it at my leisure." He looked around. "Or keep it."

"No, I could not—"

"My healer needs the help as soon as possible, Juskin. When you talk to her you'll understand."

"So, right now?"

"Yes."

Juskin sighed and closed his book. "Let me get my coat and I will lock up."

The doorbell clanged as someone entered and Rawk turned around. Weaver was standing there in deliberately martial finery, guard at his shoulder, sneer on his face.

"A bookshop? Really, Rawk, how the mighty have fallen."

"I was never mighty, Weaver."

"I'm beginning to suspect you are correct." He nodded to his follower and the man opened the door. Another half a dozen soldiers were waiting outside. "We have come to search this premises. I have reason to believe that fugitive exots are hiding here."

Rawk looked at Juskin. Juskin looked at Rawk. The old man shrugged.

"That's it?" Weaver said, obviously disappointed. "We are going to search your shop and your house and that is your reaction?"

Juskin pushed his spectacles up onto his face. "Will you stop if I complain and protest my innocence?"

"Of course not."

"Then complaining would be wasting my time and energy; at my age I don't have a lot of either to spare."

Weaver swore, then turned to the soldiers crowding the shop. "Get out of here. Back to the barracks."

"Aren't we searching, Your Highness?"

Weaver's sneer grew. "He obviously has nothing to hide. Or if he does, he has hidden it well enough to make sure nobody can find it." He swore again, glaring hatred at Juskin, then followed the guards out onto the street.

Rawk stood silently because he wasn't quite sure what to say.

"A friend of yours?" Juskin asked.

"Apparently." He checked over his shoulder, not trusting that Weaver hadn't left a spy somewhere. "Come on then, get this placed closed up so we can go."

Juskin pottered about for a while, seemingly not quiet sure what to do. Eventually, he looked around and sighed.

"You can come back, you know? If you like, you can just come down when you have some free time and sit behind the counter and hope people come in."

"I have owned this shop for..." He looked up at the ceiling as he calculated. "I've been here for nearly twenty—five years."

Rawk looked around too. He picked a book off the shelf. *The Time Between Menalor and Kirten.* It was covered in dust and there was a tear in the cover. "I think this book has been here for twenty—five years as well."

Juskin took the book and shoved it back on the shelf. "I thought you were in a hurry." He went to the door and held it open for Rawk.

If they were being followed, Rawk could not see the man in the last rush of afternoon traffic. A while ago he'd known every man in the City Guard; now, he was lucky to know half of them. Rawk took them on a winding course. He bought some pastries then, a few streets further on, a beautiful ledger that he might find a use for one day. He didn't know if he could bore the tail to sleep, but he was hoping. Their random path took them past the Tapalar mansion. It was a long time since Rawk had seen the place and it was almost unrecognizable. Yardi's workers had been hard at it. Much of the facade had been rebuilt and painted. The plants at the front had been trimmed or pulled out completely. It was almost as if Bree had come back after one of her month long holidays and declared that her next mission was to set things right. Rawk still missed her. Her laugh had been the one sure thing that would make him feel better. But he wondered what she would think of him now, an old man living off past glories and not really happy with it.

Juskin stopped to look. "Katamood hasn't been the same since Lady Tapalar died."

Rawk blinked. "You knew her?"

"*Everyone* knew her. And everyone loved her."

Rawk stared at the house. He swallowed. "Yes, well, all us humans loved her though I doubt many of the other races did."

Juskin ignored the comment. "She used to buy books from me. She was collecting books about magic, like you. She must have had quite a collection by the time she died."

"She didn't do things by halves."

"It's a shame you can't find out what happened to them."

"Yes, a shame. Come on. If we take too long Sylvia will go home."

A couple of minutes later, Rawk paused, hand on the hilt of his sword as Juskin continued on for a few steps. He looked around. The only unusual thing he saw was a man on the porch of a bakery looking around as well. The street, barely thirty yards from end to end, was otherwise devoid of life.

"Hello, Rawk," the man said.

Rawk still hadn't relaxed though. He even drew his sword as he continued to scan the surroundings. He gave a nod. "Hello. I take it you work for me."

"I'm Graft." He was as big as a bear— bigger than Thok— with a close-cropped beard and a crazy mess of hair. Graft collected a shield from the ground near his feet and came slowly down the stairs.

"What's going on?" Juskin asked.

"Can't you hear it?" Graft asked. "It's like a tinker's van in the rain."

Rawk couldn't hear anything. But... "Can't you smell it?" He could smell a forest, rich and loamy and green, scents that were out of place in the riot of the city.

And a moment later, he sensed the portal opening and spun about. The shifting, slivery sheen hung in the air for long seconds. Then it sputtered, flashed, and the moment before it winked out of existence, a creature came through. One creature, walking as if it had all the time in the world. It was the size of a small dog but walked on all fours like it wasn't really serious about it at all. Its white fur was glistening with rain.

"What in Path's name is that?" Rawk asked.

"Should we kill it?"

The creature looked from Graft to Rawk and back again, then it turned and made it's slow way to the bakery.

It slipped through a hole and the timber paneling and under the building.

"Ummm... No?"

"Seriously?" Graft took a couple of steps closer. "It looks like an easy claim to me."

"Well, yes, but... I'll add a couple of hundred ithel to your pay."

"All right then." Graft smiled. "Thank you." He sheathed his sword but kept his eye on the hole the creature had used as he made his way back up onto the porch.

Rawk watched the hole too, as he caught up to Juskin.

"You seem to be a nice employer."

Rawk shrugged. "It's just money."

"As said by a man who obviously has a lot."

"Well, you shouldn't complain. I employ you now, after all."

$-$O$-$

In the office beneath the *Hero's Rest,* Grint and Celeste were sitting with Sylvia. The dwarf was tapping out a rhythm on the edge of the bookshelf as he perused the titles. The two women were reading quietly.

"Have you even left the room today, Sylvia?" Rawk asked

The elf looked up. She shook her head and went back to reading for a moment before sighing and putting the book down. "I do not have time, Rawk. If there is a spence— if they are real— they must be stopped."

"Surely they are less of a threat than a sorcerer seeing they can't do anything on their own."

"Creating magic is exhausting, Rawk. After Wenadean's Ford I spent the next week in bed."

"Me too," Rawk replied. He smiled around at the others, but they may not actually understand if they didn't know he had been fighting in the company of Princess Rose Ware. Celeste gave him a questioning look, but he cleared his throat and looked away. "So, it isn't like that for a spence?"

"Honestly, I do not know. But I know if I used enough power to open a portal I would be lucky to be alive."

Juskin cleared his throat. "Hello, you must be Sylvia," he said. "I am Juskin."

Sylvia's eyes narrowed. "You own the book shop?"

Rawk smiled. "*I* do now."

"You bought a book shop?"

"Well, I bought the stock. Juskin works for me."

"Doing what?"

"Security. Grave robbing. You know, the usual stuff."

Sylvia raised an eyebrow.

Celeste smiled. "If he followed you around, he could steal from your victims before they were buried."

"I never thought of that. And while I'm not out killing people, perhaps Juskin could be your assistant, Sylvia."

"I'm not sure..."

"How many languages do you read, Juskin?"

"Four."

"And how many do you speak?"

"Just the three."

"*If you don't mind my asking, though you probably do...*" Juskin asked in elvish. He pushed his spectacles higher on his nose. "*Are you Silver Lark?*"

Rawk held his tongue.

"No." Sylvia shook her head. "I do not need an assistant, Rawk." Rawk could see the lie, both of them, in her eyes, but it was unlikely Juskin would. He probably didn't believe her anyway.

"I think we have to trust Juskin, Sylvia," Rawk said. "He has been responsible for finding a lot of the books you have been searching through. He is smart— smarter than me, even. He can help."

Sylvia sighed. "Then he should stop wasting time and find a book."

"What am I looking for?"

"You know of spences?"

"I have heard the legends."

"Well, find the proof."

Juskin smiled and went to stand beside Grint at the bookshelf. He pulled out a slim volume. "Fardon Kakain mainly concerned himself with the elder magics of the north, but he dabbled in more esoteric areas occasionally." He clasped the book in his hand and continued to search. "Ah. Brenda Glyn's *Breathing Magic*. That probably won't help."

"Why not."

"It is a romance. Did that come from me or somewhere else?"

"No idea."

"And *Time Dizial* by Finigal March? It has been many years since..." He quickly scanned the other titles, muttering to himself, before turning to face Rawk. "You have Lady Tapalar's collection? All of it?"

Rawk nodded. Shrugged. "I'm not sure if Travis has collected all of it yet."

"I thought it was lost. I could sell those books and live in comfort for the rest of my life. I didn't supply them all but she showed me once." He swallowed and repeated himself. "I could sell them and live comfortably for the rest of my life."

Rawk took a breath, keeping himself under control. "Well, if I ever want them sold, I know who to talk to."

Some time later, Rawk looked up from his book and smiled. Sitting in a room full of people silently reading. Who would have thought that could feel so good?

"What's that grin for?" Grint asked, looking up from his book on the history of Falian magic.

And Rawk remembered why they were all reading and sighed. "Nothing." He looked around at the others.

Sylvia was still reading but Celeste had stopped to see what was happening. She pushed her dark hair away from her face.

"Who wants to get something to eat?" Rawk asked.

Grint put down his book and stretched. "I can't. I've got to go and help some people with a fireplace."

"At this time of night?" Celeste said. "I hope you are being well paid."

Grint laughed. "Not a chance. It's Hater and Fis. I'll be lucky if I get a sandwich."

Rawk looked at Sylvia. "How about you Sylvia?"

"Pardon? What?"

"Do you want to get something to eat?"

"No, thank you. I think I will stay here a while longer."

Juskin nodded. "I shall stay too. This is fascinating." He tapped the cover of his book.

"Very well. Celeste? Just you and me then?"

She looked around. "I guess so."

"Come on then. I know a place."

"Well..." Celeste looked around the library. "Should we keep reading?"

"If I read any more I'm going to fall asleep," Rawk said. He looked at his latest book. "Dane Hage may be the most powerful sorcerer that has ever lived, for all I know, but he writes the most boring books in the world."

Celeste looked at her own book. "It cannot be any worse than this." She threw it down on the table, earning an annoyed glare from Sylvia, and rose to her feet. "Show the way."

Making his way across *The Vault* a minute later, dodging the first of the night's patrons, listening to their mutters about Fermi going back where they belonged, Rawk decided he needed start using the other stairs more often. He seemed to notice the comments more than

Celeste, or perhaps she was just well practiced at hiding her reactions to the bullying.

Across the far side of Placton Square, just two minutes walk away, was a small establishment that sold pies and pasties. It was hardly more than a hole in a wall but the queue was long and rowdy.

"This is it?" Celeste asked. She looked disappointed.

"Yes. Why?"

"Nothing, I suppose."

"I admit that it doesn't look impressive, but the food is wonderful and the view from the dining room is about the best there is."

She looked around, examining the view, but didn't say anything.

They had barely joined the queue when the owner saw them and called them to the front.

Rawk held up his and in protest. "No, I—"

"Come, come. The great Rawk does not wait in line." The line wasn't that long.

"Really, I...." But it was quicker and easier to just give in. Rawk sighed as he made his way past the other customers; some of them didn't look happy, but they didn't say anything. He got a pastie with flaky pastry and bulging with meat and vegetables. He was going to choose for Celeste as well, but thought better of it. "What would you like?"

"I don't even know what they are."

So he got another pastie and two bottles of apple cider.

"So, where do we sit?"

"Come on."

He took her back to the *Hero's Rest* and led the way up the stairs.

"We're eating in your room?"

Rawk smiled but she quickly looked away. "No." There was one more flight of stairs beyond his door and it led all the way to the roof. Not long ago it had given access to a small attic but the dwarves had changed everything when they put the huge water–tank on the roof.

Rawk walked around the tank, running his hand along the smooth, even stone. "This stuff is amazing," he said. Part way around was a smaller, insulated tank that had a hearth beneath and a pile of wood beside.

Celeste nodded. "Concrete is easy to make; there are only a couple of ingredients and it comes out like a paste."

"You take all the romance out of it."

"I didn't know you were the type to worry about romance."

"I don't worry about it, as such," Rawk said, "but in my line of work it isn't something that can be ignored."

He finished half a circuit of the larger tank. Katamood was laid out before them, a sequined blanket folded and crumpled on the end of a bed. The river was a dark line with just a few spots of light where ships were taking advantage of the tide, to come or go or whatever it was they were doing. The canal and the accompanying work sites were even darker. Idle machinery dotted the length like grazing animals but all was quiet. Overhead, the night sky was lit by the brilliance of the stars. He heard Celeste gasp. She moved to the rail and looked out silently at the lights.

"It's beautiful," she said eventually. She took a deep breath, eyes shining.

Rawk looked up at the stars of the Swarm, curving away above their heads, and down at the lights of the city. *"Between heaven's stars above and the life sparks below,"* Rawk quoted, quite proud of himself.

Celeste turned to look at him. "You read *Kepler Venagoon*?"

He shrugged and cleared his throat. "I own a book shop now, remember."

"You also own a tavern but I don't see you drinking lots of ale." She smiled and Rawk couldn't look away.

"I do sometimes, just to keep my cover."

They stood silently for a while, between heaven above and the sparks below.

"It wasn't like this before the tank was installed. It was just roof and there wasn't any easy way up."

"I've never seen Katamood like this. It looks different. It looks clean and full of possibilities."

Bree would have loved it on the roof; Rawk could imagine her dangling her feet over the edge and shouting challenges at the night. But even knowing that, he still couldn't imagine that she would embrace it with such openness. "This is the best view in the city. Weaver got a higher spot, but he sees ocean and farmland more than anything else. I'm blocking his view of the city."

"He wouldn't be very happy about that?"

Rawk laughed. "He pretends he doesn't care. But I'm annoying him more than usual at the moment, so I wouldn't be surprised if he comes and steals the *Rest* just so he can kick me out."

"Can he do that?"

"Ultimately, yes, but it would be very bad for business and he knows it. Businesses and investors are unlikely come knocking if they think he'll just come and take what they work for. If he knew I owned it, that might be a different matter."

"How have you kept it secret all these years?"

"I've kept a lot of secrets. Business secrets are due mainly to Yardi. She worked everything out right from the start. I just supplied the money. I wouldn't have much at all without her."

Celeste turned away from the view to look at him. "She is a good friend?"

"The best."

And back out at the city "Never anything more?"

Rawk glanced at her. "Long ago, when we were kids. Then I left to be Hero and that was that."

"Your wandering must have made things difficult."

"Lots of people wander and still manage to have adult relationships. I think I was using it as an excuse most of the time." He cleared his throat. "Here, eat this before it gets cold."

He handed over one pastie and opened the other as he made himself comfortable on the bench Travis had somehow lugged all the way up the stairs.

"Do you come up here often?"

"Not as often as I'd like. Never with someone else."

"This is delicious," Celeste said around a mouthful of food.

Changing the subject? Rawk wondered.

After that they ate in silence for some time, staring out over the city as it lived and breathed below them.

Rawk was just breaking the seal on his cider when a noise disturbed him. For a moment he thought it was an exot and he wished he'd brought his sword, but he saw the same black kitten he'd seen earlier in the day. He stared at it, and it stared back. And when he recognized it he laughed loud enough to nearly scare it away.

"What's so funny?"

"It's the demon, I'm sure of it."

Celeste eyed it suspiciously.

"Don't worry, it isn't an actual demon." He waved his hand. "A while ago some people wanted me to evict a demon from their attic. Turned out it was just a kitten yowling because it was trapped under some stuff."

"And you rescued it?"

"Well, I certainly didn't kill it. And now it seems that he's found me." Rawk dug a bit of meat out of his pastie and blew on it to cool it down. When he was satisfied, he held it in his palm and reached out. "Come on Demon. I won't hurt you." The kitten backed away and wouldn't come closer, so Rawk put the meat down nearby then backed away as well. The kitten crept forward to eat the food, and delicately took the next bit from Rawk's fingers before skittering away nervously.

While he watched the kitten, Celeste returned to the rail and look out over Katamood. "What is that noise? Can you hear it?"

Rawk went to stand by her side. There was a rumble of sound, a roar, coming from the far side of the river.

"It's a riot," Rawk said. It was hidden, wherever it was.

A few minutes later there was a spark of color, a flash from down where the makeshift city filled the square. And a minute later the spark had become a fire.

"*Fire breathes new life into the forest.*" He thought that Words of Wisdom might have been a bit less literal than that.

"Pardon?"

"Nothing."

The blaze grew quickly, hungrily licking at the old buildings. Rawk could hear bells.

"That's the..." He waved his hand as he tried to think. "The dwarves who put out fires." Did they realize there was a riot? They were likely to get themselves killed before they managed to put out any fires.

"The fire department."

Rawk shrugged. He could hear shouts and screams. The clash of weapons.

He wanted to go and help, but he was a long way away. He moved a little bit closer to Celeste.

"I've got to go," she said suddenly.

"What? Why?"

"I have to make sure my grandmother is all right."

"Where does she live?"

"With me, half a mile from the square."

"I'll come with you."

—O—

Rawk hurried over the bridge, panic growing. The world to the east had fallen strangely quiet just a few minutes earlier, not like any riot he'd heard before. The rumbling and the shouting had been moving as they made their way down the hill. First tumbling out from beside the river, then climbing the side of Mount Grace. Now to the east, now to the west. Once, the clatter and din had died down to almost nothing though the orange glow of the fire had continued to spread. Smoke was tightening its grip on the sky, slowly squeezing all the air out of it.

Celeste was struggling to keep up and he forced himself to slow down. And he still didn't have his sword. They'd already been out the door of the *Rest* and a block down the hill before he realized, though he'd missed it just minutes earlier when disturbed by Demon. How could he not notice when he'd carried a sword on his hip for most of the last forty years?

But it had been too late when he first realized and it was even more too late now. His dagger would have to do.

The ramshackle, flotsam town in the square was half a mile away, if it still existed, but the riot had passed along this street not too long ago. There were no people left now, none that were still standing anyway. In the flickering darkness it was hard to tell how many of the sprawling figures were still alive. His dagger felt ridiculous in his hand, given the circumstances. Rawk muttered to himself as he moved slowly forward. He wanted to tell Celeste to stay where she was, to go back to the *Rest*, but he was worried that the safest place was where he could keep an eye on her.

Further down the street, they finally found some people. There were about a hundred locals— rough, desperate people with nothing to lose— who were staring down at least three score of armed, trained warriors. There could not be many City Guard left to actually guard the city. Rawk wanted to say something, he wanted to stop what was about to happen, but he knew there was nothing he could do. It was just a matter of who was going to blink first in the thickening smoke.

Rawk called out as the soldiers charged. And a moment later he found himself face to face with one of them. The man had a wild look in his eyes; he knew he wasn't looking at a soldier, and that was all he cared about.

Rawk waved his dagger and stepped around a loose, wild attack. "Do you know who I am?" he shouted.

The man wasn't thinking well enough to look.

"Weaver won't be happy if you kill me." Rawk ducked another attack and spun in close. He rammed his elbow into the man's kidney, then straightened and struck again on the side of his face. There was a crunch and a groan. Rawk didn't have time to worry about the details. He looked around for the next threat, almost panicking, seeing enemies in every shadow, expecting an attack with every noise or movement.

The number of civilians quickly diminished leaving more of the City Guard to battle those who had any fighting ability at all. Rawk temporarily disabled two more before Celeste called out. A man twice her size closed in on her with a calculating smile on his face. Rawk ran, slashing at the guard's hand as he reached out. The man bellowed with pain and backhanded Celeste out of the way, flinging an arc of blood, before turning to Rawk.

"I'm going to kill you for that..." The man hesitated as he recognized who it was. And Rawk ran him through with his little blade.

He grabbed Celeste's hand and pulled her to her feet. She gasped and he turned to see another soldier behind him.

"Rawk?" the man said. But it didn't seem to matter because Rawk found himself stepping in close to block his opponent's arm with his own, even as he was nodding in reply. He slashed with his dagger. The blow struck home and Rawk turned and grabbed Celeste's hand before he saw the result. He didn't *want* to know the result. He ran.

Her hand was warm in his, sweaty, surprisingly soft. She struggled to keep up but didn't complain. Rawk finally stopped in the shadows by the mouth of an alley. The sounds of the riot continued, though it seemed that it would not last much longer. The billowing smoke diffused the glow of the fire.

"Are you all right?" he asked.

Celeste nodded as she tried to catch her breath. There was a bruise growing on the side of her face, a huge blue and black swelling that went from her eye to her ear to her chin. A line of blood was dribbling away from a cut lip, down her chin and neck.

Rawk looked at her hand, still in his, and decided he should let go. "I killed a soldier," he said. "Maybe two." 'Maybe two' was worse than 'Definitely two' because that last man might be the only witness to what had happened. *I should have made sure of it. One or two would not make any difference in the end.* Unless, of course, someone witnessed the second killing and not the first. Rawk reined in his roiling thoughts. He could go forever like that and it still wouldn't help. The dice were thrown now and could not be called back.

Celeste took his hand again. "You had no choice."

Rawk grunted. "Do you think the other guards will see it that way? Do you think Weaver will?"

"Weaver is your friend."

Rawk shook his head. "I'm a criminal now." But he had done similar things, killed people, in a dozen different situations in the past. He wondered why it was this instance that bothered him so much. He swallowed, took a deep breath. "Weaver and the Guard may not know it yet, but that doesn't change the facts. Come on."

They kept to the backstreets. Several times they hid in the shadows as groups of locals rushed past. They hid a couple of more times, in deeper shadows, when troops of soldiers went past. And once they skirted around a small, narrow street where a barricade had been set up. But mostly it was quiet. Mostly, people stayed inside and hoped the trouble passed them by. But Rawk wondered what would happen tomorrow. He doubted it would be long before Weaver sent trouble knocking on doors.

Celeste took him to building around towards the western side of Mount Grace. A small, plain door divided a group of shops on one side and a weaving factory on the other. Rawk could hear the clacking and clicking of the looms. The workers probably didn't even know what was going on outside their doors.

"Does that go all night?" he asked. The sound had set his nerves on edge even before they reached the door. Admittedly, his nerves were pretty close to the edge before that anyway.

Celeste shrugged. "Sometimes. Not often though." The bruise on the side of her face was a livid purple stain, even in the thin overlay of light from the distant street lamps. She had wiped the blood from her chin and it now marked the sleeve of her tunic. Her face was wet with tears.

She opened the door with a shaking hand and led the way through. Beyond, they climbed some steep, narrow stairs that creaked alarmingly, then followed a hallway past at least ten doors on each side and right to the end. Inside, the room was smaller than the rooms that Rawk had given to Biki. There was two yards of kitchen bench with a sink and tap at one end and a pile of clean dishes at the other. The table, which was pushed against the wall, had flowers carved into the corners. The bed, against the other wall, had another bed built over the top of it. If Rawk had *Kaj* he'd be able to touch one wall with his fingertips and the one opposite with the tip of his sword.

An old fermi woman, with a bent back and bright eyes sat at the table peeling carrots. She barely looked up from her work until she noticed Rawk had come in with her granddaughter.

Celeste's shoulders slumped and she hurried to sit down at the table, as if it had been nothing more than the tension that was keeping her upright. "Are you all right, *mab*?"

The old woman stared at Rawk for a moment before turning to Celeste. "Of course I am," she grunted. "What happened to your face? What happened to his arm?"

Rawk looked at his arm and saw that the sleeve of his shirt was covered with blood. The wound was stinging but he hadn't thought it all that serious. Seeing the blood, he wondered if he should get it looked at.

Celeste gasped and hurried to pull a box down from the shelf above the kitchen bench.

"I saw you once," the old woman said, looking at Rawk. "You were sitting outside a tavern down by the river as if you owned the place. People fawning all over you."

"Maybe I did own it."

The woman squinted as she looked at him.

Rawk shrugged. "I didn't, but I could've."

That earned him a smile. "You can call me Matilde. So, what are you doing here with my Celeste?"

"We came to check on you."

"What for?"

"There's a riot."

Matilde looked around the room.

Rawk looked as well. "Obviously it isn't here, exactly, but we didn't know that at the time and you don't know where those things end up anyway."

The old woman pointed to a cudgel, lumpy and dark, leaning in the corner behind the door. "I'm too old to let things like that worry me."

"We're all too old," Rawk offered.

"You aren't old."

"Matilde, you have no idea."

"What? You're knees ache? It takes you five minutes just to decide you do really need to get out of bed in the morning? When the weather is cold you can barely move your fingers? You can't see properly?"

"Well, yes."

"Just because you can't go around killing people like you used to doesn't mean your life is over. I used to dance at the Mesiarne you know? They paid me a fortune. The crowd used to throw coins and flowers."

"People throw walnuts at me."

"Really?" Matilde smiled.

"Apparently it doesn't mean what they think it means."

Celeste finally got the box back onto the shelf and brought a bandage and a small jar back to the table. "Take off your shirt," she said. Rawk did as he was told, carefully peeling the sleeve away from the wound. Celeste gasped then started to dab at the ragged cut.

"I still dance, Rawk. I just do it at home. Or in the little dance hall just down from... Well, it isn't there any more, is it." She gestured to the club. "Just because you're old, it doesn't mean you have to go quietly. It doesn't mean you can't dance whatever dance you want. I'll beat the stuffing out of anyone who tries to tell me otherwise."

"Remind me not to sneak in here at night."

Matilde smiled. "You wouldn't have to sneak; I'll leave the door open for you."

"*Mab!*" Celeste had finished with the ointment, whatever it was, and started working on the bandage.

"How long have you been living with Celeste?" Rawk asked.

"Only a couple of weeks. I just need to find some work."

"You still work?"

"Of course. You think I sit around here all day peeling carrots?" As if reminded of her task she started peeling again.

"What do you do?"

"I used to work in a laundry but Weaver knocked that down for the damn canal as well."

"You can't blame Weaver for the canal. Apparently it was Thacker's idea. Or a dwarf's, at any rate."

"You're defending Weaver? Get out of my house."

"Firstly, it isn't your house. And secondly I'm not defending him; I'm just saying. There are dozens of things you can blame Weaver for that really *are* his fault."

Matilde grunted again. "The zaka fruit rots at the top."

"Does it?"

"I don't know."

"So you just made it up? It sounds like something Words of Wisdom would paint on a wall."

"Maybe."

"And what about all the other fruit that doesn't rot at the top? Talk about cherry picking your homilies to suit your needs."

Rawk winced when Celeste tied off the bandage.

"You really need to get Sylvia to look at it."

"It isn't that bad."

"It needs stitches."

"Now?"

"Yes."

Rawk glanced at Matilde. "I don't suppose you want me to stay to protect you?"

"You won't be any good to me if your arm falls off." She looked him up and down. "Well, you might be useful for *something* with only one arm."

"*Mab!* I'm right here; I really don't want to hear you talking about things like that."

"Are you jealous?"

Celeste grabbed Rawk's hand and pulled him from the room, closing the door loudly behind them. Rawk pulled free for a moment and looked back inside. "Lock the door behind us. If I want to get in, I'll knock."

And Celeste pulled him away.

But Sylvia wasn't home. The door to the shop was locked and there were no lights upstairs.

"She must still be reading in the library," Celeste said.

"You don't need to come with me."

"I think I do. You will do something silly like not get her to look at your arm."

"She's my healer. I get her to look at things all the time."

"So you want me wandering the streets on my own? With Weaver's men around looking for trouble?"

Rawk sighed. "Pull your hood up."

They walked down the hill, avoiding likely trouble spots like large squares and using one of the less iconic bridges. Nobody was going to wage a battle on the old timber boards of Messa Bridge down near the cattle yards.

The streets were quiet. There were noises nearby, around corners, in the shadows, always just out of sight. Rawk kept his hand on the hilt of his dagger and kept wishing for his sword. His eyes darted about, examining each old man that they passed. A troop of soldiers bustled by, heading down towards the river, taking no notice of a couple out for a walk now that the trouble seemed to have passed.

And up the hill on the other side, all the way to the *Hero's Rest*.

The front door was locked. Rawk knocked loudly and a few minutes later Mykle called from the other side.

"Go away. Were closed."

"It's me. Let me in."

The door opened a crack and Mykle looked out. The barman was as big as a tree but nervous around people at the best of times. He checked one way, then the next, and opened the door the rest of the way. Rawk slipped in, pulling Celeste with him.

"What's going on?"

"Waydin led a dozen men in a while ago and herded all the non-humans out."

"There were non-humans in here?" Rawk didn't mind, but it would have been unusual.

Mykle shook his head. "Just Biki."

"They took her?"

Mykle laughed. "Of course not. Travis told them she had already gone home."

"What about Sylvia?"

"She wasn't here, I don't think. They are moving all the non—humans to the south of the river."

"She isn't here?" Rawk almost went back out the door, but if Sylvia wasn't at home then he could spend all night looking and still not find her. She was probably fine. "Where's Travis?"

Mykle motioned over his shoulder towards the kitchen.

Everyone was in the kitchen. Travis was talking to Kalesie. Kalesie was shouting at Biki. Biki was staring at her shoes. Valen was hiding in a corner. There were some chambermaids and serving girls hiding with him so he was probably having the time of his life. The ostler was standing by the back door, looking very embarrassed, and Natan was fanning himself with a cabbage leaf nearby. There were five other people as well— Rawk assumed they were all residents though he only recognized one of them.

"What's going on?" Rawk asked.

Kalesie glared at him. "Ain't none of your business."

"Travis?"

Travis sighed. "Kalesie doesn't think I should have hidden Biki from Waydin."

"Is that all?"

Travis raised an eyebrow.

"Well, it doesn't really matter what Kalesie thinks about that, does it?"

"I suppose not."

"Either she goes or I do," Kalesie shouted. "And that damn fermi as well. I'll not have them in my kitchen any more."

"Go home, Kalesie," Rawk said. "There won't be any more cooking to do today anyway."

"You can't tell me what to do."

"Travis?"

Travis sighed. "Kalesie, either shut up or leave."

"But you'd send me?"

"I'm not sending you anywhere. If you shut up you can stay. But neither Biki or Celeste are going anywhere."

"If I go I won't be coming back. I've had about enough of this place. You'd choose a stinking dwarf over me."

Travis looked at the dwarf in question. "Biki is the best worker we have." He said it reluctantly, as if not wanting to admit something like that.

Kalesie stormed over to the door. She grabbed her cloak from the peg and swung it around her shoulders. The drama was lost when it caught the handle of a pot and upended black, greasy water all over the floor. The old woman soldiered on though, fumbling with the clasp for a moment before violently pulling open the door.

"I won't come back," she said. "My son's been asking me to work with him for years." She looked around, obviously waiting for someone to stop her. The ostler tipped his hat to her. He was probably just being polite— Boke didn't have a confrontational bone in his body— but Rawk liked to think he was being ironic.

The door slammed and bounced back open, then there was silence in the kitchen.

"Do you think she will be back?" Natan asked.

Travis laughed. "She'll be back."

Rawk looked at his arm. "So, how are your stitches these days, Travis? If I don't ask I'll get in trouble."

Celeste was glaring at him.

While Travis worked, Rawk tried to think of something else. He was watching the door when Demon poked his head through the gap.

"Nobody make any sudden moves," Rawk said. "Valen, find some food for the kitten please."

The lad did as he was asked and Demon crept in to sniff at the bowl when it was set on the floor. It seemed he like the raw chicken more than he disliked the attention.

Wensday

RAWK SAT UP IN BED AND LOOKED AROUND.

"Good morning, Travis. It's been a while."

Travis was sitting in the chair reading a newspaper. "It has, hasn't it? I normally slip away before you wake up." He smiled.

"That's just creepy. Now I'm going to imagine you sitting there each night watching me."

Travis' smile grew. "Thank you."

"So, to what do I owe the pleasure?" Rawk stretched carefully. His knee hurt, his back ached and his arm was numb beneath the bandage. Just another morning.

Travis folded the newspaper and threw it onto the bed. "The world is falling apart."

There was one of the amazingly accurate pictures on the front page. It showed citizens facing off against the City Guard. "This can't be from last night. It has to be from the day before." He read the story that went with it. He was mentioned, getting up on the stage to talk the people out of doing anything silly.

"So there was another riot last night? That's what set everything off?"

"I guess so." Rawk skipped through a couple of pages. There was another story about him having dinner at *The Sky Tree*. It made a big deal out of the company he was keeping. "Do you really think Kalesie will be back?"

"Yes."

Rawk sighed. "But you aren't going to let her work again."

"She's been here a long time, Rawk. Longer than I have."

"Well, it's about time she retired then. Give her a couple of hundred ithel and send her on her way."

"Are you sure?"

"Is the *Rest* open this morning?"

"No."

"Well, it's a good opportunity for you to find another cook then."

Travis sighed as well.

"Ask Juskin."

"Juskin can cook? He's a man of many talents."

"I meant ask him to help you look. He works for me now."

"Doing what?"

"Whatever we think he can do. He can help you with the day to day management stuff." Rawk shrugged. "He is also helping Sylvia. Actually, was she here last night?"

"Not that I know of. I think you should go and find her though; my stitches will hold you together well enough, but it was a pretty bad wound so you should get her to look at it. And give you some medicine."

Rawk got to his feet and found a shirt on the floor at the end of his bed. He had a sniff then pulled it on carefully. A minute later Travis was following him down the stairs towards the cellar. They discovered Juskin still in the office, sitting in Sylvia's favorite chair and snoring loudly. He had an open book on his lap and a pile of three more on the floor by his side.

"He's dedicated," Travis said.

"He was sitting around reading books on magic; he probably does that for fun at home."

Juskin snorted, stirred, and came slowly awake. The old man rubbed at his face and made a cursory attempt to straighten his shock of hair. "What is the matter?" he said. He looked around and jumped when the book fell to the floor.

"It's all happening," Rawk replied. "The city is falling apart."

"I said the *world* was falling apart," Travis pointed out.

"Right, yes. The world is falling apart."

"Really?"

"There was another riot. People were killed." Rawk winced as he remembered his part in the killing. Neither Weaver nor the City Guard were bashing down the door yet, so maybe nobody had seen. Or maybe they were getting reinforcements.

"What does that mean?"

Rawk sat on the edge of the desk. "I don't know."

"What are you going to do?"

"I don't know."

"He's going to see Sylvia."

"She isn't here. She left not long after you did."

Rawk looked at Travis. "I went to her place last night but there was no sign of her."

"She might have been out doing house calls."

"Perhaps. I'm going to have another look."

The walk across the city to Sylvia's place usually seemed like a long way. Today, it seemed like an endless trek. Rawk knew something was wrong, though he didn't know what. The mood in the streets didn't help. North of the river, the people were overly jovial, like a nervous youth making too many jokes on a first date. Everyone was on edge, waiting for trouble.

South of the river was worse. The smell of smoke still hung in the air. Half a block was nothing more than blackened frames and chimneys pointing accusingly into the air. There was hardly anyone about at all. The streets were almost empty except for troops of City Guard, patrolling warily like men in an occupied city. Rawk saw three troops on his way up the side of Mount Grace. He knew some of the soldiers, but none of them acknowledged him. The few locals brave enough to take to the streets hurried about their business.

When Rawk finally reached Sylvia's place, he knocked on the door. He went around the back and knocked there as well. He looked up at the windows but there was no sign of life. He looked up and down the street, as if that might be the exact moment she came home. But there was nobody. After several minutes of waiting and hoping, Rawk continued further up the hill and found the gate into Caldera. There were five dwarves sitting around nearby who had not been there the last time he visited. They appeared to be unarmed but they were obviously guards. They watched him closely as he made his way into the tunnel that would take him through into the circular valley hidden at the top of the mountain.

There was another dwarf at the spot where the tunnel took its first turn. He looked up from his whittling for a moment and gave a small nod. Rawk went around the corner, then back the other way. At the far end of the tunnel a dozen men— dwarves, elves, fermi and others, all waited. These ones *were* armed. There were a score more onlookers milling around nearby.

"Hello, Rawk."

Rawk looked around for the speaker. He finally spotted Rake amongst the armed men. He normally guarded Thacker, as far as Rawk knew, so this might well be an official guard post.

"Hello, Rake. Did Thacker send you here?"

"Of course. Just as a precaution, so we can escort any of Weaver's men safely to a meeting."

"Of course. Where *is* Thacker?"

"Where do you think?"

Rawk nodded and headed for the nearest tram station. Caldera was much more crowded than the rest of Mount Grace. In fact, it looked as if a lot of the residents from outside had sought the safety of the valley. The tram was crowded and Rawk was forced to hang half out the door as the contraption made its way along the tracks. His injured arm burned.

He jumped off before the tram came to a complete halt and regretted it. His already-sore knee twisted painfully but he tried to ignore it as he hurried across the road to Thacker's office. There were another dozen guards, dwarves for the most part. They certainly looked like they knew what they were doing. Rawk slowed as he approached. He looked for the leader and was saved the trouble of asking when someone stepped forward.

"We can't let you in there, Rawk."

"I need to see Thacker."

"You are a known associate of Prince Weaver."

"Well, obviously."

"So we can't let you in."

"Tell Thacker I don't know where Sylvia is."

The dwarf wrinkled his nose as he thought. Eventually, he spat onto the perfect cobbles and looked over his shoulder. "Bracken, go tell Thacker that Rawk is here."

A minute later, Thacker came out the door and strode down the steps. The leader of the guards looked like he was going to have a fit as he hastily tried to rearrange the protection. Thacker ignored the activity.

"What's going on, Rawk?"

"Have you seen Sylvia?"

Thacker looked around, as if that might be the exact moment she turned up. He shook his head. "No. Should I have?"

"She isn't at home. And she isn't at the *Rest.*"

"Surely she still does other things."

"Not that I know of. And she would tell someone if she wasn't turning up when expected. She's nothing if not thorough. And polite."

"You're right, of course." He gave a decisive nod. "I'll send some people out to see if they can find her."

"Thank you. I'll let you know if I see her."

Rawk headed back the way he'd come. He decided he would go home via Sylvia's place, just for one more look. But she still wasn't there.

An old lady was peeking out the half open door of a glass blower's workshop across the street. "She isn't there," she said.

"Do you know where she is?"

"They took her."

"What? Who took her?"

"The City Guard. They were waiting for her. Grabbed her right off the street and dragged her away. *I* couldn't do anything."

"Of course you couldn't. Do you know where they took her?"

"How could I know that?"

"Of course."

Rawk headed back down the hill as fast as he could. The streets were quiet but half way to the river he saw a goat cab. He waved the driver to a stop and climbed in.

"To the palace, quickly."

"I can't go all the way up there," the dwarf said. "Not today."

"Right." He'd probably be arrested on sight. "Just take me as far as you can then."

He got the goats moving with a soft whistle and soon they were trotting along noisily. He kept looking back at Rawk.

"What is it?"

"There's a rumor about you."

"There normally is."

"About last night."

Rawk almost said, '*There usually is,*' but his heart wasn't in it. He didn't say anything. The dwarf seemed to get the hint, for he fell silent too.

At the bottom of the hill, Rawk shouted for the driver to stop and the dwarf pulled on the reins.

"I thought you wanted to go to the palace."

"I do. But look."

Not far away, Clinker was hiding under the porch of a butcher shop. He obviously wasn't doing a very good job. Rawk called out to him and the lad grabbed his satchel and hurried over.

"You're rattling again," Rawk said as he shifted over to make room on the seat.

"Kikum stole my blanket."

"I thought you weren't fiends with him any more."

The driver got the cab moving again.

"I'm not. I think he's still allowed to steal my stuff if he isn't my friend."

Rawk sighed. "What else did he take?"

The lad shrugged. "I had some new shoes. I think he was looking for my money though."

"Sylvia still has it?"

Clinker nodded.

"Good lad."

The goats trotted along the edge of the canal— deep and empty and seemingly perfectly smooth— for quite a way before turning onto a bridge.

"My brother helped design this bridge," the driver said, breaking the long silence. The pride was obvious, but Rawk wondered if he would have been just as proud had some random dwarf designed it. As long as it was a dwarf. "The two bits fold up so boats can get underneath."

Clinker smiled. "I already told him that, Harris."

"Did you?" The dwarf laughed. "I think you're too smart for the rest of us, lad."

They clattered over the planks. On the stone pillar on the far side of the bridge was a scrawl of white writing. "A sharp sword won't stop the sun from rising— Words of Wisdom." Rawk swore under his breath. He wished the graffiti artist would either shut up or get on with whatever he was going to do.

A hundred yards short of the river the dwarf pulled his cab to a halt under a tree who's bare branches offered barely any shade at all. The goats were glad of the rest and took the opportunity to scratch and nibble some bark.

"How much?" Rawk asked as he was climbing out. He didn't really care. He had a handful of coins ready to pass over.

"Nothing," the driver said. "You paid last night."

"Take Clinker back up to Caldera. And Clinker you have to tell Thacker that Sylvia has been arrested."

"She has?"

"Yes. I'm going to talk to Weaver right now."

Rawk shoved all the money into Harris' hand and hurried forward. He climbed the back of the next bridge. On the far side of the river members of the City Guard were watching, waiting to turn away any undesirables—namely anyone who wasn't human. Or maybe humans too, if they looked like they belonged on the south side of the river. Rawk nodded to the men as he hurried through.

He would have run up the hill if his knee allowed it. His knee and his back and his arm. He walked as quickly as he could.

$$-O-$$

Rawk stalked across the palace waiting room. At first, he thought it was crowded with all manner of people, but after a second look he revised his opinion. It was crowded with all manner of humans. He'd noticed before that only humans went to see Weaver but had never really given it any thought. Now he knew why. Firstly, Weaver didn't really run the lives of most of the non–humans, not in the day–to–day at any rate. That was Thacker. And even if Thacker wasn't around the dwarves probably realized that Prince Weaver wouldn't do anything for them, unless their problems happened to coincide with his. Which was unlikely.

Rawk ignored the queue and stopped in front of the receptionist's desk.

"Is Weaver in?"

"He is not seeing anyone at the—"

Rawk pushed around the back of the desk towards the private door beyond. The two guards stepped forward to block the way but backed down when he glared at them. He visited regularly enough and they knew he wasn't going to hurt Weaver. Rawk grunted. They thought they knew. He pushed through the door, ignoring the complaints from the penitents gathered behind him. Five minutes later he was outside the door to Weaver's private study. The guards here were veterans. They were closer to Weaver. They weren't about to let him through. They weren't even going to knock to see if Weaver wanted to see him.

Rawk didn't even bother asking. He stood in front of them for a moment. Then he attacked. He hit the first man flush on the nose, knocking him out cold, and turned on the second. He knocked the wind out of him with a knee to the stomach and finished it off with an elbow to the side of the head.

Taking a deep breath, Rawk took stock. He thought he might have broken his wrist. Possible the stitches on his arm had pulled out. His knuckles were bruised and bleeding. Shaking off the pain, he opened the door and went inside.

Weaver was sitting with his feet up on the windowsill, wine in one hand, newspaper in the other. "I said I was not to be disturbed."

"Sorry, I didn't get the message."

Weaver almost fell of his chair. He got his feet down to the floor and spun around. "How did you get in? Sargan knows better than that."

"I didn't ask for Sargan's opinion."

The prince looked out through the still open door. "You attacked them? Both of them?" he took a nervous drink. "Sargan is very good. You haven't lost it, have you Rawk?"

Rawk sighed. "Sargan was surprised," he said before Weaver could mention *the good old days*. "That's all. They didn't expect me to attack. I'm sure I'll pay for it in the next few days. The whole Guard will be out for revenge."

"I imagine they will. So, what made you take the risk?"

"Sylvia, my healer, has been arrested. I assume it is part of the crack down after the riots but..."

131

Weaver waved his wine goblet. "Actually, it isn't."

Rawk nodded.

"I'm not sure if you realize, Rawk— well, you mustn't, because that would be silly— but Sylvia is not a healer. She is actually Silver Lark, our old enemy."

Rawk took a deep breath. "She is a healer. Whatever she might have been in the past, she is not now."

"Really?"

"She doesn't use magic. She uses herbs and common sense."

"Are you sure? There is magic all around Katamood at the moment."

"She hasn't done any magic for years."

"Does that mean she is no longer a sorcerer?"

"She has nothing to do with the portals. She helped me find the cabal that was making them."

"Really? Then how come there are still portals opening everywhere?"

Rawk unclenched his fist. He tried to calm himself down. "Firstly, portals can happen naturally."

"Then why haven't they been happening naturally for the last ten years?"

"Maybe they have. Maybe we just didn't notice."

Weaver raised an eyebrow. He didn't do it very well; he just looked silly.

"Opening portals with magic weakens the wall between worlds and makes natural portals more likely."

"She told you this, did she? That's convenient, isn't it?"

"Weaver, she has committed no crime. She has done no magic."

"I should let her go? Is that what you are saying?"

"Yes."

"So she didn't help you defeat all those sorcerers? You did that yourself?"

Rawk didn't say anything.

Weaver raised his eyebrow again. Now it was just annoying.

"I will not be letting her go, Rawk. She is a sorcerer and doesn't belong here; the laws are clear and simple."

"The laws are wrong. You are wrong." Rawk heard noises behind him and turned to see half a dozen guards gathering around the door. A couple were helping Sargan and his companion to their feet. "Sylvia is the best healer in the city. And she does it all without magic because she is afraid of drawing attention to herself."

"I don't care who she is, Rawk." Weaver almost shouted. "You spend too much time with her..." He faltered for a moment and cleared his throat. "She is using sorcery on you and you can't even tell."

"Weaver—"

"This all started when you started seeing her."

"The wolden wolf came before I visited her. I..." Rawk's eyes narrowed. "Wait. This isn't about sorcery, is it?" He almost laughed but it caught in his throat. "This is about you and me."

"You spend more time with her than you do with me. You like her more than you like me. Don't deny it."

Rawk sneered. "I wasn't going to deny it, Weaver. Like I said, Sylvia has been helping me fight the sorcerers."

"Silver Lark. Her name is Silver Lark, and I think you would do well to remember that." He took up a grape and popped it in his mouth. "She may say she loves you now, but I imagine that could change at any moment, if she saw an advantage. Or if she thought she had no other choice."

"What are you talking about? She doesn't *love* me."

"Of course she doesn't, it's good that you see that. But even if you are only bedding her for fun, the danger is still great."

"I'm not—"

"Not in danger? That's what all the sailors say as the sirens lure them onto the rocks."

"Sylvia has shown no evidence of luring me onto any rocks, so I will trust her until she does."

"Don't you understand? It will be too late then, Rawk. If you want to screw an elf there are plenty around that are much less dangerous than Silver Lark."

Rawk knew that the conversation was never going to go anywhere. Weaver didn't hear because he wasn't interested in the truth, not unless he was the person who came up with it. "So that's it?"

"I cannot spend my whole life protecting you from sirens and sorcerers." The prince sighed dramatically. "You can see her tomorrow and perhaps when you see what she is like now, you will change your mind."

"She is innocent."

"Well, if the portals keep opening then she obviously isn't responsible and we shall see what we can work out. She's playing with your mind. She's convinced you that dwarves and..." He waved his hand. "And fermi and all the others are better than humans."

"Not better. The same. Just different people."

"They are *not* the same. They will never be the same. They are hardly more than animals. If we weren't here the dwarves would be living in caves. The fermi would be in tents."

"And they would be happier than they are now, I dare say."

"We can discuss all of this after we visit her tomorrow."

"Where is she being held?"

"The Quod, of course."

"*The Quod?*" Rawk took a deep breath and loosened his fist again. "Weaver..."

"Where else did you think I would keep her?"

"Will the Quod be enough? You're the one telling me she's a sorcerer."

Weaver smiled. "I have a supply of coran chains. She will cause no problems."

Rawk gasped. "But coran chains burn, Weaver. You know that."

"That isn't my concern." The Prince sighed and held up a hand. "Look, she's staying where she is for now, but I will treat her well. We need to talk so we can work this out."

Rawk glanced at the guards again. They looked serious. "Of course. We've been friends far to long to let this come between us."

Weaver smiled. "Exactly. I knew you would see it my way."

Rawk hesitated. "Well. I guess I should go then."

"Important Hero stuff to do?"

"Always. And I've got to keep track of a whole bunch of other Heroes as well now. I don't know why I bothered." He headed for the door, fighting the urge to rest his hand on the hilt of his sword. The guards watched him carefully.

"I'll be there first thing in the morning."

"Come up here and I'll go with you. I'll talk to her."

Rawk nodded. "Very well. I'll come back tomorrow."

On his way out, Rawk stopped in the doorway and looked Sargan up and down. The soldier wiped a dribble of blood from his chin and spat onto the floor.

"Try that again and I'll kill you. I don't care what Prince Weaver says." He grunted. "Not so tough now that I'm ready for you, are you?"

Rawk smiled. "And you're much tougher now that you've got seven friends to help." He looked over his shoulder at the prince. "Where did you find this one? He could do with a bit more training." Weaver didn't reply so Rawk shouldered his way out into the hall. Sargan and three others followed, sounding like some young bullies trying to be tough.

Rawk hardly even noticed them. He was thinking about Sylvia. She could have been at home treating sick people if he hadn't come along and insisted that she help him. Blackmailed her into helping. She was in the Quod because he hadn't been willing to admit that he was getting old. He'd needed a healer who wouldn't talk, so now she was in a cell somewhere with a magic–blocking collar around her neck.

"I should've retired." He knew that. He should've retired a long time ago.

–O–

Rawk slumped into the chair.

"A rough morning?" Travis asked. He was already pouring tea.

Rawk nodded. "Sylvia— Silver Lark— has been arrested."

Travis blinked. "What? Sylvia is Silver Lark? But... Isn't she a sorcerer? Didn't you spend fifteen years trying to kill her?"

"Yes."

"And you just..."

"People change, Travis."

"Not you."

Rawk raised an eyebrow.

"Well, yes. You have changed a lot recently, with the whole dwarf thing and..." He seemed to think it was a good idea to shut up. He added honey to the tea and set the cup carefully down on the desk. "Have you talked to Weaver?"

"Of course. He said he'd look into things. I'm going to see her tomorrow morning. Hopefully..." He rubbed at his face and took a sip of tea. When he set the cup back down he stared at the designs engraved into the surface, spinning the cup slowly on the timber surface

The door opened and Rawk sat up quickly.

But Juskin entered, pile of book in his arms. The old man looked from Rawk to Travis. "What is going on?" He started to pile the books on the floor as Rawk went through the story again.

"What are you going to do?"

"I'll talk to him again tomorrow."

"Will it work?"

Rawk looked at Travis. "He's my friend." Except he wasn't. He was something else now, though Rawk didn't quite know what that was. Spurned lover? That didn't sound like someone who would do him a favor. He cleared his throat and gestured to Juskin's books. "Have you found anything about spences yet?"

Juskin sighed. "Hints. Vague mentions. Nothing substantial."

Rawk surged to his feet and went quickly to the shelf. "Well, we have to keep looking." He scanned the shelf of yet–to–be–checked books but he couldn't really see the titles, even if he could concentrate on them. He pulled one down randomly and took it back to his desk. When he opened the first page he sat for a minute waiting for his eyes to adjust. He scanned the table of contents. Nothing looked promising, so he opened the book randomly and started to read.

Ten minutes later, Rawk put the book down and rubbed his eyes. He'd always assumed his head hurt when he read because reading was bad for you and did strange things to your brain. But he remembered the spectacles in his drawer and wondered if his eyes were the problem. He took the package out and spun it slowly in his fingers.

"What's that?" Travis asked. He was sitting on the floor in the corner of the room with a book in his hands.

"Are you still here?"

"I thought I'd help."

"You know what you're looking for?"

"Of course. But stop changing the subject."

Rawk untied the string that held the cloth bundle closed and opened it out on the table. He picked up the spectacles and held them up for Travis to see.

"Spectacles," Juskin said.

Travis looked at the old man and back at Rawk. "But what do they actually do?"

"I read about them in an old book and went to a dwarf with the idea," Juskin said. "They correct the shapes of the light entering your eyes."

"Well, that was entirely unenlightening."

Rawk laughed. "They get rid of blurry vision, if you have the right ones." With some trepidation, he sat the spectacles on his nose and hooked the wire arms around behind his ears. And he could see.

He picked up the book smiling at the clarity of the letters. He hadn't realized it was so bad. He hadn't noticed the gradual slipping of his eyes, so in the end he'd just thought blurry vision was normal.

"Do they work?" Juskin asked.

Rawk smiled. "Of course; a dwarf made them."

"Indeed."

"You look silly." Travis glanced at Juskin, as if worried he might have offended the old man.

"That may be," Rawk said, "but I can see your face clearly enough to hit you on the nose if I want." He looked at Travis closer. "I never realized your eyes were two different colors."

"You didn't?"

"No. I couldn't see clearly enough. It's amazing." He looked at the book. "The letters are so clear. And I can read those titles from all the way over here." He pointed to the new books Juskin had brought in. A few minutes ago they would have been nothing more than blobs of color. "*A Thousand Years of Magic*, by Darveen Pierce. *Lonely Darkness* by Great Hadar. And *Lalinar* by..." Rawk's eyes narrowed. He surged to his feet and rushed across the room.

"What is it?"

He pulled an ancient book from the middle of Juskin's pile and flipped it open. He stood looking at the page for a minute.

"What is going on?"

Rawk held up the book. "*Lalinar*, by Natan Galabar."

"What of it?" Juskin asked. "I tried reading it. The subject is so arcane that it is beyond me to understand anything at all. I was hoping Sylvia would be able to help."

Travis was shaking his head. "You don't think it's him, do you?"

"Perhaps."

Juskin was looking from one to the other. "What are you talking about?"

"It isn't a common name," Rawk said.

"Perhaps it was when the book was written."

Rawk removed his spectacles.

"But I like him, Rawk. I really do. He's smart and funny and he... He makes me feel special. He talks to me like it is the best thing in the world to do."

"Maybe it isn't him, Travis. Maybe..."

"Somebody talk to me. Please"

Travis sighed. "A man named Natan lives upstairs. Rawk thinks he's the spence."

"I'm not saying he is, Travis. I'm saying we should investigate. Natan is a large man, just like the spence. And he is very mysterious."

"He is not *mysterious*."

"Where does his money come from?"

"He had rich parents."

"He told you that?"

"No. He changes the subject." Travis closed his book. "You told me to chase love, Rawk, or something like that. And now you're telling me..."

"I'm sorry, Travis. I could be wrong. I'm going back to the palace right now to talk to Weaver."

Travis left the book on the floor and left the room. He didn't slam the door, he just walked quickly, silently, and was soon gone from sight.

"Damn it." Rawk followed after him a little way then paused. He knew he should probably go and talk to

Travis, but he had no idea what to say. He had no idea what to say to Weaver either, but it would still be easier. He placed his spectacle sin a pouch on his belt and took a deep breath.

Nobody tried to stop Rawk this time as he marched into the private areas of the palace a few minutes later, but a group of four guards trailed along behind, making their displeasure known.

Rawk strode through the halls, trying to work out what he was going to say to Weaver. Once he had known the prince. Once he'd known how to manipulate him into doing what he wanted. The dwarves did the same thing, apparently, convincing the prince that the ideas were his. But now, Rawk wasn't so sure. He felt like he didn't know Weaver at all.

Nearing Weaver's private study, distracted, Rawk jumped back when a door opened right in front of him. His shadows were amused. And Rawk was even more surprised when Natan stepped out into the hall.

"Natan?" He said it cheerily enough, before realization struck him. Natan may well be the enemy he'd been searching for. Did the sudden burst of fear show in his eyes? He tried to steady his breathing.

"Ho, Rawk." Natan looked around. "What are you doing here?"

Rawk swallowed. "I was going to ask you the same thing." He felt his hand inching towards the hilt of *Kaj*. Natan's eyes were drawn to the movement and Rawk put his hand on his hip instead.

"Well, I've been doing some work for Weaver."

"You have?" He decided it was the strangest conversation he'd ever had, pushing his first real conversation with Sylvia to second place. "What do you actually do, again?"

"I do all sorts of things. I am a consultant. I am a finder of things, and a finder of information. I am a hider of things too, if that's what you need."

"You're a spy?"

"If it pays well enough, though it is usually a bit strenuous for me, I must say. And all that sneaking is undignified."

"It is. I've never liked it much myself."

"Oh, I certainly see you as a running–in–with–sword–swinging type of man."

"That I am."

"Well, I don't run—"

"Undignified?"

"Exactly. And I don't carry a sword, so my work is normally of a more clerical nature."

"I see. I don't like that much either."

The soldiers were getting a bit restless. It almost made Rawk want to continue talking, but Natan seemed to be just as keen to get moving again.

"I must go, I am afraid." Natan motioned back the way Rawk had come. "I still have a few people to consultify before the day is done."

"Well, I'll see you later then." His hand was on the hilt of his sword now. It twitched. But he didn't draw. Even if he were quick enough to kill Natan before being blasted by some sort of horrible magic, which he doubted, he'd be dead a moment later because the guards were looking for any excuse to draw as well.

"I should hope so. Tell Travis I will be late back tonight."

"I'll let him know." Rawk breathed and loosened his grip.

The soldiers sneered at Natan as he went past, but the big man didn't seem to notice. "Hello, boys. So nice to see you again." He waved cheerily and patted one on the arm.

The soldier looked as if he was going to die from disgust, making Rawk wish Natan didn't now make his skin crawl too. He shook off the feeling and hurried further along the hall.

But at the next corner he stopped. He could see Weaver's door from where he stood. It was barely twenty paces away, heavy and banded with iron as if it needed to withstand sieges.

Rawk felt his hand on the hilt of his sword again. "Natan works for Weaver," he muttered. "Weaver dreams of the good old days, when there were creatures everywhere for the killing." He looked at the two men guarding the door. He looked at the men behind him. And turned and went back the way he came.

"Hey, where are you going?" The men blocked his path.

Rawk shook his head. He cleared his throat. "I want to show Weaver something, but I just realized that I forgot it."

"I knew you were an idiot."

"I'm getting old. You'll be like this too one day."

"You were always an idiot."

Rawk glanced back over his shoulder, though the door was gone from sight. "Apparently." Weaver didn't just wish the good old days were back, he was doing something to make it happen.

$$-O-$$

Rawk quietly closed the door and leaned back against the rough timber. "He isn't going to let Sylvia go."

There was a gasp and Rawk noticed Celeste sitting in Sylvia's chair, face bruised, cup of tea halfway to her lips. He would have softened the blow if he'd realized she was there. Juskin was there as well.

"How do you know? He is your friend."

"He is *never* going to let her go."

Juskin closed the book he was reading. "Perhaps if you—"

"Weaver loves me." Rawk shook his head and sighed. He rubbed his hand over his face. "He thinks I've been ensnared by Sylvia. At least he's convinced himself that that's what happened. He'll *never* let her go."

Juskin looked over the top of his spectacles. "I know a lawyer. We could..."

"The law is on his side, Juskin. It is illegal for sorcery to be used in Katamood. He can say Sylvia is opening the portals and who's going to argue? She's Silver Lark and for years I told everyone how evil she was."

"But..." Celeste put down the cup.

"He's Prince Weaver. He brought law and order to Katamood. The people love him."

"What are we going to do?" Juskin asked. "If the law is not on our side then..."

"Indeed." Rawk pushed himself away from the door and went to look at the book that Natan had written. It seemed heavier than it had before. He opened it up, as if some type of sorcery might be the cause. But it was just ancient crackling pages held between leather covers. He starred at the boxy, staccato, blurry text.

There was a drawn out silence.

"The people don't love him, Rawk." Celeste was staring at her hand, rubbing the tips of her fingers. "The *humans* love him. And even then, it's only those on the north of the river, really. The south may well be a different world sometimes."

"So, what are you saying?" He was angrier than he should have been. It wasn't Celeste's fault.

She shrugged. "I don't know. I am just saying."

"Right. Sorry. I didn't..."

"It's all right." She laid a hand on his arm. She took a deep breath. "Where is she?"

"The Quod."

Another gasp. "The Quod?" She cleared her throat. "So, will you let her stay there?"

"Of course not."

"And Weaver will never let her out?"

"No. I'm sure of it."

"Well..."

Rawk turned to look at her. "You're saying I have to break her out of prison?"

"I merely made you rule out one option. You came up with the next option on your own."

Rawk sat down at the desk. "It's not as simple as that. If I break her out, Weaver will know it was me. And he will have to put Sylvia back in prison, and possibly me as well."

"Or you leave town."

Rawk looked at Celeste. "Katamood is my home; I will *not* leave."

"Then the law has to change," Celeste said quietly.

"Weaver won't change the law. It is doing exactly what he wants it to do at the moment— putting him in control of me."

Juskin cleared his throat. "An innocent woman is being held against her will by men who are upholding unjust laws for selfish reasons. Sylvia cannot be taken from the Quod legally. So our options are, get her out illegally or change the law."

"She could be dead tomorrow. We can't change the law that quickly."

"Well then..." Juskin pushed his glasses further up onto his nose and rose to his feet.

"Where are you going?"

"I'm sure the dwarves will have the architectural drawings for the Quod somewhere."

"You're kidding."

"Do you know who we should ask? I've never been all that far south of the river before."

The old man was heading out the door. Rawk looked at Celeste and they hurried to follow.

The sun was setting by the time they made it to Caldera. Rawk's knee was aching and that was making his hip ache too, so he stopped to lean against the last of the houses before the tunnel. "I need to rest."

"We don't have time to waste," Juskin said. It looked like he could go all night though he had limped worse than Rawk. "Where are we actually going?"

Rawk pushed away from the wall, but Celeste led them past the incognito-guards and into the tunnel.

"A cave? I thought the dwarves stopped living in caves years ago."

"It isn't a cave," Celeste said. "And dwarves still live in caves, if caves are the best place available."

"Really? When are caves the best place available?"

"On the side of a mountain. Or anywhere where the weather is extreme, really. Caves generally have a very regular temperature."

"Oh, I suppose so."

"Like she said, though, this isn't a cave," Rawk said. And they stepped out into the hidden valley.

"Oh my."

Rawk smiled at the old man's expression for a moment, but then he remembered why they were there. "Do you know where Thacker actually lives, Celeste?"

"At his office."

"Of course he does."

Rake was no longer amongst the guards, but they let them through without a word. They caught the tram around to the far side of the valley with Juskin hanging on as if his life depended on it. It was busier than what Rawk was used to with locals heading home after finishing work for the day. But the crowds were quiet, which was totally out of character for the dwarves if not the others. They sat in silent contemplation, staring at their hands or out at the city. Rawk sat and stared with them.

Down on the street, a dwarf stopped by a lamppost for a moment. He fiddled with something then light blossomed at the top.

"How does he do that?"

"It's a gas lamp," Celeste told him. "They open a valve to let gas through and then light it. It is much easier and quicker than the oil lanterns up north, but Weaver won't agree to the initial cost. That's what Grint told me, anyway."

Rawk craned his neck as the tram passed the dwarf and watched as he lit another lamp.

"I think they are working on making it automatic, but I don't know if they can make it happen. That is a lot of pilot lights and a lot of gas."

Rawk didn't really know what a pilot light was. He didn't say anything. All he could think was that the dwarves were always moving into the future while Weaver was stuck in *the good old days.*

"What are we going to say to Thacker when we see him?" Juskin asked, cleaning his spectacles as he blinked out at the city, still trying to see.

"The truth."

The old man raised his eyebrows. "You think he will help us break a prisoner from jail?"

"Yes." Rawk had no doubt at all. "We'll probably have to convince him to stay at home."

Thacker didn't say he wanted to go with them, but the look on his face said clearly enough what he was thinking. "When are you going to do this?" he asked, running his hand through his hair as if it wasn't always a mess. He sat at the table in the small apartments in the west wing of the administrative building.

Rawk looked at Juskin. "Tonight."

Thacker grunted. "Short notice."

"I know. But I'm supposed to go and see her tomorrow, with Weaver. After that..." Rawk shrugged. *After that he may decide she has outlived her usefulness.* He didn't want to say it out loud.

"Well, I guess we don't have a lot of choice. Let's not even bother talking about this until we have some details." He called to one of the guards outside the door and sent him off the find a secretary. And when the secretary arrived a few minutes later, he sent the man off to find anything he could to do with the Quod. It was an ancient building, almost as old as the River Watch towers, but apparently the dwarves had information about everything.

While they waited for the man to return, Thacker sent for wine and pastries. It seemed strange to eat and drink while they sat waiting to make their plans. Rawk chewed mechanically on an apricot tart and didn't even taste it.

"It isn't your fault," Celeste said softly, laying a hand on his arm.

Rawk jumped. "Pardon?"

"It isn't your fault."

"I didn't say it was."

"But that's what you are thinking, isn't it?"

"If I'd left her alone, Weaver wouldn't have even know she was there."

"A thousand decision we make every day change the world, Rawk. If Weaver hadn't chosen that certain tavern for lunch, the City Guard would not have found you and you would not have gone to the Old Forest to kill the wolden wolf. So you would not have gotten injured and you wouldn't have needed to see Sylvia at all. So it's all Weaver's fault after all."

"Yes but..."

"But, if Pirates hadn't taken over Katamood, then Weaver wouldn't have been prince at all. So perhaps it is the pirates fault."

"Now you're being ridiculous."

Celeste raised her eyebrows and Juskin gave a short, sharp laugh. "Never argue with a woman, Rawk. I thought you would know that by now."

Rawk grunted and Celeste continued. "Sylvia values your friendship, Rawk. I believe, given the choice, she would change nothing."

"She told you that?"

"More or less. This is not your fault. So let's stop worrying about that and fix the problem."

"Right. Yes."

"And damn those pirates," Juskin said softly.

The secretary returned and thumped a large sheath of papers down onto the table. Thacker moved his chair closer, put down his wine, and looked at the first sheet. "Let's see what we can see."

After a moment of hesitation, Rawk pulled out his spectacles.

$$-O-$$

"What in Path's name am I doing?" Rawk held up two fingers in the symbol of the Great Path because he figured he would need all the help he could get. Crouching into the shadows near the mouth of the alley he couldn't see anything all that interesting, but that was sure to change quickly enough. The Quod was across the other side of the road but all he could see of it was a tall stone wall that looked like it was going to be staying there all night. He ducked back a moment later when a man walked along the top.

"Are you ready, Rawk?"

"Of course I'm not ready, Rake," he muttered. "That would be impossible."

Rake nodded. "Well, ready or not..." He looked at the dwarves and men clustered in the alley behind him. There were two dwarvish warriors. "Gunnar? Crisp?"

The dwarves nodded. But they were already focusing on the task as hand. Rawk knew he should be too, but it was hard. He was sneaking into prison to release a sorcerer.

"Kristun?" The engineer gave a nod. He looked calmer than everyone else.

And there were also five laborers. "Hobart? Are your boys ready?"

Hobart was a dwarf with a long beard tucked into the collar of his shirt and a crowbar tucked into his belt. He looked like he should be at home with his feet up in front of a fire and a grandchild on his knee. He ignored the question and asked one of his own. "Can you see the spot?"

Rawk examined the wall and couldn't see anything. But that wasn't his job, so that didn't matter. As long at the dwarves knew what was going on. Even Rake could see the spot. Rawk sighed and looked at the last two members of their party. Fabi and Frew looked like he felt. Weaver was one of them. He had taken a pirate haven and turned it into one of the greatest cities in the world. It felt wrong to be crossing him like this, even if he had become the man he now was.

They waited some more. Rawk could feel dawn approaching like a mounted charge. He felt it would arrive at any moment and just wanted to get on with the mission. No, he just wanted to be at home with his feet up. He took a deep breath and pulled on his mask. The others covered their faces as well, with masks and visors and even a scrap of cloth tied in place.

"Here we go," said Rake. He shifted his grip on his sword.

For a moment, Rawk couldn't hear anything. Then he heard the drums and the shouts and watched as the guard on the wall heard them too. There was a riot in the square on the far side of the Quod. It wasn't a big square, but it wasn't a big riot either and wouldn't last long. The guards ran along the ramparts, heading for the action, and a minute later Rawk was standing at the base of the wall, sword in hand, trying to see what the dwarves could see. Maybe there was a section of the wall that looked a bit newer than the rest, a bit rougher, but it was hard to tell. The dwarves were sure though, apparently. They had a battering ram, small enough to be held by just four of them, and they set to work, pounding in time to the beat of the drums.

Rawk watched as the mortar between the bricks started to crack, then he could see a staggered, door-sized outline appearing. "Well, what do you know?"

Rake smiled as he watched his companions work.

"It was filled in twenty years ago," Hobart said. "They needed more storage and less guards."

"I imagine Weaver didn't want to pay them."

"I imagine so."

Two more thumps against the stone and the battering ram crew stepped back. Hobart stepped forward and examined their handiwork. He ran his fingers over the bricks then set to with his crowbar. He worked at the first block for a long time, but when it finally slid free and was lowered carefully to the ground the next ones followed in a rush. And a minute later, there was a hole large enough for Rawk to climb through. He took that as an invitation.

Inside, Rawk paused to take a deep breath. He adjusted his mask and looked around. The only light was coming in through the hole they had created and the moonlight did nothing more than silver the dust they had stirred into motion. Rake lit a torch and the flames caught and gathered.

The plans had suggested there would be a large room, and they were right. Of course, the plans thought there would be an entrance, so it was marked as a guardroom, but now it was full of clutter that hadn't seen the light of day in a long time. The air was thick with must and dust, painted a flickering gold now, instead of silver, which was good because it meant it was unlikely anyone would walk in on them while they got themselves organized. Rawk stood being nervous and impatient as Hobart and his assistants brought the now—loose parts of the wall inside so they couldn't be seen from up above. They stacked them neatly near the hole and, all going well, they would slip them back into place as they left so it would take a while for anyone to realize. They didn't do it now in case they needed to leave in a hurry.

"Good luck, everyone," Hobart said and lead the work crew back the way they'd come where they could wait in the relative safety of the alley until they were required.

Rake stumped across the room to stand by Rawk. He was wearing light, black armor and a helm that covered most of his face. "Are we ready?"

Rawk nodded. Fabi nocked an arrow and he nodded too. Frew just grunted. Rousing agreement, then.

But then it was too late. Gunnar and Crisp set off, swords at the ready. Rawk wanted to go next, but Rake beat him to the door. Then Kristun pushed past, tools clanking softly in a leather satchel he had over his shoulder. Rawk grunted and went through before Frew and Fabi could beat him too. The door led to a hallway and, according to one of the dwarves that cleaned the place, just around the corner there would be a guard at a barred door. The man wouldn't have the key.

By the time Rawk got there, the guard was lying motionless on the floor. "Is he dead?"

Rake looked at the man speculatively. "I'm not sure. Knocking someone unconscious isn't like engineering."

Rawk wasn't quite sure what that meant. It didn't matter. If the guard was dead then there was nothing they could do about it now. "So how do we get past the door?" he whispered.

But Kristun was examining the lock and poking at it with some tools.

Rawk was about to ask his question again when the lock clicked and the door swung noisily open. "Oh."

Kristun turned to look back for a moment and said quietly, "Locksmiths Guild. Why did you think I was here?"

"Well..." Rawk shrugged. He changed the subject. "What's the point of a lock if opens that easily?"

"Thank you, Kristun. Are you right to keep going?"

The engineer nodded as he gathered his tools. "Probably no point opening this one if I wasn't." He stood up and waited for the procession to continue.

Rawk adjusted his mask. "How far is it?"

Rake shrugged. "Unless you can tell me exactly where she is..."

"Of course not."

"Right, then don't ask silly questions."

"You should show me some respect," Rawk said to him.

Rake smiled, the flickering light of the torch and the shadows conspiring to make it look fierce. He started walking and Rawk was forced to follow again. The dwarf kept talking as they went. "Up here is a stairwell that gives access to all the best cells." He glanced back. "Best being the ones you want your special prisoners in, not the ones that have the nice view and easy access to the fire escape."

Rawk didn't know what dwarves were talking about half the time. He didn't even bother trying to work it out any more. "So we just look?"

They started to climb, clattering up the narrow, worn stairs in single file. On the landing, the light from their torch merged with another set in a bracket on the wall. Rake set his torch on the floor out of the way.

"Yes. Tell me when you think of a better plan. Now quiet. There will be another door above." He slowed down and poked his head around the final corner.

Rawk had a look too. There was another barred door just around the corner and a guard sitting on a stool another ten yards beyond that. Safely hidden again, Rawk gestured to Fabi's bow. "I think you should handle this, Fabi." He explained the situation.

"So can I get close to the door?"

Rawk shrugged. "If you're quick. Just make sure the guard doesn't call out or warn anyone else if you can."

"You realize I'll have to kill him, right?"

Rawk took a deep breath. "It's them or Sylvia."

Fabi flexed his shoulders and neck as he readied his bow. He went up the last two steps and quickly around the corner. Rawk didn't see the release but he heard the shaft thrumming through the air, heard it hit *something* and waited for Fabi's reaction.

"Done."

Just a single, quiet word and Rawk felt they had passed the point of no return. He didn't know why this attack felt like that and the previous one hadn't. Perhaps because dwarves had taken out the last guard. Or perhaps because he had taken part in this one, no matter how peripherally. Or perhaps because there was a chance the last guard was still alive. Rawk stepped around the corner to look as well. The guard was lying on the floor, green fletched arrow in his back, pool of blood spreading slowly outwards. "Done," he agreed. He sheathed *Kaj* as Kristun went to the door and set to work. Rawk tried to keep his focus. He went back to the top of the stairs to keep watch, though they would probably hear someone coming long before they saw them. Fabi came and joined him.

"It's strange..."

Rawk nodded. "Yes."

"I've spent my whole life killing things— people, exots, you name it— but now..."

"I know. And do you know what the strangest thing is?"

"What?"

"My... reluctance started with the exots, not with people. I started to wonder if I was doing the right thing killing strange magical creatures, then started thinking about what it means to kill people."

It was Fabi's turn to nod.

"I've been out to see the duen, you know?" Rawk said.

"The what?"

"The trolls. In the forest."

"You're kidding?"

"No. They're just people. They just want to be left in peace."

Fabi nodded slowly, looking uncomfortable.

"I spoke to the father of one of the duen we killed. If anyone was going to kill me, he would." Rawk sighed. "We killed his entire family."

Fabi cleared his throat. "I think they're ready."

"What?"

"The door's open."

"Oh. Right. Let's get this over with."

The others were waiting for Rawk this time. He marched through the door without a word and they fell in behind. The passageway was cold and bare and damp. Half a dozen lamps were hanging from the wall, but only three were lit. The pale light reflected sickly off the slimy walls. Cell doors alternated on each side.

Rawk looked in the first cell. The light didn't reach into the back corners but a man stood by the door, dark hair a wild mess, eyes narrowed in suspicion. Rawk swallowed and moved on. Next there were two men, small and rat like, who could only be brothers. Not twins though. Their entire cell was bathed in light; they would never sleep. Then an old woman, dressed in rags, one eye staring off at a crazy angle. A young man, hardly more than a boy, naked and huddled in the back corner, hiding in the shadows. And a dwife. Her left arm was blistered and weeping. Her face was bruised.

There was a side passage. Pools of dark and light. More cells. Rawk didn't turn aside. He kept walking all the way to the end of the passage. He stopped there and leaned against the wall, feeling the rough, damp stone through his shirt. He rubbed at his knee.

"What is it, Rawk?"

He shook his head. "Nothing," he said quietly. "Come on."

When he started to make his way quietly up the stairs, clinging to the wall, he realized *Kaj* was still sheathed at his side. He pulled the blade free, gripping the hilt tightly. Before he reached the top, he paused, listening. He could hear something around the corner, but wasn't sure that he wanted to look. He stood for a while, heart racing, while he tried to think. He wished he had thought to bring a drink. Someone touched his arm and he almost jumped out of his skin. Kristun gave a rueful shake of his head, then handed Rawk a small square of mirror.

Crouching on the stairs, Rawk held the mirror down near the floor so he could peak around the corner.

After a moment, he motioned for the others to go back down.

"This is it," he said softly when they were back on the floor below.

"Are you sure?" Fabi asked.

"There's two guards just around the corner and two others guarding a door at the end of the hall. They all look to be awake."

"So what do we do?"

"Nothing's changed. We still have to get Sylvia out."

"So..."

"So, we kill the guards as quickly as possible. And get her."

"So, what's the plan then?"

"I thought I just told you the plan." Rawk held up a hand as he gave the matter some thought. "We all rush around the corner with Fabi at the front. He shoots someone down by the door, then we keep going."

"That's it?" Fabi asked. "Your plans haven't improved at all."

"I'm a Hero, not a general."

"Let's go then," Rake said.

Rawk hurried to make sure he was at the front with Fabi. They crept up the stairs, looked at each other, and charged around the corner. Fabi loosed his arrow almost before the guards were in sight. He started to lower his bow, but seemed to think better of it. Instead, he drew another arrow as Rawk rushed past.

Rawk ran into the first guard and knocked him over, grunting with the impact. He fell as well, sprawled on top of the man. A sword slid past close to his ribs. Crisp's sword. The guard stopped moving. Rawk jumped back to his feet, knee throbbing, and turned to the next man, but Frew was already on him. Fabi, Rake and Gunnar arrived like a small avalanche a moment later. The last man by the door was still alive, so Rawk leapt over the man he had felled and hit the floor running. Running slowly, but running. He came to a halt as his opponent raised his sword.

Rawk pushed up his mask, letting some cool air onto his face. "Do you really want to die tonight?"

"Couldn't surprise me like you did Sargan?"

Rawk smiled. "You guards must gossip like old ladies at a knitting circle."

The man sneered.

"Well, you'd better get your knitting needle ready."

Rawk attacked, low then high, and the guard slapped his sword away. But the other man had the door at his back and no room to move. They traded a couple of more blows, the clash of steel ringing around the hallway. There was no other sound. The fighting behind him was over.

"You all done there, Fabi?" He hoped they were. He was going to feel like an idiot if the guards had won. Only for a little while though. He'd probably be dead after that.

"Yeah. Wasn't much of a challenge at all."

"Do you need some help?" Rake asked. Rawk heard someone walking down the passage behind him.

"No. I think I should be all right." He attacked while he was still talking, catching the guard by surprise. But it still wasn't enough. The swords clanged and clattered. Rawk took a slight prick on his chest as he retreated, then got a slash across his arm as well. He didn't know the guard, but he was good. He wasn't flashy, but he was direct and to the point.

Rawk pressed forward again. He slashed and lunged. His knee hurt, he hurt all over, but he only needed a couple of seconds to back the man against the wall. Once, seemingly not long ago, Rawk would have finished the fight without thought. But now all he did was think. He thought about parries and thrusts. He thought about the pain in his arm and in his knee. He thought about fatigue. He thought about the cold stone beneath the soles of his boots and he though about his shadow stretching out before him. And amongst all the thoughts there was hardly time for moving, for being in the moment and reacting to what his opponent did.

Taking a couple of steps back, Rawk took a deep breath and tried to empty his mind. Another deep breath. He swayed aside and let the guard's sword slip by his chest. Push the blade away with his sword arm, spun, hit the guard with his elbow. He felt the man's jaw crack but just kept spinning and slashed him across the side.

And that was it. Rawk breathed again. His heart was pounding in a most unheroic way. His hand was shaking so he tightened it around the hilt of *Kaj*.

He heard someone step up behind him and almost ran them through. "For Path's sake, Frew, don't do that."

The other man ignored him. "That was easy."

Rawk grunted and tried not to look at the wound on his arm. "Yeah. Simple."

The guard wasn't dead yet. He was lying on the floor, groaning, clutching at the wound in his side with spasming hands. Blood pulsed out between his fingers. A moment later two of the dwarves grabbed him and dragged him away from the door. He gurgled a scream before finally dying.

Rawk felt a bit sick. "Kristun, how about that door?"

Kristun came forward with his tools and got to work. He peered into the lock and clicked his tongue. "Quite a bit more complex than the last one."

"How long will it take?" Rawk asked. "We don't have all night."

"Is that a Begmok lock?" Rake asked. "They're legendary. Almost impossible to pick."

Rawk could see the word Begmok stamped on a big piece of studded metal on the door. He groaned.

Kristun gave a nod. "Yes, Begmok locks are about the best there are." He was packing up his tools.

"Have you ever picked one?" Frew asked. "I don't want to do all of this for nothing."

Kristun nodded. "Yes, it's a Begmok. No, I've never picked one and I don't know of anyone who has, but—"

"Path, damn it," Rawk said. He hacked at the door with his sword and barely even left a mark. He tried to take a breath, to calm himself, but it didn't work. "Do any of the guards have a key?" The dwarves were way ahead of him and had already gone to check.

"Nothing," they reported, almost before he had asked.

"What are we going to do?"

Kristun sighed. "It is a Begmok," he said again, "but..." He reached up and turned the big wheel that worked the lock. There was a click, and a thunk, and the lock opened.

Rawk looked at the dwarf. He looked at the lock. Then he pushed the door open.

"Why would they not even bother to lock it," Fabi asked.

But the answer was right before them. Sylvia, naked, striped with cuts, bruised and unconscious, was chained to the wall by both hands and feet. She wasn't going anywhere.

Everyone stood silently for a minute.

Kristun cleared his throat. "Well, those locks I can do." And eyes on the ground, hands fiddling with his tools, he quickly crossed the room. He set to work immediately and it was only seconds before the first shackle fell away from Sylvia's ankle. She groaned, but didn't open her eyes.

Rawk swallowed. "Fabi, your cloak." He held out his hand without looking and took the cloak when it was given to him. He took it across to Sylvia.

"Guards coming," Rake said, motioning the dwarves to his side. Frew and Fabi went with them.

Kristun moved to the next shackle. His tools were loud in the echoing silence of the cell.

"I'd guess about a dozen, Rawk. We don't have time."

Rawk didn't move. When the second lock opened and fell away, Rawk motioned to the brass collar that encircled her neck. It wasn't attached to any chains. "Get that one next."

"We can do that later."

"No. Do it now." His tone didn't leave any room for more arguing. It was the shackle that contained her magic and it might be the one thing stopping her from waking. He wasn't sure if waking her right now was a good idea, but he knew leaving her asleep was definitely a bad idea. They had to get her down the stairs. They had to...

This one took longer. It seemed to take forever. Each second took a lifetime.

The clash of swords suddenly filled the hallway. Men screamed. Rawk had a quick look and saw that his companions had made it to the high ground at the top of the narrow staircase, but he knew the advantage might not help indefinitely. More screams.

The collar fell away and Sylvia groaned again. She writhed and blood began to dribble down her wrists. Rawk shook away some of his own stupor and finally thought to support her weight. Kristun didn't slow. He went to work on the next lock, muttering to himself, tools clenched between his teeth. When the shackle finally opened, Sylvia slumped to one side but seemed to weigh nothing at all. Rawk struggled to get the cloak about her shoulders. His fingers fumbled with the clasp. But when Kristun finally finished his work, Rawk scooped her up and immediately headed for the door.

At the top of the stairs, Fabi fired two arrows in quick succession. The first one missed, but the second one tore through the neck of a man attacking Rake. The dwarf didn't pause, shifting his attention to the next opponent. Rawk stood behind the fight with Kristun. Frew, was just in front of him, stabbing through the front line every now and then, hoping to distract somebody if nothing else. Fabi took down another two, but each shot was risky and he spent most of the time looking frustrated.

Rawk knew how he felt. He wanted to put Sylvia down and draw *Kaj*, but there was no room. If his services were required it was probably too late anyway.

A writhing mass of shadows danced on the walls.

One of the dwarves missed a block and yelled wordlessly as his hand was sliced open. Frew dragged him clear, even as he kicked and shouted and kept trying to fight, and jumped into the breach. His extra reach let him kill two men quickly and the rest back away. And that let Fabi take out another. The dead man fell backwards, hitting the stairs with a wet thud, and the rest scrambled over him as they tried to flee.

"Hold," Rake called.

Rawk wanted to give chase, but decided that holding was probably a good idea. "We don't want to give them too much time to regroup or find support." He drew in some deep breaths though holding Sylvia wasn't much of an effort at all.

"I know," Rake responded. "But killing them isn't our goal. We need to get out of here."

Kristun set to work bandaging Crisp's hand, wrapping it tightly with a bandage from his satchel and tying it off with a neat, professional knot.

"Healers Guild?" Rawk asked.

He touched the red ribbon in his beard. "Of course."

Rawk looked at the bandaged dwarf. "Crisp, are you right to carry Sylvia?"

"Yes."

Rawk handed the elf over, wrapping the cloak carefully about her thin, pale frame. "Let's go then." He started down the stairs.

On the next floor, three guards were waiting, swords drawn. They changed their minds quickly enough when Rawk strode towards them, his companions at his back. He'd hardly gone a dozen paces when they turned and fled, though it was possible they were retreating to a more secure position.

After a few more steps, Rawk stopped.

"What is it?" Frew asked.

He didn't reply. He went back to the cell with the dwife he'd seen earlier. She stared back vacantly, hardly even registering his presence. "Let her out," he said. "Let all of them out."

Frew sniffed. "We don't know what they're here for, Rawk."

"I don't care. It looks like she's learned her lesson."

"Releasing Sylvia is one thing; she's your friend and healer. But this is moving to a whole *new* thing, Rawk."

"I know. In the past we've just done what we were told. We had our quest and—"

"Exactly."

"We were hired killers and bounty hunters. We were mercenaries."

"No, we weren't. It was completely different."

"Was it? Really? We were just getting paid to do other people's dirty work."

Frew didn't say anything. He stared into the cell. "You've spent more than 35 years as a Hero, Rawk."

Rawk nodded and drew in a deep breath. "I know, but I'm feeling better now. Release them all."

"You can say Sylvia didn't break any reasonable law. How do you justify this?"

He looked at Sylvia, limp and quiet in Crisp's arms. He watched her breathing just so he was sure that she was.

She didn't deserve to be in the Quod and he doubted any of the others really did either. "Let them *out.*"

Kristun started working on the lock. When he was done he swung the door open, but the dwife didn't move. She still hadn't moved by the time the rest of the doors on the main passage had been opened. The other prisoners came out into the open one by one, nodded their thanks, or pumped Kristun's hand or slapped him on the back, before looking each way down the hall and heading the same direction as Rawk and his companions were. In a few seconds, the hall was quiet. Until the next rush came from the side passage, flooding past wordlessly.

"They might clear the way a bit," Fabi said when they had gone too.

"I hope they escape unharmed," Rawk said. "They were not released to be a distraction."

"Yes, but..."

"Come on."

There were more guards. Five came from the stairwell before Rawk reached it. Others were coming close behind.

"Rawk?"

Rawk swore. He wasn't wearing his mask. The first of the men looked familiar.

"Rawk? What are you doing here? Did you see..?" The guard seemed to see Rawk's companions for the first time. He stopped.

A moment later, an arrow whisked past Rawk's ear from behind. It missed the leader and hit the next man in the chest. Rawk winced and shrugged and emptied his mind as the guards charged. Another died with an arrow in his throat, a fountain of blood splashing on the ground, audible, even over the rush of feet. Or maybe he just imagined it.

Rawk blocked the first attack at the last moment and the man kept pressing forward. For a second, another two guards gave assistance and Rawk could barely keep up. But he didn't panic. He fought, calm and focused, ignoring everything except the dance before him. Then Rake arrived, crashing into one of the guards, knocking him back into the rest. And Frew got the other's attention with a cut across the arm.

The leader's blade flashed through the air and Rawk smiled as he flicked the attack aside.

"What are you smiling at, traitor?"

"Skill."

"And it makes you happy that you are about to die because of my skill?"

"I never said I was smiling at *your* skill." Rawk actually laughed then. He anticipated the next attack and had *Kaj* in the way almost before his opponent knew what he was doing. "It's just nice to know that I'm not too old after all." Rawk countered, drawing a line of blood. And he paused, staring at the blood.

It struck him that it was real. He might not have been able to remember the man's name, but he was someone that Rawk knew, someone that he occasionally interacted with, and now they were trying to kill each other.

So much for focus.

Rawk swayed back, letting the blade flash past his face. He pulled himself together as the other man gave a wordless shout and charged forward. Rawk blocked, stepped aside, pushed aside a swipe and ran him through.

It was very real.

"Leon."

"What?"

Rawk shook his head and looked around. Frew was just finishing off the last man.

"This was Leon," Rawk said. He breathed.

"You knew him."

"Sort of."

Kristun was starting to bandage a cut on Rake's thigh. It was going to need stitches, sooner rather than later. Others were seeing to their own minor wounds. Rawk went to the top of the stairs with Fabi and kept watch.

A few minutes later everyone else joined them and they started down towards the ground floor. The guard was no longer near the door, though if he had left on his own or with assistance was not obvious. Rawk kept moving forward, unsure what would happen if he stopped now. The storeroom was still empty, bricks waiting in the corner.

One of the dwarves rushed forward to check out through the opening.

"Nothing," he said.

"So we just climb out then?" Frew asked. "Is the distraction sill happening?"

Rawk looked around, shrugged, and went out through the hole. He couldn't see if the guards had returned to the wall above, but the sound of drums and shouting was still audible. He took Sylvia when she was carefully handed out to him and started to cross the street. The others followed close behind. Halfway across, Rawk froze when he heard a noise coming from the alley. Then Hobart stepped into the half–light. The dwarf nodded as he led his workers across to the wall. "Evening."

Rawk started breathing again and continued forward. He almost looked calm when he entered the shadows of the alley on the far side. He was sure there were no witnesses but still, there was no turning back now. No turning back.

Thersday

RAWK SAT UP. He'd been lying in bed for hours but wasn't within miles of sleeping. A dwarf healer had stitched his leg and she'd also taken a look at his arm. Everything hurt. His whole life hurt.

The door opened.

"How long have you been here?" Travis asked.

Rawk shrugged. "Does it matter? What time is it?"

"An hour after dawn. Were you out with Celeste and Grint? They didn't sing last night."

"Were they supposed to? I didn't even think we would be open."

"Yes. I had to pull a performer in off the street."

"You did not."

"I did. Well, Ferran was on the front porch, and that's close enough to the street."

"Close enough."

"So, do we fire them?"

Rawk raised an eyebrow. "Celeste and Grint? You're kidding? They get a lot more leeway than that."

Travis grunted. "Are you having breakfast?"

"No. I have to go see Weaver."

"About Sylvia?"

"Of course."

When he stood up, Rawk realized he was still wearing the black breaches and old boots he'd worn on the rescue mission the night before. If Travis noticed anything, which of course he did, then he didn't say. Rawk stripped off and headed for the shower in next room. He was pushing past the heavy tapestry that hid the doorway, wincing at the pain in his arm, when Travis spoke again.

"I spoke to Natan last night."

Rawk paused.

"I asked him what he does for money."

Rawk didn't say anything.

"He didn't answer again."

"He works for Weaver."

"He does? How do you know? Doing what?"

"I saw him in the palace yesterday. And he didn't really say. He certainly didn't admit to being a spence."

"So he could do anything. Weaver hires all sorts of people. Weaver hates magic."

Rawk nodded. He looked up at the priceless tapestry that hid the doorway. He hadn't known it was priceless when he put it there. "Take this thing down," he said. "Move it down to the office." And he slipped through into the hallway. A minute later he was examining the shower and wondering how he could use it without getting all of his bandages wet. He took a washcloth, held it under the warm water, and used it to wipe the sweat and grime from his body. It wasn't the same at all.

−O−

Rawk sat in Weaver's private study. He avoided his usual hard chair and sat in one of the overstuffed couches. The prince kept him waiting for almost half an hour. Eventually the door opened and Weaver strode in.

"It's about time," Rawk said, rising to his feet. "Let's go."

"Go where?" Weaver asked. He was dressed in a chain mail shirt and had leather gloves tucked into his belt.

"To see Sylvia, obviously." He looked the prince up and down. "Why in Path's name are you dressed like that?"

"Surely you know. Sylvia escaped, Rawk."

"What? When?"

"Last night."

"She escaped from the Quod?"

"No, I had her moved to the *Giddy Sailor* at midnight. The barman couldn't hold her though."

"Well..."

"It means war, Rawk."

167

"What? One elf escaping isn't an act of war."

"It's not one elf; it's Silver Lark. And she couldn't have done it on her own. She must have had help."

"Who says?"

"She was wearing coran chains, remember? Someone must have released her."

Rawk looked confused. "So who are you declaring war on exactly?"

"The dwarves, of course."

"Which dwarves?"

"All of them."

Rawk swallowed. He knew Weaver was crazy but... "All of them? You can't just..."

"Yes, I can."

"You're going to kill all the dwarves?"

Weaver's lip twitched. "Maybe not all of them. But enough that the rest will learn their lesson."

"You can't..." Rawk tried to think of something to say. He'd had a conversation something like this a couple of days ago. "Who'll finish your damn canal?"

"I will."

"You will?" Rawk almost laughed but managed to control himself.

"It was my idea to begin with, Rawk. I'm sure I can work out the details."

"And the sewers? And... who'll light the street lamps at night? Who'll collect your rubbish? If the dwarves stop working the city will fall apart in a few days."

"Rubbish." Weaver seemed to enjoy his pun. He paused for a moment to smile. "You've been talking to too many dwarves, Rawk. They are not important at all. There are more than enough humans to do the work."

Rawk doubted there were enough people at all, even if they were all willing to do the work that the dwarves did. Even if they were capable of it. "So, you're declaring war on the south of the river?"

Weaver nodded. "They will learn to not defy me."

"Or they will learn to hate you. Because not all of them *did* defy you. Let's assume the dwarves did help Sylvia escape. How may do you think were involved? Ten? Twenty? The rest have no idea what happened."

"Are you on their side, Rawk?"

"Of course not. I'm on Katamood's side. And Katamood needs dwarves."

"I'm going to replace Thacker and all of his followers. I've been letting him get away with too much for too long."

"Doesn't he collect your taxes?"

"Yes."

"And what else does he do?"

"I'm not sure. And that's the problem. None of my people know what the dwarves do. They pay their taxes, so nobody has ever bothered to find out."

"Well..."

"I am assembling the City Guard. And I've been bringing mercenaries into the city for a few weeks. I have nearly five thousand men ready to fight for me."

"Mercenaries? Five thousand of them?"

"Yes. I knew there was trouble brewing. With these portals opening everywhere and the riots."

"You know they are unrelated, right?"

"What?"

"The south isn't rioting because of the portals. They're rioting because you knocked down a huge swathe of houses and businesses when you built the canal and didn't do anything to replace them."

"No, they aren't. Who told you that? If there aren't enough houses they can just go somewhere else. Nobody's stopping them."

Rawk grunted. He was starting to wonder if Weaver believed his own stories. He'd heard of men that had two personalities, like two separate people living in the same body, each doing things that the other knew nothing about.

"Will you help me, Rawk? If things keep going the way they are, Celeste and Grint will soon think themselves too important to work for you, you know. They have to be kept in their place."

"You may be right." Rawk nodded slowly. "What about magic though?"

"What about it?"

"Well, Sylvia has escaped. And there may be other sorcerers we don't know about."

Weaver smiled. "I've got that under control. I don't just have mercenaries."

"You've brought in sorcerers? Isn't that against the law?"

"I'm the prince; I can do whatever I like." He smiled. "So, will you help me or not?"

Rawk looked himself up and down. "Let me go back to the *Hero's Rest*. I need my mail and... some other things."

"Excellent." The prince clapped Rawk on the back. "Oh, this is just like old times, isn't it?"

"Yes," Rawk agreed. "I can hardly tell the difference." He left the office and hurried through the palace with two guards shadowing him.

—O—

Rawk stopped in the storage room and looked around. He knew there were mail shirts in there somewhere. He just couldn't remember where, exactly, and he couldn't remember if they were useable or merely decorative. He suspected it would be the latter. After a couple of minutes he found a pile of shirts. The second one was serviceable. But he couldn't think straight. He stood where he was, heavy mail shirt held up before him, and just stared.

"What's going on?" Celeste was standing in the doorway. She was looking at the shirt as well, as if trying to work out why it was so interesting.

"Who else is here?"

"Juskin and Grint."

Rawk nodded. "You have to get out of here. All of you. Is Biki working today?"

"I don't think so."

"Well, find out. You have to get to the other side of the river as quickly as possible."

Juskin came to stand by Celeste's side. His shock of hair was even worse than usual. "Why? What is happening?"

"Weaver is about to start a war."

"Against the south? Then surely we would be safer here?"

Rawk took a deep breath. "You will only be safe here until Weaver works out I'm not on his side. Then anyone who is a friend of mine will be in danger."

"You will fight against the prince?"

"I don't see that I have any choice." He looked at the book in Celeste's hand. "Get all the books and hide them in this room, then leave. All of you."

They hesitated, then went into the office and started to collect the books.

"What's happening?"

Rawk almost jumped. He turned to see Travis standing in the door behind him. He looked him up and down. "Nothing. Nothing."

"What's with the mail shirt then? It's been a while since you wore one of those."

"I know..." He cleared his throat. "Sylvia escaped from the Quod last night. Weaver is going to get her back, no matter what it takes."

Travis nodded. "If the dwarves helped her then they won't just give her up."

"It could get messy. I think we might need to close down for a couple of days. Barricade the doors and all that kind of thing."

"The trouble won't reach here. Weaver will send some of the Guard across the river and..."

"I know. Just in case though."

"Very well."

"Get all the customers out then hire some men."

"What about your Heroes?"

"They'll probably be busy."

"All right."

"I'm going to lock up down here. I don't want anyone coming in."

Travis looked a bit confused, but nodded.

"Go and start organizing things. We might not have much time."

When Travis had left, Celeste came from the office carrying a pile of books. "You don't want Travis to know?"

Rawk shrugged, uncomfortable. "He doesn't like dwarves much. And he does like Natan."

"He likes *you* though."

"Yes, but I'm not sure if that's enough." He wasn't sure of anything any more. It wasn't like the good old days at all. Back then, he knew everything there was to know. If he didn't then it wasn't worth knowing. Now? Shaking his head he pulled off his shirt then tried to find a gambeson amongst the clutter so he could don the mail. There was one somewhere, he was sure. "Get those books hidden then get out of here. Stick together, and send a message to Thacker so I know where you are."

Rawk finally got himself organized and hurried upstairs. In the kitchen, he realized he had skipped breakfast and grabbed a couple of wrinkled apples. He was about to head out into the taproom when he noticed Demon had returned. The kitten was sitting near the door, watching him silently.

"Hello again." He found some meat and held it out. And much braver than before, Demon entered to kitchen to take the food. Rawk scooped him up before he could escape and hurried back down to find Celeste.

A few minutes later, kittenless, Rawk stepped down from the porch and towards the river.

"Where are you going, Rawk?"

Rawk looked around and spotted Waydin coming in his direction. He tried to think. "Well..." He looked around, then lowered his voice. "I've got all those Heroes standing around the city waiting for trouble. I thought they could be useful, so I was going to round them up."

Waydin looked around too. "Weaver has lots of men. I'm not sure your Heroes will be needed."

"Do you think? Well, I'll just tell them they aren't needed then so I can stop wasting my money."

"I'll come with you."

"Did Weaver send you along to watch me?"

Waydin winced. "No."

"I'm just going to find a couple of them and tell them to find the rest. I'll be back up at the palace in about an hour."

"I don't know..."

"Waydin, bugger off. Just tell Weaver I lost you. Or I'll hit you on the head and leave you here."

"What makes you think you could do that, even if you wanted to?"

"Go away, Waydin." Rawk turned his back on the man and continued down the street. When he turned at the first corner, he saw the guard standing and watching. He didn't look happy.

A couple of quick turns later, Rawk slowed down. For a moment he wondered if he should really go and round up the Heroes, but decided not to risk it. Some of them may well side with humans against dwarves, regardless of who was offering the money. And Rawk wasn't sure he wanted them on his side if they were fighting for the money anyway. He turned down another alley and headed down the hill as quickly as he could.

He stopped at the offices of *Keeto Alata* and barged in past the receptionist.

"Rawk?" Yardi said when he entered the office. "Today you not even pretending to be polite?"

"No time. How much capital is locked up in Katamood."

Yardi shrugged. "Not a lot. Real estate, mainly. A few of our warehouses be full, but that's all." She put down her pen and sat back in her chair. "Weaver is calling up the mercenaries?"

"You know about them?"

"Of course. We brought a few boat loads in."

"And you didn't tell me?"

"I didn't know who had hired them at the time. I've had people investigating."

"Well..."

"If we lost everything in Katamood it would hurt, but we would recover. You not be broke just yet."

"Good. Good. Then just make sure everyone is safe, I suppose."

"I've got them moving to the other side of the river. I was assuming you be fighting against Weaver?"

"Yes. Against. It sounds as if you've got it under control then."

Yardi shrugged. "South of the river won't necessarily be safe, but there are evacuation plans if required."

She wrote a note and called in her receptionist. "Give this to Marcus." The lad was gone a second later. "You should go, Rawk. You don't want to get caught here."

"Of course. You should leave too."

"I have a few more things to do. I assure you, I not intend to die for your money."

"Good. Stay safe, Yardi."

He gave her a kiss on the cheek and went, hurrying back out the front and down the stairs. He was breathing a little easier. If Yardi said she had everything under control then he believed her and it gave him a lot less to worry about. That just left a lot of things he needed to worry about.

The city was holding its breath.

Everyone hurried about their business, barely looking aside, or stood and watched everyone else suspiciously. Rawk placed himself firmly in the former group, but knew that he was getting more attention than anyone else. Once he was across the river, it wouldn't matter.

"Rawk."

It took a moment for Rawk to recognize his name and a moment more to stop. He looked around and saw Clinker and a dwarf work gang looking at a wall.

"Hello, Clinker. What are you doing here?"

He pointed at the wall. "Working."

Words of Wisdom were scrawled across the timber and plaster. "Tomorrow is too late. The Prince must go." Rawk grunted. "That seems a lot less obscure than usual."

One of the dwarves nodded. It was Kristun, carrying on as if nothing had happened the previous night. "Doesn't leave a lot to the imagination, does it?"

"Leave it there," Rawk said.

"What? If we do that..." Kristun was watching Rawk carefully.

"*Today* is too late. Leave it. Everyone get over the river as quickly as possible. If you see any other dwarves or elves or fermi or on the way— or anyone else— take them with you."

The dwarves looked at each other.

Rawk sighed. "I've been talking to Weaver this morning. He's had enough and he has the mercenaries to prove it."

"Mercenaries?"

"They're everywhere."

Kristun looked at his companions, and Rawk left them to figure out what they were going to do. When he looked back, Clinker was hurrying along a few steps behind.

"Does Prince Weaver really have mercenaries?"

"Yes, he does, lad. It's going to get ugly very soon."

"Does Thacker know?"

If Yardi knew, surely Thacker did as well. "I hope so. Now you have to get across the river."

"I'll come with you."

"No, I'm making a detour first. You go. And no arguing this time; just do as I ask."

He pushed the boy gently down the hill and turned aside, heading towards Biki's place. The tension in the city seemed to grow with every breath. It was stifling, oppressive, hanging over everything like a pall. At Biki's place, he hurried inside and up the stairs.

Rawk knocked loudly but it seemed to take forever before he got a reply. The door opened a crack and Biki looked out nervously. She breathed a sigh of relief when she saw who it was.

Celeste, Grint and Juskin were waiting inside, looking like they wanted to be somewhere else.

"How do you get here so quickly?"

"You told us to hurry," Grint said.

"I know but... Well, why are you still here?"

"We got here about a minute ago."

"Very well. All right. Come on then, let's get out of here."

Biki nodded. "I was just trying to get Suki organized." She was putting her daughter's shoes on as she spoke. The little girl was nursing Demon, running her fingers through his black fur. He was enjoying it enough to lie still and quiet.

"Is that it?"

Biki looked around the room. "I'll just be a second."

"Ummm, Rawk?" Grint said from his place by the window. He motioned Rawk over and twitched aside the flowery curtain so Rawk could see. "Are they with you?"

Rawk swore. A troop of the City Guard was out in the street, weapons drawn, listening to their captain. It wasn't immediately obvious what was being said, but Rawk doubted it had anything to do with lunch.

"No time, Biki. We have to go now." Rawk grabbed Celeste's hand and pulled her to her feet.

"I can't run, Rawk," Juskin said.

"You have to."

"No, you don't understand. I really can't. I have a bad hip and... Well, I'm just too old."

"Well."

"I am human. And they won't be expecting me."

Rawk tried to think. It didn't seem to be working. "We can't just leave you. Weaver will want to talk to you eventually."

"If I can just get through the next few minutes I should be fine." He took a deep breath. "I am just going to walk out the door and across to the other side of the river. The guards will not know me."

They didn't have time to argue. "Very well. But please be careful." He wished there was someone else they could send the same way, but even regular dwarves and fermi would be harassed at the moment. Ones know to consort with him would be arrested on sight. Then he thought of someone who *could* go the easy way. He took Demon from Suki's hands and passed him over to Juskin. "Look after this guy would you?"

"Of course." Juskin took another deep breath, opened the door and stepped out into the hall. A moment later he was gone and Rawk closed the door.

"Can we go now?" Grint grabbed Suki from where she sat quietly on the bed and swept her up into his arms.

"Yes." Drawing *Kaj*, Rawk opened the door again and checked the hallway. Nobody, so he went out and headed towards the stairs. On the landing he stopped to listen. "Path, damn it." He motioned the others upwards, then followed behind Celeste, last in line. He ducked out of sight on the next floor just as the first of the Guard pounded up the stairs. Up another floor, until there were no more stairs.

"Where to now?" Grint asked. He swapped the little girl to his other arm.

There was no way out. Rawk knocked on the door to the rear of the building and, when there was no answer, motioned for Grint to work on the lock.

The dwarf grunted. "I'm not a locksmith. Or a thief."

"I could possibly break the door, but it would be very noisy."

Grint put Suki down and set to work. A couple of minutes later, the lock was broken and the door was open.

"Close enough," Rawk said. He herded everyone through and closed the door behind him. It wouldn't latch properly, so he jammed it shut with a chair.

"And now?" Grint asked.

Rawk motioned to the window at the rear of the apartment's single room. Outside, a dirty, grey–tiled roof led down to the roof of the neighboring building. He sheathed his sword and quickly climbed out.

Crouching on the tiles, he looked around. Buildings crowded close. It seemed that the roofs were sewn together like a patchwork quilt. They were hardly distinguishable from the never–cleaned plaster walls. All he could see was a long grey and brown landscape of mountains and valleys. There was no clear way out. Rawk turned about and lifted Suki out through the window. He sat down, held her close and slid down the roof. He hit the gutter at the bottom of the valley and grunted when he hurt his knee, but the little girl was suddenly enjoying herself.

"That was fun, was it?"

She nodded and gave a small smile.

"Well, I'll see what else I can organize for you."

But next he carried her up the opposite roof and stopped at the peak and examined the options. There weren't all that many. The next slope lead down to the nothing of an alley and the gap across to the next building was too far to cross. Grint stopped by his side, grabbing his arm as he tried to get his balance. He examined the possibilities as well. "This is going to be fun."

"Suki and I were just talking about that, weren't we?"

The little girl didn't say anything.

Celeste and Biki clambered up but there wasn't time to rest. Rawk sent them shuffling along the ridge towards where it butted up against the blank plaster wall of another building. There was no window or any other obvious way to get inside, but it was the only route that didn't involve leaping across alleys or falling onto cobbles. At the wall, Rawk put Suki down with her back against the plaster, and looked around. He went carefully down the slick tiles to the gap. Grint stayed at the top and tapped the wall experimentally.

"Down here," Rawk called softly, beckoning them down with him. The wall by his side continued when the roof he was on ended, so the alley ended at a dead end. There was a balcony on the end wall and its rail just a couple of feet lower than his position.

"Just one level," Rawk muttered, shaking his head.

"That isn't going to be easy," Grint said a moment later, letting go of Suki's hand and putting her safely against the wall again.

"Have you got a better plan?"

He grunted. "I don't even have a worse plan."

"That's what I thought."

"And you and I might be able to do it, but I don't know about anyone else."

Rawk shrugged. "There's a little ledge just down there…"

The dwarf leaned out carefully to look. "Yes, there is." He looked from the roof to the ledge to the balcony, as if calculating. "It still won't be easy."

Rawk nodded. "I'll climb down and then…" Yes, and then? He was about a foot taller than anyone else and probably a lot more used to jumping and climbing and…

Celeste sat down on the edge of the roof, dangling her legs out into nothing, then reached out, found a handhold and slowly lowered herself down to the ledge. Rawk wanted to reach out to grab her, to pull her back, but she stretched her leg across to the rail, found another spot for her hand and pulled herself after her foot. A moment later, she stepped down onto the balcony and brushed off her hands.

Rawk grunted as she waved to the others. "It's easy," she said, though the look on her face suggested otherwise. "You come across, Grint, then Rawk can pass Suki over."

Grint looked at Rawk and did as he was told. He was shorter than his sister but managed to jump over to the balcony with minimal effort. The next bit was going to be the problem. But Rawk didn't hesitate. He didn't have time. And if he paused to think anyway...

He got the little girl onto his back, holding on tight, then wondered if it would be better if she held on to the front. He didn't know. He couldn't think. But every delay was bringing Weaver's men closer and probably making Suki more scared. So he carefully lowered himself onto the ledge. There was barely room for his feet.

He was being choked and could barely breathe, but he managed to mutter some encouraging words as he worked out what he was going to do next.

"Keep your eyes closed, darling," he said. He looked down and wished he could keep his closed as well. He stretched across towards the railing. He could feel his foot beginning to shake and willed it to stillness. Suki's weight was pulling back out into the nothingness. She clung to him tightly, breathing into his ear. Rawk froze for a moment and he did close his eyes. The little girl wasn't crying. She trusted him. He shifted his hands, and managed to lean sideways enough for Grint to complete the transfer. The dwarf hugged Suki for a moment before putting her down.

Rawk took a deep breath and was over. He smiled at Suki and clenched his fist around his shaking fingers Biki started across almost straight away. When she made it to the ledge, she looked down and it seemed she might never move again.

"Look there."

Rawk looked towards the mouth of the alley and swore. Three of the City Guard were staring up at them.

"Is that Rawk?"

Rawk swore again and turned his attention back to Biki as the men started to run down the alley. He called her across, but she couldn't move. "Come on, Biki." But the dwife shook her head and clung to the wall. Down below, the soldiers were starting to climb. A couple more paused at the entrance to the alley, then headed off to find another way into the building.

"I can't."

"You have to do it. Suki is waiting."

That got her attention. Biki looked at the little girl, who was crying now, sitting on the rough boards by Grint's feet. "Help me," she said.

Rawk reached out and took her hand. "Jump and I'll pull you over."

She did, but it wasn't much of a jump. Rawk grabbed her other hand and pulled her towards the balcony. She landed half over the rail, winded and hurt. Rawk was flat on his back, but the other's rushed to help, dragging her over onto the balcony. When Suki went to her it wasn't immediately obvious who was comforting whom.

"We don't have time for this," Grint said. He pulled Biki to her feet and picked up the girl. "They could be here any second."

Rawk stood up and shouldered open the door into the apartment. Inside was quite a bit larger than Biki's apartment, but it was shabby and unloved. There must have been a second room with the bed. Rawk went to a door and reefed it open. Yes, the bedroom. He swore and went to the other door. He looked up and down the hall, trying to decide which way to go but there was nothing to give him a clue. "This way."

They'd barely gone anywhere at all when two men appeared out of a doorway. "There they are."

Rawk drew his sword, even as he turned to urge everyone in the opposite direction. There were more men at the other end of the hall. The first ones were closer, so Rawk turned back and charged. He killed one man in the initial rush, slicing him across the leg and running him through. But *Kaj* got stuck in a rib and he couldn't pull the weapon clear fast enough.

He ducked a swing, blocked another with his arm against his opponent's arm. The wound from the riot screamed at him. No time. He punched once and kicked, blocking out the crunch of bone and the scream of pain. He pulled *Kaj* free with a jerk and pushed past his companions before the second set of guards could close the gap. The men slowed but kept coming.

"Keep everyone moving, Grint," he said. "Not too fast though. We don't want to run into trouble before we know it's there."

The dwarf grunted.

Rawk's knee was aching. His arm was worse; there was blood soaking through the bandage.

Walking backwards after his companions, Rawk carefully stepped over the two dead guards. He smiled at the remaining men. "Are you two ready to die today?"

They slowed slightly and looked at the dead men. One of them shifted his grip on his sword.

"Is it worth it? Just for Weaver?"

The men looked at each other.

"He won't even know. Say you didn't see us."

He kept backing away until he was at the top of the stairs. He listened as his friends descended to the floor below.

He heard Grint say, "More trouble, Rawk." He doubted the guards could hear.

"Are you coming or not?" Rawk asked them.

They stopped and Rawk turned and ran. He nearly tripped on the stairs. He crashed into the wall at the landing and barely stayed upright. On the floor below, Celeste was standing at the top of the next flight of stairs, listening.

"There are more guards," she said softly.

"Do you know how many?" Rawk put a hand on her shoulder for a moment. She was shaking, sweating.

"I don't know for sure." She shrugged. Rawk felt the slight rise and fall of her shoulder. "A few, though."

"Right."

"Grint is looking..."

And just then her brother came back out through a door. "If we go through that last apartment we can get down to ground level easy enough." He glanced at Biki and her daughter.

Rawk squeezed Celeste's shoulder. He smiled at her. "Let's go then." He wanted to touch her bruised cheek and had to quickly look away.

"There's someone there," Celeste said.

A guard came around the corner and up the stairs. Rawk pulled Celeste out of the way and was distracted enough to almost lose a leg. He stepped clear at the last moment, more through luck than anything else, and countered quickly, trying to keep the guard on the stairs. He could feel Celeste watching him, though he was sure everyone else had disappeared after Grint.

"Go, Celeste. We don't have time."

"No. I..."

But he heard her turn and leave as he batted aside an attack that would have sliced through his ankle and pushed forward some more. His opponent couldn't do much at all, but Rawk couldn't reach properly either. After a couple of more ineffectual exchanges, Rawk snatched a torch down from the wall and threw it. The solid piece of timber and iron got past the man's defenses and struck him a solid blow on the face. He gave a cry of pain and tumbled down the stairs.

Rawk grunted in surprise and raced into the apartment behind his companions, slamming the door behind him. He dropped the old style timber latch down to lock it, though he wasn't sure it would do much good against someone who was really determined. He didn't intend to hang around to find out. Sheathing *Kaj*, he made his way to the room's only window and watched as Celeste climbed carefully down the wall, holding a horizontal piece of the exposed frame as she walked down a diagonal. He wanted to shout some encouragement, but was loath to distract her at all. She looked so serious, concentrating fiercely as if to keep her mind away from the fall. Rawk decided he was worrying enough for the both of them. He gripped the edge of the windowsill as if his hands were the ones keeping her safe.

When she was almost down and no pursuit had materialized, Rawk climbed out the window as well and followed her down. Once on the ground he wrapped his arm around her. "Well done. Where are the others?" He tried to let go, but she clung to him for a second. He could feel her shaking.

Eventually, Celeste stepped back and wiped tears from her face. She motioned down the alley. Biki, Grint and Suki were huddling behind a pile of wooden crates not far away.

"Come on then." Rawk checked the window but there was still nobody there. He pushed Grint aside when he started to pick up Suki and swung the little girl around onto his back. "You have to hold on," he said. She laughed and wrapped her arms around his neck.

"What if you need your sword?" Grint asked.

"Let's just hope I don't."

They moved quickly down the alley, pausing at the end before hurrying out onto the main street, trying to look as if they weren't a group of fugitives. Rawk tried to get his bearings. "Where are we?"

"I know," Biki said. "But where are we going?"

"We're going over the river, as quickly as possible."

"This way, then."

Rawk followed, trying to keep an eye on their surroundings as he talked to Suki and avoided running into people and kept up with Biki and...

It was a few streets before he worked out where he was. And it was only a few minutes after that when they caught a glimpse of the river. Rawk started to think they might make it. Even when he saw a pair of guards loitering on a corner he just kept moving, not bothering to say anything to the others. The city went right down to the river at Coover Bridge with buildings dabbling their toes in the water. The fact that they didn't have any open space to cross might have been good, if they'd been able to get a good look at who might be waiting for them. As it was, they stood in the mouth of an alley for a couple of minutes, trying to look for trouble. That was what Rawk was doing, anyway. He didn't know what they others were doing.

The nearby buildings were grimy and as rickety as the bridge itself and Rawk thought that the people living to the south of the river might get a bit of sympathy from those in this area, but he wasn't willing to bet his life on it.

"We can't stand here all day," he said eventually.

Grint grunted, as if he was willing to give it a go. He sucked on his teeth for a moment then called Suki over. "You walk with me, darling. You're being very brave." Biki took her other hand.

Rawk took a deep breath. "Let's go." They made their way quickly towards the bridge.

Someone called out to Rawk and he almost stopped. The person called again and he realized it was just a woman, probably wanting to get him into bed. The timing wasn't great. He supposed the timing was never really great, but he hadn't let that stop him in the past. He kept going, not even looking back.

As they approached the bridge, Rawk saw two men trying to keep an eye on things from a low porch in front of a haberdashery store. Neither was in uniform, but Rawk knew John Conter and doubted he'd ever bought a nice piece of clothing in his life.

"Trouble," Rawk muttered dropping back a couple of steps. "Just keep walking. Don't stop, no matter what. And try not to run; Weaver may have them looking out for you, but they may be distracted by me." If they stopped they wouldn't get moving again.

Rawk and his companions joined the crowds and moved between the last of the buildings that held hands with the bridge posts at the edge of the river. Ten more yards and they would be onto the warped, ageing planks but the guards finally spotted them. They called out, and moved to intercept.

"Keep going," Rawk said. He stopped and took a couple of steps back, trying to gage if the guards were concentrating on him or the entire group. The others kept going. Only Celeste even looked back. Rawk willed her on, feet twitching as if his were the feet that were going to get her over the bridge. He drew *Kaj* and turned back, advancing on the men.

He smiled. The men hesitated. They looked at each other, and advanced some more.

"You two really think you are going to be enough?" He tested his footing, but the cobbles were about a hundred years old and were as smooth as the top of a table.

They hesitated some more, then Conter called out and there was an answering call from the other side of the river. "Maybe not," he said. He had a smile of his own.

Rawk risked a glance over his shoulder and saw a group of five City Guard topping the crest of the bridge like a roll of thunder on the ancient planks. They ran straight past Celeste and the rest of the group, so it wasn't all bad.

"Come on then."

Rawk charged at the two men. He knew Conter would worry him about as much as a prickle in his sock, so he attacked the other man first. A low attack, dance around the reply, lunged into a gap. Then he spun away as blood started to flow from a not—really—serious cut across his opponent's chest and swung wildly at Conter. He was in the clear, so he turned and ran along the street, parallel to the river, shouting and waving his sword to clear a path. The soldiers followed, pounding along behind.

Between the buildings on his left he could see momentary flashes of mast and boats and beyond them the buildings on the far side of the river. They seemed to be miles away. After a hundred yards of dodging crowds, leaving a trail of outrage, he realized how out of shape he was. Once upon a time, not that long ago, he'd exercised every day, working out in the gymna and just *doing things*. Now...

But thankfully, the City Guard were no better. Most of the time they stood in doorways or sat in the barracks. Katamood was normally such a peaceful place that they didn't even take their sword—work all that seriously. They were probably going to get a rude surprise in the next few days.

After two hundred yards, Rawk was really struggling. He looked back over his shoulder and discovered that there were only two men still following. And they were gaining on him. He turned away from the river, taking a couple of random turns, tying to confuse anyone who was still doggedly bringing up the rear, if not the closer two. In a dim alley, amidst a snowdrift of trash, he turned to fight. While he waited for the men to reach him, he leaned on *Kaj* and drew in great, heaving breaths.

He knew both of them. Petu and Darvid. Darvid was a sneaky, conniving individual who would probably hang back and see how things went. Petu, on the other hand, was an arrogant bastard who had every reason to be arrogant.

"Worn out, old man?" Petu asked as he approached. He took off his jacket and untied the lace on the collar of his shirt. He was young and lean and if Rawk had known who it was, he probably would have kept running and risked the heart attack.

"I'll be fine in a moment. Thank's for your concern."

Petu sneered as he drew his sword.

Rawk stood up straight and twirled his own blade around, trying some fancy tricks that didn't really prove anything at all but normally impressed the crowds. There was no crowd and Petu wasn't impressed. Darvid didn't really seem to be paying attention.

"Come on then," Petu said. "Let's get this done."

Raising his sword, Rawk crouched and winced as his knee gave a twinge of pain. It hadn't liked all the running and was probably going to like this even less. "Yes, let's. I have places to go."

"Weaver isn't going to let—"

There was no finesse to Rawk's attack. He just swung hard and fast and pushed Petu back, though both of them knew he wasn't really in any danger. But that wasn't really the point. All the action had brought Rawk close to Darvid who, apparently, still wasn't keen to get involved. But he didn't seem to think he was in any danger and stayed where he was.

Petu took one more step back and Rawk spun aside, slashing Darvid across the throat. He didn't pause to watch the man fall to the ground, turning his attention back to Petu. The man seemed shocked. He was standing, mouth open, looking at his companion. His mouth flapped a few times, but nothing came out.

"Welcome to the grown–ups' game, Petu. Have you ever actually fought anyone outside the training arena? It's a bit different out here, isn't it?"

He seemed to gather himself. "It's all the same in the end," he said. "It's just sword against sword." But he glanced at Darvid again before he attacked.

Rawk danced *Kaj* in the shadows of the alley, clattering it against the other blade. He moved smoothly through the rubbish, ignoring the pain in his knee. He smiled. He tried to look calm. He thought he was succeeding, but he didn't know how much longer he would last. He was always half a moment behind. He was always racing to catch up to the next attack. He wasn't sure if Petu had noticed, or if the lad was still thinking about Darvid.

It was obvious when Petu finally started to get his head into the fight. Rawk was pushed back constantly— there was no longer any back and forth— and he spent so much time defending that he hardly had the chance to make a counter attack of his own. He was sweating. *Kaj* suddenly seemed to weigh twice as much as it did a minute ago.

When his knee gave out, Rawk was almost relieved. Almost. He glanced around, hoping for a miracle, and almost missed the woman stepping out of a darkened doorway with a cudgel in hand. Petu didn't see until the last moment either, and by then it was too late because the woman knew what she was doing. She hit the guard a solid blow across the chin and then a backhander across the back of the neck. He fell like a sack of wet wheat.

Breathing a sigh of relief, Rawk used *Kaj* to lever himself to his feet. "Thank you," he said.

The woman nodded and spat onto the cobbles. She was older than she looked. "Don't like them guards, Rawk. Trouble makers, the lot of them."

Rawk almost said, "*Not all of them are like that,*" but restrained himself. The good men didn't need his defense against this old woman and she didn't want to hear it anyway. "And they're worse every day," he said instead.

She nodded.

"What's the quickest way to a bridge?"

The woman spat again. "Don't be stupid. No way they going to let *you* across a bridge now."

"So..."

"So take a boat. Them guards ain't got the brains to think of that."

"What about Weaver?"

She laughed. "He ain't even got the brains to work out them dwarves is playing him like a fiddle."

"Pardon."

"He thinks he got all these great ideas but he's just doing what they tell him to do."

"You know about that?"

"Of course. Everyone knows if you ain't got two coppers to rub together you go to the dwarves for help. And once you friends with 'em they tell you everything."

"They don't tell everyone. They aren't stupid."

"That's what I was just saying." The woman sniffed. "Anyway, like I was saying, go hire yourself a boat. You'll be across the river in no time."

"Thank you. I think I will. So, what's the quickest way to a boat?" Rawk listened to her directions, such as they were. "Thank you. Stay safe; it's going to get bloody very soon." And he slipped the woman ten ithel as limped away.

This time, there was a street running right along the edge of the river. It wasn't the best location in terms of being discovered, because there were trendy cafes looking across the street and the river, but there were plenty of little boats ferrying supplies from across the other side. Boutique ciders and ales, produce, pastries from the huge dwarf bakeries that churned out such things all day long.

But there were none of the City Guard in evidence and he could spend all day wondering if someone else might give him away, so Rawk stood up straight, tidied his shirt, and marched across the street like had nothing to fear. Except he had his hand on the hilt of his sword. And he kept looking around.

At the edge of the river he looked both ways. The tide was out and there was a two-yard drop down to the water. There were a dozen small boats tied up between two flanking ships, but only three of them had any occupants. Rawk would borrow a boat if required but he'd always considered things like rowing to be below him, so it could turn into a long, slow journey. So he headed towards the closest. An old woman was sitting at the oars.

"How much to take me across the river?"

She looked up at him. "What's wrong with the bridge?" She pointed. There was a bridge just fifty yards away. Rawk couldn't see any guards there, but he was sure there would be.

Rawk shrugged. "I just feel like a boat trip today."

The woman shook her head. "I ain't an idiot, Rawk. On your way. Go visit your dwarf friends."

Rawk muttered but didn't say anything to her. A moment later, she called out for the Guard, and he wished he had. He looked back towards the bridge and saw a commotion. "Damn you, woman."

He hurried to the next boat. "Twenty ithel if you take me across the river." The normal rate would be about five. Maybe less. The owner of the boat was a young man with long hair and a missing ear.

He looked towards the bridge as well and Rawk moved on before the 'No' got out of his mouth. He should have gone to the last boat in the first place. The dwarf was beckoning him forward and untying the rope that held his small skiff to the stone wall. Rawk moved quickly, but when he looked up, he saw half a dozen guards coming from the other direction. They would beat him there.

Rawk swore and drew his sword. But there were six of them and that was too many, no matter who they were. He slammed *Kaj* back into the sheath and went over the side of the wall right where he was, quickly scaling down a ladder into a sorry looking boat at the bottom. For a moment the dwarf looked at him as if he was crazy, but then heard the men approaching. He pushed his boat out into the river while Rawk worked at the knot holding his own craft. His fingers fumbled with the rope and after an agonizing moment he gave up and drew his dagger. He sawed through the rope and pushed out as well, just as the first of the city guard stuck his head out to see what was going on.

Rawk took up the oars and tried to get himself organized. He almost succeeded in capsizing the boat but survived with just some wet feet as water sloshed over the side. Guards were climbing down to other boats, shouting to each other, sending out waves as the little craft rocked and danced. The movement didn't help Rawk as he fumbled about with the oars and didn't really do much at all. A boat bumped along side of his and Rawk spun about, brandishing his oar, sending out a long arc of glistening water droplets. The dwarf smiled when Rawk almost brained him.

"I can go somewhere else if you like."

"Sorry."

The dwarf had a hold of his boat and was keeping it steady. "You may want to come over here. I can't row both of them."

"I can't even row *one* of them." Rawk threw down his oars with relief, then undertook the nasty task of getting out of his boat and into the other. He imagined it looked comical to those watching, but he was very aware of his pursuers and what they were up to. One was working at the knot in a rope. He had forgotten his sword for the moment and was working with clumsy fingers as Rawk had done.

In the end, Rawk gave up on his dignity and simply rolled over the wale and into the other boat. He was a sorry mess, covered in squashed mangoes and peaches, as the dwarf started to row. When he got his head above the painted timber he noticed they were heading upstream. "Wouldn't it be quicker to go that way?" He pointed directly across the river then sucked some mango from under his fingernail.

"Yes." The dwarf worked at the oars like an expert and they were opening up the distance to their pursuers. It looked like most of them hadn't handled an oar any more often than Rawk. "But over there isn't really designed to handle boats like this. It would be like scaling a sheer cliff."

He seemed very calm. Rawk looked back and saw that most of the guards were still floundering. Only one boat was under control and moving smoothly forward but it was still slow and falling further behind by the moment. A minute later and it was lost from sight as the dwarf rowed the boat around the prow of a merchant ship that was tied up in the middle of the river.

Rawk grunted. "That was easy." He tested his sore arm, clenching and unclenching his fingers.

"It may not be over yet."

Rawk tried to see where they were going but the timber cliff of another ship blocked the view. "Right. What's your name?"

"Gabe."

"Well, Gabe, either way, thank you very much."

"Nobody was buying my fruit anyway."

"I'll buy it. How much for the lot?"

Gabe examined the sacks and baskets. "A hundred ithel."

Rawk raised his eyebrows. "That seems expensive."

"It is. Now that I think about it, that's probably why nobody was buying anything." The dwarf gave a bark of laughter.

"Well, I'm more than happy to pay, but I don't have the money on me."

"Of course. I know where to find you."

The boat following them came around the ship and into view. "Are you sure?" Rawk asked.

"You'll be in The Quod, won't you?"

"Probably in the cell next to yours."

"Exactly."

"Well, I think it would be better for all of us if that didn't happen though."

"I was thinking the same thing myself."

The skiff turned again, ducking in under Faldamon Bridge, slipping between old, half rotten pylons. Out the other side the dwarf grabbed a metal spike that had been driven into the stone wall that lined the side of the river. Before he'd tied off, a half dozen other boats, full of all sorts of cargo, were crowding around. In a moment, the boat was hidden in plain sight and the dwarf was scrambling up more of the spikes to the flat ground above. Rawk followed, not quite as quick. He had a look back and saw an old man in Gabe's boat, shifting an umbrella over to protect himself from the sun as he made himself comfortable.

Rawk smiled. "Thank you, Gabe. I'll get you your money as quickly as possible."

He shook the dwarf's hand and headed up the hill. After a few steps he couldn't even see the river.

There were still troops of the City Guard marching around the southern side of the river. They no longer marched as if they owned the place, but they were there. Before he'd gone a hundred yards, Rawk had to turn aside and after a couple of minutes, discovered he was a bit lost. He stood on a clean narrow street that he was didn't want to call an alley, as he tried to get his bearings. It was a moment before he realized that all he had to do was find the hill and climb. He would find himself eventually. But before he had the chance, somebody else did. Rawk heard him coming before he saw him.

"Hello, Rawk."

"Hello, Clinker. What are you doing?"

"Looking for you."

"Really?"

"Yes. I saw Grint and the others at the bridge and they said you were trying to follow." He shifted his satchel from one shoulder to the other. "I saw you a while later but you lost me before I could catch up."

"I was trying to lose the Guards."

"I guessed that. Are you going to see Thacker? Sylvia is with him."

"She made it?" Rawk was more relieved than he wanted to admit.

"Of course."

"Come on then. Let's go." He waited for Clinker to lead the way.

$$-O-$$

The two dwarf guards let Rawk straight through into Thacker's office. Clinker came too.

Everyone was there. Frew and Fabi were leaning against the wall, looking as if they weren't sure they wanted to be there. Whether it was the occasion or the company was hard to tell. Sylvia, Biki and Celeste were sitting. After a moment looking at all the serious faces, Clinker went to join Grint and Suki playing in the corner.

"Glad you could make it, Rawk," Thacker said.

"I'm glad *everyone* could make it." He had a nod for Sylvia and a smile for Celeste.

"Celeste said you had some trouble."

"Other than a dwarf charging me a hundred ithel to row me across the river..."

"Who was it? I'll have a word."

Rawk waved the offer away. "It was Gabe someone. But I squashed his mangoes and I offered anyway."

"Very well." He straightened some papers on his desk. "So, what happens now?"

"I don't know."

"That doesn't help. I assume Weaver will want to get Sylvia back at any cost."

"It will be a bit embarrassing for him if he doesn't. He embarrasses himself every day but he generally doesn't even realize. Today, he *will* realize."

Thacker nodded. "And you?"

Rawk rubbed his face. "I don't know. He can't link me directly to the Quod, but the fact that I came over here..."

"Means it won't matter."

"I'm embarrassing him too, just by consorting with the likes of you."

Thacker smiled. "I can understand that."

Sylvia shifted on her seat. "But how will he react?"

Frew laughed and Rawk turned to look at him. The little Hero shrugged. "Weaver has never been known for his subtlety."

Rawk nodded. "Apparently he has been bringing mercenaries into Katamood. He's ready for a war."

"A war?" Sylvia said.

"So it is today then?" Thacker leaned forward in his chair.

"It is according to Words of Wisdom, who ever that is."

"I knew it was coming."

"So what are you going to do?"

"Block the bridges, first of all. Rake?"

"Yeah, Thacker."

"Get Machan to call up the militia. I need fifty men with machinery on each bridge by nightfall."

"All right."

"We need to keep letting locals back over this way for a while, but don't let them go the other way."

"Can northerners go back north?"

"Civilians can, yes."

Rake nodded and hurried out.

"Will fifty men be enough?"

"Fifty men and machines; yes. For now, anyway." Thacker looked around the room, then called to the guards outside the door. "Who's out there?"

The two dwarves poked their heads around the corner to look.

"Right. Jurdy, go find Hatch. Tell him Machan is calling up the militia and we need some of them to sweep through the city, starting at the top, to find any of Weaver's men— guards or mercenaries. Disarm them if possible and lock them up. Otherwise, kill them."

"So it's really happening," Rawk said after Jurdy had left. It felt strange. He'd fought battles regularly enough during his life, but he wasn't normally in on the planning meetings. He was just a Hero. His usual method was to stand at the front, wave his sword and look heroic. He was good at that. Well, he used to be. He wasn't so sure any more. "I want to help. Where are the militia mustering?"

"Several places. Just out the front, first of all, but that lot probably won't see any action for a while."

"Where else then."

Thacker's brow furrowed. "Do you know Lamond Square? That will be the main gathering point. And we will be moving our headquarters to the *Burning Tree*, which is down there."

Rawk shrugged. "I don't know neither the inn or the square by name, apparently."

"I can take him." Clinker stopped playing and rose quickly to his feet.

"It won't be safe out there soon, Clinker."

"But it is now."

Rawk knew he could spend ten minutes arguing, then the boy would just follow him anyway. "Very well then." He turned to Frew and Fabi. "Thank you for your help rescuing Sylvia. You are now released from your employment."

"You don't want us fighting with you?" Fabi asked, looking offended.

"Of course I do, Fabi. But I want you to fight with me for the right reason. Let's not be mercenaries, just this once."

Fabi smiled. "I'm with you. I'm independently wealthy, anyway; I just do this for fun."

"Don't we all?" said Rawk. He resisted a sigh. He had enough money that he could have retired ten years ago and lived like a king for the rest of his life— like a king of a *small* country, admittedly—while good men like Fabi were just trying to get by.

"Frew?"

"I don't have anything else to do."

"The dwarves make great beer."

He seemed to give it some thought. "We can save that for later."

Rawk clasped both their hands. "Thank you. It seems that Clinker is taking me to Lamond Square. Will you come?"

"I don't think I've ever fought on the side of the militia," Frew laughed. "They usually can't afford us."

Fabi laughed too. "We can set up a payment plan, if they like."

Rawk grunted. "I thought we weren't going to be mercenaries."

"Oh, right. Sorry."

A few minutes later, Rawk limped down the stairs from the council building and into the middle of a standoff. It took a moment to realize. There was hardly anyone on the street, so he should have seen it straight away, but he still needed sleep. And he had a lot on his mind.

To his right a group of about a dozen people stood, hands on the hilts of their swords. Rawk knew a few of them. The ones he knew were all Heroes. Some of them were men and women he'd been paying to stand on street corners waiting for exots. Perhaps the rest of them were as well. He turned to look at Frew for confirmation but it didn't matter. He wouldn't be paying them any more. He started moving towards them but then wondered what they were all staring at. He looked back over his shoulder and saw another group of men and women. They didn't look like much... Except... at least four of them were sorcerers who he'd had run–ins with over the years.

The Heroes drew their weapons and started moving forward. The sorcerers became still, concentrating.

Rawk tried to get his brain working. He imagined it rattling and shaking like one of the dwarvish steam engines, an old broken one, until it finally started to move. "Hey there, Londa," he said, moving quickly out into the middle of the street.

The young Hero seemed to notice him for the first time. He blinked. "Hello, Rawk." He was barely into his twenties but his hair was already going grey. The lad nodded to Frew and Fabi as well.

"What are you doing here?"

Londa narrowed his eyes. "We've come to fight."

Rawk nodded. "To fight who?"

"I assume we're fighting, Weaver. You're here, after all."

"So, you aren't actually here to fight sorcerers?"

Londa looked at the sorcerers. "Well..."

"You know that this whole thing with Weaver started because I released a sorcerer from prison?"

"No."

"Well, it would have happened anyway, but I got it moving a bit earlier than expected. I snuck into the Quod, with some help, and got Silver Lark out before Weaver did anything permanent."

"You helped Silver Lark? But she is your sworn enemy."

"Sworn enemy? Well, it was never anything as official as that— there wasn't a ceremony or anything— we just battled each other a few times. But that was a long time ago. She's been helping me with a few things recently, so I thought I should return the favor."

"But *they* haven't been helping you, have they?" Londa motioned to the sorcerers with his sword.

Rawk turned to look. The sorcerers were still there, but seemed to have relaxed slightly. "No, they haven't, but they haven't attacked me either. As far as I know they haven't attacked anyone. Have you ever battled a sorcerer?"

"Of course."

"Really? I would've thought you were too young."

"Well..."

"Cox," Rawk said to one of the older men. He was whip thin and almost seven feet tall. "How long since you fought a sorcerer?"

"Five years. Maybe. It was over in Mapet."

Rawk recognized someone else. "And Graft? How long since you came against a sorcerer?"

The big man shrugged like a mountain range during an earthquake. "Longer than that I reckon."

Rawk turned to the sorcerers. "Jako, it's been a while." Rawk was surprised the old man was still alive. He walked with a cane and squinted as he tried to focus his eyes. It was doubtful he'd travelled very far to get here.

"Twenty years, Rawk."

"And you've been in Katamood the entire time?"

"Not the entire time." He smiled. "I did visit my sister a few times. But mostly." The old man hobbled forward so he could get a better look. "You're looking old," he said when he was only a yard from Rawk.

Rawk laughed. "So those bad eyes of yours stop you from seeing mirrors?"

Jako laughed too, a rumble that set off a fit of wheezing.

"Are you all right?"

The sorcerer waved the concern away and took out a handkerchief to wipe his eyes.

"So, what are you doing here?" Rawk asked him.

"We've come to help."

"You came to help fight Weaver?"

"Of course."

"You don't want to fight Londa?"

Jako squinted some more. "Which one is he? This boy?"

Rawk laughed, but wasn't sure if that was the way to go about avoiding a fight. "Yes, that's him. He's only young, but he's done some good things."

The old sorcerer had turned his attention to someone else. "Now there's a face I know. Keegen."

The Hero nodded. "Hello, Jako. How's your leg?"

Jako waved his walking stick in answer to the question. "How's your stomach?"

Keegen glowered. "I still can't eat spicy food." But he gave a bark of laughter and shook his head. "I suppose it could've been worse."

Jako tapped his bad leg. "Yes, it could."

Rawk looked from the sorcerers to the Heroes and back again. "It appears that all animosities are in the past," he said. "The days when Heroes and sorcerers battled are long gone. And now, today, we have a common enemy."

The Heroes grumbled. The sorcerers didn't move; perhaps they were holding onto spells, waiting. They were too far away for Rawk to know for sure.

"We're on the same side and our chances of success increase dramatically if we work together."

Keegen pushed through the Heroes and went to stand in front of Jako. "You're smaller than I remember."

"I'm smaller than *I* remember."

The two of them laughed and Keegan held out his hand to shake. "I've guess I've worked with people more despicable to you. I once worked with a Gibbian master—thief who ate dogs on a regular basis. Easier to catch than rats, he said."

Jako shook his hand.

After a moment, a few more sorcerers crossed the gap and warily eyed the men that half an hour ago would have tried to kill them. Perhaps many of them had never spoken to a Hero previously.

Introductions were made—Rawk recognized names from both groups—and awkward small talk was exchanged for a few minutes.

"So, we're all just people, right?" Rawk said after a while. "No terrible monsters here at all?" He got grudging nods of agreement. "Good. Now, Jako, why don't you take your friends inside? Thacker is there, and Sylvia— Silver Lark— is too."

"Silver Lark is here?"

"She's been in Katamood almost as long as you have, I think."

The sorcerers headed off and Rawk turned to the others. "How many of you are working for me at the moment?" They all were. "Well, I have some bad news."

"What?" Londa asked. Of them all, he seemed the most put out by this recent turn of events.

"I'll pay you all for today— that is, if I live through the next week and still have any money left at the end— but I won't be paying you any more than that."

"Why not?"

"Because I don't want to fight beside mercenaries. You fight because you want to. Because it's the right thing to do."

"And if we don't want to?"

"Then off you go. But if I see you fighting for Weaver, I'll make a special effort to go and say hello."

"Weaver will pay," Londa said.

"I'm sure he will. But you do know he has a sorcerer working for him? He's the one who's been opening the ohoga portals to let through the exots."

"Weaver hates magic."

"Yes. But he hates living a boring life more. He hates being normal, even if he is a prince."

Cox nodded. "I'm with you. Weaver has always taken too long to pay."

Frazen agreed. "And if he's employing a sorcerer he is also a criminal, breaking his own laws."

Rawk smiled as the others joined the fight.

Keegan smiled as well. "An army of Heroes," he said. "We'll be unstoppable."

It *sounded* great.

–O–

Rawk looked around the corner. A short way down the street was a tavern and sitting on the front porch were a dozen men, in three groups. They tried to look like everyday patrons, but every one of them was a trained warrior. They were the first real group Rawk and his followers had come across. A couple of individual men and sometimes as many of four had been spotted, but they had all retreat very quickly or surrendered if that was not possible.

"So?" Rake asked.

"This lot aren't going to run away." Rawk scratched at his beard as he turned to examine the militia crowding into the alley behind him, wondering how they would do in their first real fight. There was Rake and another of Thacker's guards. Plus Fabi and Frazen, a Hero with one missing arm and a small fountain of hair spraying from the top of his head. The rest of the group were militia— men and dwarves and elves. They all had reasonable, proper weapons but none of them had done anything more than train a couple of hours a week, just in case.

Frazen had a look at the mercenaries as well. "Don't like it much," he said.

"Me either." He turned to Rake. "Can we find some more militia to help us? Odds of two–on–one are not in our favor. Not by a long shot."

"Maybe we could. But I don't know how long it would take."

"Come on then." Rawk sighed. "We can't surprise them from this distance so let's go and ask them to surrender."

"Is that likely to work?" one of the dwarves asked.

"No."

"Oh." The dwarf shifted his grip on his sword.

Fabi and Frazen led the way around the corner. Rawk saw all the mercenaries turn to look. And when the dwarves came around the corner as well, they were on their feet in an instant, weapons drawn. A few of them came down the stairs to the street.

A tall whip of a man sauntered along the porch so he could get a better look. "This looks like it could be fun," he said. He tossed back the last of his ale and threw the tankard onto the floor.

"We can escort you back across the river," Rawk said. "Or you can die."

Someone laughed.

"You can report to Weaver about what's happening. He's sure to be impressed and reward you accordingly."

"We've got the prince's money already. Now we're just waiting for the action he promised."

Rawk laughed too. "Normally I'd tell you not to count on Weaver coming through on his promises, but tonight you might just be in luck."

The tall Whip drew his sword and jumped down to the cobbles. Those still on the porch followed him. "We were told it would be a week or more yet."

Rawk drew his sword. "Well, we don't work to Weaver's timetable."

A couple of dwarves seemed to take that as some sot of signal because they charged silently forward. The rest of the militia joined in and Rawk swore as he was swept along as well. He didn't know what he'd been planning to do, but charging the more experienced force had not been one of the top options. Sensibly, the mercenaries stayed where they were and readied themselves.

Rawk tried to get to Whip, but the surge pushed him away and he found himself fighting a bear of a man with one milky eye and a surprisingly light sword. He traded blows for a moment, distracted by the man's strange smile. He eventually swatted away a lazy riposte and stabbed him in his good eye. And in the twenty seconds all of that took, the battled has shifted inevitably in favor of the mercenaries.

Militiamen were falling. An old man here, with a knife in his throat. Beside him, someone young enough to be his grandson— though he was human and two foot taller— took a slash across his thigh and went down amongst the press of bodies.

Glancing at Fabi, Rawk wondered if a withdrawal was possible. The defensive formation they were facing would help, making a quick chase difficult, but he still didn't like the odds. Just when he was about to call anyway, hoping the militiamen would know how to retreat in an orderly manner to avoid leaving themselves open, there was a shout from inside the tavern. Then one and another and another of the patrons rushed out onto the street. Soon more were streaming out, almost fighting each other to get out the relatively narrow door. When a dozen or more were arrayed in the street, makeshift weapons at the ready, their disparate shouts became one and they charged forward.

With the mercenaries trapped in the middle of a now vastly superior force, it was only a matter of time. They must have known that, but still they fought on.

Rawk pushed past some militia to get at Whip. He pulled the last dwarf away, saving him from a knife in the stomach, and set himself to fight.

"It's over," Rawk said above the rumble.

"Not yet."

Perhaps he merely meant this one little battle amidst the large. If he thought anything else, he was overly optimistic. Rawk ducked a swing and pressed forward, not really thinking he would find his mark, but setting the pace for the fight, building up expectations with short, stabbing linear attacks. But when the mercenary backed into the couple of his men who were fighting the rearward battle, he paused for half an instant and Rawk changed his attack. He stepped forward and to the side. He swung low, which caught Whip by surprise. And he surprised him even more when he aborted the attack and spun the other way. When he stabbed the man, he was facing the wrong direction. He held the pose for a moment, then thought better of it and turned to face the enemy. But there were none left. Caught between the two groups of locals, they had succumbed quickly.

"Well done," Rawk said to a chorus of cheers. But looking around, he saw several fathers and sons who would not be going home to their families tonight. His mood quickly soured. "See to the wounded," he said. And while people more capable than he did just that, he helped search the mercenaries for anything useful and then moved them to the side of the road. Someone was already heading towards Caldera to let Thacker know a clean up crew was needed.

Rawk crouched by the wall and leaned his head back against the whitewashed plaster of the wall. Fabi sat by his side.

"Now I know," Rawk said.

"Know what?"

Rawk looked around at the dead militiamen. He wondered who was going to have to tell the families. "I know why I never fought with the peasants." He cleared his throat. "It's much harder to think of them as expendable, as nothing more than pieces on a gaming board."

But he didn't have time to think. He couldn't afford the luxury of sitting around mourning the losses and he certainly couldn't sit around feeling sorry for himself. Not when other fathers and mothers and children were dying elsewhere.

Pushing himself back to his feet, Rawk looked over the remains of his small army. He grunted. "We won here," he said to them, "but we can mark that down to luck. If anyone charges at the enemy again without my say so I will cut you down myself. You put all off us in danger and I don't want to die tonight. And I don't want anyone else dying either." He looked to where the dead had been lined up near the side of the road. "It's going to happen, more of us will die, but it will happen less if you listen to orders. This isn't a game. It isn't training. You need to listen or I will make you go and tell the families of the dead why they aren't coming home."

Nobody said anything.

Rawk's lips twitched. "I know you aren't professional soldiers, which is all the more reason for you to do what you're told." He turned on his heel. "Now, leave this to the clean up team and follow me."

–O–

Rawk had captured five mercenaries in a beer garden and avoided two larger groups, slinking away with his militia behind him because he knew that they would be lucky if anyone made it out alive.

It was late, the sun was long gone. He was about to head for home, wherever that was going to be, when Frazen touched his arm.

"You hear that?"

He couldn't hear anything, and was so tired that he was almost beyond caring. But he paused and cocked his head and tried to listen. There was a fight, a battle, somewhere nearby. He didn't have the energy to swear, but he sighed and looked around. "Which way?"

Frazen looked around too and gave it some thought. He pointed to the east.

Fabi cleared his throat. "The River Tower?"

Rawk nodded. "Come on then."

The main street of Fek Bazaar was strangely quiet in the hissing light of the street lamps before they arrived. Stalls stood silent along the sides of the street, locked and covered. Normally there would be private guards patrolling but tonight there was nothing. Just the sound of the battle growing louder, shifting in the stillness.

A minute later, they broke into the clear at the edge of the square surrounding the solid, square base of the tower. There was a troop of mercenaries, professionals with matching uniforms and cold, hard eyes, fighting a ragtag group of locals. It wasn't immediately obvious if the mercenaries were trying to get into the tower or trying to get out. It didn't really matter. Rawk gave a shout and led the charge. It was doubtful anyone heard him.

Running past two dwarves, who seemed to have control against a huge opponent, Rawk came to the aid of an elf. The man was struggling against a red haired opponent but moved aside confidently enough to let Rawk in as well.

"I am glad you could make it," the elf said. He batted aside an attack but was driven back a moment later by a lightning quick reply.

Rawk jabbed into a momentary opening that closed quicker than he thought was possible.

"Oh, I like to turn up at the most dramatic time."

"Well done, then; you succeeded."

"Would you two shut up," the mercenary said. "Dying is a serious matter." He attacked furiously and it was all Rawk could do to keep his skin on one piece.

"You be serious then. You're the one who's about to die." Rawk danced around to the side and threw himself forward for a reckless moment. He blocked one attack, barely, then paused. The mercenary tried a second time and a dwarf at his back clobbered him over the head with a club.

"Thank you," Rawk said. He straightened and wiped sweat from his brow. "So, what's going on here?" he asked.

The dwarf was already gone, but the elf answered. "There are men inside the tower. Perhaps as many as fifty. This lot are trying to break them out."

"Any action from inside?"

"No. The seem happy to let these ones do the dying for now."

"Well, let's oblige them. What's your name?"

"Red Raven."

"Well, Red, nice to meet you. You've got some experience?"

"It's Raven, actually. But yes, Hopola, most significantly."

"Really?"

But there wasn't time to find out more. The two turned as one when a mercenary came towards them. Rawk blocked a high, clumsy swing and the elf ran him through. And they stepped over the body and deeper into the fray.

And after a moment it was like it had always been. The world— the moment— crowded close. Screams and shouts, the clash of steel on steel. All the sounds merged, and then combined with the smell of sweat and blood, and the cold touch of fear to create an entirely new sensation that was never the same from moment to moment but always the same from fight to fight, from year to year. Rawk breathed in the *thing*, tasted it, felt it crawling across his skin like ants, saw it dancing behind the eyes of men all around him.

Then he blinked, and it was gone, and he was fighting a pair of men, one as big as a bear, the other as cruel-faced as a rat. They worked as one, flowing through the chaos as if they danced.

Rawk didn't like dancing. He stood his ground amongst the whirling blades. He was a rock compared to Raven's willow tree. He hardly moved, letting his blade do the work, while the elf flowed around the enemies' weapons. And when Rawk finally saw an opening he *did* move, lunging forward and twisting. The Bear's blade whistled as it skimmed past his ear. When he slashed across the man's thigh and arm and neck, Rat was distracted for half a second, more than long enough for Raven to finish his work there as well.

And they moved forward again, heading for where the fighting was the fiercest. They cut down men as they went, helping an over stretched dwarf, then an old man who was tiring quickly. They barely paused. Rawk distracted a grizzled veteran and the woman fighting him expertly stabbed him in the eye with her light, switch of a sword. She nodded her thanks and moved on to someone else with hardly a pause. She didn't block anything— her blade was useless for that— but nobody could get close.

Rawk almost slipped in blood. He kicked a head and it rolled away across the cobbles like a ball in a sick children's game. He paused to breathe and almost lost his own head. Raven saved him, pushing him aside. When he got himself organized again, Rawk expect to see the elf with a knife in his heart. That was always the way it worked in the stories. That was the cliché. But Raven was fighting with cool concentration. The rest of the world didn't seem to concern him.

Stabbing one mercenary in the back as he passed, Rawk left the elf to his business— he'd be fine— and pushed further into the fight. He headed towards the banner, though the effort was as clichéd as his savior dying in the act would have been.

A woman with a scimitar and a round shield attacked from his left. He spun to face her, but a dwarf almost cut off her leg from behind. Rawk kept going and the dwarf fell in behind.

"Where are we going?" He had a long grey beard and a horned helmet. He looked very serious about his work.

Rawk pointed.

"The banner? Good idea." The dwarf battered aside a pike and ran the owner through with his wicked looking sword.

Rawk almost lost his head but ducked in time. He slipped, swinging as he fell, and got lucky. But he fell into a pool of blood that was growing larger by the moment and got up sticky and feeling horrible. He wiped his hands and arms on the man he had just killed and marched forward again. Raven was back with him, guarding his right as the dwarf guarded his left.

They detoured slightly to help two women fighting four mercenaries. Rawk slashed his way amongst them, cutting one down and distracting the others for long enough. They didn't die immediately, but they were suddenly on the back foot and it didn't take long.

Party expanded by two more, Rawk surged forward. The dwarf went down when someone hit him on the side of the head with a sharp−edged shield. Frazen came from nowhere and disemboweled the attacker before Rawk could do anything. Fabi was with him, bloody and smiling grimly. Nobody had time to check on the dwarf.

A group of a dozen or more emerged form the chaos and came at them from the side. Rawk's little band somehow formed a defensive line, fighting side−by−side, pushing forward. They were out numbered though and the advance could not last. But it didn't matter. In the mess of the battle the smaller fight disintegrated almost as quickly as it had started.

Red Raven was gone again, currents swirling him away. One of the unknown women left and another two joined. Frazen rushed off to help a dwife whose club was not going to keep her alive long. It was amazing she'd lasted as long as she had.

Rawk spotted the banner again and started moving. He didn't look who was with him. They either came or they didn't.

He took a slice across his shoulder that burned. He almost dropped *Kaj* to grab the wound. But it wasn't as bad as if felt. He spun around, in time to block another attack and cut off a couple of the woman's fingers. She *did* drop her sword and collapsed to the ground with a wail of pain. Rawk left her staring at the bloody stumps.

Two minutes later he had finally made it to the center of the melee.

The pole holding the banner had been rammed between two cobblestones and five men stood around the base. If Rawk knew anything at all, then the big one with the crested helm was the leader. If the scars that covered most of his visible skin was any indication, he'd been in the business long enough to learn a thing or two. He was still at least ten years younger than Rawk.

The man looked at Rawk and smiled "You look like a man who thinks much of himself," he said.

"I try to think as little as possible."

The mercenary wiped at his drooping moustache and stepped forward as he readied a huge, two-handed sword. He used it one handed, flicking it around like switch.

Rawk raised an eyebrow. "*I* think much of myself? Are you going to dance, or are you going to fight?"

The mercenary paused for a moment. He obviously didn't like being baited very much.

"Come on. I've had a long day and I've still got things to do."

But the other man regained control and started to circle slowly.

Rawk took a deep breath and threw *Kaj* at him. The hilt hit the man in the arm, but it was still a surprising tactic. And while his opponent was getting over the shock, Rawk darted forward and punched him in the throat. He took the man's dagger and slid it into his heart while he lay on the ground, struggling to breathe.

"Like I said, I've had a long day."

Rawk picked up his sword and looked around. The battle seemed to have paused for a moment and he wondered if everyone was going to throw down their weapons. But that cliché went the way of the others and the screams and clashes of weapons rang out again. Rawk knew that the pause had never even happened. He swatted aside an attack and let Red Raven kill the man.

"You're back," Rawk said.

But the elf was too busy to reply. So Rawk left him to it and kicked the banner over as warriors swirled around him. Then he turned to fight again.

He continued for what seemed like the entire night but was aware of the fact that the arrival of his militia group had turned the tide of the battle and the ebb and flow of the fighting quickly decreased. He fought on, thinking it couldn't last much longer, hoping to stop as many mercenaries as possible from getting away.

−O−

Rawk wiped his sword on a dead man's shirt and all it did was smear the blood all over the blade. He didn't really care. He would see to the weapon when he got the chance but all he wanted to do now was sleep. Things had really gotten out of hand.

"Do you realize who this other lot were?" Fabi asked. The big man had taken a seat on the edge of the cistern. He was looking at a wound on his arm. It didn't look all that serious and the flow of blood was already starting to decrease.

"Should I?" Rawk thought of sitting as well, but he decided that he would probably fall asleep if he did.

Fabi pointed to one of the red sashed mercenaries that had turned up shortly after Rawk took the banner. Shortly after he'd thought the battle was winding down. "They're Vanoof's Cohort."

Rawk's eyes narrowed as he looked at the corpse again. "Really?"

"I worked with them a few times over in Januze."

"I thought they were supposed to be good."

Fabi shrugged. "Last I knew they'd taken heavy losses at Midditole Crest. Maybe they hadn't really recovered."

Red Raven gave a bark of laugher as he joined them. "I imagine this will set them back a bit as well."

Rawk looked around the square. There was a layer of corpses with hardly room to spare for walking between. Unfortunately, many were locals. Not far away, tangled amongst the dead, were a couple of men that Rawk had fought with earlier, including the dwarf who'd been hit with the shield. Perhaps if they'd been able to help him sooner...

They'd been close to overrunning the enemy, then Vanoof's Cohort had come. And more locals. It had turned into a major battle. "We can't keep doing this. We might win, but the city won't survive anyway."

"Katamood will survive," Red Raven said. "But perhaps it will not be the city we knew."

Rawk didn't know if that was a good thing or a bad thing. He'd come to appreciate the city even more recently, but mainly the parts that endured in spite of Weaver's attention. He sighed. "I don't care how many more mercenaries there are around here, I need to sleep." People had come to care for the wounded again. And they could do a better job than he could. Again. "Come on. You too."

Red Raven looked surprised. "Me?"

"Yes, you."

So Rawk led Fabi, Frazen and the elf up the hill, all the while wishing Thacker would move his head quarters closer.

A lifetime later, they stepped into the *Burning Tree* and looked around. There were a few people there, from a few different races, but it was as quiet as a church. And Thacker and his advisors were nowhere to be seen.

"Maybe Thacker already left," Fabi said, running his fingers through his beard, trying to remove the tangles.

Frazen grunted and Rawk said, "I don't think I can make it all the way up to Caldera without some food."

His companions didn't complain when he headed towards an empty table down in the back corner. He sat down and closed his eyes. The chairs scraping across the rough wood floor seemed very loud.

It had been a long night and a long day that followed. He'd managed to get some sleep, but it wasn't enough. And he doubted he'd be getting enough sleep anytime in the next few days.

"Hello, Rawk."

Rawk opened his eyes and looked at the woman. For a moment he wondered if he knew her. Or perhaps she was just someone who thought he was their friend because they knew his name. Then he realized it was a serving woman. "Hello."

"Would you like an ale?"

"Yes, thank you. Four ales."

She started to walk away.

"Wait."

"Yes?"

"I don't like ale."

She narrowed her eyes, as if he'd said he didn't like breathing. "You don't like ale?"

"No. I never have."

"Then why..."

"Because that's what Heroes do."

"I thought Heroes did whatever they wanted."

Rawk laughed. But he didn't know if he was laughing at her naivety or his own. "Can I have some apple cider, please? Three ales and a cider. And four meals."

"Very well."

He watched her go and when he turned back, discovered Clinker was standing by his table. "Are you still sleeping on the street?"

The lad shrugged. "Sometimes. Sometimes I sleep in Kristun's workshop. Why?"

"You have a new blanket I gather? Well, we need to get it out of your satchel so you can't sneak up on me."

Clinker smiled. "But maybe I need it for sneaking up on other people."

"Like who?"

He shrugged. "Prince Weaver."

"You don't go anywhere near Weaver, do you hear me."

"Why not?"

"His spies probably saw the two of us talking. If not, you're a dwarf, and that is more than enough reason for him to hate you."

"How would I get near Prince Weaver?"

"I don't know. Have you had anything to eat?" Rawk got his knife and fork out of his belt pouch, tested the edge of the knife, and set them down on the table.

"Not today. Nobody's got time to organize food."

"Sit down then."

Clinker pulled a chair over from another table as Red Raven and Fabi made room for him.

"So you do a lot of work with Kristun?"

"Some. He helped me with my wall cleaner so I helped him with some other stuff. I sweep his floor— just with a normal broom— and fetch things for him."

"And has Thacker offered you a job yet?"

"He gives me work sometimes. But things have been busy lately, so I don't think he's really thinking about things like that."

"Fair enough, I suppose. You really shouldn't be this far down the hill though; it isn't safe."

"Nowhere is safe."

"Well..."

Keegen entered the tavern and looked around. He spotted Rawk and, after a moment, sauntered over. "How goes it?"

"It goes well enough. We've made it through the day." Rawk sighed, looking around at his companions. There were a good many people who hadn't. A good many *good* people.

"And you?" Franzen asked.

Keegen nodded. "Well enough. We almost lost Long Bridge this morning."

"I heard."

"Londa held back the reserves too long. We got lucky, otherwise we would have been overrun before they got there."

"I thought he was promising."

"Me too. Now he's off sulking somewhere. We can't even find him."

"He'll learn. Leading soldiers, whatever the sort, is different to fighting a few wolden wolves. I was down at the South River Watch." Rawk told him about the battle. "I reckon there must be a few men in that tower if they are willing to send that many try to break them free," he finished.

"Maybe it isn't about how many. Maybe it's about a particular person."

"Like who?"

"How should I know?" He shrugged. "All I can say is thank Path for the river. It's the only thing saving us at the moment, I think."

Rawk agreed. He thanked the waitress when the food came and ordered another two bowls, one for himself and one for Keegen, as he slid the one intended for him across to Clinker. The boy started eating straight away.

"So how did *you* get across the river this morning anyway?" Rawk divided his glance between Franzen and Keegen.

The former gestured vaguely. "We went up the river a couple of miles and borrowed a boat. Then we just walked back."

"Nobody tried to stop you?"

"There was a boy with a wooden sword," Keegen said. "We gave him a few ithel and he let us pass."

"Traitor." The extra food came and Rawk started to eat. "So, have you seen any of the others? Our army of heroes?"

"Frew and Graft were down at the bridge this morning. Cox and Donovan found some mercs holed up in a warehouse and almost had to burn them out."

"That wouldn't have been a very good idea."

"I know. Neither of them are the sharpest knife. Luckily Taffy was there. She did something or other..." He waved his hands as if that would explain the sorcerer's actions... "And they all came pouring out soon enough."

Rawk nodded. "Good. Maybe there's hope after all."

"Hope for the fight, or hope for Heroes and sorcerers?"

"Right now, they probably go hand in hand." With a sigh, Rawk cleaned off his spoon. "I need to sleep," he said. He didn't know if it was going to happen, but if he stayed where he was it most certainly wouldn't.

Faraday

RAWK WOKE WITH A START. Blinking and looking around, it took him a moment to work out exactly where he was.

"I was beginning to wonder if you were going to sleep through the rest of the day," Sylvia said. She was sitting in the corner of the room with a cup of tea in one hand and a book in the other, with a long, slim finger marking her place.

The meeting room near Thacker's office. He sighed, wondering if he could go back to sleep and wake up in another life, but stood up and stretched his back. It didn't help. "Is that something you can arrange?"

The elf gave a small smile. "Perhaps, but I am not sure if anyone else around here would be thrilled with you missing the excitement."

Rawk grunted. Fighting beside Red Raven the night before, he'd come to the conclusion that there were people around here who were better suited to the task than he was. He said as much to Sylvia.

"It is as much about your presence as your skills, Rawk. You started this fight, so they need you there."

"I did *not* start it. Weaver has been bringing in mercenaries for weeks. We were still friends then."

"Well, perhaps you did not start it, but you certainly brought it forward."

"And where *is* everyone else?" He looked around, as if he might have missed them sitting in the corner. He remembered reporting to the room after the battle to take the South River Tower and his late dinner. He remembered talking with Thacker and his leadership team. He couldn't really remember the details though, and he'd fallen asleep before the meeting ended.

"They went for breakfast."

Breakfast sounded good. But first... "So..."

"Yes?"

"Well, Weaver knows you're here and any of his followers will kill you on sight."

"Are you trying to comfort me?"

"No. It's just that there's nothing stopping you from doing magic."

The elf narrowed her eyes.

"Could you fix my knee? I'm rubbing on the cream every day. Well, most days. Some days. Look, I've been pretty busy. But it just hurts constantly. And my arm." He waved the bandaged appendage at her as if that was all that needed to be said on the matter.

Sylvia sighed and shifted in her chair. She looked down at her book for a moment. "I have a confession to make, Rawk."

It was Rawk's turn to narrow his eyes.

"I can no longer do magic."

"Pardon? What?"

She cleared her throat. "I have lost my ability to do magic. Well, anything other than the most basic of spells."

"After the Quod?"

"No, before that. Years ago."

"But I saw you kill Balen."

"Yes, you did. But I did not do it with magic."

"He was on the other side of the room. There was thunder. There was..."

Sylvia picked up a bag from the floor by her side. She looked inside then carefully pulled out a...

"What is it?"

"Kristun calls it a pistol."

It was made of timber and metal but that was about the only thing that was obvious about it.

"What does it do?"

"It kills people from the other side of the room. I thought we established that."

"Do you throw it?" It looked heavy enough to hurt if you were hit with it, but he wouldn't rely on it being fatal, even if they did stand in the one spot and let themselves be struck. But she hadn't thrown it at Balen anyway.

"You have heard and seen the explosions that the dwarves use while building the canal?"

Rawk nodded.

"Well, the pistol uses a smaller explosion to propel a lead ball fast enough to kill."

"So that thing throws a lead ball at people?"

"Yes. Very quickly." She held the thing out for Rawk to take.

Rawk wasn't sure he wanted to take it though. But she kept holding it out, so he crossed the room and carefully took it from her hand.

"It will not harm you."

"But..."

"It is loaded, but remains uncocked."

"What does that mean?"

"The ball and the powder are in place, but there is a lever that needs to be pulled back before anything can possibly happen. And another lever after that, under normal circumstances."

Rawk still wasn't sure, but he looked at the contraption, turning it in his hand. It *was* heavy, and beautiful, but it was still hard to believe it could kill someone. He handed it back to her. "So you didn't use magic to kill Balen? You used that thing?"

"That is correct."

"What about Queel?"

Sylvia winced. "I threw acid in his face."

That sounded slightly... brutal. "You've been lying to me?"

The sorcerer looked at her hands.

"I can understand at the start, but after that..."

"Perhaps I was lying to myself as well, Rawk. Do you think I like my weakness? Once I could raze buildings and heal torn flesh. Now I can light a candle with magic, but it hurts. I can boil water, but I must rest for hours afterwards."

"But you let me go into a room full of sorcerers."

"I attempted to stop you."

"You let me... Well, yes, but still."

"Let us talk about lies, Rawk. When did you hurt your knee? When you fought the wolden wolf or before that?"

Rawk cleared his throat. "It wasn't a wolden wolf. It was a little girl's pet."

"How many people know about the aches and pains you live with every day? Is it just me?"

"No. There are lots of others."

"Travis hardly counts."

"There's also—"

"Celeste and Grint do not count either." When he opened his mouth to speak she held up her hand. "And if you are about to say Juskin, then I do not believe you."

Rawk looked around the room again. "Where *is* Juskin? Did he make it?"

"Are you changing the subject? Yes, Juskin arrived safely not long after you left with the militia."

"And Demon?"

"The kitten is also safe. I believe he is in the care of Clinker at the moment."

Before Rawk could change the subject some more, the door opened and Rake hurried into the room. "Good, your awake."

"Yes. I haven't had breakfast though."

"We can organize something, but it will have to be after the meeting."

"What meeting?"

Another dwarf came in. Then some humans. And Red Raven. Soon the room was filling with people and Rawk found a seat along the wall before they all filled up.

When Thacker eventually entered the room, Rawk wondered if he should stand up and salute. In the end he stayed seated, too tired to even give the idea too much thought. Lots of other people, mainly dwarves, seemed keen to do so now that he was in charge of an army, makeshift though it was.

Thacker slumped into his chair at the head of the conference table. "We think we just cleared the last of the mercenary units from south of the canal."

"How many are between the canal and the river?" Gannon asked. He was an experienced human soldier, but he was so old that he may well have been retired for the last thirty years.

Thacker winced. "About three hundred died at the South River Watch," he glanced at Rawk. "They were good, experienced units and we did well to get them as we did."

"You seem to be avoiding the question, Thacker," Fabi said. His arm was bandaged but his beard was still messy enough to have a squirrel and a couple of birds living in it.

"Perhaps." He checked a sheet of paper, though Rawk doubted he really needed to. "We estimate there are about a thousand left."

Rawk groaned. "How many people did we lose at the Watch?"

"About four hundred."

Rawk shook his head. The militia had outnumbered the mercenaries by a good amount and still it had been touch and go several times. And all they had done was clear the square— they hadn't actually taken the tower. "We can't keep doing that; it isn't acceptable. These aren't professional soldiers. They are people who need to go home to their families."

"You don't need to tell me that, Rawk," Thacker said angrily before getting a hold of himself. He rose to his feet and paced to the window and back. "We're working on some things."

"Like what?"

"We have some engineers and whatnot coming. They shouldn't be long, hopefully."

"And are the bridges secure? That thousand could turn into five thousand very quickly."

"We have men at the bridges and they are ready to demolish them if required."

"And how long will that take?"

"About a minute."

Rawk raised an eyebrow but remembered the weapon Sylvia had shown him and the explosions that were gouging the canal through the rock.

A minute later Kristun ga Meyer hurried into the room, arms full of a lopsided stack of dirty, dog–eared papers. "Sorry I'm late." He looked up and suddenly seemed overwhelmed by all the eyes on him. Perhaps he had expected to be meeting with just Thacker. A few more dwarves, with satchels and papers and boxes, came in behind him and looked just as surprised.

"Don't worry, Kristun. Just give us some good news."

"Right. Yes. I'll go first, shall I?" He looked back at the dwarves that had come with him. He cleared his throat. "Well, I've been working on some designs for small, mobile siege engines recently that should be useful." He shuffled through his pages and pulled out a diagram of a strange machine. "I have a couple ready to go in my workshop and one smith and one carpenter could probably make one a day."

Thacker nodded. "I'm sure we can spare more people than that. Do they work?"

"I've done some testing. No problems so far. I've done about fifty tests with one of them. The range is only about fifty yards with scatter–shot but it's a nice low trajectory."

"Fifty yards is plenty in the city," Gannon said.

Kristun shrugged. "I never really thought about that."

"Fifty tests? Well, that's fine. As soon as we're done here we'll organize some assistance for you." Thacker noted that down. "What else have you got?"

He shuffled through his papers. He shuffled back the other way. "I've got a kind of rolling wall. You use it to block a street then slowly push it forward..."

"I am not sure how useful that would be," Red Raven offered. "Unless we have one for every street I imagine the enemy will just go another direction."

Gannon pursed his lips and scratched at a scar on his weathered cheek. "But if we did have a couple we could use them to hold a beachhead on the other side of the river."

Raven nodded. "Perhaps you are right." He turned to Kristun. "I apologize."

Kristun shuffled his papers some more. "I have an idea for a cross bow that is basically just for holing ships."

"An idea?" Thacker asked.

"I haven't tried it."

The other dwarves presented the same range of good, bad and never–even–tested ideas that might win them the war or set them up as the joke of historians for a thousand years. And around the suggestions they built a plan that might just let them live through the next couple of days.

The meeting broke up as quickly as possible so the experienced soldiers could get back out into the city to help with the fighting. Thacker finally moved his head quarters to the inn and Rawk attached himself to a militia unit.

For the next hour, he moved through the streets with about fifty men, flushing out small bands of mercenaries, capturing some and dealing with the others as quickly as possible. They suffered very few losses, but Rawk thought he could feel the tension building, like a storm on the horizon, building towards something big.

He followed Hapa through the twisting streets. The sorcerer was a plain woman with short green hair and a weak chin but had proven useful on a few occasions throughout the morning, little things that had made the difference. Like now. She'd been living in the crazy warren surrounding Fek Bazaar for a couple of years and knew the area like the back of her hand. Rawk knew the basics but he had the feeling he would wander around in circles for the rest of the day if they became separated.

When they finally reached the South Watch where the river met the Bay of Kata, they stopped to stare at the remains of the previous night's battle. The bodies of the locals had already been removed, the wagons rolling up the hill in a convoy with pipers and drummers marching along beside. The mercenaries had been dragged into several piles and were waiting to be loaded and carried away as well.

A huge dwarf, cloth tied over his mouth and nose, saw Rawk and wandered over.

"Hello, Yed. Just another day in the office?"

The dwarf nodded a greeting and turned to look at the work as well. "It's the biggest mess I've ever had to clean up. Falling Leaves was a walk in the park compared to this." He grunted. "A couple of the boys think we should just leave them here. That would get the bastards out of the tower soon enough."

Rawk looked at the tower. The door had been barred from the outside, so nobody was going to be leaving any time soon. Perhaps not until they were hungry. "So where are you taking the bodies?"

"South. We're working on a couple of barrows."

"The farmers aren't complaining?"

"They're near Weaver's hunting lodge."

Rawk grunted. Weaver hated hunting. The lodge was used for drinking and not much else.

"Are you all right?" Yed asked.

"I'm fine..." But Rawk realized Yed wasn't looking at him. He was looking at Hapa. The sorcerer looked very pale. Her mouth was working silently. For a moment, Rawk worried that the woman was casting a spell.

Hapa blinked and turned abruptly. "No. I'm fine. It's just..."

"You've never seen a dead person?" Yed asked.

"She's seen quite a few this morning, Yed," Rawk said.

She nodded. "I have, but..."

Rawk turned to look at the scene as well. "Not quite on this scale." And for a moment it concerned him that the piles of dead men, the blood and the entrails and the stench, didn't concern him at all. "You get used to it," he said.

"I don't want to get used to it."

"No. I suppose not."

There was a shout from somewhere back along the river. Then nothing.

"Tinder," Yed shouted.

Another dwarf hurried up. "Yeah."

"Go see what's happening."

Tinder gave a lazy salute and headed towards the source of the sound.

Yed looked around. "Has anyone seen my sword?"

"You didn't make some of this mess, did you?" Rawk asked. "I didn't see you anywhere." It would be amazing if he had seen a particular person amidst the madness of the battle.

"Not this one." The dwarf waved a hand towards the west. "I was over by Kela Road last night."

A minute later there was another shout. A warning. Yed had found his sword and led the way, lumbering towards the west. Rawk hurried to catch up as a large contingent of workers downed their tools and snatched up weapons instead.

They raced out of the square and along the edge of the river. A sleek sloop bobbed at the head of a long line of ships as the bank dipped under a bridge. They didn't make it that far. A swarm of men came around the corner of a warehouse, swords drawn. When they saw Rawk and his companions they paused for a moment then, as one, gave a wordless shout and charged forward.

Rawk swore and drew *Kaj.* "Hold the line," he shouted. There wasn't a line, but one quickly formed with Rawk at the center. "Hapa, can you slow them down."

The sorcerer didn't reply.

"Anything."

In a moment it would be too late.

Rawk's breath caught when he saw Londa, the young Hero, at the head of the charge with his sword drawn and a while look on his face.

"The little bastard," Rawk said. He almost didn't want a distraction.

There was a noise, a bone chilling screech, like nothing Rawk had ever heard. The charge faltered as the men and women slowed to look around. Rawk kept his focus, staring at Londa, lip twitching. He didn't know if the noise was Hapa's doing or something else. It didn't matter. Either way, the more immediate threat was standing in front of him. He wanted to start a charge of his own now, but didn't know if anyone would go with him or if they were all still looking for the source of the noise.

Eyes on Londa, he charged anyway. As he neared the enemy, a huge mercenary got in his way. Rawk cut him down, slashing his throat and, while the blood was still spraying, stabbed another in the stomach. Then Rawk was surrounded, ten yards from his target and on his own.

He spun and parried, twisting his knee, jarring his elbow, working against two men and a woman, slapping away attacks as quickly as he could. Cox arrived from somewhere, and the old man used his reach to advantage. He kept the enemy at bay, grim and silent. The militia finally arrived in force, letting out a war cry as they crossed the small distance between the two forces.

Rawk felt the clash, heard the cries of pain, noticed that Cox had been carried away by the ebb and flow, but tried to keep his attention on the details of *his* fight. He wanted to find Londa but all he could do now was survive. For a few seconds he dodged and wove but each movement sent a flare of pain through his leg. He was not going be able to keep it up for long. So he pushed forward while he had the chance, spared as little thought as possible on the lesser threats around him while he concentrated his efforts on a short, barrel chested brute who's dark eyes stared soullessly out from beneath his helmet. The stranger didn't care much for finesses but his blade was always where it needed to be. So Rawk dispatched a woman when she stumbled on an uneven paver, and sliced another man's arm enough to end his fight, before he managed to find a chink in the brute's defense.

He saw the man's eyes go wide with shock when *Kaj* parted two of his ribs. But Rawk pulled the blade free and turned away before he saw the ending.

Rawk's whole body ached. His mind was a riot of thoughts that were being held back by a wall of fear and exhaustion and the need to just keep moving.

As ever, the mercenaries were out numbered but did not give up. Their experience told, but it was not a story Rawk was willing to listen to. He killed a bald–headed man just as he was about to take a dwarf's arm off at the shoulder. He slipped on the growing pool of blood. Heart racing, he fought from on one knee for a lifetime of seconds, deflecting the blows from a woman's long, etched scimitar before she too slipped and he sliced through her leg just below her mail breech. He took a glancing blow from a mace that deadened his arm. He would have died then, but Yed punched the man in the face with his massive fist even as he held off another with his sword.

Rawk shook his arm to get the feeling back. When he found a horrible dull ache he set to work again. He ran a boy through, watching the surprised look on the lad's face as his sword clattered to the ground and he fell back with a wet slap. He left a slash in an old man's shirt that was getting redder by the moment. The man kept fighting for a long time before realizing he may be in some trouble.

And as always, Rawk eventually looked around for another opponent and realized that the fight was over. His consciousness suddenly expanded like a man taking a deep breath after being underwater and he could see more than just the person in front of him, the sword and subtle shift of eye and weight. He could see the world and feel the little aches and pains that he had not noticed in the moment of the battle. He stepped back from the carnage, wincing as his knee flared with pain, and sucked in a deep breath. And again.

"Do you think there are more?"

Rawk looked around and saw Yed not far away, putting pressure on a wound on his arm but looking unconcerned. "I don't know. Probably." There was no way to tell without knocking on each door and hoping someone answered. "We have to make sure there are no small groups of militia. We have to get as many men as we can together so the mercenaries don't think it's worth the fight."

But there *were* more.

Rawk listened to a rumble of sound and watched as a large group of militia came around a corner just beyond the bridge. At least three score of them, running hard. And right behind them, pressing hard, were mercenaries. A lot of mercenaries. A hundred or more.

Yed groaned. Rawk thought swearing was more appropriate. "No time for rest," he shouted and stalked forward, hoping the militia would stop and turn when they realized they had reinforcements instead of just charging over the top of them.

He had barely gone a dozen paces, stepping over dead mercenaries and dead militia and Cox, who had a neck wound pumping blood onto the cobbles, and Londa with dagger still protruding from his eye, when he heard another sound. At first, he didn't know what it was. It sounded like the roar of a group of men, but it was so loud, so kaleidoscopic, that he wasn't quite sure. And coming out from among the buildings on the far side of the river was a tidal wave a men, mercenaries by the hundred, by the thousand. They were taking the opportunity to surge across the bridge and join the fight.

Rawk stopped. He swore again though he thought groaning might be more appropriate. He swallowed and stared. "Ummm... Hapa." He looked around for the sorcerer and saw her standing, dazed and staring, not far away. "We need a distraction, Hapa. A... miracle. Anything? Please." If they had enough men, and they didn't have the first group behind them, they could have held the enemy on the bridge, bottling them up before they could bring their numbers to bear, but they didn't have enough men, and they did have the enemy at their back as well, so they couldn't. Rawk swallowed. He thought it was strange to stand on the banks of the river and watch as his death stormed across the bridge in front of him.

The first of the mercenaries reached the top of the arch. They picked up speed as they started the descent. And the rumble of their charge stopped. A boom of thunder swallowed it. Thunder like Rawk had never heard before. He ducked and covered his ears as the ground shook. People stumbled and fell. The boats and the river trembled. A quickly spreading cloud of dust enveloped the bridge. A moment later, the ships danced, thumping against the docks, tangling their spars as they rocked and rolled, pushed by a wave that surged down the river and out towards the bay. The battle ended before it had even started and everyone turned to stare.

When the dust cleared the bridge was gone. There were just short fingers of stone projecting from each side of the river, pointing out into nothing. Bodies and parts of bodies clogged the water, shuffling towards the sea, almost leaping up when sudden surges of water met the incoming tide. A minute later, there was another clap of thunder, and another, each further away than the one before. And for the next five minutes the ships fenced with spars and masts as more waves and the army of the dead fled for the sea.

Rawk looked at Hapa. "That was a bit more distracting than I expected."

Hapa's eyes were wide, her face pale. All she could do was shrug and shake her head.

Trying to get his mind working again, Rawk gathered some militiamen about him and headed towards the mercenaries already on this side of the river. They were stunned, still staring at the bridge that was no more.

"Throw down your weapons."

Rawk turned and saw Rake standing on a wagon fifty yards away. The dwarf called out to the mercenaries again. They did as they were asked. First one, then another, then a dozen all at once. A minute later, they were sitting on the road and dwarves were moving among them collecting weapons. Everyone stole surreptitious glances towards the bridge. Rawk could still see bodies floating past and he wondered if each of the explosions he had heard had been another bridge falling. And had there been mercenaries on all of them, charging across in what they thought would be the final assault?

"You turned up just in time." Rake came to stand by Rawk. He stared out at the river as well.

"I was just thinking of the drama, as ever. Though I do think the whole exploding bridge thing was more helpful." Rawk looked at the two fingers of bridge pointing out over the river. Dust was still floating in the air, like early morning mist. Some of it was red. Then he looked at Londa, lying nearby. "Another chance to cliché has passed me by," he said.

"What?"

"I told Londa that if I saw him fighting for Weaver I'd kill him." He gestured at the body. "Someone else beat me to it though. Come on, I need a drink. Is it lunch time?"

Rake nodded. "I know just the place."

—O—

There were guards outside the *Burning Tree* this time and the square was overflowing with the bustle and hum of activity.

"That wasn't very nice of you," Rawk said to Rake. "I thought we were going for a drink."

"You can have a drink if you like. Thacker will probably even pay."

"Great."

Inside, the inn was filled to overflowing this time but hardly any louder than when he had turned up the previous night. Thacker sitting with Grint at a shadowed table in the back corner with two serious looking men standing close by, hands on the hilts of their swords.

Rawk made his way through the crowd.

"How goes it?"

"Thacker. It still goes, which is better than it is for a lot of people."

Thacker nodded.

"And how is our war going?" Rawk sat down when he was offered a chair.

Grint grunted and Thacker sighed. "It could be better. Weaver seems to be happy to throw mercenaries at us all day long— it's just money, after all. But he doesn't seem to realize that if this keeps going there won't be any people left in the city."

Rawk grunted. "Win or lose, I don't think there will be anyone left south of the river. If Weaver wins and *you* somehow manage to make it out of this alive will you stay? Will all the thousands of dwarves who are being cheated stay after this? It will only get worse for them. Weaver will lose either way— Katamood will never be the same."

"Well, I don't know how much longer we can hang on, Rawk. Even with the bridges gone..."

"You blew up all of them?"

Thacker shook his head. "There's one left and it is rigged to blow."

Rawk shook his head. "I don't think Weaver will find many volunteers to lead *that* charge."

Grint sat back in his chair. "That's what everyone else is thinking as well. So we find ourselves in a bit of a stalemate."

"So then, we all just sit around here pretending the other side of the river doesn't exist?"

"We all know Weaver won't do that. If we let him sit he will eventually come up with the idea of flanking us, if he hasn't already. He would be a fool to keep throwing men at us over the river."

Rawk said what they were all thinking. What most people south of the river were thinking. "Surrender?"

Grint threw down his pencil. "That's the same as losing. Like you say, who would stay here if Weaver wins?"

There was a moment of silence and Thacker gestured towards the door. "You've got a visitor, Rawk."

Rawk turned and saw Celeste standing in the doorway. "Me? She'll want to see Grint." She wasn't moving, silhouetted against the light.

Celeste hurried through the crowd and came to a halt by the table. She glanced at Grint, then Rawk. "It is good to see you are well. Both of you." And she looked at Thacker. "All of you."

Thacker grunted. "I stubbed my toe on my desk this morning. That's about the most danger I've been in all day."

Rawk wasn't sure that Grint had been close to any action either. "Your desk looks really heavy, Thacker," he pointed out. "That would hurt."

"Oh, it did."

Celeste was looking at her own toes. "I hear the fighting was terrible this morning." The bruise on her cheek was a livid, purple patch.

Rawk nodded and took a deep breath. "Yes. Weaver just keeps sending men against us. Thankfully he hasn't worked out how to send them in large groups yet.

When he does..." Rawk shrugged then remembered his manners. He rose and gestured Celeste to the seat.

"No, thank you—"

There was a commotion by the door and Rawk dragged his eyes away from Celeste to look. Red Raven was standing there, silhouetted like she had been but not looking nearly as good. He was sweating and breathing hard, as he looked around the room. He spotted Rawk and gathered himself, before hurrying through the now silent crowd.

"Thacker. Rawk." He nodded. "Weaver wishes to talk to you."

Rawk narrowed his eyes. "Talk to who?"

"He won't want to talk to me," Thacker said. "He wouldn't lower himself to talk to me as if I was in charge."

Raven nodded.

"Well, you're coming though," Rawk said. "You *are* in charge, so you can make any decisions."

"Gannon's in charge." Thacker grunted. "Very well, if I must."

"Come on then."

Out of habit, Rawk checked he had everything. Sword. Utility belt with his dagger, snacks, and his cutlery. And his spectacles. Maybe one time he'd find a way to win the war in one of the pouches as well. "Right." He sighed and headed for the door.

"Rawk."

He turned and looked back at Celeste.

"Be careful. Don't try to be a hero."

He nodded and started to turn. But he stopped for a moment before hurrying back to her. He cleared his throat and looked around. Everyone was watching him. "You be careful too. You should go back up to Caldera."

"If the fight reaches even this far then all is lost."

"I know. But you should go." He gave her hand a squeeze. When he looked around the room this time he discovered that nobody was watching him now. They were all busy with drink or reports or conversation.

When Celeste went to say something, to argue again, he leaned in and kissed her on her uninjured cheek. "I need you to go. Just in case."

She stared at him for a moment, eyes wide, then smiled slightly. "I will go," she said.

Rawk turned and hurried to the door. He glanced back once and saw her, hand on her cheek, watching him go.

Outside, Rawk started down the hill without looking around. His heart was racing. He couldn't think. He licked his lips, tasting Celeste's skin, feeling her warmth. Before he'd gone two steps, Thacker called to him, breaking the spell, motioning towards a row of waiting goat cabs. Rawk climbed into the seat of the nearest and they started down the hill.

The edge of the river was crowded with warriors. Most were just normal men and women— bakers and cobblers and merchants and a hundred other types— but they were warriors nonetheless. It was in their eyes. In the way they stood. In the way they spoke. They shuffled aside as best they could in the crush to let the cabs through.

A rumble followed Rawk along, growing to a cheer as he neared the water. Rawk was glad they didn't have any walnuts.

The goats finally came to a halt near a hay wain that had been turned on its side as a barricade just a few yards from the river. Rawk hopped down into the shade and was joined a moment later by Thacker and Red Raven.

"So I'm just shouting from here?"

Raven shrugged. "He's on the northern stub of the bridge."

Rawk rolled his eyes. "Of course he is." His bald head was sweating. His arm itched under the bandage.

"What do you mean?"

"That's nice and dramatic, isn't it? Is he wearing a cloak?"

Raven glanced at Thacker. "Perhaps. I didn't really take any notice."

"I imagine he's brought some men with him to wave big fans so the cloak billows around him." Rawk loosened his shoulders and his neck.

"There is some breeze today."

"Come on then."

The three of them, plus two more warriors, headed for the tail of Dragon Bridge and started to climb towards the crest. Twenty yards up, the bridge ended in a ragged stump where the dwarves had demolished it. Rawk stopped near the edge. Weaver was thirty yards away, cloak billowing.

"Hello, Rawk."

"Hello, Weaver. Haven't you got some gold to count, or puppies to torture, or something?"

"I want this to end, Rawk."

"So you're surrendering?" He clapped his hands together. "Excellent."

Rawk saw Weaver's mouth twitch.

"This went better than expected."

"Do you take anything seriously?"

"Seriously? You want me to take this seriously? All right then. If you want this to end, and you aren't here to surrender, then offer your terms."

Weaver didn't respond.

"That's what I thought. Even *you* know your terms are ridiculous."

Still, the prince said nothing.

"Come on, Weaver," Rawk bellowed. "Name your terms. You want me and the leaders to turn ourselves in? And everyone else should back to work as if nothing happened? As if you haven't tried sent mercenaries into their homes. As if you haven't destroyed their businesses. As if you haven't tried to take everything from them in a petty fit of rage."

Taking a deep breath, he thought of Maris, killed by exots coming through Weaver's portals. He hadn't actually loved her, which made her murder even worse. She just died because Weaver could not control his rage. His voice dropped to almost a whisper. "In some cases you have taken everything, Weaver. But here you are, asking for more.

"Now, name your price, so I can tell you where to shove it and we can get back to the fighting."

"I just want you, Rawk. As ever. As always."

Rawk shook his head. "Even if I went over there, Weaver, with flowers in my hair and a smile on my face, you still wouldn't have me, and you know it."

Weaver glared for a moment. "It has come to this, has it?"

"I don't know, has it? This is all about you, Weaver. You can stop this. We don't want to fight, but we cannot surrender. This ends when you leave Katamood, or when you die."

"Just remember, you called this down upon everyone, Rawk. This is on *your* head." He started to turn away, but stopped. The prince smiled at Rawk. "I thought you were in love with Maris. And I thought you were in love with Sylvia. I was wrong. I got the wrong women, didn't I? But not this time. This time I got the right one." His smiled broadened. "So that makes two out of four. That isn't too bad, really."

He turned away, cloak swirling dramatically, and called to some of his followers.

Rawk's heart was beating wildly. He stared after Weaver, unwilling to believe what he had heard. Then he turned and ran down the bridge.

"Dragons!" someone shouted.

"DRAGONS."

Rawk slowed and turned back. He walked backwards through the crowd, eyes scanning the sky. There were dragons rising from the palace. A dozen of them. Each was at least twenty yards long and looked as fierce as a cornered cassaluk. They were bright colors— red and green and blue and gold— and each had a rider on its back.

"Take cover."

The creatures raced southwards, skimming over the tops of the buildings, screeching a chorus that set Rawk's nerves on edge as he pushed his way through the square. He didn't want to start a stampede but he wanted to run. He didn't want to escape the dragons, he wanted to return to the *Burning Tree* as quickly as he could, before it was too late, if it wasn't already.

But the dragons kept coming, crossing above the river, and a hundred arrows leaped into flight to meet them. Rawk stopped to watch and saw most of the shafts bounce harmlessly away from the thick, scaled hides. A second volley had the same effect.

Then they were over land again and the dragons breathed long gouts of liquid flame into the retreating militia.

Rawk saw a woman batting at her burning dress, but the flames clung to her hands and she was screaming before he could get to her. She rolled about on the ground, but all that did was set the cobblestones on fire as well.

Red Raven dragged Rawk away before he could go to help. Others did what they could, but her screams followed them away from the docks and in amongst the streets.

They stopped to look back and saw the dragons coming around again.

"I must go to the *Tree*," Rawk said, but he didn't mean it. No matter how much he wanted to go, he would not leave this battle to the militia.

Raven didn't say anything.

"In here." Rawk said after a moment. He led the way into an old stone building. Inside was a bakery but Rawk broke the door in the back and thumped his way painfully up to the second floor, and from there to the third. He found a bedroom with a window that looked to the north.

Outside, buildings were already starting to smolder. The tree near the edge of the square was blazing, sending out crackling flames that leapt towards barricades.

Across the other side of the river, a hundred men emerged from one of the streets. They carried between them a long platform with struts on the bottom and six legs sticking up n the air .

"What is *that*?" Raven asked.

But it became obvious soon enough. The end closest to the water was quickly chained to two stone blocks, the other end fitted into some type of contraption that...

There was a hiss and clang and the end of the platform rose up into the air, teetered at the perpendicular for a moment, then fell over the river, hitting the water with a great splash and the wharves with a crash and a storm of dust.

Rawk looked at Raven. "I think we'd better talk to Thacker about dwarves who aren't where they're supposed to be."

Raven nodded but was still looking out the window. "Perhaps some other time. At the moment, we have more pressing concerns."

Mercenaries were already streaming over the newly made bridge. It flexed and wobbled but held their weight. And with the attention of the few remaining defenders captured, more men were approaching the far side of the river with boats and rafts to add to the ones already afloat.

Raven leaned out the window and looked down. Then he sprang through the opening and was gone.

Rawk look out as well and saw the elf leaping down to the ground from the roof of a ground floor porch.

"Is he crazy?" *No, he's an elf.* Ignoring his knee, Rawk took the stairs two at a time and raced across the square. Militia were already defending the end of the new bridge and holding their own for the moment, keeping the enemy bottled up on the wobbling planks. But if too many of the boats made if across...

He stopped by the edge of the river and stared. There were already a hundred boats making the crossing. Some of them only had one man on board, others had ten or twelve, all with weapons ready.

"Great Path," Rawk said. This was it then. Weaver had finally decided that he wasn't going to get what he wanted. And if Weaver wasn't going to get it, then nobody was.

Rawk tried not to think of what might be happening at the *Burning Tree*. Who had stayed behind?

Taking a deep breath, he looked at the men and women waiting around him. "Those men don't fight for their family," he shouted. "They don't fight for their homes and their shops. They don't fight for what is right. They fight for money, and sometimes, today, money is not enough."

The militia cheered, brandishing their weapons. Rawk would have been a lot more confident if those weapons had all been swords, or maces and flails. There were far too many rakes and hoes and staves for his liking. And for a moment, he wondered if he should send them on their way. But the ones who would leave had already done so— these people would just be disheartened by such a suggestion.

He swallowed and took a deep breath as the first boats reached the bottom of the wall below him. "Don't let them reach the top," he said. "Let the river do the rest."

Rawk kicked the first man in the face and nearly had his leg chopped off at the ankle by the second. He stumbled away, panting, sweating, and was pushed back towards the action by the crowd waiting around him. He needed more room. All the front line did. But even if such a thing could be created in the surging mass, there was too much noise for the order to be heard. So Rawk concentrated on stabbing and thrusting and tried not to get tangled with those beside him.

A dragon screeched, and Rawk looked up, feeling the sound twisting amongst his nerves. The creature spat and twenty yards away a handful of people burst into flames. There were militia and mercenaries alike and they suddenly had no thought for the battle at all. Some of them jumped into the water but the screams kept going.

Killing another man, Rawk sent him tumbling into the water as well, creating an avalanche of mercenaries that left him on his own for a moment. Overhead... He tried to keep his thoughts on something he could control but he hunched his shoulders, as if that might save him from the fire, as if that was really all that much worse than a slow death with a knife wound in his stomach. To his left, away from the bridge, he saw a tight cluster of men collapse, almost as one, as they were pounded with arrows from a barge in the middle of the river. And half a dozen mercenaries surged up the wall and into the breach.

Rawk was too far away. He watched, knowing that the first few seconds would make or break everything. And the mercenaries pushed the locals back, edging away from the water. Soon they'd made enough room for another boatload of men to get their feet on dry land. And that was it. It was all over.

"Don't be a hero," Rawk muttered, thinking of Celeste and what Weaver's men might be doing to her. He couldn't help her now, so he charged towards the enemy he could reach. He called for archers, but there were none. Or if there were, they didn't hear, or if they did they were too busy doing something else. Men fell in behind him though, drawn along by his urgency. They arrived in time for the third boat, crashing into a group of mercenaries that had pushed through the militia line.

Rawk swung wildly, hoping the help wasn't far behind. They were taking their time. He killed two men, or good enough, running one through and sending the other head first over the wall and onto a boat. There was a sickening thud and a loud crack. It wasn't immediately obvious if it was the boat or the man that made the latter noise.

Taking the chance to look around in the spare moment, Rawk discovered that he fighting with just a few locals. The rest were dead or dying, or had been forced further from the river. Mercenaries were coming up the wall by the boatload now, all the way to the makeshift bridge and almost to the edge of the square in the other direction. Rawk swallowed. It wouldn't be long. They would be over run soon. More boats were on the river, ferrying men across in ever increasing number. There were already more than enough to win the battle, but more were lining up on the far side, ready to launch their boats.

"To me," Rawk called, dragging his attention back to his more immediate surroundings. He couldn't do anything about the men in the boats. All he could do was concentrate on those within reach of his sword. And that would be more than enough in a moment.

"Hello, Rawk."

Rawk blinked in surprise. "Fabi! What are you doing here?"

Fabi looked a bit confused. "Fighting."

"I thought, a long time ago, I told you to find another line of work."

"You did. This is just a hobby; I'm not getting paid."

"Well, I have the feeling you are going to enjoy today then."

The big man looked out at the river and smiled sadly. "I imagine you're right."

"Come on." Rawk looked at the militia gathering around him. Makeshift soldiers, many of them with makeshift weapons. "Give them hell."

And they charged towards the largest knot of mercenaries who had gathered not far away to organize themselves as quickly as they could.

By the time Rawk reached the first man another dozen had joined the group. Two died almost instantly, and another handful took their place. Rawk shouted and swung his sword. And he knew that for every man he killed, at least three or four of his own followers met a similar fate.

It wouldn't be long.

There was a slight reprieve when the next wave to come over the wall suddenly caught fire. But by the time the shadow of the dragon had passed the next surge had scrambled up to join the fight.

A dwarf on Rawk's left died with a dagger in his chest. On the other side a woman stumbled away from a mace strike only to be impaled on a pike. And another died and another. They shouldn't be fighting. They should have all left... He tried not to think about it. He tried not to think.

"Look to the river. Look to the river."

Rawk didn't know who was calling, whether it was friend or foe, but it didn't really matter. He turned to look at the river again, expecting to see a whole flotilla of mercenaries making their way across. There *were* a lot more boats than before, hundreds of them, but they seemed to be making their way *down* the river, not across. And in the first one was a man in a fluttering butterfly cloak and...

Rawk smiled. Opok stood in the back of the boat. The old duen raised a huge bow and fired an arrow as long as a javelin into a crowded boat. One mercenary died with the arrow in his chest and he took another three into the water with him. A man fell from the sky, an arrow in his chest, and knocked a hole right through the bottom of a skiff. Overhead, his uncontrolled dragon attacked on of its fellows and others scattered

A hundred more huge arrows were loosed, some towards the sky, others towards the river, as the duen turned towards the southern shore. They cut a swath through the enemy, using maces when they came close enough. The fear they created seemed almost as deadly.

Half the boats reached the shore and duen started leaping up onto solid ground. And the mercenaries now had an enemy at their backs, a huge enemy who fought with a cool, silent ferocity that was unnerving.

It took only a matter of minutes for the enemy to break and run, though where they thought they were going to go when everyone south of the river was totally against them was anyone's guess.

Rawk looked around. "Fabi, I have to..."

Fabi was lying on the ground not far away, blood slowly leaking from a wound in his chest. Rawk rushed to the other man's side.

"No, no, no." He slid to a halt and tried to pick Fabi up but he was too big and couldn't do anything to assist with the movement. Rawk cradled the other man's head in his lap.

"Rawk." It was a whisper. Such a soft sound should not have come from such a big man.

"Yes, Fabi. I'm here."

"We've got things under control here. I've got them sorted out."

Rawk nodded.

"Go and find her. Make sure she's all right. Path be with you."

Rawk turned and found Opok walking closer. Zid was by his side, the soldier carrying his helm under his arm. "Can you help him, Opok? I have to go..."

The duen nodded somberly and quickened his pace.

"I'll talk to you soon." And he gently laid Fabi down. "Don't be a hero." He winced when the other man coughed a spray of blood onto his shirt, and rose quickly to his feet. A moment later he was racing through the remains of the battle. His knee throbbed with every step, but he paid it no heed. He would have run all the way back up the mountain, but a dwarf blocked the way with his goats and buggy.

"Hop in, Rawk. It will be quicker."

Rawk recognized Harris. He hesitated for a moment, then threw himself into the passenger seat.

The dwarf got the goats moving, pushing them as hard as he could.

The goat ran all the way to the *Burning Tree*.

There were dead and injured people lying on the cobbled street outside the inn. Some were soldiers or militia, armed in one way or another. Gunnar was there, staring silently at the sky, blood dribbling from his ear. But there was an old lady as well, and a girl with pigtails and a green dress. Rawk searched the faces but could not see Celeste. He ran in side and looked as well. Inside was worse than outside. A small area had been cleared to look after the wounded. Tables and chairs had been shoved quickly into the back corner where people were just starting to work at moving them even further. Nobody had gotten around to doing anything with the obviously dead yet.

Rawk could not see her there, either. He had a quick look out through the backdoor, then raced back out onto the street. He saw Sylvia, kneeling over a dwarf on the porch of the cobbler's shop next door.

"Where is she?" he asked her. "Where is Celeste?"

Sylvia looked up. She had a cut on her cheek and a haunted look in her eyes. "Were they looking for her? She left before they got here. She said she was going home."

Rawk nodded. The elf said something else, but he didn't hear. He was already running, heading towards the house Celeste shared with her grandmother.

But he was coming from a different direction. He wasn't sure where he was going and became lost in the maze of streets. He stopped in a narrow street, whitewashed walls towering above him, and looked around. For the first time, he noticed the people. The whole city seemed to be lost. People were fleeing. Some were carrying their entire lives on their backs— clothes and valuables and children. Rawk wasn't sure where they were going. He wasn't sure if they knew, though perhaps the three inns in West Port would doing a roaring trade tonight.

He stopped someone and asked, "Do you know where Celeste and Matilde live?" The woman didn't know. The man he asked next didn't either. Or the dwarf after that. He was ready to shout at the next person as his frustration grew, as his desperation grew. But nobody knew. He thought to ask if anyone knew where there was a weaving factory. And someone pointed him down a street.

"A hundred yards."

"Thank you," he shouted back over his shoulder as he ran, pushing past people. He was only vaguely aware of them struggling to stay on their feet, to keep their precariously packed lives balanced.

He found the factory and the small plain door that divided it from the shops. He almost knocked the door off its hinges as he charged through. He pounded up the stairs and down the hallway, right to the end. And he stopped. The last door, the one that led to Celeste's flat, was partly open. Rawk drew his sword. The rasp of the blade against the sheath sounded loud in the half-light. The only other sounds were coming from outside. It might well have been some other world. The creak of the door as he pushed it open sounded like the screech of a banshee.

There was a man lying on the floor, jaw smashed, blood dribbling from his mouth. Sitting beneath the window, dark coat making her hard to see in the shadows, breath rasping in her throat, was Matilde. When Rawk gasped, the old lady struggled to raise her head. Her hand clutched at the haft of her club, but she didn't have the strength to lift it.

"Leave her alone. Don't come near..."

"Matilde," Rawk said. "Mab." He dropped his sword and rushed to her side. "What happened?"

"Rawk? They took her."

"Yes, I know. I know that. I mean, what happened to you?"

But the front of her coat had come open as she lost the strength to hold it as well and it became all to clear what had happened. The blood staining her dress was thick and dark. And there was a lot of it.

"I'll get help. Wait here."

The old woman gave a wet cough of laughter. "I'm not going anywhere." She was barely audible. She barely had the strength to move her lips. "Too late for me. Celeste. Promise."

"Of course. I promise. I'll get her back. And Weaver will pay."

But Matilde didn't hear. The faint flutter of her breathing had stopped and her head fell forward once again.

"I'm going to break his neck, Matilde. But I'm going to do it gently, so he's alive for what I do next." He kissed the old lady's hand and laid it gently in her lap. Fighting back tears, he collected his sword and headed back the way he'd come. By the time he returned to the street his eyes were dry and his hand was aching on the hilt of *Kaj*.

He stalked back towards the river, moving against the tide of people. He was aware of them moving out of his way, but he hardly saw them. He made it all the way to the battleground beside the river. There were no warriors there now, just dead people and survivors. And looking at the stump of the bridge, pointing out towards Two Watch Hill and the palace on top like an accusing finger, he wondered why he had come all this way. He wondered where the last intact bridge actually was. He was in the midst of deciding weather to go and look, or to find himself a boat, when he heard someone call his name. Thacker was standing not far away with Opok, Zid, Red Raven and the leaders of the river defense.

"Rawk," the dwarf called again.

Rawk ignored him and headed for the river. At least until Opok moved to bar his way. He pulled up short, looking the duen in the eye. "Get out of my way, Opok."

"Prince Weaver be taken your wife?"

"She is not my wife. She's..." What was she? Rawk wasn't sure. How could he be? She was a fermi and a dwarf. A few weeks ago he would have avoided being seen in public with her. Now... "I have to find her."

Opok shook his head. "If Prince Weaver has taken her, then you cannot simply be marching up to his palace and ask."

"I was not intending to ask." Rawk tried to step past Opok, but the duen moved to block his way again.

"I cannot let you go."

"Do you think you can stop me, old man?"

"Yes."

He said it with such calm certainty that it made Rawk pause. He had killed duen, but none of them had known magic. And, magic or not, Opok probably had more cunning than all of the others put together. Rawk crouched where he was, surrounded by a snowdrift of bodies, and put his head in his hands.

"Today's fighting seems to be over— the men stopped trying to cross the river and the dragons have gone for now— so let us be going with Thacker and talk of what can be done."

$$-O-$$

Rawk dully watched Opok squeeze in through the door of the meeting room. The duen stood uncomfortably, shoulders hunched, working out what to do next. Eventually he moved to the side of the room, freeing up the doorway so others could enter. Zid came in, calm and in control, and went to stand by the window. More men and women entered, bloodied and weary. They had just won a major battle, but they looked beaten.

Red Raven strode in the door last. "I don't know who you are or what your story is," he said to Opok, "but you turned up just in time."

"If we had turned up sooner..." Opok responded. He sighed and crouched down so he didn't have to stoop beneath the ceiling. "There was much debate amongst our council. Many hours of arguing." He looked towards Zid, who was sitting alone near the window. "If Zid had not declared his intention to return, with or without us, we may still have be arguing."

"Well, I'm glad he did," Thacker said. "Another five minutes and it would have been all over."

Rawk shook his head. They had been too late. Fabi was dead and Celeste was gone. He looked at his hands as the others talked around him. He had never thought that Weaver... But the prince had said 'two out of four'. Maris, Sylvia, Celeste and... Lady Tapalar? Rawk knew that his secret love had been killed by General Ramaner, but had Weaver given the order all those years ago? Even then? Rawk clenched his fist, felt the wound in his arm pulling painfully under the bandage. His jaw was clenched.

"But what is to be happen next?" Opok asked.

Thacker rubbed at his face. A blue and white guild ribbon came away in his hand and he threw it down on the table. "Can you fight the dragons with magic?"

Opok glanced at Sylvia and shook his head. "I cannot. Even if I could be hitting one of the creatures with offensive magic while it was flying, which I could not, I am be doubting that my strongest spells would have any success."

Rawk saw blood on his bandage.

Thacker turned to look at Sylvia. "What about you? Can you do anything?"

She cleared her throat. "No. Not even twenty years ago. I explained to Rawk that using magic in battle is like fighting with a two-handed battle-ax and a helm that keeps slipping over your eyes; you cannot see and fight at the same time. Also, and Opok may be able to confirm this, it seems that the dragons also have some magic abilities, or some magical qualities at the very least, that would allow them to counter or dodge sorcerous attacks."

Opok nodded. "I believe that to be true, though like Silver Lark, I am uncertain."

"But you shot some of the riders," Thacker said.

"Now they knowing what we can do, I doubt they be flying low enough to hit in future."

"So how do we continue this fight then?" Rake asked. "We can't sit on this side of the river all day waiting for them to come and get us. And we don't have the numbers to stage a major assault."

Rawk surged to his feet and several people close to him reared back. "We can't give up." He almost shouted.

"I wasn't suggesting that," Rake said.

"It sounded like it."

"I am sorry I could not save your friend, Rawk," Opok said. Everyone suddenly looked uncomfortable. "The world turns on moments. In some moments it be the rush into action that saves us. In others it be the stopping to think."

"We will not save Celeste by sitting around here talking."

Grint grunted. "And we will not save her by dying as we try to cross the river. We need more than hope or desire here, Rawk."

"What about those pistol things?" Rawk asked spinning about to find Sylvia in the crowd.

Sylvia gasped.

Thacker's eyes narrowed. "What pistol thing? I don't know what you're talking about."

Rawk looked at Sylvia. "Was it supposed to be a secret? I mean a secret from everyone, not just me?"

Sylvia shrugged. "Kristun was not certain of the pistol's effectiveness."

"Kristun has a weapon?" Thacker asked. "Go and get him, Rake. He's in the Garner Room working with some engineers."

The inventor came back with Rake a couple of minutes later.

"What's this pistol Rawk's talking about?"

Kristun tugged at his nose with thick fingers. "Well, they're not ready, are they. There's only about five currently in existence and there's still a lot of work ta do on them."

"It seemed to work fine to me," Rawk said. "Sylvia killed someone with it."

Kristun nodded. "They have a tendency ta blow up if you aren't careful."

"And you let Sylvia have one?"

The dwarf looked a bit embarrassed about that. "Yes, well... She assured me she would only use it if there was no other options. And the charge cartridges I gave ta her were really only half full. It wouldn't do much harm at a range of more than fifteen yards.

"Enough," Thacker said. "Do you mind telling the rest of us what in the Great Path's name you are talking about."

Kristun glanced at Sylvia and sighed. "I've been working on something. A weapon. I call it a pistol."

"So I gathered. And it can kill at fifteen yards?"

"The range is better than that, if you want ta risk losing your hand. Or your face."

Thacker didn't say anything. But the look on his face was clearly encouraging elaboration, and quickly.

"When they do exploding at the canal, they make sure nobody is standing anywhere close."

"Of course. So they don't get hit by flying stone or something."

"Right. People could die from stuff like that."

Thacker nodded slowly, as if realizing the implications of that thought.

"So I wondered if I could do a smaller explosion and direct the blast, and the shrapnel, very precisely."

"And you did?"

"Yes. Well, most of the time."

"And you've used this weapon, Sylvia?"

"Yes," Sylvia confirmed. "Just the once. Balen was only five yards away, at most."

"Bows are more useful," Kristun said. "It takes me about thirty seconds ta load a pistol. I could get quicker with practice, I assume, but we don't really have the time. And I wouldn't be confident of hitting anything that was more than about ten or fifteen yards away anyway."

"The dragons have got longer range than that."

Kristun shrugged.

"Well, go and make some more of the things anyway. Get some help. All the help you need."

Kristun nodded and hurried from the room but Rawk shook his head. How many of the weapons could they make? How many would work without killing the person using it? It was useless. Celeste needed help sooner than that. "Forget the war."

Everyone turned to look at him. Opok grunted, obviously confused.

"We can't win the war. Weaver has more men and most of them are experienced. We've got coopers and bakers. Even if we could win, it could take weeks of fighting and Celeste doesn't have that long."

The conversation had gone full circle. "We cannot give up," Red Raven said.

"I know that. But, like we told Weaver, this ends when he leaves Katamood or when he dies."

"He isn't going to leave," Grint said.

"Exactly. So I'll go up to the palace and kill him."

"Just like that?" Sylvia asked. "It sounds like a fine plan."

"It isn't a plan, and you know it. It's an idea." Rawk shrugged. "Getting across the river is the biggest problem.

After that, I'm sure I can find my way up the hill without being seen."

"And, what, you stand out the front and challenge him to a duel?"

Rawk winced. That would be a lovely cliché, the cliché to end all clichés, if he could conjure it. But Weaver had already admitted he was no match for Rawk in a fight. He was unlikely to strap on his sword and come outside. "Well..."

"He might come out if you insulted him," someone suggested. "He's that kind of man."

"He is," Thacker agreed, "but I doubt even he can be goaded that far."

Rawk sat back. "It's a shame he didn't get those secret tunnels he's always talking about."

"He wanted secret tunnels?" Thacker suddenly stood up and went quickly to the door. He poked his head out, said something to the guard outside, then went back to his seat. "He wouldn't have found a dwarf who would build them for him anyway."

"Why not?"

"People who build secret tunnels for other people normally end up dead." He sat back and gave a satisfied smile. "We actually have something better than one of Weaver's secret tunnels though."

"We do?"

"Yes. I should have thought of it before."

"Well?"

"We have tunnels that he doesn't know about." A guard came through the door and Thacker was up out of his chair again. He took a big sheet of paper from the dwarf and dramatically rolled it out on the table. The effect was ruined when it instantly rolled back up again and the momentum almost carried it right off the end of the table. But Red Raven rolled it out again and people held down the corners. Thacker continued, face flushed slightly. "Well, Weaver would know about them if he gave it some thought, but it's unlikely that he will." He pointed at a red line that ran right to the keep at the center of the palace.

"Soooo, what do we have, exactly?"

"We have the sewers."

"The sewers? That sounds like a crappy tunnel to me." Rawk waited for the laughter, but it didn't come. He was actually a bit relieved.

"We can get all the way there without him knowing." Thacker looked down at the plan. "Probably."

"Unless he's thought of them. Or one of his men has thought of them."

"Exactly. But *I* didn't even think of the sewers."

"You want me to go in through the sewers?"

"I thought we'd established that already. But not just you. That's ridiculous. A small band of twenty or so."

"No, I'll go alone."

Red Raven shook his head. "*That* is ridiculous. We know you want to get Celeste back but all it would take is for a couple of guards to see you..."

"Ten people then," Rawk said.

"We can talk about it later. The sewer hatch there brings you up in the corner of the keep. It could be blocked by something but we won't know until we get there."

"It's going to smell," Rawk said.

"Yes it is."

"How long will we be in there?"

Thacker looked at the plan. "There's an access point here," he said, pointing to a place close to the palace wall. "But unless we take time to chase the guards off the wall we'll be spotted for sure. The next access is down here." He calculated. "It will be about two hundred yards all up, I would think."

"Two hundred yards?"

"Yes."

"In the pipe where the shit goes."

"Yes."

"It's going to smell."

"Still yes."

Rawk sighed. "Can we go tonight?"

Red Raven shook his head. "You know we can't, Rawk."

"Do I?"

"Getting across the river is the hardest part, remember?"

"Oh. Right."

Gannon pushed up beside the table and examined the area of the map around the river. "So, only one bridge remains?"

"Yes."

"We attack over the bridge as a diversion. Rawk and his party can cross via boats further upstream."

"That's potentially a lot of lives lost just for a diversion," Sylvia noted.

"Yes, but there will be people watching the river. We need to get their attention."

"We don't know if Celeste has even that long," Rawk pointed out.

Grint grunted. "If she is not already dead she will live that long at least."

"Tomorrow morning, then." It seemed a lifetime away, and might well be. Celeste's lifetime.

Thacker nodded. "Early. And we have a lot to do before then."

They were still talking themselves in circles when Rawk left, trying to find the one thing that would turn the battle in their favor. Rawk didn't think there was anything to find. He would cross the river while an 'army' created a distraction and he would leave them to their fate while he went to find his old friend and kill him. Then it would all be over.

Outside the administration building, he stopped on the top step and looked out at the city. There were not many people about. Most of them were down by the river— stopping Weaver's mercenaries from crossing, or searching the streets for those that had yet to be rooted out— or holed up in their homes, waiting for their loved ones to return.

"I've been waiting for you."

Rawk's hand went to the hilt of *Kaj* but a moment later he recognized the voice. "Hello, Yardi." He turned saw her sitting on a bench further along the porch. "I'm surprised you aren't off finding a way to make money from this fight."

She shrugged. "I already know how to do that. I just wasn't sure you be appreciating some of the methods."

"Have you eaten?"

They walked down the street together. Not all of the street lamps had been lit, so they spent a lot of time in the dark, moving with a thin stream of people. They stopped at tavern where the tables had spilled out onto the street. Most were empty, despite Caldera being overflowing with refugees, but Sylvia was sitting at one table with Grint, Juskin, Clinker, Biki and Suki. The elf waved him over.

"I didn't see you leave the meeting," Rawk said as he sat down.

"I knew nothing of planning battle when I was fighting them in my youth. I know even less now."

Rawk had to agree. "Well, they're still going up there so I'm not sure that they know a lot either."

Sylvia had a small smile. "Men like Gannon and Red Raven do, thankfully. And hopefully we do not have to survive much longer. If you are successful in the morning..."

Rawk didn't want to think about that. "Are you all eating?"

But Sylvia couldn't let the talk of the fighting go. "How do you stand the waiting?"

"Firstly, you don't think about the waiting. You don't talk about the waiting."

"Sorry."

He shrugged. "Practice. But that doesn't even help all the time. It's much easier when it isn't personal, apparently. Or maybe it's much easier when you are younger."

Grint shifted in his chair. "You will get her back, won't you?" It looked like the dwarf had aged a decade in the last few days. Or perhaps it was just since the afternoon.

"I'll get her back."

"I know you will." But he didn't sound convinced. Maybe that was the way of dwarves in Katamood, always thinking the world was against you.

Rawk wasn't sure either. It seemed a long way up to the palace.

"She will be all right, Grint." Biki laid a hand on Grint's arm and he nodded.

Rawk cleared his throat and changed the subject. It wasn't very subtle. "I hope you're looking after Demon, Clinker."

The lad smiled and folded back the flap on his satchel. The kitten poked its head out into the light and looked around. When it saw Rawk, it climbed out, padded across the table and nuzzled against his hand.

"He's never done that before," Clinker said. "He doesn't like people much."

"Some animals are like that." Rawk petted Demon's head and scratched behind his ears. "But when he does make a friend, he will be the most loyal animal you have ever seen because he knows how rare real friends are. And he will do anything for you."

"Really?"

"Well, he might make some mistakes because he's just a cat and sometimes might not understand how those things are supposed to work, but he'll try his best." He turned to look at Sylvia and she had another smile for him. She touched his arm for a moment, then took a sip of her spiced wine. And Rawk looked at the others. But they weren't just his friends. They were his family. Even Juskin, with his spectacles and crazy red hair. Two people were missing though. He didn't know where Travis was and wasn't sure what he was thinking any more. And Celeste...

Grint obviously got the allusion because he shifted uncomfortably in his seat and looked intently at an interesting building across the street.

When the silence stretched on, Rawk clapped his hands together. "What are we all eating?"

"They have roast beef here, I think," Biki said. "I will go and get us some."

"I'll pay." Rawk started fishing for some money, then just handed the dwife his entire purse.

Grint went with her and the two of them came back a couple of minutes later with two trays barely big enough to contain all the plates of roast beef and vegetables. Rawk pulled his cutlery from the pouch on his belt, polished the knife and then set to.

"Here's your purse."

"Thank you." He looked around the table and cleared his throat. "If this doesn't go well," he said, concentrating on his meal again, "Yardi may have to leave Katamood. But, if you ever need anything, go and see her. I'm not sure what will be left if... But there should be enough."

Grint grunted. "No offense, Yardi, but I'd like to keep dealing with Rawk."

Rawk concentrated on his roast beef with much more intensity than was necessary, cutting the meat with his bone handled knife as if it was the most important task in the world.

Satyrday

IT TOOK A MOMENT FOR RAWK TO PUSH ASIDE THE DREAM, though he didn't want to. Bree had been there walking amidst a menagerie of exots, petting them and feeding them treats. It had been a nice dream, though he wondered if it would have turned violent if he had not woken when he did. Would Ramaner or Weaver have been in the next cages? He thought it ironic that with all the dangerous creatures in the world, men always seemed to outdo them all. But lying in the dark he clung to her memory as long as he dared, and listened to the sound of all the warriors sleeping around him. Being a great Hero and all, he probably could have gotten himself a private room the night before but it hadn't felt right. A lot of these men, or men like them, would be attacking a superior force over the bridge very soon, just to get him across the river. The least he could do was keep them company for a few hours.

The sounds of the city came to him through the window, and he could almost pretend that everything was back to normal. The tram was rattling along the tracks and a blacksmith was battering away at something. But the former was probably overloaded with soldiers and the latter was probably making a weapon of some kind, working up until the last minute. Once again, just to get him across the river.

There was no signal, nothing in the outside world seemed to change, but the men started to wake. The sound of breathing in the room changed, a shifting of the wind. The men were silent at first but, as more woke, soft conversations started to creep about the room like early morning mist.

Rawk stayed where he was for a few more minutes, letting the peace settle on him as if he might be able to carry it with him for the rest of the day. Eventually, he climbed to his feet, shook his knee to unlock it as he collected his sword and belt from the floor, and hobbled through the flotilla of sleeping-pallets. He nodded to men as he passed. He clasped hands with some, touched some on the shoulder. He didn't know what to say, so he didn't say anything at all. He looked at faces and wondered who would not be around by the time noon come around. Possibly, many of them wouldn't even make it 'til dawn. In the hallway, a rushing dwarf nearly knocked him over and they apologized in unison, the sound like a thunderclap in the stillness. The dwarf didn't slow but Rawk stayed where he was, rubbing at his face as if he could scrub away the last few weeks so he could sit in the *Mason's Hammer* and tell Waydin he wasn't interested in killing a wolden wolf. But it wouldn't matter. Weaver was already in love, and everything that came after was inevitable, sooner or later.

"Rawk!"

Rawk jumped and turned to find Thacker with a small group of advisors heading his way.

"How long?"

Thacker stopped and took a deep breath. "Our army is already starting to gather amongst the buildings down near the river. It will probably be an hour before we are ready."

"And what is the time now?"

"Four hours past midnight."

Four in the morning was too early. Five would be too early as well. "In Frenable they wouldn't start a battle before midmorning. This time of day is uncivilized."

"War is uncivilized, Rawk." Thacker said. He looked around at his advisors as if he'd forgotten something. "There has been a slight change of plans."

"Oh."

"They're likely to have a lot of sentries watching the river. We can't guarantee you could get across without being spotted and if you're spotted then you will probably die."

"Yes, thank you."

"So you will cross the bridge with the diversion."

"I will? I'm not sure I'll be able to slip through the battle lines without being spotted either."

"Not far over the bridge, there's an access point for the sewers. So you and your team can climb in there."

Rawk pursed his lips. "You want us to go all the way up the hill in the poo pipes?"

"Of course not. You can just go a hundred yards or so then come up into the streets again."

"That's all right then. I think. So who else is coming?"

Thacker motioned back over his shoulder. They are gathering in the meeting room for breakfast. You might as well join them. We'll send someone to collect you all soon enough.

In the meeting room, a spread of food had been laid out on the main table. Four dwarf soldiers— Rake, Crisp, Heron and Poe— were standing together. Red Raven, bow by his side, and Frew, were sitting with a young man that Rawk recognized as a sorcerer. And Buzt, the big, dragon tattooed man from Zid's jentre was on his own in the corner with his sword and oilstone in his lap as if he had been sharpening his sword or was about to start. Rawk hoped he was finished, for he knew the sound would set his nerves on edge. And standing by the window, looking out over Caldera, was Sylvia. Rawk didn't feel like eating, but he took some cold chicken and some bread and went to stand by her side.

"Hello, Rawk."

"Hello, Sylvia. Why are you here?"

She turned to look at him and gave a small smile. "You and I started this battle together, Rawk, I intend to be there to help you finish it."

"But you can't—"

She pulled her pistol from her pocket. "I have this. And you never know, I may find a rapier to use as well, instead of the war hammer."

"Just make sure you come out alive."

"You are worried for my health? How far we have come."

"I'm not worried about you," Rawk said with a smile. "You have all of Clinker's money."

Sylvia smiled. "So you are worried about a dwarf then? I believe my point stands." She took a deep breath. "But I am sure the boy will do fine, come what may."

"Who's that?" Rawk gestured to the sorcerer with Frew.

Sylvia glanced in his direction. "That is Drace. He will do well enough as well, as long as he can hold his nerve."

As long as he can hold his nerve. Rawk knew the feeling. He went over and greeted the young man. If they were going to fight together, to die together, he should at least say hello. But after the greeting, Rawk didn't know what to say. He put the piece of chicken on his bread and ate mechanically. Outside the sound of the machineries of war were joined by the murmur of people as the city awoke from its restless slumber. "It is going to be a long day."

Drace nodded nervously.

It wasn't long before a dwarf poked his head around the door. Everyone looked up at him and he suddenly looked nervous. "There are cabs waiting for you down on the street," he said. "It's time."

Rawk nodded, as if the statement had been just for him. Rake handed him a pack. "What's this?"

"Food. Water. A map of the palace."

"Right." Rawk had a look inside then slung the pack over his shoulder. He checked that he had everything else. Cutlery in the pouch on his belt. Jerky for snacks. His dagger. Spectacles. *Kaj* sheathed at his side. Old habits that, for a moment, made it seem like it was just another day. Not a day when he was planning to kill one of his oldest friends even if that friendship had been in question for some time.

–O–

The goats pulled the cabs down through the city and every window seemed to hold a candle to light the way. People watched from the soft light and Rawk could feel the weight of all the expectations descending on him the further they went towards the river. They clattered over a bridge across the canal and it seemed to Rawk that the machines down in the depths were silent for the first time in months, though he knew they stopped every night. And beyond, the streets were lined with people. At first it was civilians, watching silently. Rawk didn't know whether to wave or stare straight ahead. And the whole time he imagined how the goat would react to a storm of walnuts. But there were no nuts and no ribbons and no cheering and soon the civilians gave way to militia— civilians with weapons. Men and women who would soon be charging across the bridge just so Rawk could sneak along in their wake with his smaller army.

He remembered what Keegan had said after the confrontation between the Heroes and the sorcerers. He turned to Frew and gestured out at the men and women crowding back against the building along the side of the street to let the goats past. "There's Keegan's army of heroes."

Frew looked around. He gave a small nod, more to himself than anyone else, and stayed silent.

The darkness and the silence hung heavy. All those people watching, with hardly a sound to touch the night. Thousands at parades and after battles had cheered Rawk, but this silence touched him more and sent a shiver down his spine.

A block from the water, the goats stopped and Rawk climbed to the ground. Thacker was waiting, surrounded by advisors as ever, though now they were all silent. It was too late now, the stones were cast.

Rawk gripped the dwarf's hand. "So, this is it?"

Thacker nodded. "I guess it is. I'll see you when you get back."

Rawk nodded, took a deep breath. And for the first time, he wondered if he would get back at all. He knew he could beat Weaver in a fair fight, but the odds of that situation arising were slim at best.

Thacker took a deep breath too. "Where's Kristun?"

The engineer appeared out of the crowd, pack on his back, pistol in his belt and another, with a longer barrel, in his hand. He also had a bow slung over his shoulder.

"How are they looking?"

"How do you think?" He gave the long pistol to Thacker. "They've had about an hour of training and are expected ta go into battle."

"What's that?" Rawk asked.

"It's a pistol."

"Well, yes, but..." Rawk looked at the weapon. "It doesn't look like Sylvia's," he said.

Kristun shook his head, looking as excited as a Hero with a new sword. "Longer arrows are more accurate. I didn't know if that would transfer ta the pistols anyway but I thought I'd give it go."

"And?"

"It's definitely better with the long barrel. I call this one a musket. I hit a five-inch target four times out of five at about thirty yards. That could improve with more practice, obviously. The range is, maybe, a sixty yards. Though that could improve too, I suppose, once we get things worked out properly."

"And now the militia have them as well?"

Kristun nodded. "Thirty pistols and ten muskets."

"Can they hit anything?"

The dwarf shrugged and scratched his cheek. "I reckon the noise will do as much as the lead pellets. We only need a couple of minutes ta get into the sewer."

"We?"

"You need *someone* along who knows what they're doing. Not with hand-ta-hand fighting, of course, but anything else that needs doing. Like at the Quod."

"You can use that bow?"

"I've never killed a man, but I've been working with bows, trying ta improve them, for a few years now. So we'll see, I suppose."

"Are you sure?"

"Of course."

Rawk gripped his hand but Thacker interrupted before he could say anything. "The other things are ready?"

Kristun nodded, tugging at his beard. "I think so." He looked up at the sky. "The wind was in our favor half an hour ago but now..."

"Someone is keeping an eye on it?"

"Of course." Kristun looked offended that things could be otherwise.

"And they know what they're doing?"

Kristun hesitated and Thacker raised his eyebrows. "If those things..."

Kristun nodded. "Luker should be able ta handle it."

Thacker took a deep breath. "Right, well let's get this war finished."

But he didn't move. He waited for Gannon to start moving towards the river. Rawk followed. He moved through the waiting militia and still there was no sound beyond the soft shuffling of their feet and the whisper of their breath. That would all change soon enough. In the stillness, a commotion coming along behind caught Rawk's attention. He stopped and was surprised to see Juskin painfully rushing to catch up.

"You really can't come, Juskin," Rawk said once the old man had caught his breath.

"No, no, no. I don't want to go, Rawk, heaven's no. I just... Good luck. Path go with you on this journey." The old man held up his two fingers. "Or something like that, I suppose."

"Well, this is a strange journey, to be sure," Rawk said, "and if the Great Path is around here somewhere, I shall be pleased enough for his company." *A journey?* he thought with a grunt. *Huh.*

He shook the old man's hand and once again wondered how he had happened along all these people so late in his life. Whether it was *too* late was yet to be seen.

Rawk was directed into an alley with his companions and told to wait. He got a shock when he saw a creature in the dim light and a lifetime of habit had his sword in his hand in a moment. But Opok stepped from the shadows, empty hands held before him.

"Don't be sneaking around on a day like today," Rawk said.

Zid stepped out in the half–light as well.

"I be sorry, Rawk."

"I'm just a bit jumpy and *Kaj* is the solution to most of my problems these days."

Opok narrowed his eyes. "*Kaj?* Your sword be named *Kaj?*"

"Yes, I named it after Atine's wolf thing." He held up the weapon so the duen could see it better.

Opok examined the weapon. "Do you be knowing what *Kaj* means?"

Rawk looked at the sword, twisting it so it caught the feeble predawn light. "Well, no."

Opok cleared his throat. "It be meaning *little princess.*"

"*Little princess?*" Rawk heard muffled laughter behind him. Keegen could barely contain himself. Red Raven and Sylvia were smiling and the dwarves suddenly thought there was something interesting in the sky. Rawk looked back at the sword. "*Little Princess?*" He gave a grunt. "Maybe I should have thought of that possibility before." But he smiled and laughed quietly himself. "I like it though. All theses warriors being killed by a little princess."

Gannon came back into the alley. "We're ready. We'll send you out when you need to go. Don't waste time when you get to the other side; we'll want to pull back as quickly as possible if there are any problems."

Rawk shook his head. *Any problems.* There were going to be problems.

He didn't hear the signal, when it came. He wasn't sure if there was one, or if the myriad of men and women who made up the militia simply decided that they'd had enough of the waiting. One way or the other, the great mass surged forward and after a few moments, someone signaled for Rawk and his team to insert themselves into the flow. Rawk didn't know who the woman was, or if she knew what she was doing, but he grabbed Sylvia's hand and stepped out of the alley. He hoped the others followed as they were carried along the street, bustled and bumped, trying to stay together.

They entered the intersection with the street that ran along beside the river and for a few seconds the pressure was relieved. Then more of the militia joined the main flow from other, smaller streets and the press was doubled. They kept going, up the slope of the bridge towards the crest.

There was a chorus of thumps from siege engines to the south and Rawk ducked instinctively as he heard the shot whistling over his head. He heard it hit to the north, a hailstorm shattering against the roads and buildings and men. People screamed, pummeled by the fist—sized stones. When his team reached the top of the crest, there was another thump, a volley from engines held in reserve, trying to catch them by surprise. The sound of pain and suffering increased. Then another sound filled the air and Rawk ducked again as a flight of arrows came from the enemy. The south returned fire, five volleys, one after the other, in quick succession.

From that vantage point at the top of the bridge, Rawk could see down to the far side of the river. Torches lit scenes of carnage but also showed thousands of more men waiting for the real fighting to begin. And up ahead, the front edge of the militia reached the end of the bridge and crashed against the mercenaries. The siege engines and arrows had softened the middle of the defense, so the line buckled.

There was a screech and Rawk looked up. A pair of dragons raced down from Two Watch Hill. As they reached the bridge they both let out a stream of the burning liquid, spraying it onto the militia that crowded the bridge. The fire went over Rawk's head, but not twenty yards behind him, people started to scream. Arrows and siege engines returned fire to little effect. More dragons were coming to join the fight. And coming to meet them from the south...

Rawk gaped and stared but the longer he looked the more confused he became. There were... things, floating out over the river. Silken bags with boxes hanging beneath were drifting with the breeze. He looked around for Kristun and shouted over the hubbub. "Are they yours?"

Kristun looked up and nodded. "Balloons. And they're working, so far. The most important bit..."

The dragons came in a bunch, lining up with the bridge, and the first one shot a blast of fire at the balloon floating before it.

And the bag exploded, a huge fireball lit up the sky. A second bag, and a third was caught in the blast and they exploded as well. A dozen dragons were engulfed in the flames. It seemed as if the creatures weren't affected at all, but the men riding on their backs were on fire. Some swatted desperately at their clothes. It wasn't going to help. Others had already succumbed and fallen. They screamed the whole way down and hit with a sickening thud.

The crowd of mercenaries they fell into didn't do much better. The front line was wavering, fighting on instinct alone as their thoughts focused on what might come next.

The whole mob, mercenaries and militia, surged and thrummed, a mad mass in the flickering light of the torches and the fires. Shadows and light warred between the buildings.

Rawk licked his lips, unsure what to think of the situation. "Now that they know what the balloons do, the dragons are unlikely to spit fire at them again. They'll just let them pass by."

Kristun was smiling grimly. "I thought of that. The next wave will explode on their own, but getting the timing right will be the problem. That's out of my hands though."

Down at the end of the bridge, Gannon was trying to push the advantage. The whole world was filled with sound; the ground and the air pounded with it. And the armies continued to ripple like the surface of a lake in an earthquake.

Rawk was twenty yards behind the front lines when those engaging with the enemy threw themselves down onto the ground. Behind them was one rank of kneeling militia with muskets and pistols. And behind *them* was a similarly armed rank on their feet. They fired in unison. The sound of one pistol, indoors, had been deafening but even here, out in the open, two dozen of them was unbelievable. If he hadn't known what was going on, Rawk thought he would have fled himself. Many of the mercenaries did. Of those that stood their ground, many of those closest to the bridge were overrun by the charge that followed.

A minute later, Rawk found himself with his companions twenty yards north of the river. Militia, hacking and swinging and shouting and dying, surrounded them. A young man who worked at the pie shop died with a sword through his eye. And a fermi woman, a big as man was trying to hold in her stomach. Someone else just fell and it wasn't clear why. But Rawk was not allowed to help. He wanted to help. He looked around and found Kristun, Rake and the other dwarves a few yards away. Heron and Crisp, were kneeling on the ground, working at a metal plate. They soon had it out of the ground and were gesturing the others forward.

Rawk examined the fight pushing in close around him. The shouts and screams and curses of dying men and women. He didn't know which of the sounds were coming from friends and which from enemies. He wanted to stay, but the best thing he could do was enter the sewer so everyone else could withdraw. He followed Sylvia and waited while Buzt and Frew helped her down then followed themselves. Rawk crouched on the edge then lowered himself down. In the drain he couldn't see much past the end of his sword and didn't want to touch anything, so he shuffled along behind the others. A short time after that, darkness enveloped them completely as the cover was replaced.

Standing in the dark, Rawk tried to keep his breaths shallow. It seemed to be a long time before Rake lit a torch and the cold, grey cement walls of the drain came into view. They were in chamber about five yards to a side that was mostly filled by a hulking, cast–iron machine. It had large pipes coming and going. It looked like some strange monster crouching in the dark.

"What's that?" Frew asked.

"A pump," Kristun explained. "Gravity gets the shit to this point, but it needs a bit of help from here."

"And the big pipes?" They were nearly a yard across, much bigger than those further up the hill.

"That's what carries the shit."

"You mean it isn't just in these tunnels?" Rawk said.

"Of course not. That would be crazy."

"Then what's the smell?" Breathing still wasn't a pleasant experience, but the taproom of some taverns smelled worse.

"The pipes need to be vented to make sure there isn't a build up of gases."

"Well, it isn't as bad as I was expecting," Rawk said.

Kristun grunted. "The drains are flushed every day."

"What?"

"A whole heap of water is put through the pipes every night, when the tide is going out, to get out as much mess as possible. It hasn't been happening for the last few days— we wanted to make things as unpleasant as possible for Weaver— but Thacker made sure they did it last night."

"Why didn't someone tell me all this? I thought I was going to be walking through shit up to my knees."

Rake smiled. "Where would be the fun in letting you know?"

"Really?"

Kristun grunted. "I'm not too sure I'd like to be down in here with a torch if they hadn't been flushed recently."

"Why is that?" Sylvia asked.

"Methane, the gas made by animal waste, is very flammable."

"Then perhaps we should proceed," the elf said, "before the people of Katamood begin their day."

Buzt said something too, in his musical language, but nobody could understand him. He seemed unperturbed by the idea. He stood, smiling slightly, shoulder stooped under the low ceiling.

Rake carefully moved to the front of the line. "We won't be in here too long. There's a street not far from here where the street lamps haven't been lit, so we just have to make sure we come out in the right place."

"There are dwarves working for Weaver, you know."

Rake nodded and didn't look happy. "We know. They were diverting food from the refugees. And they obviously helped design those bridges... We think we know who they are and we'll deal with them once this is over."

"Good. So, let's finish this so Thacker can sort that out too." Rawk wanted to draw his sword but in the confines of the drain, in the middle of the line, that seemed crazy. He could imagine poking Frew in the ribs every step of the way. So, shoulders hunched beneath the low ceiling, hand on the pipe that ran along the side of the drain, he followed Rake's flickering torch, trying not to breath too deeply.

Several minutes later they stopped at an intersection while Rake and Kristun consulted a map and talked about distances. Rawk had no idea how far they had travelled and he wasn't sure if the dwarves knew either.

"How did we end up here, Frew?" Rawk asked quietly. "Following some dwarves through a stinking drain. Once we get into the palace, Weaver's men will smell us coming a mile away."

The other Hero grunted. "I try not to worry about things I can't control." He shrugged. "I've been in stranger situations anyway. I once spent two days lying under a dead sheep in the corner of a cave while I waited for a grupo to fall asleep."

"At least you would have been warm."

"It was the middle of summer. In Lakash. Warm wasn't the half of it."

"Oh." It felt strange, standing there talking about life beyond the tunnel. Rawk wasn't sure that the world out there even existed any more. Beyond this one patch of torchlight it seemed that everything was just a story about somebody else's life.

Rake had gotten his bearings and the line was moving again, turning onto another drain that went off the main one at forty-five degrees. It was slightly smaller and Rawk hoped they didn't make too many more turns or they'd be crawling. He followed along, watching shadows dancing on the floor. Drace and Buzt, both walking along silently for their different reasons, were behind him. Poe and Heron brought up the rear. It was probably sensible—they dwarves small enough that they didn't have to duck and would be able to fight more freely in the cramped space— but Rawk had a feeling Buzt could easily outfight them both.

Soon, the smell didn't bother Rawk any more. They came to another intersection and Rake paused for just a moment before carrying on straight ahead.

"I don't think the Great Path will find us down here if we get lost," Drace said softly, holding up two fingers to call the god's attention.

Rawk looked into the branching drain as he passed. "I don't know; this might be the kind of place he likes." Like Frew said, it was just one more strange path he'd traversed in his life.

A couple of minutes later Rake called a halt. "We've arrived," he said softly. He snuffed his torch while Crisp worked on a hatch above their heads. Rake had to help, but after a few minutes of grunting and cursing they slid aside the metal plate and let pale moonlight down into the drain. Rake poked his head out into the world for a look, then the rest of him quickly followed. Rawk hauled himself out not long after, banging his bad knee on the rim, and limped into an alley not far behind Frew.

"That was easy," Drace said when he was crouching in the shadows as well, but his rapid breathing and the shaking of his hands against the plaster wall beside him suggested otherwise.

Rawk rubbed at his knee. "You're doing great, Drace. Just make sure you know you limits."

The sorcerer looked at Rawk and nodded.

"What now?" Sylvia asked, trying to wipe her hands on her clothes.

Rawk shrugged. "Now we just get up the hill as quickly and as quietly as we can."

"That sounds easy, too."

Rawk tried to work out where they actually were. It was all unnervingly quiet, as if all the life had been sucked out of the city. Lights peeking around curtains and sniffing under the doors did nothing more than accentuate the darkness. It felt nothing like the city that had once been awake at all hours of the day.

Apparently Kristun could read minds as well as tie bandages and make flying explosives. "We're not far from the *Keeto Alata* warehouse."

Rawk looked out at the main street and examined the building over the other side. He pursed his lips as he thought. "Right. I think I know where we are. Come with me."

He checked to make sure they were still alone then hurried eastward. He turned up the hill at the next street, then east again after that. When he reached Carker Square he stopped in the shadows and watched for activity. He was unsure if Weaver had ordered a curfew or if everyone had just decided that it was a good idea to stay at home, but either way, the place was completely deserted.

"Where are we going?" Rake asked. He was eying the mouth of Mistook Alley suspiciously.

Rawk smiled.

"I really don't think that's a good idea," the dwarf said.

"We'll be fine."

"Yes, but how long will it take us if we have to fight every cutpurse and murderer on the way."

"Two hours."

This time Rake looked at *Rawk* suspiciously. "How did you come up with that number? It would take about fifteen minutes just to walk the alley, even if we were left unmolested. But beyond that calculation..."

Rawk sighed. "I have no idea how long it would take, Rake. I just picked a number."

"Oh. Right."

"Look, obviously it's dangerous, but so is walking around out here, especially with nobody else around; a patrol will spot us instantly. So let's just hurry up and do it." He took a deep breath and led the way across to the mouth of Mistook.

When everyone had gathered nervously, Rake struck a flint and relit the torch that he had snuffed and Rawk plunged into a flickering darkness that seemed much worse than the one in the drain, even with his shadow dancing on the ground and on the walls. He had barely gone twenty yards when someone stepped out of a sheltered patch of inky blackness and barred the way.

"Well, just when I thought it was going to be a quiet night."

Rawk drew his sword. He should already have done that. "Don't worry, we won't disturb anyone. We will be very quiet."

"I think it's too late for that."

Rawk looked back over his shoulder. "Can you actually count?"

The man leaned slightly to the side to look past Rawk as well.

"Let me save you the head ache. There are ten of us, all up. Eight warriors and two sorcerers."

The would-be thief pursed his lips.

"How many friends do you have? Who's going to be the first to attack?"

"Rawk? Is that you?"

Rawk examined the shadows above his head, trying to find the source of the voice. "Who else would be coming in here in the middle of the night?"

Something moved on a stub of balcony and a man swung his leg over the rail and climbed down to the ground. "I didn't think you'd actually be back."

Rake helpfully held his torch a little higher so Rawk could see the man's face and his perfect teeth. "Fix?"

"Course it is. Or do you have lots of friends in Mistook?"

"Well, there's Johnny..."

"He's around here somewhere."

"Up here." A silhouette waved from a window above the dwarves who were guarding the rear of the party.

"What are the odds that I'd meet you two again?" Rawk started to relax a little.

"Well, it's a strange world these days," Fix said. "Not that it wasn't always strange, of course."

"Indeed."

"You said you'd tell us a story," Johnny said.

"I did. But I don't really have time, again. Besides, wouldn't you rather be a part of the story?"

Apparently climbing was for wimps; Johnny leapt down amidst the group, and looked Sylvia up and down.

"I would not do that if I were you, Johnny," Red Raven muttered. "She could burn you to a crisp where you stand."

Johnny swallowed. "She's a sorcerer?"

"Does she look like one of the warriors?"

Rawk got the conversation moving again. They didn't have all night. "We're on a mission. When I tell this story to the kids, would you like to be someone who got killed because they were in the way? Or would you rather be someone who helped end the war."

"Do people in stories get some type of payment?"

Rawk sighed. "For Path's sake, if your whole life is about money, then yes. But if you would just like to do the right thing..."

"Who says killing Weaver is the right thing. Seems to me that's just a matter of opinion."

"Who says we're killing Weaver."

"We may be poor, Rawk, but we aren't idiots."

"Well, what's your opinion on the matter."

Fix shrugged. "He don't hurt me none."

"Well, if he wins this war, do you think the city will survive? Who will do all the work that the dwarves currently do?"

"Well, maybe me and Johnny can get a job then."

Rawk wasn't quite sure how to reply to that, but he realized he didn't have to worry when Fix started laughing.

"I reckon you've got enough people here that nobody else would bother you— we got the biggest group going these days— but we'll escort you anyway, just in case."

Rawk nodded "That would be nice. But let's hurry up about it because we're running out of time."

"Of course."

"Friends of yours?" Sylvia asked as Fix headed up the hill.

Rawk grunted and hurried to keep up. Johnny and another couple of ruffians brought up the rear. The alley seemed to have found its own course over the years, like a river carving its way through the mountains, here narrow, there wide, weaving and turning. Rawk heard all sorts of sounds from the buildings on either side, but didn't have the time to wonder what they were.

"How is your daughter?" Rawk asked Fix after a couple of minutes.

The thief didn't reply for a moment. "Can't say that I know." He cleared his throat. "One of the City Guard caught her yesterday. Mali Hagarth saw it all. They took her to the Quod."

"Oh."

"When this is all over..."

"I'll see what I can do for you."

"I'd appreciate it."

Fix held up his hand and Rawk stopped as the other man moved slowly forward. He stopped at the end of the alley, cloaked in shadows, and looked out into the world of regular people. He came scuttling back a moment later. "There's a guard station set up just up the hill. Looks like they intend to stay there for a while."

"How many? Can we go out through one of the buildings?"

"About eight of them."

Fix had a bit of a think about the second question. He nodded slowly. "We could go through a building. But it would take time. And, while I'm realistic enough to know how I feel about real work, a lot of folks around here have fooled themselves into thinking the dwarves have taken work that is rightfully theirs. Right now they're on Weaver's side."

"Right. So..."

Fix waved Johnny and his companions over. A few more came from further back, where they'd been stalking them through the alley. "I reckon we need to distract those guards, boys." He sucked on his teeth.

"What's the plan then?" Johnny asked.

"We'll just go out there and throw some stuff at them. Then we run."

"And what if some of them stay behind."

"He has a point," Frew said. "If they are the City Guard and not mercenaries then they probably like the idea of staying put and letting someone else do the exercise."

Rawk shrugged. "Well, if any stay behind then hopefully we can out run them or there's enough of us to finish the fight quickly."

"Good. Let's go then."

While Fix went through a pile of rubbish and pulled out some bottles and half rotten fruit, Rawk checked with Rake and Kristun about where they were going next.

"The access hatch we want is on the corner of Ocean Rd and Long Rd," Kristun said. "From there it will be about two hundred yards."

Rawk nodded. He shifted his grip on *Kaj*'s hilt, then wiped his hand on his breeches.

Fix had handed around the weapons of choice. "I think we should pretend to be drunk, so they're less likely to suspect a trap."

One of the thieves put up his hand. "I think, technically, I *am* dunk."

"I never doubted it, Tench. Come on then."

Seven thieves and cutthroats moved out of the alley, leaning against each other and singing a bawdy song. They staggered towards the guard post.

Rawk waited out of sight. He heard the pause, then the crash as the first bottle was thrown. For a minute there was all sorts of commotion, then the sound of footsteps and shouting. Fix and his companions ran past, followed by a handful of guards. When the pursuit had moved on, Rawk stuck his head around the corner and discovered five guards still hiding behind the makeshift barricades. The men were looking jittery, but Rawk didn't give the time to think. He hefted his sword and charged.

Weaver's men held the better position, stationed behind a low brick wall and with pikes standing at ease before them, but they were out numbered and stood looking shocked for a long time. By the time Rawk was just fifteen yards away they decided their location was no longer as comfortable as it once had been and they vaulted over the wall and took off up the street.

Rawk was inordinately pleased.

Drace wandered up to Rawk and looked up the street where the men had gone. "What if they tell Weaver they saw you here?"

Rawk shrugged. "If he hasn't already got someone guarding the sewers he won't think of it now. Rake? Where's the next entrance?"

"It isn't far."

$-$O$-$

Rawk waited silently, looking up as Rake and Heron worked on the heavy, round cover, but inside he was all over the place. This felt like the point of no return. Once he climbed up to ground level inside the keep, there was no turning back. But he couldn't have turned back after crossing over the river in Gabe's boat either. And he couldn't have turned back after releasing Sylvia. Or after killing the guard in the riot. Or... He realized the real point of no return, the first point of no return, had been a long time ago on the day he killed the wolden wolf, when he first went to Sylvia for help. Once Weaver found out, which had always been inevitable, Rawk knew the prince was never going to understand his friendship with *any* elf, let alone Silver Lark, or forgive him. And that was when he had really started to realize that he and Sylvia weren't so different after all. That had been the moment when he had really started to leave 'the good old days' behind.

It seemed to take forever for the two dwarves to remove the hatch and it made a lot of noise as they slid it aside. When the column of dim light lit up the sewer Rawk pushed them out of the way and stuck his head up into the palace. Gray light was starting to seep over the top of the wall and half a dozen torches sputtered the last of their energy around the walls.

He was looking out through the spoked wheel of a wagon, but could see enough to know that he was in the Yeoman's Yard, about thirty yards from the big, double doors that gave entry to the keep. He quietly hauled himself out of the hole and crawled to the back of the wagon where he was given some cover by four barrels that had been unloaded then left where they were. The only people in the yard were two guards in a small circle of torch light over by the door. They seemed to be half asleep.

"Do you know where we're going?" Frew whispered when he was crouched behind the barrels as well.

"Let's worry about these two guards before we start getting too excited," Rake said quietly as he joined them too.

Rawk tried to gather his thoughts. "If there's only two guards here, maybe Weaver's feeling a little bit over—confident. He might have everyone down near the river or out harassing innocent civilians."

"Do we just rush them, then?" Rake asked. "It worked last time."

"We don't want them warning anyone though, if possible," Frew said. He turned to Red Raven whose head was poking up from the drain. "Can you shoot both of them?"

The elf examined the distance, cocking his head to the side. He looked up at the wagon above his head then back over his shoulder. "Of course I can shoot them," he said, "but if one turns at the wrong moment..." He climbed out of the hole and Kristun's head appeared where he had been.

"What's happening?" the engineer asked quietly.

"Raven is going to shoot a couple of guards."

Kristun craned his neck to take a look. "Does he need help?"

"Can you hit one of the guards from here?" Raven asked.

Kristun shrugged. "I think so. And if not, we won't be any worse off."

Raven nodded. "Very well. I shall still prepare to fire two arrows."

"Suit yourself." Kristun hauled himself up and readied his bow as well. His was a much shorter, thicker affair with all sorts of odd attachments.

"Does that even work," the elf asked. The look on his face suggested he wasn't sure how he felt about it, no matter its functionality. His was just a regular thing, a piece of timber held to a curve with a piece of string.

"Of course." But he glanced at Raven's longbow and suddenly didn't look sure. He grunted softly. "It's something I've been working on for a while."

After a moment, the elf and the dwarf knelt side by side. They took deep, synchronized breaths and rose smoothly as if they had been working together their whole lives. Raven stood straight up, Kristun took a slight step to the side so he was no longer behind the wagon, and they fired.

The elf's red fletched arrow stuck one man in the throat. His second arrow thwacked into the next man just a moment after Kristun's took him in the chest. Neither of the guards made a sound, except for the soft thump as they hit the ground.

"Well done." Rawk rose to his feet and looked around. He listened to the silence, which was broken only by the sound of his companions climbing up out of the drain.

While he waited, Rawk pulled out the map Thacker had given him. He couldn't see anything with the light and his eyes conspiring against him. He cursed for a moment, then pulled his reading spectacles from the pouch on his belt and slipped them over his eyes. He cleared his throat when he saw Frew looking at him and quickly turned his attention to the map. "Weaver's private study is in the middle of the keep. His rooms are above that. I've never gone there from here, but it shouldn't be too hard." According to the map it wasn't hard at all. But unfortunately the map didn't tell him how many guards there were or where they were.

When everyone else was above ground Rawk strode across to the door and opened it enough to stick his head through into the large hall beyond. He noticed Kristun pause for a moment to look at the man he had killed, but the dwarf quickly moved on.

Shadows clung to the corners despite half a dozen torches lining the walls. Sleeping pallets crowded the floor, but luckily they were empty. It looked like they had not been slept in for a while. A woman with a washing basket on her hip passed through at the far end of the room, hurrying towards a door, not noticing anything other than what was right in front of her. Rawk slipped inside, leaving the door open so the others could follow.

"Through that door at the end there," Rawk said quietly. "Then we go right and through another two halls. Then a hallway and into Weaver's office."

"Will there be guards?"

"I assume so."

"How many?"

"Just two." There would probably be more now. "Come on."

They were halfway across the hall, weaving around the sleeping pallets, when half a dozen men came through the far door. Rawk noticed at the same time that Red Raven let loose his first arrow. He roared and charged forward. Another man went down with an arrow in his throat. And almost everyone else rushed past Rawk before he reached the enemy. He was forced to stand back and watch, cursing loudly as he looked for an opportunity to get involved. He shouted warnings that would never be quick enough. But it was all over quickly and Rawk tried to calm himself down.

"Is everyone uninjured?" Sylvia asked.

There were only minor injuries. Drace healed a cut on Frew's arm, hands shaking as he did so. Everyone else declined any assistance.

"Come on then, let's keep going," Rawk said. "And next time, make some room for me."

Frew grunted. "You worry about Weaver. How would you feel if one of us had to deal with him?"

Rawk ignored him, checking through the next door and heading down the short passage. His best chance of getting into the fights was to make sure he kept leading. Red Raven strode along by his side and Rawk wondered what would happen if he upped his pace. Would the elf match him? He imagined them racing down the hallways, trying to be the first to stick their head through the doors.

At the end, Rawk paused with his hand on the door handle. "A hall through here. It isn't as large as the next one but..." He shrugged and carefully opened the door and looked around the edge.

About twenty men occupied the room beyond. None of them saw Rawk as he retreated and closed the door again. He swallowed and took a deep breath. "I suspect that not everyone is down at the river."

"You suspect?" Sylvia asked, raising her eyebrow.

"Perhaps Weaver isn't so sure of success that he will leave himself unguarded."

"How many?"

Rawk rubbed at his beard. "Would thirty be too many?"

Drace's eyes went wide. Rake nodded.

"Well, don't be concerned because there are only twenty. Give or take a couple."

Rake pushed his helm back and scratched at his head. "Are they awake?"

"Mostly?"

"Most of them are awake? Or all of them are mostly awake?" Crisp asked.

Rawk shrugged. "I didn't have time to do a survey."

Red Raven pulled out some arrows. "How close were they to the door?"

"The closest were about five yards away."

The elf nodded. "How many of those pistols do we have?"

All the dwarves had one, as did Sylvia. Six in total.

"So, we go in there and fire." Raven shrugged. "Anyone who is not dead or running after that gets killed the old fashion way. And any assistance from the sorcerers will be appreciated."

"That sounds like one of my plans." Rawk shook his head.

"You're still alive, so they must have worked."

"Any other ideas? Sylvia?" Rawk was conscious of the fact that someone could come through the door at any moment and all options would be taken from them. "Anyone?" He sighed. "Come on then." He shifted his grip on *Kaj* and reached for the door. It started to open before he had touched the handle.

Rawk swore and charged forward, glad for the small mercy that the door swung away from him, and went through. The unlucky victim of the door wasn't going to be doing a lot in a hurry, by the looks of him, but Rawk took three steps to where he had fallen and stabbed him anyway. Leaving his sword sheathed in the man's chest, he dropped to one knee, like he had seen the front ranks do on the bridge, and covered his ears just before the dwarves fired their pistols. The six weapons, in the confines of the room, were almost deafening. He thought he could feel the heat of them. The black smoke stung his eyes. And the enemy panicked.

Rawk grabbed *Kaj,* pulling it forth with a sucking sound, as Raven let loose his fourth arrow. He charged towards the frozen or fleeing City Guard.

Rawk cut a man down. It was Danner. He was getting on and his daughter had recently had her first child. Masket was next. The big man was still thinking about the noise but managed a distracted, half–hearted swipe. Rawk ran him through as well. And Tippa still owed him ten ithel from a card game. Well, he wasn't getting that money back.

After what seemed a lifetime, much more than the seconds that it really was, Rawk lowered his sword in the newly born silence and drew in a deep breath. He knew most of the dead men. He'd talked to them, drank with them.

"Is everyone well?" Sylvia asked. She was looking for somebody to help, but Kristun was already tearing at Frew's sleeve to look at a wound beneath. It wasn't as bad as the blood suggested.

Rawk took a deep breath and tried to not look around. "Come on. The sooner this is over the better."

But before they could go anywhere, another group of the City Guard entered the room. It took everyone a moment to gather themselves. Rake and Heron had reloaded their pistols and they both fired. An arrow scratched out from Red Raven's bow. Where the former had the survivors rooted to the spot, the latter got them moving again. Another arrow flew as the guards started to charge. Then Raven dropped the bow so he could draw his sword.

Rawk blocked out the faces. For a moment he was surrounded and laying about himself without thought. He danced blades with a little man that he refused to recognize, dodged blows from other blur–faced monsters. Then Red Raven, torn sleeve flapping, cut a man down from behind and the pressure eased. And others crashed into the defenders.

Men were falling. A dwarf went down. Guardsmen. Frew was almost stabbed as he fought to keep someone away from Dace. But the guard's dark hair caught on fire and he stumbled away screaming and swatting at himself madly. Thunder from another pistol. Smoke billowing. The smell. Rawk thought he might get used to the noise, but the smell...

Soon the room was littered with corpses. There was hardly room to walk.

Rawk hunched over, rubbing at his knee. "We can't keep doing that," he said quietly, watching as Sylvia knelt over Poe. She wasn't hurrying because it was obvious there was nothing she could do. Rawk swore silently.

Rake motioned to the door they were supposed to go through. He'd just come back from checking it. "We can't go through there, either," he said. He was equally quiet, perhaps just moving so he didn't have to think.

"Why not?" Rawk thought movement might be a good idea.

"It's a hall, bigger than this."

"Yes."

"And about fifty men just entered it."

Sylvia gasped. "Are they coming this way?"

"I imagine so," Rake said. He started to load his pistol again, stuffing something down the barrel with some kind of stick. Rawk hadn't paid any attention to how it was done before, although perhaps someone had explained it to him. For some reason, the details seemed important now.

"Is there another way?" Red Raven asked. He was collecting the arrows he'd fired earlier, wiggling them backwards and forwards until they pulled free of flesh and clothes.

Rawk gathered himself and pulled the map free of his pack, tearing it along one of the folds as he rushed to get it open. He looked for a couple of seconds. "That door there," he said, pointing to one of the five doors that went out through the side walls. "It's longer but..." *But maybe there isn't an army waiting for us.*

"Go, then," Rake said, straightening from his task.

Rawk led the way to the door and had it half open when they were once again disturbed. More men were coming through the door that had caused all the problems in the first place.

Buzt bellowed and sprinted across the room, stepping on bodies like a child playing stepping stones. Heron fired his pistol and killed the first man though. Rake took down the second and that allowed the big, tattooed man to get there and keep the rest in the other room.

"We hold," Buzt shouted, his sword a blur of movement. After a moment, the man attacking him shouted in fear as his shirt caught fire. Someone else took his place though he didn't look too keen on the idea.

Rake was reloading once more. "You go. We can hold here forever, I think."

Rawk nodded, but looked at the other doors. He didn't say anything, but Frew noticed. The little Hero check on Buzt's fight, then raced to the nearest door and started dragging bodies over to block it. Four should do the trick nicely. So Rawk turned and kept going. Red Raven, Sylvia, and Kristun went with him, crowding close behind.

They raced along a hallway and burst through the door at the end. Another hall. Rawk hefted *Kaj*, looked one way and then the next as he tried to remember the map. While he was thinking someone came through a side door.

"Rawk?"

Rawk looked him up and down. "Sargan? How's your head?"

The other man drew his sword. "You won't surprise me this time."

But the look on his face suggested he was at least slightly surprise when an arrow thudded into his chest. Rawk was surprised too. When he turned to look behind, Raven lowered his bow and shrugged apologetically.

"I have had about enough of this," the elf said. "I just want it to be over."

Kristun nodded. "A man after my own heart."

Rawk couldn't argue either. Stepping over the fallen guard, he looked through the still open door. As far as he could remember, it wasn't on the map but it led directly to Weaver's private study, which certainly was. The room was empty.

"If he's not here…" Rawk said quietly as he stepped inside. Now that he was so close to the end it felt strange. Weaver had grown strange over the years, but once he truly had been Rawk's friend. They'd been through a lot together. And now…

Rawk cleared his throat and pulled the map out once more. There's some sort of meeting room nearby." He rotated the map, trying to orient himself. There were three doors other than then one they had used already. "That one," he said eventually, pointing to a door that looked much like the others. "One more passage, and we'll be there." Hopefully Weaver was as well.

He hurried across the room, moving around the familiar furniture as if in a daze. The hard chair he'd sat in dozens of times. Hundreds of times. The battleship of a desk that was normally used for holding Weaver's feet and his wine and not much else.

Just a moment later, Red Raven said, "Quiet." He cocked his head to the side. "Can you hear that?"

Rawk tried to listen. Voices. He didn't know what they were saying, but they appeared to be coming from beyond the door he had just indicated. And they were coming closer.

"What is through the other doors," Sylvia asked.

"Nothing interesting," Rawk said. "Just palace."

Raven nodded. "Then you hide back through there. I will draw the men away."

"What? Are you crazy?"

"Of course. Do you really think they will catch me?"

Actually, Rawk did think they would catch the elf. Or, if not the men that were approaching now, then some other men. If only...

"Damn it."

"What is it," Sylvia asked, looking around for another threat.

"The mushon—skin cloak. I could've given it to Raven."

"Which mushon—skin cloak?"

"Galad's."

"But..."

"I know. I don't know where it is; probably at Biki's place somewhere. But when Juskin ran up to me before we crossed the river this morning would have been the perfect time for him to give it to me."

"Juskin knows where it is?"

"No."

"Then..."

"My clichés are deserting me. I'll never work out how to tell this story properly."

Kristun cleared his throat. "I'm not sure if this is the time."

"Go. Quickly," Raven added. "All of this is meaningless, all those militia dying is meaningless, if we don't kill Weaver."

"Right." *Of course.* Rawk took Sylvia's hand and dragged her back the way they'd come.

Kristun followed reluctantly, glancing at the elf as if trying to come up with an argument that had any chance of success. "I could help," he said eventually.

Raven shook his head. "It only needs one of us to draw them away."

Rawk stood just out in the hallway. He pulled the door almost closed so he could peer through the crack and watched as Raven checked another door to make sure he could escape. Then the elf stood behind the last, overstuffed chair Rawk had sat in, readied his bow and waited.

A few moments later the first soldier entered the room. Red Raven put an arrow through his eye. Then a second man. But those behind realized what was happening and rushed through. There were eight of them, swords ready, war cries on their lips. Two more died before Red Raven turned and fled. He left the door open behind him and the final half a dozen obligingly followed.

"Do you think he will be all right," Sylvia asked as Rawk led her across the room. The sound of the men's footsteps could still be heard, getting further away.

Rawk looked to where the elf had gone. "If anyone can outrun them, I reckon it's Raven." He didn't believe it really— one elf in a palace he didn't know being chased by... well, everyone probably— but Sylvia nodded as if satisfied by the answer.

Kristun got to the door first and pulled it open. The dwarf took a deep breath, ready to keep going, but Rawk stopped him.

"I should go first."

"And why's that?"

Rawk drew *Kaj*.

"Really?" Kristun drew his pistol.

Rawk gave that some thought. "What happens after you fire?" he said after a moment. "You'll just be standing there with a useless piece of metal and getting in my way."

"Yes, but..."

"And beside that, I think we'll all go deaf if you fire that in a narrow passage."

"You may be right. But if things get desperate, just duck down and I'll shoot someone."

"Duck down and block my ears, you mean."

"Good idea. Don't cut your ear off though."

"Come on."

The passage was narrow, barely lit by the hissing oil lamps. Rawk held his breath and went slowly, approaching a small alcove that could house a guard if required. He crept closer, heart racing. And there was nobody there. He sighed and straightened, easing the tension out of his shoulders.

"What are we waiting for?" Sylvia whispered.

Rawk took a deep breath. "Nothing." He continued down the passage, concentrating on the next possible threat; the door at the end.

At the door, he paused again, hand on the handle. "Are we ready?" he whispered.

Kristun nodded. Sylvia, barely visible in the shadows behind the dwarf, hesitated then gave something like a nod as well. It didn't matter because the handle wouldn't budge.

Rawk swore under his breath. "It's locked," he said.

"No, it isn't." Kristun pushed him out of the way and started to feel around in the darkness. "It's probably a secret passage so there will just a be a catch or something somewhere." There was a click, and the dwarf gave a satisfied nod. Then he opened the door before Rawk could say anything, and stepped out into the room beyond. Rawk and Sylvia had no choice but to follow.

There were bookshelves hiding a lot of the walls and weapons on display racks and hooks took up many of the spaces between. All sorts of furniture cluttered the room, mismatched and out of date and generally overdone, much like Weaver's disguises. A huge scale model of Katamood stood on a table in the center of it all.

"A little caution might have been in order," Rawk said, as a dozen or more people turned to look in their direction, faces yellow in the light of a dozen tall, thick candles. Some soldiers, advisors, and a couple of dwarves trying to blend in with the wallpaper down the back.

Celeste was sitting in a soft, striped chair a few yards from Weaver. She was bruised and bloody. Her hands and feet were tied.

Kristun cleared his throat. "Sorry. I was a bit excited about opening the door— I wasn't really thinking." He tugged at his beard.

"Next time," Rawk said, though he didn't have much thought to spare for the dwarf of for doors. He swallowed. "Can you lock it so nobody can sneak in behind us?"

"I'll just check." He backed towards the door then turned around to see what he could work out.

"Rawk?" Prince Weaver rose from a huge, padded chair, glancing towards Celeste, as if to make sure she was still there. "How did you get in here?"

Rawk heard something break behind him and the door closed with a horrible grating sound.

"That's done," Kristun said. "How's it going here?"

Rawk was staring at Celeste. She seemed to be all right. "We're just taking a moment."

"Right? What for?"

"Well..."

Kristun drew an arrow and shot a soldier in the chest. The man collapsed against the model, upsetting some ships in the harbor and toppling one of the river towers. Shouts and curses. Swords being drawn. Another man died on the end of a brightly fletched arrow. The engineer seemed to have gotten the hang of killing people.

"What are you doing?" the prince shouted.

"Just following Raven's example," Kristun told him.

"But... You can't just come in here and shoot people." Weaver poked his head up from behind Two Watch Hill, peering between the palace and the *Hero's Rest*.

Rawk was guessing Weaver meant that you could just come in and shoot *him*. It was doubtful the prince was worried about anyone else. "Come out and fight like a man, Weaver. Let's end this."

"One on one? Just you and me?"

Rawk nodded. "That's the way you want it, isn't it? You and me? Hasn't it always been about you and me?"

"He won't put an arrow in me?"

Rawk motioned to Kristun. "No, he won't."

"I'm out of arrows," the dwarf muttered, too quiet for anyone else to hear.

Weaver slowly stood up and straightened his clothes. He was wearing a ridiculous military uniform that was nothing like those worn by the guard, or anyone else for that matter. His own ridiculous one–man army. The tunic was covered in so much gold brocade that is was impossible to tell where it ended and the dozen medals he had pinned to his chest started. He had a tricorn hat, worn in the wrong orientation, and an ornate sword that probably cost enough to buy a small town.

"If it's just us," Weaver said, "why is *she* here?" He seemed to ignore the fact that there were still a few guards left as well. Luckily none of them had a bow.

Rawk glanced at Sylvia. The elf was staring at a patch of darkness beside a shelf at the other end of the room. The candlelight refused to go in there. Rawk shivered.

"Silver Lark is here in case *he* is here." He gestured at the darkness, hoping he wasn't going to look like a fool. Or perhaps hoping he *was* going to look like a fool. His life would be a whole heap easier, and possibly longer, if Natan was on a ship heading out of the harbor right now.

But the shadow slipped away and a crow flew down to sit on the back of a chair. The bird preened itself for a moment, then started to change, swirling and blurring like smoke behind a darkened pane of glass. And a sickening moment later, Natan dusted off his black cloak and looked up.

"It's good to see you again, Rawk. It seems an age since we last spoke."

Rawk wondered how many of the crows he had seen around the city were Natan and how many were just crows. Did he have to be close to the portals to get them to open? "Well, if I have to watch you do that again, I think I'm going to throw up."

Natan ignored him. "And Silver Lark? I was hoping for someone... more."

While Rawk was distracted by the spence, the guards had sidled forward and finally charged.

Rawk swore as he hefted *Kaj*.

Behind him there was a thunderclap of sound. Sharp and almost deafening.

The guards had stopped. Apparently one of them stopped dead. He stared at the quickly growing patch of blood on the front of his uniform. As Kristun hurried to reload his pistol and the man toppled forward, Rawk attacked. The guards were standing, stunned and staring. The first died before he had a chance to recover. The second blocked and stumbled back and tripped and died with a sword in his throat.

"Who's next?" Rawk asked.

Another guard started forward. He died with a bang— apparently Kristun had finished reloading.

But there were two more volunteers who decided there was safety in numbers. Rawk drew his dagger and threw it. He'd never been particularly good at throwing daggers, but it worked this time. The guard made the bad decision to pull it out of his chest. He probably wouldn't have lived anyway, but he would have had a chance. Feeling a little bit pleased with himself, Rawk set himself to fight the final man. But whoever he was decided Kristun was the better target. The dwarf was reloading again and not really paying all that much attention.

"Kristun," Rawk shouted.

The dwarf looked up. Eyes going wide, he dropped his pistol and started to draw his sword. He was too slow. He was always going to be too slow. But he was a dwarf and stubborn and even with a sword in his stomach, Kristun managed to finish drawing his own blade and ram it up into his killer's armpit. The man screamed. Blood gushed. The two of them toppled to the floor, a dark stain of blood quickly spreading across the carpet.

Rawk swallowed and turned towards Weaver. He couldn't say anything. He had no witty remarks. All he could do was move towards the prince once more. The sooner he got him out of the way, the sooner he could help with the magician. The sooner he could... He stopped himself from glancing back over his shoulder. Though, halfway around the city model, he wondered if distracting Natan might have been the better option after all. Too late now.

Not far away, a door opened and Rawk lost his focus. His knee twisted slightly as he turned to look.

Waydin came through. "Prince Weaver, Travis would like to..." The guard's sword was still sheathed, but it whispered out when he saw Rawk. He smiled grimly. "Well, I should have known it would come to this."

Rawk wasn't paying attention. His heart sank. Travis was standing behind the guard, silently examining the room.

"Travis..."

"Rawk?" But he was distracted too. "Natan? I came to..."

"Now may not be the best time, my dear."

Rawk took a deep breath, then shook his head and continued on his original mission. He would mourn the loss of his friend later.

Weaver started backing away. Waydin started running, leaping over a footstool, knocking a wine carafe off a table. His sword slashed through the air.

Rawk ducked, rolled, cursed his knee, and came back to his feet against the side of the model table. He fended away another couple of attacks and slipped back out into the open.

"You're slow, Rawk. Old."

He grunted. "You do know why I'm old though, don't you? Because I'm good." He smiled. "Better than you will ever be."

Waydin laughed. "In your prime, yes. Now?"

Rawk parried and countered. He drew a line of blood across his opponent's arm. "You were saying?"

They traded some more blows and Rawk smiled at the line of sweat coming out across Waydin's brow. He took a moment to glance around the room. Travis was talking to Natan, seemingly pleading with him. Silver Lark was concentrating silently. And Weaver sneaking up behind him.

"That's more like the Weaver I know," Rawk muttered.

Rawk ducked a wild swing a moment before it would have taken the tip off his already short chin-beard. He angled his blade to slide an attack from Waydin past his thigh and danced back.

Weaver hadn't held a sword in anger for a long time, but with him on one side and Waydin on the other, Rawk was pressed hard.

He feinted a swing at Weaver and lunged towards Waydin. When he missed he spun away into the clear, threw a serving tray that didn't come close to hitting anyone, and backed away.

On the other side of the room, Natan pulled a sword from a display on the wall. Travis backed away, hands held up, still talking, pleading. But Natan didn't listen. Surprisingly light of foot, he slipped forward and lunged. Travis twisted aside at the last moment, darted away, and grabbed at a weapon of his own. The hilt caught on the bracket holding it. He fumbled. And pulled it down just in time to save himself from being skewered. He took the edge across his side anyway and winced as he readied himself.

Rawk hated himself for ever doubting Travis. His friend had never been one to do something merely because it was easy or comfortable. He did it because it was right.

Another jab slid past Rawk's ear, snatching his attention back to his own predicament. He slashed at Weaver. But the prince's first thought was always to run away, so the tip of *Kaj* didn't get within a foot of the target.

Waydin was on him, bulling his way forward, trying to get him on the ground with nothing more than his body. But Rawk was bigger and heavier and shoved back. He whipped his sword up, got it tangled in the material at the guard's crotch. It didn't do any actual damage, but it was enough to scare him.

Rawk took the chance to catch his breath.

Travis and Natan were still exchanging blows. It seemed surreal. One man who hadn't picked up a sword in years and another who thought anything more energetic than walking was undignified. They hacked and bashed at each other, stumbling around the furniture, before they stopped and stared, then started again. Silver Lark had moved closer. She stood just beyond the range of their battle, watching silently.

Rawk returned to his own fight, blocking and slashing as Waydin moved in quickly. Rawk started to retreat, shifting his weight onto his back foot just slightly. In that moment, he saw Waydin relax. And he lunged back in. The guard reacted, but too late. Rawk felt the moment of resistance as *Kaj* encountered cloth, then skin then cartilage, then the blade slipped neatly between two ribs and let forth a spurt of blood.

Then Rawk's knee gave a crack that sent pain up and down his leg. He grunted in pain. *Kaj* slipped from his grasp as Waydin fell backwards and he fell downwards. Lying on his side, he clutched at his knee and groaned.

A pistol fired, the noise loud in the sudden silence.

Rawk looked for Sylvia and Travis but Weaver moved to stand in the way.

"Well, this is an interesting turn of events." The prince glanced at where *Kaj* was still sheathed in Waydin's chest almost two yards away, then crouched down, leaning his cheek against the golden pommel of his own sword. He had collected a mace from somewhere. It was lying on the floor by his side.

Rawk grunted in reply. He screamed a moment later when the prince pounded the side of his knee with the mace. He may have passed out. If so, he almost wished he hadn't woken up again. His knee was nothing but pain. A whole world of pain all of its own. He could barely think. He gritted his teeth, fighting to stay conscious.

"I didn't want it to come to this, Rawk. Really. I have loved you for so long..."

"You don't love me, Weaver. You love the idea of me perhaps, the idea of owning someone like me when all the women of Katamood couldn't."

Weaver surged to his feet, his face transformed. "Don't tell me what I think," he spat. "You don't know me at all."

"And if you think I could love you, then you don't know *me*." He fumbled at his belt.

Weaver glanced towards the movement. He laughed. "If you're after your dagger, I believe it's over there in Toma's neck."

Rawk didn't look away from him. He rolled carefully onto his back, though his leg screamed like Weaver had hit it again. "Well, if you're going to just kill me when I'm lying on the ground unarmed, just get on with it. I don't want to look at your face anymore."

Weaver sneered. "Gladly." He stepped forward, and pressed the tip of his sword against Rawk's chest, right over his heart.

The sharp point dug into his skin. And he could feel when the pressure eased for a moment as Weaver drew the sword back and prepared to press it home.

Rawk rolled towards the prince. His chest pushed the weapon aside so he was no longer directly beneath it. It still seemed to bite deeply as it plunged downwards. But when he met less resistance than expected, Weaver overbalanced, and Rawk rammed his dinner–knife into the other man's stomach.

"This is for Maris and Bree and all the other innocent people you have killed." He tore the knife sideways. Blood streamed down his hand and arm, mixing with his own blood, soaking into his bandage, as the prince examined the bone handle, a surprised look on his face.

"Are you really surprised, Weaver?" Rawk gasped. He didn't know which hurt more— his arm or knee or his chest. "Did you really think you could beat me?"

Weaver tried to reply but all he managed to do was cough up a huge mouthful of blood.

"What do you think of the good old days now?"

As the prince finally toppled to the floor, taking his sword with him, Rawk closed his eyes laid his head on the thick carpet. He wondered if the prince had killed him. There was a lot of blood streaming form the wound on his chest. Perhaps something vital had been hit, though Rawk tended to think that his whole body was vital. But at least the pain in his knee didn't seem quite so bad.

"Rawk? Oh, Path. Rawk!"

He opened his eyes and looked around as best he could. "Celeste?"

She was kneeling by his side, hands fluttering as she tried to work out what to do.

Another voice. "Move out of the way." Silver Lark. Rawk couldn't see her but she sounded exhausted. He just kept looking at Celeste.

"There's so much blood?"

"Yes. Apply pressure."

Rawk groaned as someone tried to slow the bleeding. Then there was a spreading, stuttering warmth like the blush of first love.

"Are you all right, Celeste?" Rawk asked quietly, seemingly using an impossible amount of energy.

"Am *I* all right," Celeste replied, wiping at her face with a shaking hand. "I haven't been stabbed."

Rawk took that as a yes. "What about, Travis? And Kristun?"

"Travis will be all right," Silver Lark said from close by.

Rawk gave a small nod. The silence regarding Kristun was not reassuring. He cleared his throat. It hurt. Everything hurt. "You beat Natan?"

"Yes."

"How?"

"He was going to kill Travis. I shot him before he got to, but he hardly seemed to notice. He just turned on me and... I can create a small amount of magical heat, so I warmed the liquid in his eye."

Rawk smiled. "A rapier."

"Yes, and then I found an *actual* rapier and stabbed him in the throat while he was distracted."

"You stabbed him?" Rawk didn't want to move his head to look at Silver Lark, so he kept watching Celeste. The woman gave a small nod.

"I was aiming for his chest," Silver Lark's soft, tired voice admitted.

"And you're healing me," he whispered.

Just then, the warmth disappeared and Rawk could feel nothing at all.

"Barely. I need to find some medical supplies."

Rawk didn't really hear. He couldn't hear anything at all. There was just the dullness in his chest, the pain in his knee, and Celeste's face.

Epilogue

"I DON'T WANT THE JOB. Path, that's terrible idea. I think we've seen the proof that Heroes shouldn't be in charge of anything." He looked around at the others, crowding into a small chamber in the palace. Thacker at the far end of the table, looking as harried as he ever had. Sylvia and Rake on one side, Gannon and Yardi the other. Thok and Red Raven were against one wall, trying to look inconspicuous, as if wondering why they were even there. Zid and Opok had taken up position on the other wall. The duen, sitting on the floor, had been muttering quiet translations for his companion

"Are you comparing yourself to Weaver?" Sylvia asked.

"Yes. 40 years ago we were very similar."

"But 40 years..." Thacker started to say.

"No. I'm not going to run Katamood. I refuse. It's just a terrible idea." Even if he thought he could make a good fist of it, Rawk had better things to do with his time. Anything would be better.

"The people love you." Thacker tried.

"They love you too, Thacker."

"I think a dwarf running the city is a bad idea right now. The humans from the north wouldn't stand for it."

"If we put me on the throne everyone to the south would just be wondering what had changed as soon as I did anything they didn't like."

"Who then? Sylvia?"

Sylvia almost choked, though it was obvious it could not be a serious suggestion for the same reasons that Thacker wouldn't work. Opok would do a good job too, probably but nobody even suggested him as a joke.

"Well, that's why I asked Thok along. I think he should run the city." Rawk watched as the others narrowed their eyes.

Sylvia spoke for all of them. "But..."

"Words of Wisdom played a big part in the rebellion."

"That was you?" Rake asked. His beard had been shaven short so a big flap of skin could be sewn back onto his face.

Thok winced. "It was. How did you know, Rawk?"

"I didn't. It was just a guess but seemed likely."

"Either way, I don't think it's a good idea."

"Of course it is. You've studied history and politics. You may be even smarter than me," Rawk said. "And for the most part, nobody knows who you are so they can't possibly hate you just yet. And anyway, we don't really want someone who's keen for the role; I think that would just lead to problems down the track."

"No, I mean, I don't think it's a good idea to go looking for a new prince at all."

"A princess then? I don't know of any woman more qualified than you." Though even as he said it, Rawk was turning to look at Yardi. If she could run a business...

Yardi said, "No," before he could even voice the thought.

Thok sighed and said, "No," as well.

"Well—"

"Rawk, just shut up and listen for a moment." Thok seemed to gather his thoughts. "If you put one person in charge then chances are things will go badly. They will do things to favor themselves. Or their friends. Or their race. Or they won't be able to see all the problems. Or... Or they die unexpectedly and everyone is left fighting over the position again. Who would have taken over if Weaver died?"

"Right..." Thacker said slowly.

Red Raven sat up to listen.

"So you have a council."

Thacker laughed. "You can't run a city by committee. Who ever was in charge would just get rid of the people who didn't agree with him so you eventually get back to having a prince anyway."

"The committee has no say on who gets appointed."

"So... Who does then?"

"The people." Thok looked around at everyone. "Everyone who wants to be on the council puts up their hand, and then the residents of the city vote. The five people— or ten people or whatever— with the most votes are on the council. And a year later you go through the process again."

"Voting might work with small groups, but a whole city?"

"Look, I don't know all the details but it could work. It would be fairer for everyone and better for the city."

Opok rumbled from his place by the wall. "I be thinking the idea could work."

"Perhaps," Sylvia agreed. She was nodding and looking thoughtful.

Red Raven was nodding as well. "Imagine if Yardi did get elected. She would know how to get business to come to the city. Or how to help the ones that are already here. And an old soldier—" he looked at Gannon, "and a sailor and... All those people working for an area of the city that they understand."

"But who would want to do it?" Thacker asked.

"You'd pay them out of the taxes," Thok said. "Not a lot though, because you don't want them to be in it for the money."

"It *could* work," Thacker admitted.

"Right," Rawk said, "I think we should have a vote on whether people should vote?" He looked around at the others and smiled.

Sylvia shook her head and sighed.

When Rawk stood up an hour later, leaning on his walking stick though his false leg made it all but superfluous, it had been decided that Thok, Thacker, Sylvia, Yardi and Gannon would be on the first Council of Katamood, but only long enough to work out how to organize voting and getting the residents of the city to do it. None of them really wanted to job, so Rawk guessed the details would be worked out rather quickly. But he intended to leave them to it, otherwise they'd turn to him again and wonder how he'd managed to avoid the job himself. He took up his walking stick and limped from the room as quickly as possible.

Out in the hall he paused to adjust the strap on his leg. Since the engineer had added a spring to the ankle of the contraption it was much more comfortable and sometimes he forgot he was wearing it at all. As he was doing up the last buckle he was almost knocked over when Rake, Red Raven, Opok and Zid rushed out behind him, as if they'd also been having thoughts of escape.

"Is that still hurting you?" Rake asked, watching Rawk fiddle. "You should get Kristun to…"

Rawk cleared his throat. "I just loosened it while I was in there and didn't want to slow down long enough to fix it."

"Do you still need the walking stick?"

Rawk looked at the item in question. "It's more for show most of the time. Or just in case. Now that I'm used to the leg I hardly even have to think about it."

"Well, go back to Tudem if there's problems. He may need to make some adjustments when everything has settled properly."

They were all making adjustments. So many people had died under Rawk's leadership. Frew, Kristun, Heron, Crisp, Poe and Buzt. Fabi and Galad. And then there were the thousands of militia, fighting for their families and for their city. And now that small group he'd left in the meeting room was trying to make sure those deaths had a purpose.

Red Raven looked back over his shoulder. "You may all feel safe here, but I will be retreating further."

Rawk sighed and glanced at the door as well. He gave a small nod and followed the elf.

Out at the edge of Placton Square, at the top of the stairs that led to the main door of the palace, Rawk stopped again. The sun was sinking in the west and dwarves on stilts were working their way around the square, lighting the lamps. Grint, Biki, Juskin, Travis and Clinker sitting on a seat not far away. Celeste was there as well, still wearing mourning white for her grandmother but finally smiling just a little bit. They all rose and joined the new arrivals.

Rawk told them what had transpired in the palace but nobody said anything. For a minute they all stood in silence before Zid cleared his throat and said something in his own language. Opok translated.

"Zid be wishing to return to the forest, for a short time at least. And I be agreeing. We can not help here and we must be preparing our own people for dealings with Katamood."

Rawk nodded. "Thank you, Opok. You saved us all." He bowed to the duen and to the warrior in his butterfly cloak and watched as the two of them headed down the hill.

When they were gone from sight, Rawk look towards the canal. He couldn't actually see it from where they were, with the *Hero's Rest* and other buildings blocking the view, but it wasn't something that Rawk was likely to forget. The dwarves had flooded the last section that morning and the first ship— belonging to *Keeto Alata*— had passed through, rising up on the first of ten locks as it headed westwards. There were three more ships lined up ready to go through as well.

"The Age of Heroes is over," Rawk said softly.

"I'm not sure it works like that."

Rawk turned and looked at Celeste and smiled. He looked her up and down before he spoke. "Maybe not normally, but it does this time. And it didn't end today, it ended the day our army of heroes— those bakers and chandlers and wharf workers— held back professional soldiers with pistols and muskets." He shook his head. "Nothing will be the same now."

"Perhaps." Juskin came up to stand beside him, halo of red hair as wild as ever.

"No. I am officially declaring that the Age of Heroes is over and the Age of Machines has begun."

"The Age of Machines?" Grint asked.

"Yes. Machines make us all equal."

Red Raven wasn't so sure. "Having an easy–to–use machine that can kill people from fifty yards away is one thing, Rawk. Having the will and the skill to use it are entirely different things."

"It's not just the pistols. It's everything. Nothing will be the same." Rawk flexed his leg. He looked at Celeste again. "Even this council Thok dreamed up will prove my point. Regular people wont be relying on kings and Heroes and gods to run their lives. The Great Path is dead. The good old days are over, and I, for one, couldn't be happier."

They stood there for a long time, looking between the buildings towards Mount Grace. "Well, my face is aching," Rake said. "I think I'm going home."

Rawk shook his hand.

"Me too," Travis said. "You've made more work for me, as usual." He was still quiet, but Rawk thought that the banter was proof that his old friend was going to be all right.

"You wouldn't have it any other way, Travis."

Biki and Justin went with him, already working out between them what they needed to do to finish cleaning the mess Weaver had left behind. Even two weeks later it seemed that the end of that chore was no closer at all.

Silver Lark went too, heading towards the river to see to her patients.

"And when do you want us back at work?" Grint asked.

Rawk shrugged. "Tomorrow? I'll go broke if we don't start getting some customers in again."

"Fine." The dwarf nodded, looking from Rawk to Celeste and back again. "You coming, Raven?" he asked after a moment and the elf nodded. "You too, Clinker."

The lad scowled. "I was going to—"

"Let's go to the *Hero's Rest* and let Demon have a run around. He must be getting tired of being stuck in your satchel today."

"He loves it."

"Come on anyway."

Rawk shook the dwarf's hand. Then Raven's and Clinker's. "Take care of Demon. I'll come and get him soon." The kitten shoved his head out of the satchel and Rawk gave him a scratch.

When he looked around a moment later Rawk discovered that he was alone with Celeste. He cleared his throat and quickly looked away. They wondered a few steps out into the square. The crowds were starting to return. There was even a line of people waiting at the pie shop.

"Great Path isn't really dead," he said eventually. "That's impossible, because I worked out what Path is, you know."

"Really?"

The *Hero's Rest* a hundred yards away across the expanse of cobbles. Closer by was the road that led down to the richest part of town with views of the harbor and the river. "Yes. Path isn't a God. Path is just what it says it is. A path. It's a metaphor for the journey through life. Each choice we make is an intersection that sends our life one way or the other." He held up two fingers in Path's symbol.

Celeste nodded thoughtfully. "Perhaps."

Without saying anything more, Rawk turned away from the *Hero's Rest* and started to limp eastward, down the mountain.

"Where are you going?" Celeste asked after a moment.

He stopped to lean on his cane and looked down the road towards the Tapalar Mansion, though it was well out of sight around the bend. "I'm going home," Rawk said. He held out his hand to her. "Are you coming?"

She hesitated for a moment, then smiled and took his hand. Rawk walked, her hand soft and warm in his, and sighed. He knew he'd missed out on yet another cliché as he led her away from the sunset.

$$-o O o-$$

I hope you enjoyed

The Last Great Hero
Book 3:
An Army of Heroes

Please help support
independent writers and publishers.
Your money is wonderful.
So are your reviews,
comments, mentions, tweets,
emails, blogs, likes
and deliveries of chocolate.

ABOUT THE AUTHOR

Scott J. Robinson grew up in a small town in rural Australia, the kind of place where you had to make your own fun. And from a young age, his idea of fun was to create strange worlds and populate them with interesting people.

He now lives in a different small town, with his wife and three children, and still enjoys creating strange worlds. Though now, he actually finishes some of the things he starts. When not writing he enjoys photography and camping and recently retired from an amazingly mediocre cricket career.

For more information visit
www.tengama.com
or email
scott@tengama.com

Other Books by
Scott J. Robinson

The Bygone Wars: Book 1
Songs of Space and Time

After years in the army, then more years backpacking around the world, Kim thinks she's seen just about everything there is to see. But she has to admit to being a little bit surprised when the giant bats started dropping bombs. And then the aliens came. There she was, wondering what a medieval hotdog might have been filled with, and five minutes later she was battling ugly, leathery–skinned aliens, beating them over the head with a historically accurate mace. And if that wasn't strange enough, she was shown a portal to another world, with the same war being fought on the other side.

Kim knows the information she holds could be vital, but she doesn't like authority all that much, and it doesn't like her either. So, when the leaders of the Earth's defenses test her friendship one time too many she sets out to end the war on her own.

Well, just her, an elf, a giant and a dwarf who may well be completely nuts.

–O–

The Brightest Light

The Skyway Men have ruled the underworld of the skylands for centuries–– killing, stealing and doing whatever it takes of increase their wealth and power. Pistols, money and fear are their weapons of choice.

After a decade exiled to a small piece of farmland that flies the quietest windlanes, Kade is thrust back into the world of death, corruption, shady deals and dirty deeds. But it's just like old times. He doesn't know who to trust. He doesn't know who's on which side. He doesn't even know which side he's on any more.

All Kade knows for sure is that murder and mayhem aren't what they used to be.